PRAISE FOR

"Thoughtful, nuanced, exciting—*Wild Sun* delivers
a great mix of what makes science fiction
so much fun to read."

-Paul Mullie
Co-Creator of TV's "Dark Matter" and
Executive Producer of "Stargate SG-1"

"A gripping, perfectly paced read."

-Shelly Campbell
Author of *Under the Lesser Moon* and *Gulf*

"*Wild Sun* is a thrilling, science fiction adventure
that manages to blend a vintage, golden age feel
with an enjoyably modern take on tyranny...
It really does feel like the kind of classic sci fi
adventure I'd happily pluck from my dad's
bookshelves as a teenager."

-Oliver Clarke
ScifiandScary.com
(Author of *A Cat Called Hope*)

"I didn't want to put this book down...
This story is what 'Avatar' should have been."

-C. Gold
Author of the Darklight Universe series

Explore more of the Wild Sun universe:
TheWildSun.com

Follow the authors:
Instagram.com/TheAhmadBros
Twitter.com/TheAhmadBros

For more great science fiction and fantasy novels:
UproarBooks.com

Publisher's Note:
If you enjoy this novel, please leave a positive
rating and/or review on Goodreads, Amazon, or
other similar websites to let other readers know.
Reviews work! Support your favorite authors.

WILD SUN

UNBOUND

SUN

BOOK TWO

EHSAN AHMAD & SHAKIL AHMAD

Uproar
Books

1419 PLYMOUTH DRIVE, NASHVILLE, TN 37027
UPROARBOOKS.COM

UNBOUND

Published by Uproar Books, LLC.

Cover art by Lance Buckley.

ISBN 978-1-949671-13-1

First paperback edition.

To Our Tribe

1

The pale purple blooms of the flower were easy to spot amid the sea of swaying grass. Unfortunately, they were a hundred feet away.

Cerrin watched them from the shadows. She did not like straying onto open ground. Though they hadn't seen a single Vitaari in six days, exposing themselves like this was a risk. In addition to the flying combat shells and the shuttles, there was the great ship in the sky that looked down upon the whole of Corvos.

In the thirty-two days since the mass escape from Mine Three, Cerrin reckoned they had covered at least two hundred miles. They had lost eleven people in that time: nine to Vitaari attacks, one to illness, one to an accidental fall down a steep slope. There were now fifty-five of them. Cerrin knew the enemy had been damaged, but it was surely only a matter of time before they recovered enough to launch a full assault on the escaped slaves.

Most of that damage had been inflicted by the Palanian man, Sonus, and he was the reason she was taking this risk.

He was now resting in a hollow some three miles away with the most of the other rebels. It was morning; as had become their custom, they had travelled through the night along a route already scouted by Cerrin. Sonus was struggling to breathe, still afflicted by some condition of the lungs caused by laboring in the Vitaari mines. Cerrin and the other Echobe had tried various remedies, but the only one that really helped him was a combination of yilla seeds and the petals of the forest orchid. Yilla was easy to find but they had only seen orchids twice, including today. Cerrin was determined to collect some while she had the chance. Sonus was important. He understood the enemy's technologies better than any other native of Corvos; she had to keep him alive.

Still crouching beneath a thick-limbed tree, she gazed up at the sky. It was a clear day but that wouldn't make it any easier to spot the Vitaari. Unless the sun caught them just right, the white coloring of the shells made them near-invisible. The engines were only loud if close by and they had a nasty habit of appearing from nowhere.

She stood and looked for any sign of Esteann. An Echobe like Cerrin, Esteann was at ease in the forest realm that had been their home before the Vitaari invasion. She had proven herself repeatedly since the escape from Mine Three. Their differences were well behind them now and they often worked as a pair. Cerrin couldn't see her. They had split up to cover more ground and agreed to meet back at the hollow. She couldn't assume that Esteann would find any orchids, so she had to take this chance.

Cerrin was armed with two weapons. One was the five-foot wooden spear that she carried everywhere. She knew it wouldn't do much damage to a combat shell, but it was the traditional Echobe weapon and essential for protection against the dangerous animals that dwelt in the Great Forest. None of the rebels had ever passed through this particular area, though most of the plants and animals were familiar. Cerrin knew that the forest stretched for more than a thousand miles and her aim was to reach one of the areas of Old Giants, swathes of ancient trees three hundred feet high with an impenetrable canopy. The Old Giants offered permanent sanctuary. The alternative was capture, torture, and death at the hands of the Vitaari.

Her second weapon was what the invaders called an assault rifle. Though she couldn't afford to waste bullets practicing, Cerrin had already used hers several times. The weapon was heavy and unwieldy, designed for the large limbs and hands of the aliens. The Vitaari letters and symbols on its various panels meant nothing to her, but Sonus had showed her how to operate the weapon. What was called the magazine held eighty bullets, but these could be gone in seconds if the firing stud was held down. Like everything Vitaari, Cerrin hated it: the cold metal, the murderous efficiency. But the rebels possessed only seven of them, and she was glad she had one.

With the spear over her left shoulder and the rifle over her right, she pulled up the hood of the cape she'd created from some spare overalls. Though she'd not had time before the escape, some of the others had gathered bags with vital provisions and supplies. Cerrin had dyed the cape green and brown, and though it was darker than the pale grass, she hoped it would disguise her from any passing Vitaari patrol.

With a last glance up at the sky, she left the safety of the shadows and trotted across the grass toward the orchids. As she adjusted her hood, she scanned the far side of the clearing for Esteann. Orchids were generally found in grassy areas, so it was possible she too had found this field. Open terrain was becoming much more rare as they moved toward the center of the Great Forest.

Halting beside the orchid, Cerrin wafted away some flies and checked the skies once more. The only cloud was streaky and high—too high to obscure any approaching Vitaari. It seemed a shame to strip the pretty petals from the orchid but Cerrin did so swiftly, depositing her prize in the bag attached to her belt. She took every last one, knowing this chance might not come again.

A cry came from her left. Esteann.

Cerrin stood and saw her friend bolt from the trees on the other side of the field. But not toward Cerrin—away from something. Even at that distance, she soon saw what it was. Like Cerrin, Esteann was armed with a knife and assault rifle, but neither was any use against a swarm of orri. The green-striped insects were three inches long and very evasive. Their sting inflicted a maddening itch and skin inflammation that took weeks to heal. Cerrin couldn't blame Esteann for running; she clearly didn't know the best defense against orri.

Tying the top of the bag to ensure she didn't lose the petals, Cerrin ran toward her friend. Esteann was so panicked that she didn't even see her.

"Here!" cried Cerrin. "Over here!"

Esteann kicked her knees high as she ran through the tall grass. Her hair—as dark as Cerrin's—flailed back and forth as she sped across the field. Her usually calm eyes shone with fear. "What do I do? Get them off me!"

Pawing desperately at an orri near her face, Esteann lost her balance and tumbled to the ground. Cerrin pulled the pack off her back as she ran, ripped it open, and snatched out a gourd full of water. Once the stopper was free, she waved the gourd in the air above the flailing Esteann, flinging water like rain.

"Calm down!" snapped Cerrin. "See—it's already working."

Within ten seconds, the swarm had moved away, leaving Esteann lying on her back in the grass. Her anguished expression was suddenly replaced by one of embarrassment.

"Sorry. I know I shouldn't—"

"Don't worry about it. I'd run from those things, too."

Esteann stood and brushed herself off. "Did you have any luck?"

With a smile, Cerrin tapped the bag. "I did. So let's get out of here."

Once Esteann had recovered her rifle, the pair jogged away through the grass. They hadn't gone far when Cerrin heard the sound she feared most of all: a combat shell engine.

"There!" Esteann pointed to the right.

The shell was above the trees at the edge of the field, around four hundred feet away, following a route almost parallel to their own. They'd seen lone shells more often recently. Sonus seemed to think it was because the Vitaari had to search an increasingly large area.

Cerrin knew they were too far from the trees to reach cover.

"Down!"

The two Echobe women hunched low in the grass. Esteann had no cape but she too had dyed her clothes green. Cerrin eyed the combat shell as it continued onward without changing course. She knew it was not only the pilot's eyes they had to worry about. The machines were equipped with many sensors to detect movement and heat below.

The pitch of the engine changed. Cerrin cursed. "It's slowing."

From beneath her hood she watched the shell turn toward them. Like some awful great white beast, the vehicle crossed the field.

Esteann hadn't moved but Cerrin could feel her trembling.

"Sorry."

"Forget it," said Cerrin. "We'll have one chance at this. Is your rifle ready?"

"Ready."

Cerrin fitted the butt of the rifle into her armpit and placed her finger on the firing stud.

"Burst fire."

"That's the third one?" asked Esteann.

"Yes. Push the switch all the way forward."

Cerrin watched the shell advance, sunlight glinting on the cockpit window. The twelve-foot-tall armored suit had broad limbs almost as wide as the main body. It was perhaps a hundred feet off the ground, two hundred away.

"After we fire, we split," she added. "Give him two targets."

"Got it."

The drone of the shell's engine grew louder. Birds scattered. Cerrin smelt that strange hot odor, watched the engine exhausts flatten the grass. At what she estimated to be around eighty feet, the shell halted.

"He might not come any closer."

"Are you're sure he's seen us?" asked Esteann, her voice wavering.

"I'm sure. After we fire, you go left, I go right. Ready?"

"Ready."

"Now."

Flicking the hood off, Cerrin spun to her right and brought the gun to bear. She aimed at the cockpit window and fired.

As usual, it was a struggle to hold the big weapon steady, but she saw and heard the impacts. The shell lurched as the bullets struck. Esteann was not as tall or strong as Cerrin and her volley was low.

The shell ascended, air shimmering beneath it.

"Split!"

Cerrin ran twenty feet to her right, stopped, dropped to one knee and aimed once more.

The shell's arms came up. Slung beneath them were what Sonus called cannons. Cerrin knew these fired larger bullets and they tore up the ground, sending grass and dirt into the air.

She returned fire, her bullets catching one arm of the shell and causing enough damage for pieces of armor to fly off. When she let go of the stud, all seemed silent. She scanned the field for Esteann but saw no sign of her in the tall grass.

Cerrin dropped her spear and sprinted directly toward the shell, knees high to stay out of the grass. It was another lesson from Sonus, who'd told her that the vehicles struggled to fire at targets directly beneath them. Even so, cannon shells peppered the ground around her, one whistling past her right ear. Only when she was close did she raise the rifle and fire again, this time hitting one big angular foot with several rounds. A piece of shrapnel fell past her and sliced into the ground, still smoking.

The shell dropped suddenly, fumes bitter in Cerrin's nose. Bracing the rifle and ignoring the pain in her arm, she pressed the stud again, striking the bulbous back of the shell. As it turned, she readjusted, knowing she had to stay directly under it. For a brief moment, she was safe.

"Esteann?"

"I'm all right!"

Cerrin wasn't sure if there were any bullets left in the weapon, but she readied herself to fire. Before she could do so, the engine noise changed and the vehicle veered away. When the bulky arms returned to a vertical position, she knew she would survive the encounter. Trailing smoke from the rear, the shell zoomed away over the trees to the west. The Vitaari soldier inside had given up the chase.

Even if the vehicle didn't make it back, Cerrin knew the Vitaari soldier would have already reported their location. The rebels would have to move fast, not waiting for nightfall.

Only when she lowered the weapon did she again realize how heavy it was. She slung it across her shoulder once more and ran to Esteann.

"I'm all right."

"Thank Ikala. I thought you'd—"

When she saw what the Vitaari weapon had done to her friend, Cerrin did not understand how Esteann had managed to speak, let alone keep her voice calm.

She had been struck twice by the cannon shells. One had hit her right leg below the knee and there was not much left below it. The other had struck her left shoulder. Amid the red blood and the green overalls, Cerrin could see glistening white bone.

Somehow, Esteann smiled and held out a hand. "I'm all..."

She slumped back into the grass, her final breath an awful wheeze.

Cerrin dropped the gun and gazed down at the ground, still breathing hard.

Another one gone.

She had no idea how many family and friends she'd seen die

at the hands of the Vitaari. The invaders did not seem to care how many they killed.

It was some time before she could bring herself to look at her dead friend once more. Not long afterward, she dragged Esteann into the trees and covered her body with fern. There was no time to bury her.

When she returned to the hollow, some of the resting rebels sat up or stood. Without meeting their eyes, she put down her spear and the two rifles and continued down to the little stream. Here she knelt and cleaned the blood off her hands and forearms. Once finished, she found herself facing Torrin and Jespa. Both were Echobe and—like Esteann—had proven themselves very capable since the escape.

Torrin was short and powerfully built, a pretty woman with kind eyes. She so loved being back in the forest that she had made necklaces of dried flowers and seeds. The Echobe had not been permitted to wear the necklaces while under Vitaari rule, but they were a traditional symbol of connection to the Great Forest.

Most of the former slaves were thin but Jespa was exceptionally lean. His angular face and flowing black hair added to the impression of a creature built for speed. He was faster even than Cerrin and the best tree-climber in the group.

Faces grave, the pair waited to hear what had happened.

"Did you hear the shell?" asked Cerrin.

They shook their heads.

"Caught us cold. Got Esteann. I damaged it and it flew off, but they'll know where we are."

By now, others had come to the stream and word was

spreading. Cerrin decided she would wait for them all to arrive to avoid repeating herself.

"Where is she?" whispered Torrin.

Cerrin rubbed dried blood off her thumb and pretended she hadn't heard.

As the rebels gathered, she glanced from face to face. She found a smile for young Yarni, the brave girl of twelve who had kept pace during their flight as well as any adult. Towering over Yarni was Kannalin, the tallest and strongest of the Echobe warriors, who was at last recovering from the injuries he'd sustained during the breakout. Then there were the eight Palanians—light-skinned city dwellers from a far-off part of Corvos that Cerrin had never seen and knew little about.

Sonus was one of that race. To Cerrin, the Palanians always looked pale but now the shadowy grove made Sonus's face appear almost white. In one hand was the cloth he used to wipe away what he coughed up. In his other hand was a flask of water.

Cerrin found him rather quiet and hard to read, but they'd spoken a lot and she had no doubt about the man's courage and determination. Like her—like them all—he had suffered greatly at the hands of the Vitaari. She did not yet know exactly what he'd endured, but his hatred for their enemy burned as brightly as hers.

Cerrin looked around the grove, a restful place adorned by yellow-striped izrit vines. "I'm sorry to bring bad news," she said at last, speaking loudly for all the hear. "We were unlucky. A combat shell caught us in the open. I damaged it but it got away. Esteann was killed. It was at least quick; I don't believe she suffered. But you all know what this means. Get packed up and ready to move. We may not have much time."

Most of the group immediately set about preparing to march, but Torrin, Jespa, and Kannalin remained. Erras—a Palanian who had helped dig the tunnel out of Mine Three—also came closer, standing alongside Sonus. The six of them, including Cerrin, had formed a leadership group of sorts.

As the one who had led the escape and killed several Vitaari, the group mostly followed Cerrin's lead with little question, though Erras could be awkward at times. Even so, she did not want sole responsibility and she listened to any opinion offered, especially if it came from Sonus. The man knew more about the Vitaari, their machines, and their way of thinking than she ever would.

"We should head east," she began.

"Because they'll expect us to continue south?" said Erras. He was not a tall man but very broad. He had little hair upon his head and always wore a sleeveless black coat with multiple pockets that he'd made himself.

"Exactly. And it doesn't take us too far away from the Old Giants Jespa saw yesterday. We can lay another false trail."

As she spoke, Sonus erupted into another coughing fit. Turning away and wiping his mouth, he eventually held up a hand and nodded.

"Jespa, Torrin," said Cerrin, "perhaps you can scout a route?"

The pair worked well together and Cerrin had noted what seemed like a mutual attraction. They agreed and set off immediately.

"I'll get packed up," said Erras, hurrying away.

Kannalin placed a hand on Cerrin's shoulder. "Sounds like you did well—damaging the shell."

"Not well enough," said Cerrin, relieved that he quickly removed his hand.

Kannalin cast a sideways glance at Sonus. The big warrior had been interested in Cerrin since well before the escape, and she couldn't deny he was attractive; she just simply felt nothing for him in that way. It was obvious to all that he was jealous of the time she spent with Sonus.

"I'll leave you to it," said Kannalin quietly before moving away.

Yarni ran to Cerrin. "The others were all talking and making food, but I made sure I got some rest. I'm ready to go."

"Good."

In the days immediately following the breakout, Yarni had followed Cerrin around like an obedient pet. But with Cerrin undertaking more and more scouting missions and often in danger, she'd tried to keep some distance between them. At first, the girl hadn't understood. But she had other friends among the adults and now seemed to grasp the demands on Cerrin's time.

"Poor Esteann," said Yarni. "I'm frightened."

"I know. Me too. All courage."

"What does that mean?"

"Your tribe didn't say it?"

The girl shook her head.

"It means that when you're scared, you must think about the other Echobe. All those who've lived before you, all those living now, and all those who will live after our time. All feel fear: a tiny baby, an adult warrior, an old one close to death. Remembering that helps us face our own fear."

"All courage," repeated Yarni, a thoughtful look on her face.

"Perhaps you can fill this for me." Cerrin took her gourd from her pack and handed it to Yarni, who ran to the stream.

Sonus wiped his mouth. "Kannalin is right. You did well to see off a shell with only a rifle. I doubt there's a Vitaari on Corvos who's as accurate."

She shrugged. "I just point and shoot."

"Sorry about Esteann. It was very kind of her to look for the orchids. Kind of you both."

Cerrin considered telling him about the orri, about how such a random occurrence had led to Esteann's death and placed them all in danger. But she just didn't want to talk about it.

She tapped the bag. "I have some here. We'll prepare it before we leave."

"Is there time?"

"We'll make time. We have to keep you healthy, Sonus."

"Healthy may be a little optimistic." He gave a weary grin. "I'll settle for alive. This false trail—I suggest we collate what spare metal we have. Someone can take it in the opposite direction, leave it, then find their way back to us."

"You think it will work again?"

"Who knows? There is nothing else metallic in the forest and Vitaari sensor technology is designed around tracking advanced enemies. I think that's why they've not found us already—that plus the range and size of the search area."

"You told me they can also track us using heat. Surely, they can see us from above?"

"Possibly. But the picture is complicated by all the wildlife. Those climbing things, for example?"

"Karki."

"Yes. The adults are a similar size to a human. On a heat

scanner, a group of them may not appear so different to a group of us. Then there are all the other creatures you've told me about. I doubt there's any better place to hide on all of Corvos. Think of how many years you and the remnant of your tribe were able to hide in the Great Forest after most of your fellow Echobe and all of the Palanians were made slaves. But if they're coming our way, we must take every precaution. The metal should be placed in an open area."

"All right. I'll take care of it."

"No."

Already on her way, Cerrin stopped and turned, surprised by how firm the Palanian sounded. "What?"

"Give someone else the job."

"Finding the way back to the main group won't be easy."

"You cannot keep risking yourself." Sonus gestured to the others. "They depend on you."

"They must learn to depend on themselves."

"I don't think you understand how your people see you, Cerrin. I may not speak your tongue, but I've picked up a great deal in the last few weeks. They thought escape impossible; you made it happen. They thought they'd never last out here, and yet we're still going. They trust in you. They believe in you."

2

The shuttle ascended, speeding away from the vast, churning depths of the Boundless Sea. Great gray waves rose and fell, creating splashes of white on the surface that soon disappeared. The color appeared again: on a flock of birds flying low to avoid the worst of the wind. This was the only true wilderness left on Vitaar. The storm-ravaged ocean ran uninterrupted for thirty-thousand kilometers and covered a third of the planet's surface. Vitaar's two continents contained only pockets of undeveloped territory, the result of five thousand years of technological advance.

On the continent of Utur was the Banveeris plateau, the historic homeland of Circle Za-Ulessor, one of the twelve great Vitaari clans. And one of Za-Ulessor's most prominent families was the Kan Talazeers. By tradition, they resided in the city of Zeer and no less than eight branches of the family remained there, including its most notable scion, Lord Urisit-Alston Kan Talazeer, second-in-command of the Imperial Navy. His two eldest sons occupied prestigious posts within the Domain: one political, one military.

The third son, Count Derzitt Kan Talazeer, had been back on Vitaar for fifteen days, but he had not set foot in Zeer. He had instead spent the entirety of his visit in a town south of the city: to be precise, a private medical facility where he had undergone reconstructive surgery and several other treatments.

Talazeer took his eyes off the waves for a moment and caught sight of his own reflection in the viewport. He was tempted to go to the restroom and inspect his new face again but knew he had to halt this before it became an obsession. The left side of his face had been partially melted by burning fuel, causing considerable damage not only to his skin but to his circulation and nervous system. Though the doctors were pleased with the results, Talazeer felt he still looked wrong somehow. They'd assured him that this was due to swelling and that, like the itching, it would pass with time. The Count clenched his fists as he thought of the pain he had endured. And all because of one damn native rebel on that remote backwater he had been sent to command.

The native's name was Sonus and—apart from causing personal suffering to Talazeer—he had assassinated a regional governor and virtually destroyed a mining installation.

Talazeer had initially been sent to Corvos to improve production and discipline at the remote colony. This he had achieved, but that success was long forgotten now. The uprising and escape at Mine Three had brought shame to his family and his entire circle. He had not even attempted to contact his father but wondered if Lord Urisit-Alston Kan Talazeer had brought some influence to bear:

Only two days earlier, the Count had been contacted by High Command and ordered to Nexus 1. He was expected to return to Corvos, crush any remaining resistance, and ensure the damaged mine was swiftly returned to full capacity. There could be no delay. The production of aronium, terodite, and other minerals was essential for the war effort against the Red Regent.

Aside from Sonus, Talazeer had a score to settle with a primitive female named Cerrin, who had only been saved from his clutches by a traitorous Vitaari officer. Apparently, she had organized the escape to coincide with Sonus's attack in a stolen shell, and now they led a band of rebels in Corvos's Great Forest.

Talazeer unclenched his fists. The Boundless Sea was already far below them and the viewport turning black. He could see his face clearly now, and the trace of a grim smile. He did not fear a return to Corvos; he embraced it. He had a chance not only at revenge, but to turn his greatest failure into his greatest success.

Three heavy cruisers were moored at the longest dock of Nexus 1, the largest spaceport in orbit above Vitaar. The new vessels were straight from the shipyards: each more than two thousand meters long, inelegant but impressive, dark hulls emblazoned by designations in white letters. *Yersil*, *Yaron*, and *Yaxa*. All ancient Vitaari nobles—great leaders and warriors who had founded Circle Za-Ili, long the most dominant of the twelve great clans.

Upon two of the cruisers, drones were still buzzing about the hull. The hold of the third was open and loaders were delivering a series of yellow-tipped missiles. The crew filing aboard via a nearby walkway gave scale to the munitions, each of which looked to be five meters long.

"Iridium-tipped," commented the only other man in the waiting lounge. Like Talazeer, he sat on a couch facing an expansive viewport. At other docks, bulky freighters and fuel ships maneuvered slowly while smaller vessels flitted between them.

The man's uniform was green, the color of the Imperial Navy. Talazeer wore the blue of the Colonial Guard. He was more interested in personal weaponry than military armaments, so he simply nodded and drank from his glass of wine, a decent Red Eldar.

But, as he had another two hours to wait for his flight, he decided to reply. "Hopefully they can knock or hole or two in the enemy."

"I should say so," answered the Navy officer, who appeared to be drinking water. "The targeting and propulsion systems have all been considerably improved. Should give the Red Regent a nasty shock."

"Any idea where they're headed?" asked Talazeer.

The officer grinned. "I've asked—and been asked—that question more times than I can count. Nobody knows."

Talazeer had watched numerous broadcasts while on Vitaar but the media were being typically cagey about the progress of the war. Accurate information about such matters usually came only via trusted associates, and Talazeer had not been in the mood to contact his. He only knew what most people seemed to know: the Red Regent represented the greatest threat to the Domain in ten generations. Seven naval cruisers had been lost in the most recent engagement. This had occurred in the ninth sector, on the edge of Domain territory. No one seemed in any doubt that the conflict would escalate.

"To the ninth perhaps," suggested Talazeer.

"Or the third, or the thirteenth," replied the officer. "Apparently there have been incidents there, too."

"The *third?*"

"I know. That she would dare to attack there—where the Grand Fleet is based."

The Red Regent's actions had previously been defensive, a response to Vitaari expansion into areas that bordered her own. "So, they really are taking the offensive?"

"It seems that way. I would hope to see some action myself but I'm bound for the eighth."

"Protecting the shipyards?"

"Indeed." The Navy officer stood and walked over. As he had no red diagonal sash sewn into his uniform—and was therefore a commoner—Talazeer stayed on his couch. "Captain Relston Perriel."

"Count Derzitt Kan Talazeer."

The captain bowed as custom dictated before shaking hands. He then sat beside Talazeer, who was already beginning to regret being sociable. "My father says we have had it too good for too long."

Talazeer thought of his own father. He could barely stop himself cringing as—for the thousandth time—he imagined the patriarch hearing the news of what had transpired on Corvos. Even among the many proud notables of Circle Za-Ulessor, Lord Urisit-Alston Kan Talazeer was known for his relentlessly high standards and expectations.

"Do you think that's true, sir?" prompted Perriel.

"It seems the Red Regent will be a worthy foe," answered Talazeer. "By defeating her, the Domain will once again prove itself the greatest empire in history."

"Quite so." Perriel drank his water. "And you, sir, where are you headed?"

"The twenty-first sector. I cannot say too much but I lead the Guard operation on a resource colony. It provides crucial materials for ships such as those." Talazeer aimed his glass toward the cruisers.

The apparently endless line of crewmen continued to enter the ship.

Perriel chuckled to himself. "Do you know, my cousin's wife suggested that we should allow *females* to serve in the fleet."

"As what?" replied Talazeer. "If they were to be whores or cooks, I wouldn't mind."

Perriel laughed and offered his glass for a toast. "Well said, sir, well s—"

Talazeer looked over his shoulder, though he suspected he knew the reason for Perriel's sudden dismay. "What is it, Marl?"

Talazeer's bodyguard was standing motionless in the doorway. Marl was Drellen, a species nearly wiped out when the Vitaari conquered their home world. Remarkably tall and lean, Drellens possessed tough reptilian skin and unblinking bright yellow eyes. Marl's appearance routinely caused such alarm that Talazeer insisted he keep his weapons hidden beneath his black cloak.

The Drellen had saved his life on numerous occasions, and Talazeer enjoyed having such a formidable figure beside him. During the debacle on Corvos, Marl had been one of the few to emerge with any credit, besting the traitor Vellerik in single combat.

Marl stepped aside and a third man entered the lounge. He wore the same green uniform as Perriel, though his did include a sash—and numerous decorations for tours of duty and military successes.

Deslat Kan Talazeer smiled. "Hello, brother."

. . .

Deslat insisted they speak on the Fleet Deck, away from listening ears. As the captain of a long-range destroyer, he was entitled to take advantage this luxurious facility, where high-ranking staff passing through Nexus 1 could make use of state-of-the-art medical facilities, relax in a leisure suite, or simply socialize with their peers. Other than instructing Talazeer that Marl could not accompany them, Deslat had exchanged only pleasantries until they reached the Portrait Room. This was a well known corner of the Fleet Deck: a surprisingly large, well lit gallery displaying life-size likenesses of naval officers from preceding centuries.

"We were all concerned, of course," began Deslat, "but I understand your decision not to go home." He stopped his brother and carefully perused his face. "Decent work. Expensive, I expect."

Expensive didn't even begin to describe it. Talazeer's personal finances were in a parlous state. Still, a Vitaari couldn't put a price on appearances.

Deslat was tall and strongly built, with a heavier brow and jaw than his two younger brothers. The middle brother, Yeraan, was the most academic and now a senior politician in Zeer. Talazeer always took some comfort from the fact that, if not the most powerful or intelligent, he was certainly the most handsome—even now.

"I don't suppose we're here to discuss money, brother."

"Quite so," said Deslat, clasping his hands behind his back as they continued along one long wall of the gallery. Their father often adopted the same pose while walking and Talazeer had no doubt that Deslat considered himself well positioned to take over his title. This did not automatically go to the firstborn, but the son chosen by the father upon his retirement. Talazeer believed he had more than enough time to eclipse his eldest brother. As a destroyer captain, Deslat would have numerous chances to distinguish himself—and numerous chances to go down with his ship.

"How did you know I was here?"

"Father informed me."

"Of course." Talazeer was not surprised. Urisit-Alston Kan Talazeer had been in the fleet for forty years, with associates and informers in every sector. If he so desired, he could probably have tracked his son across the entire galaxy.

"You are here to represent him?" added Talazeer.

"I am. What do you know of the current situation, Derzitt?"

"Only what I hear. I was discussing the ninth sector with that fellow Perriel. Will you be heading that way?"

They reached a corner of the gallery and turned. Talazeer noted a portrait of an officer in a fleet uniform that bore no resemblance to the current iteration. The background of the portrait was a poorly rendered image of the Vitaar system, which included the home planet and its five moons, all of which were bases for the fleet.

"No," said Deslat. "While it's true that the battle there was the most significant yet, the ninth is unlikely to remain the center of the action."

"Oh?"

It seemed to Talazeer that his brother enjoyed knowing more than him. A destroyer captain would, of course, be well informed but he presumed that Deslat obtained much of his knowledge from their father. "I haven't actually received my orders yet, but I wouldn't be surprised if we are ordered to the seventeenth."

Talazeer frowned. "Seventeenth? Not much there."

Deslat gave a thin smile. "I know you're something of an expert on outposts, brother, but you're mistaken in this case. Have you heard of the Nisibia system?"

"No."

"To be fair, most haven't. Imperator Zensen has his reasons for not advertising its existence but, believe me, it will be crucial. Unfortunately, I can't go into any more detail but what I will tell you is that the situation there has certain ramifications for you. Because terodite has never been more important."

Deslat stopped and turned to his brother, observing his reaction.

"Ah," said Talazeer. In his orders from the High Command to return to Corvos, he had specifically been instructed to focus on terodite at the expense of the other ores found there, so he did not need to feign his lack of surprise. However, the knowledge that his success would only contribute to his brother's opportunity for glory did lessen the sweetness of his own chance at vindication on Corvos.

"So, you see, there are many eyes on that outpost of yours, Derzitt. There have been for some time. And recent... unfortunate events were met with considerable dismay within the High Command and elsewhere. Given your failures, you might be surprised to find yourself returning there."

"The failures were not only mine, Deslat. I was betrayed by a man I considered above reproach—a war hero, no less. I can hardly be held entirely responsible when the man in charge of security decides to side with the rebels. Why, I was only there for a matter of weeks. Even the administrator and the mine governors were caught utterly by surprise!"

During Talazeer's time away, the High Command had seen fit to recall three members of the Corvos administration. They now faced a military court and likely imprisonment. As a nobleman, Talazeer was at least spared such indignities.

"All factors in mitigation, brother," agreed Deslat. "But it was not those that saved you."

"Father?"

Deslat walked on again. "Fortunately, his reach extends beyond the navy. That is why you now find yourself returning to Corvos."

Nothing was said for a minute. They reached a corner again and turned toward the door.

"Ah, there's Verresur," Deslat said.

Another officer had entered the Portrait Room and stood by the door, waiting. The loyal lieutenant had been with Deslat for years. Talazeer always found him sickeningly deferential and annoying.

"Still with you?"

"Of course," replied Deslat. "Derzitt, do you recall when we would play andurat before I left for the academy?"

Talazeer nodded. It was a card game popular among military officers, with stakes that doubled every round. He'd been disappointed to discover no one aboard the *Galtaryax* had a head for the game.

"There is a parallel. You now return for the second round but are playing for significantly higher stakes. If you crush this rebellion and improve the terodite yields, everyone will be happy—and you can only gain. If you fail…"

They stopped close to the door, observed by Verresur.

"How bad could it get, brother?" asked Talazeer. "Be honest."

"Father will not be able to save you again. It pains me to say this, but Mother is of the opinion that you should have already forgone your title."

Talazeer had suffered reverses before, but that statement shook him. His mother was a caring woman but as fanatical about the family name as his father. The days when she had spoiled her youngest son now seemed impossibly distant.

"It's true?"

"I'm afraid so. I'm sure you can still recover but… well, failure is not something that has often afflicted the Kan Talazeers."

Talazeer shook his head. Could he really lose his title? Reduced to the level of a commoner? Those who suffered such a fate often took their own lives, not only to escape the indignity and destitution, but also to shield their families from continued shame.

Deslat reached out and placed a hand on his shoulder. "We can only hope it won't come to that."

Talazeer couldn't tell if he meant it. He thought he noticed a subtle—but smug—smile on the face of the nearby Verresur.

"As I understand it, you're to receive some help from an up-and-coming Colonial Guard officer," Deslat added. There had been only the vaguest mention of this in the orders from High Command. "An… unconventional character, apparently, but with exceptional credentials. You will have to work very closely together." He gave a knowing, playful smile. "Brother, I think you're in for a very interesting time."

3

The gap between the two trees formed a natural gate, and beyond lay a small grove of fern and moss-covered logs. The trees were not Old Giants but each was as wide as two men, the trunks dotted with fungi. Within the grove, the rebels had gathered in small groups and made beds of fern. Though there had been no rain, the thick canopy blocked almost all sun and kept the area damp and cool. It was a fine place to rest and—after four long days—the rebels were in great need of rest.

Sonus had found a small patch of sunlight close to one of the trees. He sat there now on a log, cleaning a Vitaari weapon. In the first few days of their flight, he had carried one himself but over time he had become too weak. Thanks to the remedy Cerrin had created, however, he was now feeling much better. The coughing was far less frequent and the pain in his chest and throat bearable.

Sonus wasn't too concerned about personally wielding a rifle; the Echobe had proved themselves more than capable of using them, especially Cerrin. His main aim was to keep the weapons functioning. They were daily dragged through the forest, picking up moisture and dirt. The rebels had, as usual, stopped moving just before dawn and Sonus had already stripped, oiled, and cleaned three weapons. Before her death, Esteann had helped him build up a supply of plant oil that did the job well enough. Though he'd been unable to bring any equipment with him, the rebels from Three had absconded with anything they thought might come in useful, which included a number of small tools. Sonus had put together a little kit for his maintenance work. Such efforts made him feel useful.

Though he appreciated the beauty and comparative safety of the Great Forest, he found the humidity enervating. There was also an apparently infinite variety of insects and creatures that threatened danger with every step. He had already been bitten by a snake, a sesskar (a large type of rat), and too many varieties of bug to name. Fortunately, only the sesskar bite was considered dangerous by the Echobe. Torrin had assembled her own collection of natural treatments; one of these had been used to counter the fever caused by the sesskar bite.

Sonus removed the top from his flask and drank the water within. It was one of the long, capacious metal Vitaari flasks that every prisoner within the mines had been given. The Echobe hated them—claiming they made the water taste bad—and preferred to use gourds they had collected in the forest. But Sonus had insisted that they keep them: they were too valuable to discard.

He looked over his shoulder at those within the grove. A few were still moving around but most were now sleeping. He turned back and gazed at the endless forest ahead of him. Even though they had covered great distances, the scale of the place was almost unimaginable. He wondered if the decoy metal had done the trick or if it was simply their increasing distance from Mine Three that had saved them this time.

His mind wandered across the surface of Corvos, to his fellow enslaved Palanians in the north, to the Lovirr running missions between the mines, and even to the unconquered Kinassans in their desert.

Had his connection to the fledgling Lovirr resistance been discovered? Surely, they would have spread news of the uprising and escape. How had the Vitaari responded? How determined were they to hunt down and destroy a small band of rebels that could not realistically continue the fight in any meaningful way? Sonus assumed they were now the only ones on Corvos actively opposing the invaders. That alone was reason to survive.

He had just finished with the last weapon when Cerrin returned. "I suppose you want to do this one, too?" she said, offering her rifle.

"Yes. While we have a little time."

She laid her weapon against the log and let out a long breath.

"All clear?" asked Sonus.

"Looks that way." As usual, Cerrin had several sentries out but insisted on checking the perimeter herself. Sonus wondered where she got her energy. She didn't seem to eat much and could apparently survive on less sleep than anyone.

Noticing that she was standing in the sunlight, Cerrin took a step backwards. Before she did so, Sonus couldn't help looking at the jagged scar down one cheek. The natural treatment she had employed once back in the forest had somehow added a slight golden sheen to the old wound. Sonus knew from the others that Cerrin had been attacked by the Vitaari nobleman, Count Talazeer. He thought it inadvisable to ask about that, though he had questioned Cerrin about her trip up to the invaders' ship, the *Galtaryax*. She hadn't seemed too enthusiastic about discussing the episode, though her sight of space had evidently affected her.

Sonus recalled the moment their lives first collided. It was only weeks ago, but seemed far longer. "I don't think I ever actually thanked you."

"For what?" asked Cerrin, wiping sweat from her brow.

"Getting me out of that shell."

"You did."

"Ah. I must have forgotten."

Cerrin reached for the gourd on her belt and drank some water. She then squatted in front of Sonus, an intense look in her dark brown eyes. "I didn't want to ask this while you were ill but I have to now."

"Go on."

She looked around to check that no one else was close. "Even if we get to the Old Giants, even if we recruit more people, it will never be enough, will it? Sooner or later, they'll find us."

"Given enough time, that's the probable outcome, yes. But time may be on our side. The Vitaari haven't constructed a new mine for several years. I reached the conclusion that they have no wish to *permanently* colonize Corvos. There is simply not enough here for them—just a finite supply of a few specific minerals. They might leave in two years, or ten, or twenty. We just have to wait them out."

Sonus was conscious that he was being far more optimistic than he actually felt.

From Cerrin, a rare smile. "Torrin keeps telling me that we must enjoy each day. We were slaves for so long. And we don't know how many days we have left."

"Wise words. Nobody could have predicted what we've already achieved. We shouldn't assume that we know what might happen in the future."

"What does your book tell you about what happens to us after death?"

They had spoken before about *Our Maker's Teachings*, the tome revered by religious Palanians. Sonus was not particularly religious, but his mother had been and he retained a certain loyalty to the church. "That we will be reunited with our loved ones in a place without suffering. I'd like to believe it. What about the Echobe?"

"We become shades, here in the forest."

"Are the shades conscious?"

"What does it mean—conscious?"

Cerrin spoke *Trade* well but Sonus often found himself explaining unusual words. "Like awareness, knowledge of self. Do they know what's going on around them? Can they think?"

"I don't know. But the dead are still with the living. That's what's important."

"You would like that—to dwell here forever?"

"I would."

As if in answer, some distant bird unleashed a piercing cry.

"Get some rest, Sonus."

"You too."

As night approached, they ate what they had. There had been little time to gather food during these last few days while they put as much distance as possible between themselves and the field where Cerrin encountered the shell.

Five Echobe had been placed in charge of distributing provisions and every man, woman, and child was given a precise allocation. Sonus took the typical ration of nuts, seeds, and dried fruit offered to him and ate slowly, savoring each mouthful. Though the amounts were currently meager, they had previously dined on meat and fish caught by the Echobe. Their skills had clearly lapsed during captivity, but Sonus had been impressed by the depth of their knowledge. Cerrin and Kannalin in particular were experts in tracking and hunting.

The powerful warrior was sitting next to Erras, who seemed rather unimpressed with his meal:

"I never thought I'd miss that Vitaari sludge, but at least it was substantial."

This was not the first time he and the other Palanians had complained. Sonus thought the comments ill-advised but had not yet said anything.

Another Palanian, Nuro, spoke up. She was around Erras's age and the pair seemed to be in some kind of relationship. She was not physically strong and often struggled to keep up, regularly cursing the forest. "I forgot what proper food tasted like years ago. Milk. Cheese."

"Don't even say those words," groaned Erras.

"What is this, if not proper food?" demanded Kannalin. "It could hardly be more fresh."

"No offence," said Erras, "but we Palanians actually *do* things with our food once we pluck it. We bake, we brew. If you were to see a full table on a festival day, you would never eat this bird food again."

An Echobe man answered him: "If you like the Vitaari food so much, why not head back to Three? One less mouth for us to feed. We spend every waking hour not on the march looking for that 'bird food.'"

Sonus glanced at Cerrin. She was sitting on a bed of fern with young Yarni, showing her how to whittle a spear head. She generally seemed to ignore the day-to-day conversations of the group, preferring to expend her energy on practical matters.

Sonus was considering intervening when Erras turned to Kannalin. "Any food is better than no food, I suppose. Maybe there will come a time when we can invite you to Okara for a celebration dinner."

Kannalin gave a nod of acknowledgment. Okara was the capital city of the Palanians's homeland in the south. "What is beer anyway?" he asked. "You Palanians talk about it enough. All I know is you brew it in barrels with barley, like some kind of disgusting bread tea."

As Erras embarked on a long explanation, some of the Echobe discussed the Old Giants. Much of the conversation was conducted in their own language but some was spoken in *Trade*. Many of the younger Echobe had been imprisoned for the majority of their lives, and the Vitaari had allowed only Corvos's universal tongue. What the Echobe, Kinassans, and Lovirr called *Trade* was in fact a simple version of Palanian.

Sonus gathered that it was not only the thick, impenetrable canopy and scale of the Old Giants that appealed to the Echobe. While a few were concerned about the spirits that dwelt there, many seemed convinced that it was a special area protected by their forest deities. Sonus had long since realized that the various Echobe tribes did not agree on their interpretation of such matters.

He was not the only one listening.

Koros, another of the Palanians, sat down beside him. He was an older man with deep-set eyes and sunken cheeks. Sonus had not spoken to him much but knew he'd been a government bureaucrat in Okara before the invasion. Koros was one of the few Palanians fluent in Echobe; he had learned the language from his fellow prisoners as a method of occupying his mind.

"You're listening to this?" he said quietly, one hand still holding his meager meal.

"I am."

"I know you agree that we should head for the Old Giants. But isn't it an obvious move? Shouldn't we be a bit more clever?"

"What do you suggest?" asked Sonus before eating some seed.

"What if we travel northeast? We could be out of the forest in a few weeks, then go on to our own lands. There is still much left behind that we can use. We can create our own weapons, use underground structures to house ourselves. Government House in Okara is half-underground, for example, with tunnels to many other buildings besides."

"The Vitaari cleared every last building, cellar, and tunnel out during the invasion," replied Sonus. "Who's to say they wouldn't do so again?"

"How would they even know? There are so few of us."

"Precisely. I know this is not our home but the forest—and the Echobe—have kept us alive for almost six weeks. Can you honestly say you expected us to survive this long?"

Koros held up a hand. "Sonus, I am the last person to undervalue what Cerrin and the Echobe have done. Back in Three, I had no idea about the tunnel—in fact, I didn't believe it until I saw it with my own eyes. The woman is quite remarkable. But in the long term, can it be wise for us to remain in one large group? All it will take is a single Vitaari attack and our supposed revolt is over. Can we not at least send out messengers—to the Lovirr, to the Kinassans?"

"Are you volunteering?"

Koros leaned forward. "I am not saying that Cerrin's way is not the right way. Merely that it is not the *only* way."

Sonus rebandaged his wounded ankle before the night's march began. Once that was done, he packed his bag, which had been sewn together by one of the resourceful Echobe out of Vitaari refuse sacks. Other than his tools, Sonus's worldly possessions amounted to his water flask, a blanket, and a spare shirt.

The rifles had all been claimed by those Cerrin nominated, which on this night included Erras. Torrin and Kannalin had already scouted the route, and as the rebels set off in single file, Sonus found himself just ahead of Yarni, the Echobe girl who was so friendly with Cerrin.

"Don't worry," she said cheerily as they strode through the darkened forest. "I've got my spear in case there are any sesskar around."

"Ah, thank you!" said Sonus.

He was glad to find himself near the rear of the column. Those ahead would have cleared the way and flattened the ground. Even though he was feeling so much better, he found these journeys draining. It wasn't just the energy required to stay on one's feet: they often heard truly alarming roars and screeches from the surrounding jungle.

He'd been reassured to hear from Cerrin that most creatures would stay out of their way. Apparently, there were only three animals likely to attack: the damareus, the klintara, and the black mordyn. The last was a type of snake that could grow up to fifty feet in length. They were apparently very rarely sighted, but the Echobe feared them like no other animal, believing them to be a worldly manifestation of an evil god named Skree.

"You're not coughing so much now," observed Yarni.

"Indeed," replied Sonus. "I have Cerrin and Torrin to thank for that. They've looked after me well."

"What's it like to fly?"

"Sorry?"

"You flew. You flew in one of the Vitaari shells."

"Er… yes, I did. Well, I must say it was quite frightening. They are very powerful machines."

"Did you feel like a bird?"

"To be honest, no. Shells are noisy and they don't really move like a bird. They're not very graceful."

Yarni went quiet for a while before coming up with another question. "Mine Fourteen is on a mountain, isn't it?"

"That's right. Mount Origo."

"That's where Areti lives."

"Ah, yes. One of your goddesses."

"The goddess of light."

"Have you ever seen the mountain, Yarni?" asked Sonus.

"No. You have to be at the southern edge of the forest and the weather has to be completely clear."

"Ah. Maybe one day you'll get the chance."

"I don't think so. I don't think we'll get out of the here alive. At least not all of us."

To Sonus, that sounded like something she'd heard an adult say.

"Cerrin says we will," added Yarni, "but most people say we won't. I hope Cerrin's right."

"I'm sure she's right. She usually is."

Yarni went silent again. Sonus kept his eyes on the dim outline of the man in front, an Echobe named Duspa. He listened to the sounds of the column moving through the forest. There were never shouts or cries; any messages were passed back quietly. Sonus felt concerned about how the conversation with Yarni had ended. He was trying to think of a less weighty subject to discuss with the youngster when he heard whispering. He stopped just in time to avoid colliding with Duspa. Yarni had already realized they were halting and now passed the message back.

More whispers from ahead. Beyond that, Sonus could hear something else: a rhythmic tapping sound. It did not sound organic. He was armed only with a rudimentary knife made of wood and a jagged piece of metal. He looked out into the darkness, listening intently.

He felt Yarni beside him. "What is it?"

"I don't know," he whispered back.

The tapping grew louder. The rhythm was metronomic.

The Vitaari? Some new machine?

Sonus stepped forward, tapped Duspa on the shoulder. "What's going on?"

The Echobe shook his head.

The tapping was now more like banging.

Then came the first scream. A high-pitched, spine-chilling scream that was soon matched by others. The noise was terrifying—but clearly not human.

Sonus felt sweat drip down his flanks. Yarni reached up and grabbed his wrist.

Has to be the Vitaari.

Some form of psychological warfare?

Is this it? Is this how it all ends?

Even with the screeching, a single word travelled back through the column at speed.

"Karki."

Duspa turned to Sonus. "Huge group of them in the trees ahead. They're warning us off. We're going to try and go around. Torrin says they beat sticks upon the trees to make that noise."

Sonus sighed with relief. The tree-dwelling creatures were known to be very territorial and aggressive if threatened. Duspa explained in Echobe to Yarni and the others behind them, and before long the column was moving again. Though he now knew the origin of the screams and banging, Sonus was glad when they could no longer be heard.

Calm returned but within an hour rain began to fall. It seemed to Sonus that each drop must have collected extra water from the canopy on its way to the ground because every single one felt unnaturally large. He was glad to find that Yarni had a hooded cape. He himself had only a roughly made hat but it kept the worst of the water off his face. Soon the ground was soaked and their progress slowed.

Step after step after step.

Sonus trudged along, unable to hear anything but the rain.

He should have felt downhearted but somehow even a night like this made him proud: to be here among these brave people, truly free for the first time in years.

When he had lost his two closest friends to Vitaari cruelty at Mine Fourteen, Sonus had made a fateful decision to resist or die trying. It had taken so long for him to summon that strength, and so long to plan his escape. Moments like this represented the very best that he had—and could—hope for. Torrin was absolutely right.

Enjoy every day.
And every night.

4

Mine Three still bore the scars of the breakout. It had not suffered as much damage as Fourteen, but two buildings—the armory and the generator station—were still undergoing repairs. As he strode down the shuttle ramp, Count Talazeer was relieved to see the tower appeared as good as new. He had sent instructions ahead that his visit was not to disrupt mining activity and was pleased to see a loader emerge from the mine, shifting three large containers toward the storage yard. Elsewhere, a team of natives was scrubbing equipment, supervised by a pair of guards. Another team was digging a trench for Vitaari technicians laying some subterranean cable or pipe.

Talazeer stepped off the ramp onto dark earth, Marl, as usual, a few paces behind him. Beside the Count was Deputy Administrator Rasikaar, who had escaped the wrath of High Command. His superior, Danysaan, and the governors of mines Three and Fourteen were the three recalled to Vitaar for trial. Rasikaar clearly considered himself fortunate to avoid the same fate and seemed desperate to oblige. Talazeer had reached the *Galtaryax* only two hours previous and immediately requested a shuttle. He planned to next visit Fourteen and cover the other mines over the next few days.

Though there was to be no formal inspection, Talazeer did pass through an honor guard as he approached the tower. These men were permanently stationed at Mine Three, but High Command had also diverted a battalion of sixty Colonial Guardsmen to Corvos to bolster the three hundred guards spread across the mines. The Guardsmen would be reporting directly to the mysterious military commander Deslat had mentioned.

"I... I must say you are looking well, Excellency," said Rasikaar as they neared the tower. "Very well, indeed."

"Instead of making obsequious comments, perhaps you could tell me what you know about the new commander."

"Excellency, I was being completely honest earlier. Nobody knows a thing about him—only that High Command has recalled him from some active operation. He is expected within the next day or so. Honestly, that is all I've been told."

Talazeer did believe him, but he wanted to set the tone with his subordinates immediately. "I hope so. Because if I find out differently, I will have Marl introduce you to his blade."

Rasikaar stifled a nervous smile when he realized the Count was not jesting.

The more he thought about it, the happier Talazeer was that he had reached Corvos before the new commander. He would have time to consolidate his position. Combined with the fact that he already knew the operation well, he believed he could easily establish the upper hand. The additional military force was welcome, but if he was to make the most of his return, he would have to dominate the game from the first card played. As his brother had pointed out, the stakes were high. The Count believed he could still win.

Once past the black-clad honor guard, Talazeer was met by the new governor, who had been transferred from Mine Seven in the desert region of Corvos. Despite the fact that the occasionally troublesome Kinassan tribesmen dwelt there, Governor Saarisan had never lost a man to the natives. He was an older fellow, surely well past one hundred, but known to be efficient and conscientious. Talazeer had only met him twice during his time on Corvos but at once recognized the pure white hair and slender build.

"Excellency, welcome. My apologies that the repairs are not quite complete. It will only be a matter of days."

"I do hope so, Governor. And I'm sure that you will acquit yourself better than your predecessor. After all, you could hardly do worse."

Talazeer marched on toward the tower. "First, you can tell me about your yields. And then—with Deputy Rasikaar, of course—we can discuss why you have had so little success in apprehending our enemies."

Though he didn't admit it to his subordinates, the primary reason for their ongoing failure was patently obvious. East of the tower, the Great Forest stretched away as far as the horizon, a dark green blanket, the scale of which reminded Talazeer of the Boundless Sea.

Saarisan was still talking, summarizing his actions since taking over. Talazeer saw no reason to reprimand the man. Having arrived a week after the breakout, he had overseen the deployment of relief workers from other mines and somehow kept production going. Yield was already back to seventy-three percent of the previous average, from a nadir of forty-three percent, and Saarisan pledged to reach one hundred percent within one month. Talazeer hadn't yet announced that the focus of the Corvos operation would switch to terodite. As long as *those* yields increased swiftly, he could appease High Command and begin repairing his reputation.

When Saarisan concluded, Talazeer was still staring at the forest.

"Can't we just burn it down?"

The veteran governor answered: "The records show that our invasion force did consider that option, sir. Surveys were undertaken. Unfortunately, there is only a brief period of the year when enough of the material would be sufficiently dry and combustible. It's also estimated that the forest provides up to four fifths of the oxygen within the planet's atmosphere. Without it, life would be unsustainable."

"Perhaps just before we leave, then," said Talazeer with a grin. He admitted to himself that such a tactic would not provide a satisfying form of vengeance. Even if the forest—or part of it— were burned to the ground, he might not get the chance to look upon the bodies of his two enemies. No, he wanted to see them up close—see their eyes when they realized he would take their lives.

"Rasikaar, you were going to tell me about the other mines."

"Of course, Excellency. In the immediate aftermath of the uprising, there were small attempted revolts at three other installations—Two, Five, and Eleven. Nothing on the scale of what occurred here. A few guards were injured but no fatalities.

Administrator Danysaan's last order was to authorize tearings at the three mines. One male and one female from each shift were selected at random and dismembered in front of the entire staff."

"Too little, too late, but I'm glad to hear he found some guts at last."

"Needless to say, there's been no more problems at those three locations," added Rasikaar.

"And elsewhere?" asked Talazeer, noting some apprehensive expressions among the technicians in the tower. They watched as Marl crossed the circular room to the window, his clawed feet scraping the metal floor. The Drellen stopped and stood perfectly still, arms beneath his cloak, yellow eyes surveying the forest.

"Mostly just talk, Excellency," replied Rasikaar. "Danysaan was considering an announcement to native workers that the rebels had been captured and killed. He was removed from his post before he did so."

"I'm glad," said Talazeer. "We must not stoop so low. Better to make examples of them."

Rasikaar continued, his expression anxious: "There have also been isolated acts of sabotage, some graffiti, and two attempts to assassinate guards. Perpetrators have been punished—the *actual* perpetrators, when possible. As I mentioned earlier, there's been no significant impact on yields."

"And beyond the mines?"

"It's difficult to be certain, Excellency. Given their role in transportation, we must assume the Lovirr are aware of the uprising and all the events since. We believe they must have had some role in communicating between the rebel Sonus and those here. Otherwise, how would they have coordinated their action?"

"Really?" said Talazeer. "Those funny little creatures? Not sure they've got it in them."

"It seems the only logical explanation," said Rasikaar. "No suspects have been identified yet."

"It couldn't have been Vellerik? He might have coordinated the whole thing."

"We did investigate but there was no suggestion of that. Captain Vellerik's men seemed sure that he made his decision on the spur of the moment. He was evidently mentally disturbed."

"Clearly. What of his unit? You didn't mention them, Rasikaar."

"Also recalled by High Command, Excellency. As I understand it, they are to be split up and placed with other units. If there was any rot, Command doesn't want it to spread."

"The Kinassans?"

Rasikaar gestured for Saarisan to answer.

"Though the man turned out to be a traitor, Captain Vellerik did a good job out in the desert. They've not come north of the pass where he attacked them and placed mines. Honestly, I doubt they know anything of the uprising."

"I'm not sure we should even use that word," said Talazeer. "After all, the events were limited to here and Fourteen. There are enough locals who understand Vitaari for that word to have an impact. From now on, we shall refer to it as… the incident."

The experienced Saarisan spoke up. "What is the High Command calling it, Excellency?"

Rasikaar grimaced at the older man's words.

Talazeer ignored them both. "Those still in the forest shall be called escapees."

"They *are* fighting us," replied Saarisan. "But it's not as if this is the only planet where we've encountered resistance."

Talazeer pointed a finger at the governor. "And I can assure you, we won't be encountering it for much longer. One was killed five days ago?"

"That's correct, Excellency," said Rasikaar, joining him near the viewport. "At least six have been eliminated during three separate encounters. Each time, combat shells were deployed but it is difficult for them to penetrate the forest canopy and they are not suited to a ground pursuit. They've also been utilizing crude decoys of spare metal to further avoid detection. Unfortunately, the reb—the escapees—were able to take a number of assault rifles. One of the shuttles and three shells have sustained damage."

"Excellency." Governor Saarisan gestured to a nearby screen. The footage showed an Echobe woman firing upward from a field of grass. "She put a shell out of commission on her own. Facial recognition shows that this is—"

"Cerrin. Yes, that's her."

Talazeer stepped forward and reached for the controls, magnifying the image.

There she stood, feet wide apart, the large rifle cradled in her arms. She wore camouflaged clothing and her long black hair was tied back in a tail. Sweat shone on her dark skin. Talazeer magnified the image again. Now he could see the mark on her left cheek. For some reason, it seemed to have acquired an almost golden color.

"Interesting scar," remarked Saarisan.

Talazeer could not stop himself from smiling.

. . .

He found the visit to Mine Fourteen rather shocking. Though reconstruction was well advanced, the decision had been made not to raise a new tower and the installation appeared odd without it. This had been another of Danysaan's last decisions. Fourteen was one of the less viable installations on Corvos and—though Danysaan hadn't known it—the new emphasis on terodite made it even less significant. As the shuttle departed, Count Talazeer took the opportunity to gaze out at the glittering snows of Mount Origo. For all the pain he associated with this planet, he had to concede that parts of it were beautiful.

Once back on the *Galtaryax*, he drafted the announcement regarding the new concentration on terodite. This did not include an explanation of the change but he did request immediate responses from the individual governors and Deputy Rasikaar. Talazeer needed to know how quickly the adjustment could be made and to what extent forgoing the extraction of other minerals would improve terodite yields.

With more installations to visit the following day, he changed out of his uniform into a soft robe and lay down on the couch beside the viewport. He was still accommodated in the same room: the place where he had attempted to seduce Cerrin, only for the ungrateful primitive to stab him. Talazeer had taken his revenge swiftly and would have taken more if not for the intervention of the traitor Vellerik.

On the other side of the room, Marl was occupied with what seemed to be his only real hobby. When not sharpening his sword, the Drellen used a variety of small knives to make ornate cubic carvings out of wood. Talazeer could never make head or tail of them, though Marl spent countless hours on the task and was evidently very skilled.

"What are those things anyway?" he said, between mouthfuls of candy. While back on Vitaar, the Count had purchased some of his childhood favorites. Stupid, he knew, but it made him feel better.

The Drellen was facing away from him. He stopped carving for a moment and turned to his superior.

"They are both one thing and many things."

"I'm still none the wiser."

Marl held up the cube he was working on, which was about ten centimeters wide. "Each of the six sides tells one part of a story. These stories are as old as my people. As old as time."

"Why do you make them? To keep the memory of your species alive?"

Talazeer did occasionally feel sorry for Marl. His race had been virtually wiped out by the Vitaari on what they called Kan Arle's World. Though armed with no more than bladed weapons, the Drellen had only been subjugated after decades of fighting the Colonial Guard. Some were kept as dueling champions or enslaved within alien menageries by wealthy Vitaari. A few possessed sufficient skills to remain free.

Marl had already been working for another nobleman when Talazeer bought him out of his contract. This continuing expense added to his financial concerns but he considered his bodyguard indispensable. With that in mind, he did what he could to ensure Marl had what he needed. Other than his pay, his requirements were not complicated: a decent supply of raw meat and a small supply of wood suitable for carving.

The Drellen still hadn't replied.

"Well? Is that why you do it?"

"I do it because there is nothing else to do, sir."

"Fear not, Marl. Once we track down our friends in the forest, you and I shall go hunting."

Talazeer had just drifted off to sleep when he was woken by a familiar beep. Yawning, he hauled himself off the couch and walked over to the wall screen. Marl was still quietly working away on his carving and hadn't even looked up.

"Accept."

An image of Rasikaar appeared.

"My apologies for disturbing you, Excellency, but you did ask to be notified. Commander Elezz's shuttle is approaching. I will be meeting him down in bay four. Would you like to join me?"

Talazeer gave this a moment's thought. "No. Have him come and see me in three hours. I need some more rest."

Rasikaar seemed somewhat surprised by this. "Er…"

"Three hours," repeated Talazeer.

He made sure he was ready: in full uniform, including sidearm, with a speech prepared. Marl was told to stand by the door, another measure to put the new commander on the back foot. Talazeer had studied texts about such techniques.

The three-hour mark passed.

Outraged by such rudeness, Talazeer approached the wall screen to call Rasikaar and check where the new arrival was. Before he could do so, the door buzzer sounded. Marl stood ready, clawed hands clasped in front of his cloak. Talazeer approached the door.

"Open."

The Colonial Guard commander before him was immaculately dressed. There was no sash upon the blue uniform but an impressive selection of tour and merit medals. More unusual were the pink vertical flashes across the cheeks and forehead, a strong contrast to the silvery Vitaari skin. Such adornments were currently fashionable on Vitaar but rarely seen upon military personnel. The same bright pink had been used on a few strands of the black hair. The face was appealing, the eyes a glacial blue.

"Greetings, Count Talazeer," she said. "Commander Marties Elezz."

He was too taken aback to immediately respond. Not only was the new commander female, she looked to be very young: no more than fifty. Now Talazeer recalled his brother's cryptic comment back on Nexus 1; so, this was the "unconventional character" he had mentioned.

Elezz glanced at Marl. "And you must be the bodyguard." Her voice was surprisingly deep and carried a trace of a lowborn accent. Talazeer knew that some of the more modern circles encouraged females into prestigious occupations, but among the Za-Ulessor it was unheard of. He felt anger welling up inside him. Whatever her ability and reputation, he could not avoid the feeling that this was a personal sleight.

Elezz turned her attention back to the Count. "I presume that 'sir' is acceptable? 'Excellency' does seem a bit long." Talazeer still couldn't summon a reply, so she pressed on. "I thought we could speak in the operations room. I've brought some personnel

and equipment that might prove useful. I'd like to begin operations against the rebels tomorrow."

"Er… I've decided that they are to be known as escapees."

Elezz smiled again. "Hardly matters, does it, sir? They won't
be around long enough for us to worry about what we call them."

5

They had not been as fortunate with their hiding place this time. Though equipped with a few lights, they'd agreed not to use them, so finding an adequate location in the hours before dawn was never easy. On this occasion, the best Cerrin had been able to manage was the cover provided by three huge trees arranged in a triangle. The species boasted roots on the surface: fan-like structures that helped keep the plants stable, each the height of two men.

Cerrin would have laid down to sleep but—as always—there was an urgent matter in need of attention. She waved Sonus over, but before he could reach her, Kannalin appeared from behind the nearest root.

"Sentries have just reported in. All clear." He pointed upward. "Jespa still up there?"

"He is."

"Another long night," said Sonus, now standing at Kannalin's elbow. "Though I suppose we should be grateful we didn't run into any more karki. Covered quite a distance, at least."

Cerrin spoke quietly. "Listen, I thought I saw something earlier. In the sky to the north."

"A shell?" asked Kannalin.

"No. Smaller."

"Like a drone?" asked Sonus.

"Yes."

"We've not seen those for a while," said Sonus. "They don't have the range to get this far from Mine Three. Could be something new. How sure are you?"

"Not certain. That's why I sent Jespa up."

"Ah." Sonus tilted his head.

"Lost sight of him a while back," said Cerrin. "Can't be far from the top now."

Sonus shook his head in disbelief. "Brave fellow."

Cerrin heard a whimper of pain. All three of them turned to see an Echobe woman examining her blistered heels.

"Lot of those," said Sonus. "We've come so far so quickly."

Cerrin lifted one foot. "Without the Vitaari boots, we would never have made it this far. I don't know what they're made of, but they certainly stop water from getting in."

"It's often occurred to me that we could have learned so much from them, if they'd been… different."

"And them from us," said Kannalin sharply, fingers upon the necklace that Torrin had made for him.

"Quite right."

Cerrin was glad to see Sonus looking better. He had a bit more color in his face, and Yarni had told her that he was coughing much less. Of more concern to her now was the condition of the others. Blisters and sores were one thing, but almost every night someone fell and hurt themselves. There were several sprained ankles and it was surely only a matter of time before someone broke a bone.

"We can't keep this up forever," she said. "Let's wait to hear from Jespa, but the Giants can't be far. Once we're there, we'll rest up for a while before we go looking for a place to settle."

"I'll get a forage party together," said Kannalin.

"Be quick," replied Cerrin. "The sun's already been up for an hour."

As he departed, Sonus watched him. "I don't think he likes me."

"Why do you say that?"

"Just a feeling. Maybe because I'm Palanian."

Cerrin didn't reply. She didn't have time to worry about such matters.

"He likes you, though," added Sonus.

"Forget that," she said, feeling herself blush. "What do we do? What if I *did* see something earlier? What if they're watching us right now?"

Sonus gestured to the trees above. "They'll have difficulty landing shells or ships here. Let's try not to worry until we're sure there's something to worry about." As he said it, Sonus put his hand gently on her arm. Cerrin generally did not like to be touched: especially by men—of whatever species.

But on this occasion, she did not mind.

Count Talazeer found himself back in the operations room with Commander Elezz for the third time in two days. Though his shock and dismay remained, he could not fault either her energy or enthusiasm. He gathered that the High Command would recall her once the rebel threat had been eliminated, and she seemed keen to be involved in the coming conflict with the Red Regent. She was even convinced that it was only a matter of time before Colonial Guardsmen found themselves deployed on planets to face enemy ground troops. The fact that the Vitaari had little idea what their new enemy might unleash against them in such a campaign did not seem to concern her.

Talazeer had never worked closely with a female before—certainly not one of a high rank—and he still considered the practice an insult to Vitaari tradition, certainly as seen within his circle. But other families saw things differently, and he knew that a complaint to High Command would likely fall on deaf ears. It was they who had appointed Elezz; and if she failed, the responsibility would be theirs. He just hoped she knew her place.

The new commander had not arrived on the *Galtaryax* alone. Accompanying her were a pair of Guard technicians who specialized in anti-insurgency technology. They had brought specialized equipment that included a new sensor package, long-range hunter drones, and a variety of munitions. When not in the operations room, Elezz had been drilling the Guard regiment in the loading bays. Talazeer wondered when the woman slept.

He had left Marl to his carving so there were just the four of them present. In the middle of the operations room was a large tactical display, and around it stations for specific equipment. The two technicians—who clearly knew each other well—sat side by side monitoring their own computers. They both seemed very young and much of what they discussed was indecipherable to Talazeer. They had already complained about the antiquated equipment of the *Galtaryax* and seemed to be running the drones entirely from own systems.

Elezz stood opposite Talazeer on the other side of the tactical display, gazing down at an image of the forest. The screen was marked with icons denoting previous contacts and incidents. She had spent several minutes explaining to the Count how sophisticated the hunter drones were. Apparently, they could carry armament modules and were highly adept at distinguishing heat signatures and types of movement within a variety of terrains. Though keen to see progress, Talazeer wondered about the consequences for him if the headstrong new commander brought the rebellion to an end within a day of arrival.

"I'm shocked," said Elezz, waving at one of the *Galtaryax* consoles. "This piece of junk actually has weather prediction capability. Looks like a stormfront coming in. Hopefully we'll get our first contact before then."

One of the technicians spoke without turning around. "Lightning can affect the drones, Commander, and rain greatly reduces their effectiveness."

Talazeer gazed down at the display but couldn't make much sense of it.

"What if you do locate them?" he asked. "What then?"

"One of the shuttles is on standby, with modules already loaded. We can be down to the surface within an hour."

"The munitions you mentioned. Won't they simply destroy the area? I would like the leaders taken alive."

"With respect, sir, that may not be possible."

Talazeer could not believe she was already contradicting him. "Then you need to *make* it possible, Commander."

Elezz scratched her cheek, drawing attention to those novel pink flashes. "Count Talazeer, we also have non-fatal stun gas. If conditions allow, we can use that."

"Ah."

"*If* conditions allow."

"Meaning what?"

"Meaning there is a storm coming. Gas does not work well in rain."

"I see."

Talazeer spent the next few minutes familiarizing himself with the display. He worked out enough to realize that the storm would hit the forest within two hours. Then, when Elezz turned to consult the technicians, he examined her. Her uniform was on the tight side and he did approve of her athletic yet shapely figure. Her hair was also pleasantly sleek and he approved of her perfume. Even so, he also couldn't deny the temptation to slap her across the face. He imagined pinning her down on the display and pulling her uniform off.

His reverie was broken by the bored voice of a technician.

"Commander Elezz, I think we have something."

When Jespa finally returned, his lean, bronze frame was dripping with sweat.

"Three hours?" asked Cerrin when she and Torrin met him at the bottom of the tree. She had been unable to even consider resting while awaiting his report.

Jespa dropped to the ground, breathing hard. "You think you could climb any faster? The branches thin out a bit higher up, and I had to climb out a long way to get a decent view." Wincing, he pulled a splinter out of his left thumb. "Wanted to check every direction."

"And?" asked Cerrin impatiently.

Jespa rolled his eyes with frustration. She knew he had just put in a tremendous effort but she needed to know.

"And I would tell you straight away if I'd seen something!"

"Calm down," said Torrin, who often admonished Jespa for his impetuousness.

He made a face at her. "Nothing—apart from a crested hawk." Jespa beamed.

The hawk was a creature beloved by the god Nestar, who was said to know the Great Forest better than any other deity, even those who'd created it.

"I followed its flight—it was heading right for the Old Giants. Nestar helped me! Helped *us*. Only a few days now."

"Good work, Jespa."

He seemed genuinely surprised by the compliment. "Dark clouds coming in from the west. We could get pretty wet. And now—if you don't mind—I really need a lie down."

"Go ahead."

As Jespa departed, Torrin gave an encouraging smile. "Nothing from the sentries either. You look worn out, Cerrin. I'll tell everyone about the rain, so at least they have a chance to get shelters up."

These "shelters" were little more than sheets hung from branches but they were better than nothing. For all her knowledge, Cerrin wasn't adept at making much apart from weapons. Between them, the Echobe and the Palanians had come up with solutions for most of their problems.

She now felt her tiredness in every limb. And though she followed Torrin's advice and walked to where she'd left her gear, she didn't expect to be able to sleep. Despite what Jespa had told her, Cerrin couldn't shake the feeling that she *had* seen something. She sat down quietly to avoid disturbing those already asleep, then leaned back against the root and closed her eyes.

"He is with you."

The voice came from Murrit, a middle-aged Echobe woman who had been a guider before the Vitaari came. Every tribe had one—usually a woman, an individual with great knowledge of the gods and spirits. They often inherited the role from a parent and were also charged with learning and telling traditional stories. Cerrin knew that their return to the forest perhaps meant everything to the guider. Many was the night that she had distracted the rebels with her tales, some of them hopeful and encouraging, as many dark and disturbing.

Cerrin's family had believed more in the spirits that dwelt within the forest rather than the deities who created it, but she had long devoted herself to Ikala, god of battle. He had become popular during the battles with the Vitaari, and Cerrin had continued to give him offerings and prayers. She believed he watched over her and her trust in him gave her strength.

"Ikala is with you," Murrit clarified, and it was not the first time she had displayed such insight. "I have some uriop here." The guider tapped one of several bags hanging from her belt. The pale-yellow fungus could be found in almost every part of the Forest. Cerrin had never tried the stuff but knew it was supposed to open the mind to the spiritual world. She also knew it could unsettle the mind and lead to addiction.

"It could help you commune with Ikala," added Murrit.

"I don't need it."

"You might hear his voice," said Murrit, eyes twinkling. "You might even *see* him."

"I feel he's with me. That's enough."

"As you wish. Something to help you sleep, then?"

"That, I definitely don't need."

Talazeer could not believe he'd actually had to convince Elezz that he should join the mission.

It was true that his position within the Colonial Guard was largely ceremonial—as a nobleman he was entitled to choose any of the armed services and enjoy trappings such as rank, privileges, and uniform. And it was also true that he hadn't undergone any actual military training. He was, however, chief administrator of the Corvos operation. The High Command directive had made it quite clear that while Elezz was to lead military operations, he was still in overall charge.

Rasikaar had gleaned that she possessed outstanding familial connections within Command and had distinguished herself on previous assignments. The deputy—and indeed the rest of the staff—had seemed rather taken aback but, like Talazeer, they bore the whims of their superiors on Vitaar with practiced silence. Elezz was here to stay and might even be an unwelcomed sign of things to come. Rasikaar had heard that Circle Za-Klinnon, who considered themselves progressive, had even appointed a female governor.

Just before their shuttle left the *Galtaryax*, the deputy also reported an enquiry from the office of Viceroy Ollinder, the new viceroy who had replaced the official killed during the rebel uprising. Ollinder's staff wanted to know if the rebels had been neutralized. Talazeer told Rasikaar to inform them that the threat would be dealt with within a matter of hours.

Commander Elezz sat a few meters away from the Count,

gazing out at the dark cloud they were using to cover their approach. The new drones had identified what the technicians seemed certain was a group of at least fifty humans in one location. They had only a limited time before the storm complicated things. Elezz was clearly determined to take this chance.

She was certainly well prepared. Talazeer, Marl, Elezz, and one of her techs shared a seating module with half of the Colonial Guard troops arrayed behind them. The shuttle could accommodate various modules, and this one took up the front quarter of the hold. The Guardsmen looked a tough, experienced bunch. Their unit was based on Vitaar in the city of Ulitann, where a specific type of tattoo was popular among fighting men. Clusters of small green triangles adorned their cheeks, necks, and forearms. All were equipped with camouflage body armor and helmets with flip-down visors. Their chief armament was the assault rifle used almost universally by the Guard, but these had been augmented: some with mini-missile launchers, others with flamethrowers. The soldiers seemed especially keen to use these and watch the forest burn.

When Talazeer had arrived in the loading bay on the *Galtaryax*, he'd been surprised to see little resistance or cynicism from these hardened soldiers toward the new commander. Whatever Elezz had done to establish herself in the first days of her rule, it seemed to have worked.

Behind the seating module was a large equipment module containing four of the new hunter drones. The technician's computer was linked up to a display screen affixed to the front wall of the hold. From what Talazeer had overheard, the drones would be used first due to the difficulty of getting the soldiers on the ground. Alongside the drone module was another containing descender lines—the low-tech but only available method of transferring the soldiers to the surface.

Talazeer leaned forward to catch Elezz's eye. "Those lasers on the drones—lethal, I suppose."

"Of course."

"You will consider the gas, Commander?"

Her annoyance was clear in the tone of her reply. "As I said, sir, I will make my decisions based on how the operation develops. The whole point of bringing a range of equipment is to provide tactical flexibility."

Though the shuttle was not a military vehicle, two pods had been fitted to its short forward wings. One contained explosive ordnance, the other gas.

Talazeer leaned back, hand on the rifle between his legs. This was his hunting weapon and he now imagined himself down in the forest, peering along the sights as Cerrin and Sonus fled. He had loaded the rifle with low-velocity ammunition and would aim to wound.

Beside him, Marl sat holding his own rifle, a rare weapon from some remote system. It was entirely white and constructed of an odd plastic-like material. Whatever it was, the rifle fired something that looked a lot like a laser beam. Marl favored the weapon because of its lightness and precision. He also claimed that it had not required a replacement part in five years. Talazeer had only recently learned that the weapon was a gift from a former client.

Light suddenly filled the seating module as the shuttle burst out of the cloud. Talazeer felt a lurch in his stomach as they descended.

"The Wild Sun," said Elezz, gazing out of a viewport. "That's what the natives call their star, correct?"

"Quite so," replied Talazeer. "Apparently, it refers to solar flares and some nonsensical beliefs. The natives are certainly *wild.*"

Elezz gave a thin smile and turned to her technician. "How's the signal?"

"Stable, Commander. Three kilometers. See there."

Now tiny yellow dots appeared on a scan of the forest.

Elezz tapped the comcell on her collar to communicate with the pilot. "Altitude, three hundred meters. Don't slow down until you have to, then hover fifty above the canopy." She turned to the tech once more. "Ready the drones."

He sits in the darkness beside his mother. His hands are over his ears but he can still hear the distant screams. She prays.

Then he hears the blasting engines of the alien craft. Everything within the house shakes. Dust falls.

His mother holds his hand. They tremble.

The door is blown apart.

They're inside.

They're coming.

Sonus only awoke from the dream when someone called his name. The first thing he saw was Cerrin's eyes, and for once they sparkled with fear. Around him, the rebels were grabbing their belongings and springing to their feet.

"They're *here!*" yelled Cerrin. "The Vitaari are here!"

"Where to?" someone yelled. "Where do we go?"

Yarni appeared from somewhere and threw both arms around Cerrin.

Once on his feet, Sonus looked upward. Through a few gaps in the canopy high above, he could see metal.

"Shuttle?"

"Think so," said Cerrin, now also looking up, rifle already over her shoulder. "We have a route prepared."

"Who knows it?" Sonus asked.

"Torrin. The others must go with her. We can stay and keep the Vitaari busy."

Though his mind was abuzz and his body cold with fear, Sonus nodded. Kannalin and the other rebels with rifles were already trying to find a good firing position.

Almost everyone else was looking at Cerrin.

"Follow Torrin! She knows where to go."

Torrin pulled on her pack, passed her rifle to Sonus, then set off between two of the three trees. The rest of the rebels formed a line behind her and marched away. Erras was helping the frail Nuro, who seemed to be in a daze.

Sonus watched as Kannalin and the others raised their rifles, looking for the shuttle. "Not yet!" he yelled. "Don't give away our position—the others have no protection."

"But we have to distract them," countered Cerrin.

In the end, the argument did not matter.

"No!" shouted Kannalin.

Sonus and Cerrin turned to him, saw him staring in horror in the direction of Torrin's group.

Death had come silently. Two of the fleeing rebels had already been cut down. Sonus looked on in horror as a slender green beam sliced through the trees, striking a woman in the head. She took what looked like two normal steps, then collapsed, smoke rising from her skull.

"Drones!"

Then Sonus saw it: a hovering metal device not unlike those he had repaired for the Vitaari. It was oval, no more than a meter tall, with a coms array on top and a weapon hanging below, mounted on a movable arm. The machine shifted position and the weapon altered its aim.

Another green beam.

Another body on the ground.

The hastily arranged column now descended into chaos as the rebels fled in every direction. Despite Torrin's best efforts, the others understandably sought cover wherever they could.

Cerrin was the first to react. She sprinted ten paces toward the drone, dropped to one knee, and fired. In an instant the machine launched upward, only to reposition itself and return fire.

A patch of grass was transformed into smoldering ash. Fortunately, Cerrin was no longer there.

Another beam sliced through the forest. Yarni screeched and hurled herself toward the ground as the green light incinerated a branch in front of her.

Readying his rifle, Sonus spun around and spied the second drone maneuvering fifty feet above. He ran to the nearest tree, leaned into the cover, and raised the weapon.

"That's seven confirmed kills already."

"Very good," replied Elezz coolly.

"*Not* good!" snapped Talazeer. "What if one of them is Cerrin or Sonus?"

Elezz cleared her throat and dragged her eyes off the screen.

"Count Talazeer, I cannot effectively conduct this attack while trying to avoid killing *two* specific individuals. We did discuss this."

"Third and fourth drones prepped, Commander," added the tech.

"Launch number three. We'll keep the fourth one in reserve."

Another voice came through the internal coms system.

"Commander, this is the pilot. The stormfront is almost on us. Heavy rain. We can cope with the winds for the moment but they will quickly worsen. Maintaining position may be difficult. Then there's the danger of lightning."

"Understood," replied Elezz. "Stand by."

The tech spoke again: "Commander, we have them all within a space of two hundred square meters. Four standard explosive charges will blanket the area. Fatalities predicted at ninety-five percent."

"No," said Talazeer. "I want prisoners."

"Sir," said Elezz patiently, "we have a chance to take them *all* out. Right now."

"Why not use the gas?"

"Why not use *us*?" This question came from one of the Guardsmen sitting behind them.

"Who said that?" asked Elezz.

"Sergeant Guldar, Commander."

"Well, Sergeant, if you think you can drop three-hundred feet through that canopy and land without getting a bullet through your backside, you're welcome to try."

The sergeant didn't answer.

Talazeer unstrapped himself and went to stand in front of Elezz. "Commander, with respect, I want prisoners—not skeletons. These bastards are to be made examples of. They will be sent to every mine on Corvos and pulled apart. We must take at least some of them alive. I'm asking you to use the gas."

"*Nine* confirmed kills," added the tech.

"Is it raining?" asked Elezz.

"Not yet, Commander."

"Recall the drones. Prepare to drop a full spread of gas."

6

The drone zoomed behind a tree, only to reappear and fire. Sonus threw himself to one side, but the green light was aimed several feet to his left. Someone cried out—Kannalin! The big Echobe dropped his rifle and pitched forward into undergrowth.

Shaking his head to keep his mind focused, Sonus scanned the trees and spied the drone again. Up on one knee, he adjusted his aim and held the firing stud down. Grimacing at the percussive thump of the rifle, he saw bark explode off the tree. The drone shot upward. He wasn't sure they'd actually hit one yet.

Duspa ran past him, then dropped down to help Kannalin, who was clearly in pain. The rest of the rebels were scattered all over, staying low or sheltering behind the tree roots.

Cerrin was still trying to get a clear shot. With her gaze and rifle still aimed upward, she moved toward Sonus.

"Duspa! How is he?"

Duspa didn't look up from Kannalin's wound. "Caught him on the shoulder. Bad but he's alive."

Sonus continued to scan the trees, rifle ready, but he saw no glimmer of metal, no flashes of green.

"Where's Torrin?" he asked.

"Not sure."

"Then you'll have to lead everyone away."

"No," replied Cerrin. "We have to fight back. We have to cover the others."

"I think the drones have gone."

Before Cerrin could reply, something thudded into a patch of fern about twenty feet away—a metal canister about a foot long. Hatches at both ends sprang open.

Instinctively, Cerrin, Sonus, and the others threw themselves down.

No explosion came.

"Another one over here," yelled someone.

Sonus detected a slightly bitter odor. He had smelled it before—during the invasion—and he knew exactly what it was. He also knew what to do. He reached for the water flask hanging from his belt.

"It's gas! Use your flasks—breathe the air inside. Use your flasks!"

Two people close to the canisters had already begun to cough and lurch around. But Cerrin and the others were reaching into their packs and passing on his instructions. Even in that moment, Sonus realized that the Echobe's dislike for the metal flasks would be to their advantage now: without water inside, the empty interiors would contain more breaths of untainted air. His own mouth clamped shut, Sonus shook his flask—half empty. It might be good for two or three gasps, but he needed to get as much distance between himself and the canisters as possible first.

At least half of the rebels possessed the composure—and the time—to retrieve their flasks. Others were pawing at their eyes and a few were retching and staggering. Sonus had seen this before, too. In seconds, they would collapse into unconsciousness.

He spent enough air to shout, "Follow Cerrin! Clear the area!"

Hearing this, she shouldered her rifle, gestured westward, and started running. Sonus directed others after her. More rebels nearby toppled over. He knew he couldn't help them.

But perhaps there was something else he could do. The gas canisters were not aerodynamic or fitted with any kind of guidance system. That meant they had been dropped straight from the shuttle above. *Directly* above.

Sonus twisted open his flask and took his first gasp of air, then fought against coughing up the water that came with it. He resealed the flask and stuffed it into his overall pocket. Tucking the rifle butt into his shoulder, he aimed at the canopy. The foliage and the dark clouds made it impossible to see the shuttle, but he knew it was there. He reckoned he had about half a magazine left and he kept his finger down until every bullet was gone.

"Commander, we're taking fire."

"*Small arms* fire, pilot," retorted Elezz gruffly.

On the screen, the locations of the gas canisters were now displayed alongside the escapees. Talazeer noted that some were already motionless.

"Commander, this is not a military vessel," countered the pilot. "We've already sustained damage to the rear landing struts. If possible, I'd like to take us up a little."

"Very well."

Talazeer tutted.

"Problem, sir?" said Elezz, her voice angry.

"How will we get down there now to clean up?"

She did not reply.

"Not good," said Marl, pointing to the right. On the narrow viewport on that side of the shuttle, drops of rain had appeared.

Poor Vanna was on her knees. Eyes bloodshot, nose streaming, the elderly Palanian woman reached out to Sonus. He had forced himself to ignore the others, but he just couldn't this time. He knelt down and gripped Vanna's hand.

A stupid, terrible mistake.

He inadvertently breathed in through his nose and the effect was immediate. He actually felt the burning gas travel down his throat and into his lungs. He staggered. By the time he regained his balance and composure, Vanna had collapsed.

Fingers pinching his nose shut, Sonus opened his flask and sucked the last air from it. Then, eyes running and lungs on fire, Sonus bolted after the others.

He caught up with the stragglers and was astonished to see the wounded Kannalin among them, lurching alongside Duspa. Despite the pressure building in his lungs and throat, he somehow resisted the temptation to breathe.

The tech pointed at the tactical display. "Looks like a group on the move there, Commander."

"Drop one canister ahead of them, one behind. Pass the coordinates on to the pilot." Elezz turned to address the troops.

"Sergeant Guldar, the shuttle will soon descend again. Take the first half of your men and fix your lines."

"At once, Commander."

Guldar issued his orders and soon fifteen troopers were heading for the rear of the shuttle. Other than weapons, helmets, and armor, they were equipped only with light packs.

Elezz turned to Talazeer. "We'll go down with the second group, sir. Is this your first time on a descender line?"

Talazeer admitted to himself that he hadn't really thought all this through.

"Yes," he replied, trying to sound confident. "Should be exciting."

They seemed to be past the worst of the gas, so Sonus at last allowed himself a breath. He was relieved to see Erras and Jespa with the group and now realized that as many as two-thirds of his comrades were still on their feet. Though there were many desperate glances back toward those they'd left behind, the rebels kept moving.

Sonus only stopped when he saw Cerrin and Duspa standing over Kannalin, unconscious on the ground. The laser had burned through his shirt and left a blackened wound on his shoulder.

Then Duspa fell to his knees, coughing and retching.

"We have to go on!" said Sonus. He had left many others behind; Cerrin would have to do the same.

Instead, she shouted at Kannalin to wake up. She slapped him across the face but still he didn't stir. Duspa was not capable of helping so she aimed a fierce glare at Sonus.

"Help me!" she spluttered.

"We can't. We have to save ourselves."

"Kannalin!" Cerrin pleaded with her fellow warrior. Her usual composure seemed to have deserted her.

Sonus did not see the next canister drop but heard it crash through several branches and strike the ground. Within seconds, he could feel it in his eyes.

"Cerrin, we have to go! Now!"

Already weakened, Duspa collapsed onto his side, eyes rolling.

Sonus grabbed Cerrin's arm and pulled her up. She did not resist and he was thankful that she at last understood.

But the gas was taking effect. Together, they staggered toward the others—but Sonus was stunned to see some of them rushing back toward him. Then he realized that another canister must have been dropped in front. They were trapped.

He could taste the acrid gas in his throat again, feel his eyes stream. Vision blurring, he fell to his knees, Cerrin beside him. She turned to him, eyes splintered by red, head lolling. Watching her strength fail, it seemed to him that the whole rebellion was fading.

Then he realized the water on his face was not tears but rain. Within moments, it became a downpour.

Sonus cupped his hands and used the rain to wipe his eyes and nose. He opened his mouth, drank to clean his throat. And as he hauled himself to his feet, he realized Cerrin had also recovered herself.

And they were not alone. Some were rising to their feet, others simply lay in the mud, letting the rain pour down on their faces. Even Duspa was on his knees again, a bizarre smile of disbelief on his face.

Cerrin met eyes with Sonus.

"Let's go."

. . .

"Why is that group still moving?" asked Count Talazeer.

Again, Elezz did not answer him.

"The rain," said the tech dispassionately. "The gas is virtually useless now. The drones, too—heat sensors will be all over the place."

Elezz cleared her throat before speaking. "Pilot, there should be no further danger from small arms fire. Get us as low as you can."

Talazeer could understand her annoyance but surely they would be able to continue the attack? He turned around and saw Sergeant Guldur and the others, now attached to the lines affixed to the roof. The shuttle swung sharply around. Talazeer lost his balance and almost fell onto the seats. Ever quick, Marl flashed to his feet and grabbed his arm.

"I'm fine, you dolt!" snapped the Count. "I was simply reaching for my rifle."

The Drellen scratched his teeth together and withdrew.

"How long until we're down, Commander?"

Elezz flicked her sleek black hair off her shoulder. "For Guldur to reach the ground and secure the site? For the lines to be retracted, and for the second group to descend? In torrential rain and increasingly high wind? Quite a while, sir. Quite a while."

She unstrapped herself, aimed a final, disconsolate glance at the display screen, and then walked over to the viewport. The only thing visible was rain.

. . .

Keep moving. Just keep moving.

Though she didn't want the others to know, Cerrin had lost the escape route. She wasn't even sure how much time had passed since they fled the Vitaari—it might have been twenty minutes; it might have been forty. She had lost her spear and her pack, and had only the rifle on her back. Without her cape, she also had no protection from the rain. But she plowed on, her overalls soaked through.

Brushing rainwater from her eyes, she did not allow herself a thought of her fallen friends. She simply gazed ahead, kept her stride long, and found the quickest, easiest way through the forest. She was trying to follow a southward path but her priority was simply to put distance between the survivors and the enemy. They would drop troops; of that she was sure. The Vitaari must know they'd killed many. Would they now pursue the survivors through the forest? Were they determined to end it here and now? Today?

She knew the rain had given them cover. Their only chance was to use what start they had.

Just keep moving.

She only stopped when she had to: when Sonus and Jespa caught up with her and physically blocked her path.

"Please, Cerrin," said the Palanian. "They're exhausted."

"Perhaps *you* are."

"We *all* are," countered Jespa. "Just a few minutes. Just let us get a breath."

When she saw the desperation and weariness on the faces of those behind her, Cerrin gave a reluctant nod. She cursed as she scratched at her arms—some plant with long hairs had irritated her skin.

Sonus still had his flask with him. She watched as he used three large fronds of a nearby plant to fill it. He offered it to her first. Cerrin drank, then passed it back to him.

"Yarni!" The horror of realizing she hadn't seen the girl was matched by shame that she hadn't thought of her until now.

"She's here," said Sonus, reaching out and holding Cerrin's shoulder. "She's with us."

"Thank the gods."

"We should see who else is."

Cerrin held her breath. Had she forged ahead so relentlessly because she didn't want to know how many had been lost? She shook her head. "How long since the attack, do you think?"

"An hour at least," he said.

Four miles, at best. Not good enough.

But her people were exhausted, barely able to catch their breath. It might be days before their lungs fully recovered from the gas. She walked among them, checking for any injuries, trying to focus her mind on who was there and not who was missing.

She listened to them whisper among themselves. Some seemed convinced that the rain had been sent by the gods. Was it possible? Cerrin thought Ikala unlikely to have provided a means of retreat. Nestor, perhaps.

Cerrin passed Erras and two other Palanians. And then, a surprise. A wonderful surprise.

As Yarni leaped up from the ground, Cerrin dropped to her knees and embraced her. Sitting nearby was Torrin. The left side of her head was a livid red, but she somehow smiled.

"You made it."

Torrin pointed at her head. "Just a burn. Another inch toward me…"

Cerrin reached out and the two women held hands.

Yarni did not remove her arms from Cerrin's neck. "Sorry," said the girl. "I couldn't keep up with you."

"Don't you worry. I'm just glad to see you. Rest here."

She gently pulled away from Yarni and found Sonus helping an Echobe woman with a deep cut on her calf.

"Your prayer," said the woman, staring at Cerrin with wet, gleaming eyes. "Your prayer to the gods for rain. That's what did it."

Cerrin didn't have the heart to tell her she had made no such prayer. Sonus stood and ushered her aside to whisper in her ear. "Thirty-five. We lost nineteen."

Cerrin closed her eyes for a moment. Now she *did* think of the others. Of Kannalin.

"No serious injuries," added Sonus. "Nothing to slow us down."

"Torrin can lead for a bit. I'll hang back, see if they're coming after us. How many rifles?"

"Five left." Sonus tapped his. "This one's empty."

"I've got at least half my bullets. Will they keep coming?"

"Yes, but it will take them some time to get down to the ground."

"I'll go now," said Cerrin.

"Don't get too close." Sonus gestured to the others. "Can we give them ten minutes?"

"Five."

．．．

Count Talazeer had never seen such heavy rain. He had actually rather enjoyed using the descender line but now understood Elezz's point about negotiating the thick canopy. The downpour had slowed things even further and he was drenched by the time he landed.

Marl and the commander were already down. The Drellen was surveying the scene of the attack. Several dead rebels lay close by while a few survivors were being shackled by the soldiers. Talazeer did not immediately see Cerrin or Sonus among them.

"You all right there, sir?" asked Sergeant Guldur. Even by Vitaari standards, he was exceptionally tall—three meters, at the least—and broad shouldered. The sergeant was clearly not concerned by appearance: he bore several scars, including a very unsightly wound upon his forehead. Talazeer couldn't imagine why anyone would want to look so ugly, even a warrior.

"Fine, thank you."

"Looks like we got a few of the little rats, anyway."

"How many so far?"

"Ten. The men are still looking."

Examining the site, Elezz had donned a peaked cap and a long, gray coat. As Talazeer approached, she bent down and picked up a rifle.

"Commander, are we not pursuing the… escapees?"

"Double escapees now, aren't they?" She murmured this, then continued in a louder voice: "A pursuit, sir? In which direction?"

"We can't track them?"

"With what, sir? I told you about the effect of the rain on the heat sensors."

"We know they were heading west."

"They *were*. They may not be now. We are looking for signs of a physical trail but they have quite a head start."

"Marl and I shall join the search."

"As you wish."

Talazeer thought the commander ought to be showing a bit more enthusiasm but waved Marl over. "Come, we must find their trail."

The two yellow eyes swiveled upward. "In this?"

"There may still be signs, you idiot!"

Marl ground his teeth again but dutifully followed.

Talazeer strode through the forest to where the troopers were concentrated. Two men were carrying a native woman who seemed to be regaining consciousness. At his feet was a dead Palanian with a face that seemed to have been caved in by a drone laser. He noted how most of the natives still wore the clothes and boots issued by the Vitaari. They all looked filthy.

"It's rather pathetic—when you see them like this."

"Is it?" remarked Marl.

"What's that supposed to mean?"

The Drellen said nothing, and also ignored the wary glances of Sergeant Guldur's men. They passed two more bodies, then came upon two soldiers studying a thick patch of fern.

"Anything?" he asked.

One man held up a broken frond. "Someone came this way, sir."

Another Guardsman farther away waved them over. "*Several.* The boot prints are washed away, but there's a line of trampled shrubs over here."

Talazeer pointed down the path. "Marl, take a look. You know about such things."

"I'm sure," remarked one of the soldiers.

"Watch your mouth," snapped the Count.

The Guardsmen looked on as Marl moved past them with his uncannily smooth gait. His slender, scaled arms did not appear from his cloak until he stopped beside a broken branch and inspected it, turning it over with his long, clawed fingers.

"Well?" asked Talazeer. He did not regret persuading Elezz to use gas in place of explosives but knew a successful pursuit of the rebels would be the best outcome all around.

"A number of them did come this way. A large group—more than twenty."

"Ah. Continue on, Marl, see how far you can follow the trail. I won't be long."

With a spring in his step, Talazeer hurried back to where the men had gathered around Commander Elezz. The natives who were able to stand had been cuffed and placed in a line. There were seven of them, most gazing dolefully at the bodies of their fallen comrades. Elezz was talking to Sergeant Guldur, discussing how to get the captives and corpses back to the shuttle.

The rain was only a drizzle for the moment, but black clouds remained overhead. Glancing up, Talazeer could see only the descender lines, not the ship.

"We've found a trail," he announced. "I am happy to lead the pursuit."

"You're sure?" asked the commander.

The Count decided to be diplomatic. "Your men saw it; Marl confirmed it. A sizeable group. That many people leave clear signs on vegetation, even in weather like this."

Elezz adjusted her cap. "I appreciate your enthusiasm, Count Talazeer, but we cannot risk you in such a way. The shuttle can't remain overhead for much longer, not with more storms coming in."

"They have only a short lead on us, Commander. I've no doubt we'll catch them quickly."

"They know the territory, sir. Might I suggest a compromise?"

"Please."

"Sergeant Guldur can lead the pursuit. You and I will return to the shuttle with the prisoners. If the remaining rebels are sighted, we can come back with more men. The storms may even have passed by that point."

Talazeer could see the appeal in that; in truth, he wasn't overly enamored by the idea of traipsing through the sodden forest. But he was excited about the prospect of chasing his enemies down, finally making use of his hunting rifle.

Elezz hadn't finished: "I might also remind you that we must minimize the personal risk to yourself. The Domain has already lost a regional governor to these rebels. Part of my job here is to protect you, regardless of your personal valor."

Talazeer rather liked how she said that, and could see the logic of her suggestion. "You raise a fair point, Commander. I have other responsibilities that I must consider. I shall, however, leave Marl with Sergeant Guldur. He can keep me appraised of their progress."

Elezz gestured for the sergeant to move. "Hourly updates to me."

"Of course, Commander." The hulking sergeant tightened his helmet strap and jogged away through the rain.

Elezz walked over to the captives. "Now, let us see what these prisoners can tell us. Perhaps they know where the others are headed. They will understand me, won't they?"

"Oh yes," replied Talazeer. "We ensure that they all speak basic Vitaari so that they can take instruction."

"Good."

Unsure of what precisely the commander had in mind, Talazeer followed her.

Of the seven captives, four were male, the youngest not much more than a boy. It was he that Elezz approached first.

"Hello," said the commander softly. "What's your name?"

"Nartinn," said the boy, his hair soaked, rain running down his face.

"Well, Nartinn, we need your help in apprehending those who escaped. Where were you all going before we attacked? What is their destination?"

Another captive—an Echobe man, and a large one for his kind, though not quite to Talazeer's elbow—stepped next to the child.

"Don't tell them anything, Nartinn," he said. It seemed he had been struck by a laser blast but somehow survived. His shoulder was red and blistered, and bits of his clothing had fused with tissue. Despite this, he looked up at the Vitaari with grim defiance. "Not one thing. We're dead anyway. We must give the others every chance."

"Powerful words and a compelling sentiment," said Elezz, "but rather unrealistic."

She was not especially tall for a Vitaari female: Talazeer guessed around two and a quarter meters. But given the size difference with the natives, it was easy for her to lift the boy up by the cuffs binding his hands. Dangling there, he grimaced with pain. Elezz turned the lad so that he faced the others and placed her spare hand upon his head.

"I'll ask again. Where are they going?"

The boy closed his eyes and did not answer.

Elezz gripped hard, her gloved fingers pressing into Nartinn's skull.

"You've seen tearing," added the commander. "This will be worse."

Talazeer almost intervened. He had seen tearing, too, but knew he would never be able to do it himself. He didn't mind a bit of blood but seeing limbs come off was really quite unpleasant. The noise was also rather awful. And then there were the screams.

Elezz dug her fingers in.

Nartinn begged in impressively clear Vitaari. "Please don't... Please don't hurt me."

Then he stopped talking, because Elezz was already hurting him.

The big Echobe man stepped forward and three rifles instantly trained on him. His face was a mask of rage. "No more. No more. Just leave the boy alone. The Black Hollow. They're heading for the Black Hollow."

"Really?" said Elezz. "And what exactly is that?"

7

On and on, through high grass and fern, around great clumps of undergrowth and fungi, past trees tiny and huge.

Rain came again in late afternoon, soaking through every bag and item of clothing. Sonus often found himself next to Yarni and he carried her for a time when she felt faint. Though he had only recently recovered from his illness, some of the girl's strength seem to transfer itself to him. Where he had previously been one of the slowest, now he kept pace and encouraged others onward. Perhaps it was simply that they all knew this was a race for their lives, the only way to win more days of freedom—a chance for another chance.

Torrin led the way superbly, despite her injury. Jespa never seemed to stop: he moved constantly up and down the line, cajoling others to keep going with kindness and humor.

And Cerrin... Surely, she covered twice the distance of anyone else. She would bring up the rear for a while, then drop back to search for signs of pursuit, somehow always finding her way to the column again.

Three times Sonus heard that she'd seen no trace of the

Vitaari. If soldiers were on their trail, they were some distance behind.

When Torrin called a halt, Cerrin went scouting for a fourth time. This patch of forest seemed more vines than trees. They hung in great clumps from every branch and snaked across the ground. Scattered across the area were crimson prayers, a beautiful type of flower that resembled two clasped hands.

Sonus and Yarni sat down against some vines. Jespa seemed the only one with any energy left and he collected up the remaining gourds and flasks, filling them from hollows in the surrounding trees. Sonus was about to summon some comforting words for Yarni when he realized she was asleep on his shoulder.

It was Yarni who woke Sonus to announce that Cerrin had returned. Though many of the rebels slept on, others surrounded her, including Torrin and Jespa. Sonus had heard the gossip about those two particular Echobe, and in recent days he'd noticed it too: the glances, the hushed conversations. It was wonderful to see.

As he stood and joined the others, Sonus realized how cold he was. Rubbing his hands together, he felt water from his sodden clothes run down his legs. The only sense of warmth came from the few glimpses of sunlight far above.

He and Cerrin exchanged nods. She was even wetter than the others and as dirty as the gun she carried over her shoulder.

"How far?" asked Jespa.

"Maybe a mile," said Cerrin. "They're crashing through the forest in full armor, so they're not hard to spot. Loud, too."

The others shook their heads or cursed.

"Then we must go on," said Sonus.

"Yes." Cerrin pointed southward. "But not that way. I found a kill site. Two dead boar, very young. Something must have taken the mother."

"What could have done it?" asked Erras.

"Those boars are very dangerous. At first, I thought of a damareus. But there wasn't enough blood."

"A mordyn?" said Jespa, eyes wide.

Some of the Echobe made a sign over their hearts. Sonus had seen this before; apparently it was some appeal to the gods.

Erras let out a long sigh. "Just when you think it can't possibly get any worse."

"Actually, it's good news," said Cerrin. "I found its trail."

Torrin smiled, apparently understanding how this could possibly be a positive development.

"Please explain," prompted Sonus.

"Mordyn live in the water, except when they hunt," replied Cerrin. "Usually lakes and ponds. The Vitaari can track us across land but not across water."

Feeling rather tired after his forest excursion, Count Talazeer thought he would head to his quarters. If there were any developments on the ground, he would hear immediately from Marl. As he exited the loading bay, soldiers passed by, escorting the seven prisoners. Talazeer stopped for a moment and watched the natives, the big man and the young boy among them. All walked with heads bowed, still bound, dwarfed by the hulking Guardsmen. There was no detention area on the *Galtaryax* but another bay had been adapted for the purpose; the prisoners would be kept in a storage container.

"Sir, we shall begin interrogating them immediately."

Talazeer turned to find Elezz right behind him, as usual accompanied by one of her faithful technicians.

"Of course," said the Count. "Though I'm sure we'll have the others by the end of the day."

"I wish I shared your certainty. There are only four hours of daylight left. Guldur just reported in. They're still following the trail but have not yet sighted the rebels."

Talazeer didn't think it was the moment to remind her about using that word. "Odd. Our men are bigger, stronger. Professionals."

"The natives clearly understand the terrain. They're also running for their lives."

"I have confidence in Marl and our troops, Commander."

"I do wish we could have resolved this earlier in the day, sir."

Talazeer was not surprised the forceful Elezz wouldn't drop the issue. "I am well aware of your feelings on the matter but let me be clear. By executing them in full view of the remaining slave population, we can crush any remaining thoughts of resistance. Perhaps a live broadcast to every installation? Could be very effective."

He could see by her expression that his words had made some impact. "I suppose it could, sir."

"Very good. I shall be in my quarters. Feel free to alert me if necessary."

While he spoke, Talazeer noted the approach of Rasikaar. He knew what this would be about. "Deputy, in light of today's events, I'd like to postpone the remaining mine visits until tomorrow."

"As you wish, Excellency. I'm actually here to ask the commander if her technical staff could advise us."

"Advise on what?" said Elezz.

"The sensor array has picked up an unusual reading. A cluster of madrin particles has been identified in the upper atmosphere."

"What are they?" asked Talazeer.

"A waste product of anti-matter drives," explained Elezz. "A form of technology used by the Red Regent."

An hour after Cerrin's return, they found the lake. It was perhaps half a mile long, sixty yards across. Sonus knew he should have been glad, but it was not a sight to raise the spirits. The water was a murky green, thick with weeds and lilies. The banks were lined with overhanging trees and obscured by dense tangles of roots. Worse than all that, however, was the knowledge that they had purposefully tracked an enormous snake to this place.

The rebels gathered near the bank and stood in a circle, every pair of eyes glancing fearfully around.

"Wish there was time to build a raft," remarked Erras. Beside him, the frail Nuro anxiously eyed the water.

"Too noisy," said Cerrin. "In any case, we needn't worry about the mordyn—hopefully it's just eaten."

"And what if he's still hungry?" added Erras. "Or he's got a mate around here somewhere?"

"This is our best chance," said Cerrin firmly. "They'll likely stay away from a big group."

Sonus was still gazing at the water, trying not to imagine the giant reptile that could be lurking in its depths. Cerrin had positioned them near a relatively clear section of bank. To get into the water, they would need only to negotiate some oddly shaped bushes with star-shaped orange blooms.

She pointed across the lake. "Straight over and we come out there." The area she identified was beneath a large tree with a sprawling network of roots.

"Hard to get out," said Torrin, soothing her burned face with a wet leaf.

"Hard for them to pick up the trail," replied Cerrin. "They'll probably walk around."

"They won't swim?" asked Jespa.

"With all their equipment?" said Erras. "I doubt—"

"No more talk," said Cerrin. She took her pack off and held it up. "These can all be sealed. Get plenty of air in and you can use them for floats. Good swimmers, give them to those who need them. Two minutes and we're in the water."

She hurried over to Sonus. "We need to keep the rifles dry, correct?"

"If possible, yes." Sonus had already given this some thought. He pointed at a nearby fallen branch—it was as long as a person. "That should do it."

The pair of them moved some detritus aside and pulled the branch clear.

"Not much of a swimmer myself," confessed Sonus. "I grew up in a city."

"You don't need to be."

Sonus lowered his voice. "Could they catch up while we're still in the water?"

"Yes," said Cerrin. "Which is why we have to be quick."

Fear drove them on. With both hands on the branch, Sonus kicked hard, eyes fixed on the distant tree. The noise of the splashing and the gasping breaths of those around him seemed terribly loud, but he told himself not to look back. If the Vitaari reached the lake, there was nothing they could do.

Nobody said a word; all their depleted reserves of energy were directed toward crossing the lake. Cerrin clearly didn't need the branch but wanted to stay close to the rifles and help Yarni, who was positioned between them. If Cerrin's relentless courage and energy provided one form of inspiration to Sonus, the child offered another. Halfway across, she summoned a smile, as if this were some pleasant morning swim.

Shortly afterward, Cerrin told the other two to stop; she wanted to check on the rest of the group. As she'd suggested, the stronger swimmers were staying close to the weak. But though they had only thirty yards to go, the pace was terribly slow. Erras and Nuro were holding on to the same thick branch, but despite Erras's help, Nuro was clearly struggling.

"Got to speed up," she said loudly. "Keep going!"

They set off again but seconds later someone cried out.

"Did you see that? Something in the water!"

This drew everyone's attention, but Torrin soon dispelled the fear: "I saw it. A jori fish. They're harmless."

The last part of the crossing seemed to pass with agonizing slowness. As they approached the roots, Sonus snatched a quick look over his shoulder. He saw no sign of their pursuers on the bank.

The agile Jespa swam to the front and swiftly found the best way: through the overhanging roots, over clumps of weeds, up a slope of thick mud. Cerrin left Sonus and Yarni on the branch and began escorting the slowest. Others like Torrin did the same and soon the rebels were pulling and scrabbling and sliding their way up onto dry ground. Only Erras and Nuro were yet to reach the bank, but even they didn't have far to go.

He couldn't be sure, but judging by the way Cerrin and Torrin glanced repeatedly around, Sonus assumed they were in prime mordyn territory. As he imagined some great beast sliding around his legs, he felt his hands begin to shake.

"It's all right, Sonus," said Yarni. "We'll be out before you know it."

"Just cold, that's all."

He continued to watch as the others followed Jespa's path to safety. At Cerrin's insistence, Yarni went ahead of the remaining adults and soon only Sonus and a handful of others were left in the dark water. He'd already concluded that Cerrin had made yet another strategic decision. The vegetation around the lake was very dense and it would surely take the Vitaari some time to re-locate their trail, if at all. And there had been no further sign of the shuttle, so it seemed the pursuing soldiers were on their own.

"Could they go any slower!" hissed Cerrin, pushing off the bank to go and assist Erras and Nuro. They were no more than ten feet away, but Cerrin was only halfway there when Nuro disappeared. There was no warning, not even a cry. One moment she was beside Erras, the next she was gone. He simply stared at the water, unable to take it in and react.

Cerrin took a few strokes forward, then dived below. Erras tried the same but came back up not long after. He flailed around in every direction but there was no trace of Nuro or movement anywhere else. She had simply vanished. Cerrin then emerged, hair plastered to her face.

Sonus heard some exchange between them but couldn't make out the words. Erras did not move. Cerrin quickly grabbed the branch and kicked hard, guiding them both swiftly to the bank. The stunned Palanian was gazing blankly ahead, not making eye contact with anyone.

Sonus grabbed him under the arm and moved him through the tangle of roots. Cerrin went to fetch the weapons still on the branch, but froze.

"Stay absolutely still," she said quietly. "And don't turn."

Sonus closed his eyes to keep from being tempted to turn and look. Instead, he held his breath and listened for any soft splash in the water or slither through the mud. But it wasn't a mordyn that had caught Cerrin's eye.

"Vitaari," she said.

"How many?" asked Sonus, opening his eyes again but not daring to turn.

"Three," she whispered. "More coming now. Looking across. They're doing something with their helmets. They're—"

"What is it?"

"Not sure," continued Cerrin. "Maybe they heard something. They're all looking in the same direction. Moving away."

Thank the Maker.

None of them moved again until Cerrin gave the all clear. Sonus guided Erras through the rest of the roots and onto the muddy bank. Poor Erras simply sat there, staring back at the water while the others removed the rifles, which had been tied to the branch with vines.

"Was it the mordyn?" asked one of the others.

"Don't know," said Cerrin.

For the first time since he'd reached the shore, Erras looked at Cerrin. His eyes were still on her even when the lake was far behind them.

. . .

Somehow, the rebels of Corvos found the energy to keep moving. The weather had changed and they eventually halted beneath a wide beam of evening sunlight, drying their clothes and warming their faces. The Echobe had once more showed remarkable skill in foraging even as they moved, and there was again a handful of food for everyone.

Even after years of endless labor within the Vitaari mines, Sonus wasn't sure that he'd ever been so tired. He was sitting on damp soil, rifle in front of him, dozing. Around him, the other rebels had either fallen instantly asleep or were silently occupied by their thoughts, no doubt reliving the terrible hours since their flight from the Vitaari. Several people were quietly sobbing. As for Erras, he had still said not a word. There were now only seven Palanians left.

Cerrin appeared from behind Sonus and knelt down. She had acquired another spear from somewhere and placed her rifle in front of him.

"I replaced the bullets. We should collect the spares, see what we have."

"Agreed." He would have helped her but wasn't sure he could even get off the ground. As usual, Cerrin looked as if she could easily do it all again.

"Was it the mordyn, do you think?" Sonus asked quietly.

Cerrin nodded. "How could they be so slow? Even the children got across quicker."

Sonus thought this harsh, even for her.

"My father saw one once," added Cerrin. "Once they have hold of you, it's over. A human is no challenge."

Sonus didn't want to talk about it anymore. "I imagine he was a great warrior, your father."

Cerrin picked up a mottled leaf and turned it over.

Sonus added, "If you don't want to talk about it, no problem."

"I don't mind. It's just that I know so little about you, Sonus—your life before. I know you were an engineer. I know that you went to the University. But what about your family?"

"I was at home during the invasion. Mother liked to spoil me—she'd cooked a special meal for my birthday, even though it wasn't for another week."

Sonus had not often talked of such things, even with close friends. But he knew there would have to be give and take if he were to learn more about Cerrin. He was quiet by nature but she was… enigmatic. She seemed to give only what she wanted to.

"No brothers or sisters?" she asked.

"No," he replied. "They'd only wanted the one. So that they would have enough money for a good education."

"That is far-sighted."

"I suppose it was. I sometimes felt a lot of… expectation."

"I was an only child. Except… well… when I was nine, my mother fell pregnant. I think it was a surprise to them both. But the baby was stillborn. It was a terrible time. I felt disappointed that I'd never get a little sister, then guilty at my selfishness."

"Perhaps that's why you're so close with Yarni."

"She doesn't give me much choice. But perhaps you're right."

"Your mother recovered?"

"She did. A strong woman. She taught me a lot, but my father taught me more. In some Echobe tribes, females almost never leave home but not ours. He instructed me as he would a son. I was fortunate."

"I think we are all fortunate that he did."

"He used to say that he was *not* a great warrior. He was not the quickest or the strongest or the best shot. In fact, he was clumsy—he used to drop arrows. But he was crafty, and he understood animals and he usually made the right choice. Other, better warriors were happy to be led by him. He died bravely."

"So did my father," replied Sonus. "Mother and I saw him killed. She asked me not to fight so I didn't. Perhaps it was shameful but I wanted to be around to protect her. She lasted only two years on the mountain. The cold."

"My mother died as we ran from the Vitaari." Cerrin paused, looked around the forest. "We were some of the last caught. It seems so long ago." She turned the leaf over in her hand, then dropped it. "Do you fight for *them*?"

"For them. For my friends at Mine Fourteen. I was very close with two in particular. They…"

Sonus had not spoken to any of the rebels about Karas and Qari. It was still too painful.

Cerrin said nothing nor made any gesture. But the flash of kindness in those brown eyes put Sonus at ease. "Karas… Qari… when they died, something changed inside me. I knew I had to escape. How many times did you try?"

"Six." Cerrin grinned. "But the Vitaari only knew about three."

Count Talazeer had written and rewritten the reply at least ten times. And now that he had sent it, he was panicking that he had struck the wrong tone.

The message from Deslat had arrived with his brother's usual immaculate timing. He was, of course, enquiring about Talazeer's progress with both the terodite and the rebels. Without making any definitive comment, Talazeer had reassured his brother on both counts. There was no point pretending that all was well; he had no doubt that his father had sources in High Command—possibly even on Corvos itself.

All he could hope for was an element of fortune on Corvos and an element of patience back home. Despite the ultimatum, surely a man of his father's experience would be realistic about these things?

At the sound of raised voices, Talazeer was drawn back to the here and now.

Within the operations room, a technical discussion of considerable complexity continued. Even Commander Elezz seemed perplexed by the issues surrounding anti-matter drives and madrin particles. Talazeer stood over the tactical display, which still showed the area of the attack. He gathered that Elezz was planning to send out the hunter drones again. He had spoken to Marl only minutes earlier: it seemed that the pursuers had lost the trail at some lake.

With a frustrated shake of her head, Commander Elezz walked away from the techs.

"Any conclusions?" asked Talazeer.

"Not even a consensus. Analysis shows that there *are* madrin particles present but we cannot be sure of the origin. It's true that they are associated with anti-matter drives but they are also associated with certain cosmic phenomena. I'm not sure it's something we should concern ourselves with, though this lot are getting rather overexcited."

One of the techs stood and crossed the operations room.

"Excellency, Commander—I'm afraid we can't raise Sergeant Guldur."

According to Marl, the soldiers were performing reasonably well but the Drellen seemed to think he'd have made more progress on his own.

"It can't be the storm," added the tech. "It's already passed through that area."

"Keep trying. Count Talazeer?"

He retrieved the comcell he used to communicate with Marl. Though small, it was an expensive device with exceptional range and a durable power cell. The Count thought it essential that he always be in close touch with his bodyguard.

He keyed the call button but it just kept beeping.

"Strange," said Commander Elezz.

"Not necessarily," said Talazeer. "Marl often goes silent when he's hunting."

Sonus wished that he and Cerrin could continue talking but an eager Jespa had just appeared.

"What now?" said the Echobe.

"We need to start heading west again," replied Cerrin. "We must still make for the Old Giants. We'll stop when it gets dark."

Sonus felt he had to intercede. "West? Is that a good idea? The Vitaari have prisoners now. They may already know where we're going."

"What alternative is there?"

"Perhaps we should speak with Torrin and Erras, make the decision together."

Cerrin's eyes narrowed. She stood and dug the point of her spear into the soil.

Sonus reckoned he knew what she was thinking. Again, her leadership had kept them from danger, bought them more time. She trusted her own judgment and who could blame her? He just hoped that she still valued the opinions of others. "Very well," she said.

A minute later, five of them were gathered beneath the vine-covered boughs of a tree, the evening light already fading. Erras had refused to attend, so old Koros had come in his place. Cerrin wafted an insect away but said nothing. Sonus spoke up.

"Cerrin believes we should continue west toward the Old Giants. We know the advantages and it is not far. I am still fully prepared to go along with it. Koros did mention another idea."

The old Palanian seemed a little surprised by this but made his contribution. "We could head northeast, with the eventual intention of leaving the forest and seeking refuge in Okara. Or what's left of it anyway."

"Your old capital city?" said Jespa.

Koros nodded. "There are plenty of hiding places there. And the Vitaari won't expect it. There's a good chance they already know about the Old Giants from the prisoners."

"I agree," said Sonus. "We're all fully aware of what the Vitaari do to... what they are capable of."

"But we have come so far," said Jespa. "It will take weeks to reach the western edge of the forest."

"I understand," said Sonus. "That's exactly why they won't expect it."

"Perhaps they will *expect* us to change plans," offered Torrin. "Perhaps we should just keep going to the Giants."

"We Palanians call that a double bluff," said Koros.

They all looked to Cerrin. She dug the spear head into the soil again. "The Echobe will not leave the Great Forest. Either we live here or we die here."

Sonus had not expected a different answer and, after their earlier conversation, it pained him to oppose her. Yet he felt he had to counter.

"Cerrin, we are not all Echobe."

"*Most* of us are. We can perhaps lay a false trail or take an indirect route, but I will continue on to the Old Giants. Anyone who wishes to take another path is free to do so."

None of the others replied. Sonus would have liked to raise several other points but he simply didn't have the energy.

"Gods and spirits preserve us." Jespa had whispered this, and he was now gazing, open-mouthed, at a wall of vines not ten feet away. Something was moving within them, and in seconds a strange, blurred shape appeared.

Cerrin lifted the spear and let fly.

The projectile snapped in half and fell to the ground.

The strange blur suddenly acquired form: humanoid form.

Soon they could see what looked like a man of average height, clad in a metallic suit that somehow seemed liquid. The liquid metal now melted away from the head, leaving a remarkably pale, almost translucent face not unlike that of a Palanian.

"Greetings," said the stranger. "My name is Toll Maktar. I am here to help."

8

Count Talazeer waited another hour and then announced he was retiring to his quarters. Commander Elezz didn't seem particularly impressed. The Count didn't particularly care.

Tired, wet, and cold after his time in the jungle, he stripped off and showered. To protect his still-sensitive face, he made sure the water wasn't too hot before stepping under it. Once clean, he applied his usual selection of scent and skin conditioners, then put on a robe.

There had been no further contact with either Marl or Sergeant Guldur. Elezz's technicians seemed as confused as the *Galtaryax*'s communications officer. They were also clearly preoccupied by these strange particles but unsure if the two matters were related. Talazeer felt that the commander needed to relax a little. Despite the communication issues, there was no chance that Marl or the troops had come to any harm.

The Count acknowledged to himself that his insistence on not using explosives had spared the rebels but at least they had prisoners now. And if the hunter drones had found them once, why couldn't they do so again? He did not regret his intervention.

His reckoning with Sonus and Cerrin had been delayed, but it would still come.

Walking through to his bedroom, he removed his robe. Now naked, he opened another of the boxes of candies he'd brought from Vitaar. They were unhealthy, of course, and he never had more than three per day but the taste did make him feel better. It reminded him of happier times, innocent times.

He climbed into the bed—which was not very comfortable—and settled beneath the covers. He was relieved not to have taken part in the pursuit of the escapees. It would now seem an embarrassing failure. Wondering what Commander Elezz looked like naked, Talazeer nestled into a pillow and closed his eyes.

The stranger stood in silence while they spoke. It was an oddly quiet discussion because nobody dared raise their voice. Once all of the rebels had overcome their shock at the appearance of the being called Toll Maktar, they had to decide what to do. On closer inspection, his skin was actually quite odd, with pulsing veins and the outlines of bone and ligament clearly visible. His strangely square face seemed rather inexpressive, the eyes a lifeless gray. The interloper had not yet added much to his initial statement.

Cerrin hadn't said much either, because she was standing right in front of him, rifle aimed between those gray eyes. She could not avoid the suspicion that this was some elaborate Vitaari trick.

"We *cannot* stay here," insisted Torrin. "Believe me, I wish we could stop and rest but we can't."

"Did you listen to the man?" countered Koros.

"*Man?*" said Jespa. "I wouldn't be too sure about that."

Koros turned to Sonus. "Are you going to say something?"

The old Palanian had already tried—and failed—to persuade Cerrin to lower the rifle.

"I'll speak," said Sonus. "But not while Cerrin holds our guest at gunpoint."

"Our guest?" said Jespa. "For all you know—"

The liquid metal began to move once more, sliding down from Maktar's shoulders and up from his feet. In seconds, it had coalesced within a cube attached to his belt, no wider than a hand. Beneath it, he was wearing only black. The color was in sharp contrast to that pale face and Cerrin now noticed that his nose, mouth and ears were delicate and small. She wasn't sure she could ever trust those unblinking, dead gray eyes.

Maktar had various items attached to his belt. He now pointed at the cube. "You see what this does, yes?" He then aimed a white finger at a second device. "Translator. That's why we can understand each other. Fortunately, I was able to obtain some basic data on what you call *Trade* from the Vitaari archives."

The third item was a small black globe. "And this is what we call a defender. It searches for—and disables—nearby weapons systems." Maktar pointed at Cerrin. "That is a Mark Eight Assault Rifle. The firing stud uses a senso-relay to activate the actual trigger in the barrel. My defender can block the senso-relay. The weapon is now useless. So, you might as well listen to your friend and lower it, yes?"

Cerrin instead advanced and touched the rifle to his head. "All right if I just test it out?"

"Cerrin," warned Sonus.

"Go ahead," replied Maktar. It might have been the translator but Cerrin found his tone dry and rather arrogant, as if he was mocking her.

She didn't touch the firing stud.

"Sorry about breaking your spear," added Maktar. "The burst gauntlets are part of the armor. It has defensive and offensive capability."

Cerrin lowered the gun and raised a fist. "Suppose I just punch you in the face?"

"That might actually work."

Koros was the first but not the last to laugh. Sonus also chuckled.

Cerrin didn't have any laughter in her. "How do we know you're not working with the Vitaari? How do we know they won't be here in five minutes?"

"You did well at the lake," replied Maktar coolly. "But do you really think the Vitaari soldiers just walked off in another direction of their own accord? I led them some distance away and disabled their communications. I must admit I'm surprised by their operation here. That ship of theirs looks ready for the scrapyard."

"You mean the *Galtaryax*?" asked Sonus.

"Yes." Maktar pushed aside a twig hanging close to his face. "It's a pity I didn't arrive in time to intervene earlier. You appear to have lost a number of people when they attacked."

Cerrin said: "You're here to help? How, exactly?"

"I will explain all, yes? But even with that Vitaari patrol out of the way, this is not a good location. Only a mile east, there is a more suitable area."

Sonus nodded, clearly ready to follow this suggestion. Cerrin could not believe how easily he accepted all of this, took the stranger at his word. Koros and the other Palanians also seemed eager to do so.

She took Jespa's spear and aimed it at Maktar. "Don't think your device will stop me throwing this. You can walk in front of me."

"As you wish."

Even Cerrin had to admit that the area Maktar had identified was ideal. She'd never seen this particular type of tree before. None was taller than fifty feet but each possessed a broad trunk and only three or four branches. These branches were low and so thick—some five or six feet across—that they provided excellent cover, especially as they were currently adorned by dense leaves.

It hadn't taken long to get there, and Cerrin had stayed right behind him every step, spear at the ready. She half-suspected Maktar might have eyes in the back of his head—or some device to achieve the same effect—and she was not about to simply accept him at his word. This was another alien, and aliens had brought only destruction to Corvos. She could not always take on board the views of Sonus and the Palanians. They did not see things the same way as the Echobe. Her instincts—and perhaps the will of the gods—had kept them alive so far. If those same instincts told her that this Maktar was another threat, she would kill him.

When the rebels gathered beneath the branches to listen to him, she did not sit like the others. She stood with spear in hand, silent and watchful. Such was the interest in the stranger that all attended, even Erras. Cerrin was surprised—but also grateful—

when Sonus came to stand beside her. Two flashlights on low settings hung from the branches, casting them all in a faint glow.

Toll Maktar clasped his hands in front of him and spoke. The only other noise was the rustle of the leaves above. His calm, even voice carried easily. There was sometimes a short delay due to the translator and, though he spoke *Trade* clearly, Cerrin found some of the pronunciation strange.

"I come from Ikasar, in the eleventh sector. It is not a planet. It is a moon. You are fortunate here to have a planet and two moons. Our planet was destroyed centuries ago. It was struck by an asteroid and within weeks became uninhabitable. Only a fraction of the population survived and escaped to the moon. Those first pioneers found themselves in a dead place and, though we already had a small settlement there, we had to transform it into our new home. My people survive there still, three hundred and two years later. We can only live there because of artificial shields, under which we grow food and raise children and live as best we can. The place called Ikasar is now that moon, for we have nowhere else."

When he paused, several hushed conversations broke out. Like most Echobe, Cerrin had known little even of Palanians and Lovirr. The idea of beings from other planets had only become real—horribly real—with the invasion of the Vitaari eighteen years previous, when she had been a young girl. The occupiers made no effort to educate their slaves but information had spread during the intervening years. Even Cerrin—who had been one of the last caught—knew the name of Vitaar and other worlds. She was also one of the few, perhaps the only one, who had seen her planet from space, though that experience still seemed a dream.

"You must forgive us," said Sonus. "We have only met the

Vitaari. This is difficult even for me and I am a scientist. We are very ignorant of other worlds, of what lies beyond."

"Nothing good," remarked Jespa, a sentiment Cerrin whole-heartedly shared.

Kannalin would have agreed, too. He was still alive when they'd left him. She hoped he'd died before the Vitaari found him. She hoped they all had.

"How far is it?" asked Yarni.

"Very far," answered Maktar. "But I have a fast ship."

"Where is the ship?" asked an Echobe man.

"Close."

"Do the Vitaari know that?" asked Koros.

"No," said Maktar. "My ship is called *Spectre* and she's well named. The Vitaari do not know of my presence on Corvos."

Sonus spoke up. "Perhaps you can tell us exactly *why* you're here."

"Many years ago, Ikasar received an emissary from another race, a very powerful and influential race—the First Empire. They had taken over many of the systems close to ours. Sometimes they conquer by force—like the Vitaari—but sometimes they prefer to make alliances and arrangements. That is how Ikasar has survived. We have no natural resources now but we are creators, inventors. All of my equipment is Ikasaran, even the *Spectre*. The First Empire had no interest in our dead moon, but they were very interested in our technology. An agreement was made by the men and women of my parents' generation. The leader of the First Empire is the Red Regent. In return for guaranteeing the safety of Ikasar and supplying certain provisions, she makes demands of us."

"This regent is a woman?" asked someone.

"I believe so," replied Maktar, "though no one's actually seen her. No one that I've ever met has even seen one of the creatures who lead the First Empire. They have dominated our universe for millennia—they have absorbed so many cultures and peoples and ideas. It is said that there are only a few of them, the rulers. They are said to be immortal and the Red Regent is the oldest of them all. I have travelled far and wide and come to the same conclusion as our scholars. There was nothing before the First Empire. There might be nothing after."

"What about the Vitaari?" asked Sonus.

"In recent years, Vitaari expansion has led to conflict with the Red Regent. Most predict full-scale war. So once again, the Regent needs Ikasar. Agents like me have been sent to many systems, in ships like the *Spectre*. We monitor Vitaari communication networks. We know where they face resistance, where natives are already fighting them. The Red Regent wants allies. Anyone who fights the Vitaari is an ally of hers. I meant what I said: I *am* here to help."

Then came a lengthy pause as the listeners absorbed all they had heard.

"How, exactly?" asked Sonus. "Can you get us out of here?"

Cerrin was surprised by the question. Where did Sonus think he could go?

"No. My ship is small. And this is not a rescue mission for a few. I am here to help the whole of Corvos, if I can. But this is merely a starting point. My job is to decide how best to assist the fight against the Vitaari."

"You mean *all* the peoples?" said Erras, who had moved closer while Maktar spoke.

"Yes. I know the basic history since the invasion from what

we've gleaned from Vitaari communications. What do you know of this desert people, the Kinassans?"

Sonus answered: "They caused the Vitaari more problems than most because they are spread out and inhabit the remote lands. There are also fewer mines there. I believe there are still thousands of tribesmen free in the south."

"And the Lovirr?"

"Collaborators," said Jespa. "Cowards."

"Not all," replied Sonus. "Some are part of a resistance movement—they allowed us to coordinate my escape with the breakout at Mine Three." He gestured to the group. "Everyone except me comes from that mine."

"Do you know how I could contact this movement?" asked Maktar.

"I only dealt with one man," said Sonus. "He may even have been uncovered by the Vitaari by now."

"The Kinassans—what weaponry do they have?"

"Nothing advanced," said Sonus. "Blades, bows, and such like. But they are a tough, durable people."

"Like the Echobe," replied Maktar.

"In some respects," said Sonus. "We Palanians perhaps thought ourselves superior, but the invasion proved we were simply more vulnerable. The Echobe held out far longer. The Kinassans do still, though I'm sure the Vitaari could wipe them out if they really needed to. The Kinassans are the only race that still numbers in the tens of thousands."

"And the Echobe? What are your numbers?"

Torrin spoke up. "Nobody can be sure but it is something we used to discuss in the mines. There must have been more than sixty thousand Echobe spread across the Forest. And there must still be a few here, hiding out. Within the mines there are no more than four thousand."

Another Echobe man spoke up: "I have heard that number, too. I believe it was an estimate from the Vitaari."

Sonus weighed in again. "There were once around two-hundred thousand Palanians. There are no more than eight or nine thousand still alive, almost all within the mines. I cannot believe there are not a few still scattered around Palanian territory, particularly in the mountains. But most were killed or enslaved. A great many died within the mines. Tens of thousands."

To Cerrin, Maktar did not appear particularly affected by what he heard. She looked around and saw many visibly upset by this brief summary of her planet's recent history. She was more concerned with the future.

"What exactly can you do for us?" she asked. "Can that ship of yours destroy a mine? Or the *Galtaryax*?"

"No, but even if it could, I would not risk it. I am not here to fight a war myself."

"Weapons, then?"

"I may be able to supply you with weapons, yes."

"We need more like this," said Jespa, holding up a rifle. "To defend ourselves."

"I understand," said Toll Maktar. "But there are conditions. I realize it will take time to gather strength, but you cannot only defend. We need you to *attack*."

Summoned by Commander Elezz after only six hours of sleep, Count Talazeer walked along the corridor in a daze. He had been dreaming of his family home back on Vitaar, a pleasant family occasion during which his mother had prepared him some of his favorite foods. He sneered and shook his head at the thought of it, gripped by shame. Pathetic imaginings. Childish.

He didn't suppose he was going to hear anything good from the commander. There had been no contact from Marl and so it seemed likely that the *rebels* (as they continued to fight, he couldn't deny the term was accurate) had escaped. Though she probably wouldn't say so, Elezz undoubtedly blamed him for this state of affairs. It was undeniably a reversal, but he was not overly concerned; Cerrin and Sonus would face his justice and vengeance. Before they died, they would know he had beaten them. Their deaths would show the rest of the natives that the single flame of hope had been extinguished.

He had not been summoned to the operations room but to loading bay three, where the prisoners were kept. As the doors parted and he entered the bay, he was not surprised to see Elezz already present. Four guardsmen were lined up along the cargo container where the prisoners were being held. Other than a few other containers, a stack of metal girders, and some fuel barrels, the rest of the bay was empty.

The commander did not look tired. Talazeer wondered how much surgery she'd had, which stimulants she took. "Sir, did you enjoy your rest?"

He didn't feel this deserved a reply. "No more word from the forest?"

"Actually, we've just picked something up. Guldur and your bodyguard lost the trail. They believe there was some attempt to divert them. It will be sunrise soon. I'm going to recall them."

"Why can't they keep looking?"

"They've been on the ground for fourteen hours, sir. With no chance to rest."

"I see. So, you'll be sending the hunter drones?"

"We will. But I want a reserve plan." She turned toward the container. "This might be of interest you. Would you like to accompany me?"

"Why not?" As he followed Elezz to the container, Talazeer realized he was hungry. After this, he would sleep a little longer, then have some food sent up. He would also ask for some meat for Marl, though he supposed the Drellen might have found something to his taste in the forest.

At Elezz's order, one of the guardsmen keyed the switch that opened the container. It was a metal box about fifteen meters long, five high, and five wide. The seven prisoners were shackled to a bar and they blinked and bowed their heads as light flooded the space. With a soldier beside each of them, Talazeer and Elezz walked past the captives. The Count again felt a slight pang of sympathy for the young boy who the commander had questioned in the forest.

"My apologies for your poor treatment."

This was not how Talazeer had expected Elezz to address the prisoners.

"We should be rewarding you after your cooperation. I am glad that I was able to… persuade you to do so. It makes everything so much easier. Now that the rest of you have confirmed what—" She aimed a finger at the big warrior. He was slumped against the wall and did not appear to be faring well. His shoulder was covered in dried blood and his arm had been badly burned.

"Kannalin." Another prisoner gave his name.

"—what Kannalin told us about the Black Hollow, we have identified a possible location. You might not believe this, but I am a fair person." As she spoke, Elezz looked every one of the captives in the eye. "Your reward shall be medical treatment—you will find none better in this quadrant. The guards will escort you to the medical bay now. Have no fear, we want you to be healthy so you can work. Once the treatment is complete, you will be returned to the mines. Guards."

As the soldiers entered and began unlocking the shackles, Elezz looked on, a half-smile upon her pretty face.

When the last of the prisoners had been taken out, she turned to the Count. "There is such a place as the Black Hollow, and they described its location accurately. But our behavioral analysis shows that they were lying."

"Then why not torture them?"

"Oh, we will. If necessary. But there is a more reliable—and practical—method of tracking the remaining rebels down. How can I put this? Not all the procedures executed by the ship's surgeon will be strictly *medical*."

9

It was agreed that the exhausted rebels needed to rest. Sonus was not surprised that Cerrin insisted on two guards for Toll Maktar, who greeted this with a faint smile and now sat with Jespa and another man watching over him. The interloper was playing with some bracelet-like gadget around his wrist. Sonus felt sure that his arrival was something to be welcomed. As he had discussed with Cerrin, their eventual destruction at the hands of the Vitaari seemed almost inevitable. From the mouth of Toll Maktar, he—they—had learned about a previously unknown conflict, the consequences of which might have huge ramifications for their lonely struggle. The thought of such a powerful force challenging the Vitaari gave him a surge of hope.

Yet, despite the incredible events of the last few hours, his body had never felt so weary. For some reason, the rat bite had begun to ache again and his feet throbbed from all the walking. And now that the imminent danger was past, he could feel the after-effects of the gas. He, Cerrin, and many others had vomited several times and their eyes were sore. Torrin had provided a tonic from her limited supply, which at least eased the symptoms a little.

Only one light was on—beside Maktar and his guards.

Everyone else appeared to be asleep, including Cerrin. She lay in the shadows with Yarni, hair half-covering her face. Across her knees was the gun; propped up beside her, a replacement spear.

Though he felt certain Maktar was genuine, Sonus ensured he had one of the five remaining guns with him. He slept with both hands upon the cold metal.

He awoke with a start, fingers already gripping the rifle, but soon realized all was well. Most of the rebels were still asleep, though a few were stirring. Through the branches, he could see the sun daubing its first colors onto the dark sky. Then he saw someone coming his way, silhouetted by the dawn light. It was Torrin and she too was holding a rifle.

"He wants to talk to you. Cerrin's already there."

"Very well."

Sonus stood, told himself to ignore his various aches and pains, and accompanied Torrin back past the resting rebels. Some had covered themselves in thick fronds from the tree, others shared blankets and huddled together. As usual at such moments, Sonus felt a profound sense of togetherness and loyalty toward every one of them. Though most were not of his race, the horrid few weeks had created an incredible bond between these people, the like of which he had not seen—even within Mine Fourteen.

Cerrin watched him approach. Maktar slowly stood, his oddly delicate face yellow in the light's glow. "It seems to me that you two are the closest thing this group has to leaders, yes?"

"Well, I suppose—"

Cerrin cut Sonus off. "Yes. Why?"

"It occurred to me that this must all seem very strange, perhaps even unbelievable, to you. I wondered if you might like to see the *Spectre*. It's only a short walk from here."

"Why not show everyone?" asked Cerrin.

"I would prefer not to. It is much easier to deal with two people than many, and, as I said, it is a small ship. Also, some might find the experience… overwhelming."

Sonus felt a shiver of excitement.

It seemed that Cerrin was curious, too. She turned to Jespa and Torrin. "You'll watch the camp?"

"Of course."

"You can walk ahead of us again," Cerrin told Toll Maktar, wielding her spear.

"As you wish."

The forest was still cloaked by gloom. There were many twigs and branches on the ground and—with none of them speaking— the cracks and snaps were the only sounds to be heard. Sonus noticed that Maktar was using the bracelet to guide him and they soon reached a small clearing.

"Where is it, then?" demanded Cerrin.

Seconds after a couple of taps on Maktar's bracelet, the ship materialized.

"How is that possible?" whispered Sonus.

Cerrin simply gazed, eyes unblinking.

The ship was shaped like a tear, with a rounded stern that narrowed to a sharp bow. The surface was silver and the only obvious features were a small viewport above the bow and a black hexagonal structure affixed to the stern. The ship seemed to be hovering a yard above the ground.

Cerrin recovered from the shock swiftly. "Neat trick but that thing can't be more than thirty feet long."

"About that," said Maktar, "depending on the feet. She's designed for speed and stealth and can only accommodate two; three in an emergency."

Sonus's head was swimming. "That vessel can travel through space? From planet to planet, system to system?"

"One of our specialist technologies involves the use of anti-matter. You see the black module there at the stern?"

"I see it."

"More powerful than any conventional trans-light engine and a fraction of the size. There are many other design features that make the ship very hard to detect."

"Any weapons?" asked Cerrin.

"No. Insufficient space and that's not what she was built for. Would you like to see inside?"

"Of course," said Sonus, already on his way.

Cerrin didn't move. "We get inside, the door shuts, you fly off and deliver us to the Vitaari."

Maktar again replied calmly. "With respect, if I wanted to do that, I already would have."

Sonus felt the distance between him and Cerrin growing. He wished she could take a more logical view. "Cerrin, without this man's help, they'd already have us."

"Maybe he's just trying to win our confidence."

Maktar put up both hands. "If so, then it appears I have failed."

"Open it up if you want. I'll take a look from here." Cerrin's grim countenance was rather undermined by the coughing fit that ensued.

"From the gas, yes?" observed Maktar. "I analyzed the composition. You were lucky it's not lethal. Most Vitaari variations are. They have exterminated many of their enemies through such means. Do you know why they might wish to take you alive?"

"Possibly for interrogation," suggested Sonus. "Make sure they get all of us. Or perhaps to put us back in the mines."

Maktar walked across the clearing and touched the bracelet. A hatch appeared in the side of the ship and a narrow ramp unfolded. Maktar strode straight in. Sonus took one step along the ramp, then hesitated, looking back at Cerrin. She stood there, framed between a great white flower and a cluster of vines. Beyond the bravado, Sonus detected fear.

"It will be all right."

She simply tapped her thumb against the shaft of the spear.

Sonus continued along the ramp and into the craft. If anything, the *Spectre* was even smaller than he'd imagined. To the right was a door, to the left the cockpit, with one wide seat facing a display area below the viewport.

Maktar said something in his own language, which seemed to feature a lot of short words and changes in tone. The vessel hummed into life, activating lights and the main screen. Maktar leaned over the back of the seat, studying one display in particular. "No Vitaari ships in the area. The ground troops aren't any closer. It appears you're safe for the moment."

Aware that this was what the stranger would say if he wanted to win his confidence, Sonus didn't move.

Toll Maktar spoke again. Beside the door to the rear compartment, a hatch opened. He walked over and retrieved a flask of liquid, which he drank from. At another word, a second hatch opened and he spoke again. From within the hatch came several whirs and gurgling noises.

"It will produce a treatment to help with the after-effects of the gas. I'm afraid I can't make enough for everyone." He offered the flask. Beneath the ship's bright lights, Sonus saw a pinkish hue to the liquid within.

"And what's that?"

"A water base with nutrients and proteins. You can live on it, if you have to. Ah yes, I also have these." As Maktar approached the rear door, it slid into the wall. Sonus saw that the compartment was smaller than the main space though it seemed to contain more storage. Maktar returned with a large, square container which he placed near the hatch. He lifted the lid and took out a small rectangular package. "There are two hundred in here. Concentrated rations. From what I can gather, your physiology is similar to most of the Core species. These might taste odd but just one will keep you feeling energized for hours. I live on them when I can't get any real food."

"Thank you. Those could be very useful." Sonus watched Cerrin come close to the hatch. Instead of climbing the ramp, she approached across the ground, her shoulder at the height of the door. Eyes narrow, she surveyed the interior of the ship.

"Similar to the *Galtaryax*?" Sonus asked.

She shook her head.

Toll Maktar turned and leaned back against the seat. "That was part of my analysis. The Vitaari military presence here is—comparatively—weak. If we can at least make initial steps toward resistance, I'm confident that more assistance will be forthcoming."

"You mentioned weapons," said Sonus.

"I wish I was in a position to offer more. But I should tell you that there are over a hundred planets where natives like yourselves labor for the Vitaari. The First Empire cannot and will not help them all. In fact, I was on my way to assist another rebel group in another quadrant when I was diverted here. I do hope I haven't wasted my time."

An automated female voice spoke.

"Ah. It's ready." Maktar crossed to the hatch and took out a rack containing five small vials of liquid. "This should alleviate the worst of the symptoms." He offered the rack to Sonus, who took a vial. The liquid inside was clear.

Maktar also took one and drank it. "To put your mind at ease."

Fully aware that Cerrin was watching him, Sonus raised his vial and drank the contents. It tasted vaguely sweet. "Thank you."

Maktar walked past him. "I'm sure we both agree that time is important, Cerrin. We must discuss what happens now. Won't you come in and sit down?"

She rested the tip of her spear against the base of the hatch. "You want to talk, let's talk." She glanced at Sonus. "But if he drops dead, so will you."

"You have a lot of spirit," said Maktar.

"No doubt about that," added Sonus.

Count Talazeer and Commander Elezz stood outside the medical bay, watching as the ship's surgeon prepared the native. The others had all been treated and returned to the container. Elezz seemed keen to keep up the good treatment so they had also been supplied with a meal.

"They're not going back in the mines?"

"That's your decision, sir," said Elezz. "I was merely trying to win some measure of trust. They could still come in useful as bargaining chips."

"I still like the idea of a broadcasted tearing."

"Of course. But I'm sure we can agree that the apprehension of the remaining rebels is essential."

Talazeer didn't correct her terminology. He was feeling rather weary, though had at least eaten some breakfast. "It is."

"Quite a specimen, our friend Kannalin," observed the commander, her face close to the window.

The unconscious Echobe was lying with a sheet covering his lower half. His broad frame and defined musculature were indeed impressive. The surgeon was attending to his burns and wounds before carrying out the procedure Elezz seemed so excited about.

"Of the races here, they seem the strongest."

"Physically, certainly," replied Talazeer. "Hunter-gatherers, really. The desert people are not much more advanced. Only the Palanians and the Lovirr had any form of civilization."

"The four races were clearly very isolated. Coming here is like stepping back in time to another epoch."

"The Drellens were similar. And what's that planet in the Lal-Bek system? They're all cannibals."

The commander's comcell beeped. "Deputy Rasikaar here. We've picked up a signal from Sergeant Guldur's party. They've reached an open area, requesting the shuttle."

"Stand by." Elezz brushed a strand of sleek black hair away and turned to Talazeer. "Shall we recall them, sir?"

This seemed to the Count an admission of defeat, but they could hardly be left there indefinitely.

"I suppose so. What about the hunter drones?"

"The same shuttle will redeploy them. They can stay in the air for six hours."

Talazeer gave a nod; Elezz gave the orders.

Within the medical bay, a new figure had appeared. It was one of the commander's technicians, and he was carrying a small case which he passed to the surgeon's assistant.

Seeing a row of injectors, Talazeer recalled a conversation from his early days on Corvos. "A pity that our truth drugs are not effective on the natives."

"Partially, as I understand it, but so damaging to their brain chemistry that gleaning clear information becomes impossible. Hence the reliance on torture here in the past."

"Quite so. Commander, I'm not particularly partial to surprises. Perhaps you can just tell me what that thing is."

"As you wish, sir. It is an implant—a very sophisticated implant capable of adapting to any humanoid species. This technology was developed during the occupation of Vaklan Te, where many anti-insurgency techniques were perfected. The device will not only allow us to track Kannalin but also see and hear what he does. Provided the ship's surgeon carries out the procedure correctly, there should be no scar and our friend will be none the wiser. If we do not find the rebels with the hunter drones, Kannalin will lead us right to them."

With Cerrin still observing from outside, Toll Maktar showed them several images on the cockpit screen. The first was of

Ikasar, a dead gray moon covered by great transparent domes where his people dwelt. Then came a very complicated rotating three-dimensional map that illustrated the extent of the Vitaari Domain and the First Empire. Sonus grasped most of it but asked many questions. He was relieved when Cerrin asked one, too: she wished to understand Corvos's location in relation to the Vitaari home world. Sonus could still not marry the great distances involved with the comparatively short periods of travel. He had a hundred more questions for the agent.

The third image featured a planet that Maktar had already pointed out on the map.

"Xerxa Minor. Twenty-eight hours' flight time."

Sonus gazed at the surface of the planet, which was almost entirely white apart from a few mountain ranges.

"I appreciate that it does not look inviting. The surface temperature is minus one hundred and twenty degrees. I don't know what measurements you use for such things but, believe me, that's cold. There were no indigenous people but part of one continent was hollowed out by the Vitaari for weapons testing many centuries ago. When they left, the place was colonized by all manner of people seeking refuge. It's fairly lawless but there is a large settlement called Unt. It has a spaceport and—of more interest to us—a weapons market. If we can come to an agreement today, that is where I would obtain them from. I have been allocated sufficient funds."

"What weapons?" asked Cerrin.

"That would depend. Obviously, we're limited by what I can carry on the ship and what we can obtain on Xerxa. I think I can say with some certainty that we can get a weapon for every adult in your party."

"A rifle?" asked Cerrin. "A gun that can kill Vitaari?"

"Certainly. I would also like to get some ordnance. Mines, for example."

"What are they?"

"Explosives."

"For what purpose?"

Sonus felt he could answer that one. "For attacking Vitaari installations."

"Or stationary vehicles," added Maktar. "But, yes, primarily installations—Mine Three is the most obvious target, and the others within striking range of the forest. I believe there are four that you could realistically—"

"Wait." Cerrin now walked up the ramp until she stood in the doorway. "We cannot leave the forest. Surely you've seen enough to understand that."

Maktar stepped toward her, his facial veins again visible in the artificial light. "Not now, of course. But I cannot justify purchasing weapons for a group that will never engage with the enemy. With respect, rebels need to *rebel*. You must take the fight to the occupiers."

Though glad to see Cerrin engaging in the conversation, Sonus was less encouraged by her attitude.

She shook her head. "I wish we could, believe me. But we just lost a third of our number."

Maktar spoke confidently. "With my help, that needn't happen again."

"You talked about conditions. What are they?"

"I believe that, properly armed—and with my advice—you would be in a position to launch your first attack within fifty days. Assuming all goes well, I can be back from Xerxa Minor in three or four. You will need to consolidate a base—perhaps the Old Giants you've spoken of. Then I suggest that you leave behind those unable to fight and form a number of small fighting cells. One of the cells can carry out the first attack, perhaps at Mine Three, yes?"

Sonus wasn't sure of that approach. He was, however, sure that without the agent's assistance, the rebellion would die.

Maktar continued: "My superiors need to know if you can *continue* the fight. Perhaps another target would be preferable. Mine Twelve is only forty kilometers from the southern edge of the forest." Maktar gestured toward the screen. "I can show you."

"Forty kilometers of *open ground*!" said Cerrin, her brow furrowing. "We've only survived this long because we know the territory. We *will* fight back at some point, but for now we have to stay alive, gather strength. There are still people in this forest. They will help us."

Sonus wasn't sure he could logically refute any of that. With only a few Palanians among them, it was always likely that Cerrin and the Echobe would decide the rebels' future. He just hoped he could bring these two together. He wasn't sure there would ever be another opportunity.

"Fifty days is not very long," he told Maktar.

"It is to the First Empire. Taking the initiative will be crucial."

"Gods," said Cerrin. "You bargain like some Lovirr trades-man. As if buying as a few weapons is such a problem for this First Empire."

"They do not have limitless funds. And I can just as easily buy them for the Kinassans, yes?"

"You'd likely never see them again," countered Sonus. "The

Palanians and the Echobe represent the best chance for Corvos. And for the First Empire."

Maktar clasped his pale hands together. "I need a commitment."

"The Echobe will not leave the forest until we are ready," said Cerrin. "That might be fifty days, it might be fifty months. No one on this planet would like to see the place running with black Vitaari blood more than me. But for now, we must concentrate on survival. I started this—I don't need you to tell me what to do."

Toll Maktar pointed to him. "As I understand it, Sonus also made a significant contribution."

"He killed many of them, true, and got himself out," said Cerrin. Do you know how many I got out? More than sixty."

10

"The space man has a suit that protects him and a ship that can fly to other planets. But it's small so he can hide from the Vitaari. And he lives on a moon under big bubbles with other people. And he is friends with the Red Regal, who is the enemy of the Vitaari. He is our friend."

Cerrin was pretending to be asleep. After returning to the temporary camp, she had been struck by a desperate urge to rest. After answering numerous questions, she'd waved the others away and laid down. Jespa and Torrin had done their best to divert those seeking more information, and now young Yarni was trying to explain the situation with Maktar. Cerrin had asked Ikala for guidance and was certain about what she wanted to do, but knew it was only fair that someone explain what was being offered.

Then Sonus returned with the agent to do just that. He gathered the rebels beneath the broad branches and they listened, rapt. Cerrin joined the rear of the group and conceded to herself that the Palanian made his explanation balanced and fair. She now thought it unlikely that Toll Maktar was in league with the

Vitaari, but by staying in this location for so long, they had already taken a risk.

Cerrin usually preferred to lead by example rather than by clever words. But she needed to get her message across. She was about to step forward when Murrit gripped her arm and spoke quietly. "Girl, the gods are with you. You know their will. Do not listen to this… space man."

Cerrin did not need Murrit to tell her what the gods would think, at least not the god that mattered to her. She shook herself free and pushed her way through the crowd. The rebels turned to her.

"We must make a decision quickly. For what it's worth, I believe the offer is real. I have seen Toll Maktar's ship, I have seen pictures of his home and a map that shows the Vitaari planets and those of his allies. But as you have heard, if we accept his offer, we are bound to him and his masters. They have their own reasons to control us. Honestly, I doubt they can be as bad as the Vitaari. But we fought for freedom and I will not lead anyone out of this forest until we are ready. I believe we should fight back but only when the time is right. This is not it. I will leave within the hour. Anyone who wishes to join me, get ready now. I will not stop until I reach the Old Giants."

Though she'd not said much, her voice was hoarse and she gratefully accepted a mug of water from Yarni. Cerrin had glanced at the agent while speaking but seen no obvious reaction. She also noticed Murrit, who was nodding approvingly.

The rebels turned their attention to Sonus. "I understand Cerrin's view," said the Palanian. "And our immediate priority *must* be to find a safe place. But sooner or later, we must also fight back." He gestured to Toll Maktar. "We do not know if such an opportunity will come again. Imagine what we could do with weapons, with allies. With such help, we can make the idea of a rebellion a reality. I think in this case we should vote, and my vote is that we accept this offer. If it has to be me that leads the first attack, so be it."

They had not made decisions in this manner before but Cerrin had no objection.

"An attack will bring retaliation," said an Echobe woman.

"They've *already* retaliated," countered a male voice.

"But if we make ourselves strong, they might just leave us alone."

"Can I vote?" asked Yarni, causing a few chuckles.

Torrin suggested anyone with an opinion to offer raise their hand. More than ten did and all were heard. Cerrin listened carefully, but not one of them affected her view and she could tell most of the Echobe were siding with her. She could not stop glancing at the shaft of sunlight high above. The day was getting on.

Sonus stepped forward again. "Does anyone else have anything to say?"

"May I contribute?" asked Toll Maktar.

Cerrin realized then that she really disliked that eerily pale face of his. "You're not part of this group."

"I'd like to hear it, Cerrin," said the old Palanian, Koros.

"Very well."

"Thank you," said Maktar. "The First Empire is far from perfect, and I sometimes wish my people were not dependent on it. But the Vitaari are worse—far worse—and I wish to see them defeated. If you refuse my offer, there will not be another one. In most cases, five or ten agents are assigned to a planet where we believe intervention can tip the balance. I was sent here alone because your situation is perilous—even with help, you face terrible odds. I truly believe this is your only hope."

"*She* is our only hope." This came from an Echobe man, who pointed at Cerrin. "I will follow wherever she goes."

Erras snorted at this, drawing considerable attention. But for now, he said nothing more.

"We should vote," said Koros.

"Me too?" asked Yarni.

"I don't see why not," replied the Palanian, and it was agreed that the three other children be allowed to participate. With Nartinn now gone, Yarni was the youngest.

Only eleven voted with Sonus: all of the remaining Palanians and four Echobe. Cerrin would not hold it against them. In truth, there were still doubts at the back of her mind. The thought of arming everyone was an attractive one. But she had already lost a third of those she'd broken out of Mine Three. Her job now was to protect them, not lead them back into danger.

"There it is, then," said Koros, clearly unsurprised by the result.

"Pack up," said Cerrin to the assembled rebels, who immediately began preparations.

Feeling a hand on hers, she turned to find Yarni looking up at her. "You don't trust the space man?"

Cerrin didn't have the energy to explain. "It's not that."

"I voted with you," said the girl.

"Good. Yarni, you'll just have to trust me. I will trust in the forest and the gods to protect us."

Yarni squeezed her hand, then let go. "I'll go and pack my blanket."

Cerrin was next approached by Sonus, his face grave. "This is a mistake."

"We'll see." She felt the doubts rise up again. Their alliance had been strong while it lasted; it had helped them both, and the whole group. And during their conversation earlier in the day, she had felt a new closeness with this man. She wished they could have agreed. Perhaps it was inevitable; Echobe and Palanian would never see everything the same way.

"The Forest has protected us so far. Are you coming with us?"

Sonus did not reply. Erras and the other Palanians had gathered just behind him.

There were several things she wanted to tell him, among them an apology for what she'd said in the clearing; no one could doubt his courage and determination to help others. But, as so often happened, the right words wouldn't come.

"What will we do?" asked Koros, as Cerrin walked away.

Sonus's mind was whirling. He hated the idea of leaving Cerrin, especially parting on bad terms. He hated the idea of the group splitting. But above all, he hated the idea of losing this opportunity, watching Toll Maktar fly back to the stars.

Koros and the others turned and he became aware of the agent behind him.

"It is unfortunate that your group does not contain more Palanians, yes?" said Maktar. "Perhaps you would accompany me to the *Spectre*, Sonus. I would like to leave you some supplies, at least."

"Could I speak to you for a moment?"

As the other Palanians joined the Echobe in preparing to leave, Sonus ushered Maktar to a quiet area.

"What will you do now?" he asked.

"I will attempt to make contact with the Kinassans—assess their willingness and ability to take up the fight."

"It won't work. You think the Echobe are willful? The Kinassans take orders from no one."

"I understand that they created considerable problems for the Vitaari during the invasion."

"True, but they are an insular people. Of all the races on Corvos, they were most hostile to others. Over the centuries, we and the Lovirr sent envoys to the desert lands. Most had their heads chopped off."

"A warlike people, then. Fearless?"

Sonus realized he wasn't making his case well. "Yes. And they will have to be part of the rebellion at some stage. But they are not the right ones to start it—to lead, to organize."

Maktar gestured to the group. "The decision has been made."

"Listen to me, there are thousands of Kinassans in the southern mines. Did any of *them* work out how to make a gun from pieces of scrap? How to access Vitaari buildings? How to steal and fly a combat shell? How to blow a mine to pieces? How to bring down a Vitaari ship? Did *anyone* else, for that matter?"

For once, Maktar's inscrutable face seemed to change, the gray eyes studying Sonus intently. "Not that I'm aware."

"I did. I did it all. I worked with the Lovirr, now I'm working with the Echobe. I can learn about weapons and other technologies. I am the best chance you and the First Empire has to take the fight to the Vitaari."

"Not Cerrin? I believe it was you who told me she is the best warrior among you all."

"She is a fine warrior. I believe I am a better *leader.*"

Sonus believed no such thing. He did believe it was the right thing to say and the right time to say it. "Let me come with you to Xerxa Minor," he continued. "You said we can be back here in days. Give me that chance and I promise you won't regret it. With those weapons, I will give you your war."

"You speak well, Sonus. I read the Vitaari report about Mine Fourteen but perhaps I didn't fully appreciate your achievements. We will do as you say. If all goes well, we should return to Corvos in four or five days. I suggest you tell your friends."

Sonus first informed Koros, Erras, and the other Palanians. They were shocked and frightened for him but they also understood. He told them to stay with the Echobe no matter what occurred. He told them to stay loyal to Cerrin. Koros assured him. Erras said nothing.

Sonus would have preferred to talk to Cerrin alone but she was with Torrin, Jespa, Yarni, and several others. All had their packs on and were ready to move.

"Cerrin, I'm going with Maktar. I'll return with the weapons. We'll find you."

Jespa glared at him. "Didn't we just vote? Didn't we just make our decision?"

"You're right, Jespa. But I would never forgive myself if I gave up this chance."

Cerrin held his gaze for a moment, then looked away. Sonus couldn't read her face; there was an intensity, a spark of something, but she kept it to herself.

"You're going with the space man?" asked Yarni.

"I am, Yarni."

"Will you tell me all about it when you get back?"

"Of course."

Cerrin thumped the tip of her spear into the ground and looked back at him, her expression now softer.

"The other Palanians," said Sonus, "you'll look after them?"

"You know I will," she said. "Be careful, Sonus."

"I will. May your gods watch over you."

Maktar had supplies to leave behind for the rebels, so Koros came with them to the clearing. Although he'd been eager to see it, Koros quailed when the ship appeared from thin air. Afterward, he was mostly silent and avoided looking at the alien. After years under the thumb of the Vitaari, the sight of such advanced technology held no awe for the old Palanian, only fear.

Along with the rations, the agent provided two cases of pills. One was something called an antibiotic, he said, and treated infected wounds. The other could reduce pain and fever. The two Palanians parted outside the *Spectre*, Sonus promising to return soon. With that, he made his way once again into the little ship.

So small. Such thin metal walls. Sonus felt suddenly light-headed as the door slid shut.

Maktar was already sitting in the seat and invited Sonus to join him.

Sonus stared down at his feet, which were now heavy and reluctant to move. "I just noticed how muddy my boots are."

For the first time, he heard Maktar laugh—a brief, harsh laugh unlike any he'd heard. "Take off your boots if you wish. There is a spare locker under the seat. Just press it and it will open."

Sonus did just that, but didn't sit down. "I probably smell terrible. I expect we all do."

"Do not worry. There is a washing system in the rear compartment. A bed, too, if you're tired."

"I don't think I'll sleep." Sonus tried to smile but only twitched his lips. The agent didn't seem nervous at all, and why would he? Falling upward through the air and into space was nothing new to him. Sonus had expected himself to be excited, not scared, but his hands were starting to tremble.

He forced himself to sit down and lean back in the seat, which could easily have accommodated three.

Maktar said, "It's strange to think of space travel as something new. On Ikasar, we are with the stars all the time. Though I'll admit there's something wonderful about real air."

Maktar spoke a few words of his own language. The *Spectre*'s display screen was very long, and it now divided into four sections. One showed the ship, another looked like a tactical readout, a third seemed to be purely navigational. As for the fourth, Sonus had no idea.

The lights flickered and the ship began to rise. There seemed to be no engine noise.

"No manual controls at all?"

"Only in exceptional circumstances," replied Maktar. "I usually use voice. There is a thought-control mode but I find it distracting."

"The words on the displays, this is your language?"

"Yes. We use a similar numerical system to yours—and the Vitaari—but the symbology is different. Would you like to see your friends?"

Without waiting for an answer, Maktar changed one of the displays. Sonus hadn't realized how high they already were. His experience in the combat shell had been brief and intense; now he had the time to appreciate the astonishing speed of the *Spectre*. Having spent what seemed like endless days staring at dirt and branches and leaves, he was now given a god's eyes view of the thick, green canopy.

And in that moment, his fear was gone. Only awe remained.

There wasn't a single sign of the rebels… until Maktar spoke again. Then, thirty-four orange dots appeared, all moving eastward in a line.

"Heat?"

"Movement. Limited range but the sensors are superior to what the Vitaari have." Maktar held up the bracelet. "I can monitor anything the ship can through here. Very useful at times."

Sonus leaned forward. As the *Spectre* gained height, the orange dots grew smaller, then finally disappeared. He thought of Cerrin, and he wished the moment of parting had been different.

Maktar pointed at a section of forest. "There begins what you refer to as the Old Giants. I suppose they will be there by the time we return. Cerrin is right—the area will present considerable difficulties for the Vitaari. But it is only twenty kilometers across. I'm not sure they will be able to base themselves there for long."

"What's that?" asked Sonus, pointing at a huge body of water to the northwest of the Old Giants.

"A lake of some kind. Quite large. You don't know its name?"

"I didn't even know it was there."

The ship shuddered. Sonus felt a lurch in his stomach and an odd sensation in his ears. "How high are we now?"

"Just passing five kilometers. Don't worry, the—"

Something beeped. Toll Maktar leaned forward and spoke.

The tactical display changed. Maktar gave more instructions and the ship seemed to alter course again.

"Vitaari shuttle. Don't worry, they've no chance of spotting us in that old thing. On their current trajectory, they're headed for the remaining ground units."

"The soldiers are still on the ground?"

"Yes. Five kilometers from where we spent the night. I was monitoring them the entire time."

Sonus's heart leapt into his throat. "What if they're not just picking the men up? The hunter drones arrived just before the shuttle last time. Perhaps they launch them from it."

"That's possible."

"Is there anything you can do?" Sonus stared at the strange and impassive face, feeling his panic rise. The rebels could be captured by nightfall. What was the point of taking Sonus away to the stars to procure weapons if there'd be no one left for him to return to? "We have to give Cerrin a chance to get away!"

Maktar kept his dark eyes on the screen indifferently. "Wait a moment. We'll have to get closer."

Once again, the display showed the forest below but now Sonus could see the edge of it. He tried to locate Mine Three but guessed it was too small. Then the view disappeared.

"We're in cloud cover. As I told you, we have no weapons but the defensive pods include a beam impactor. I can't attack the shuttle but I might be able to stop the drones from transmitting."

"The ship operates independently of your instructions?"

"Yes. It is intelligent. If I fall unconscious, it will do what it can to revive me, then fly me home. If I don't return, it will come and look for me. It's not as capable as what we humanoids have up here—" Maktar tapped his head— "but for a ship, it's pretty smart. I've only had her two years but the *Spectre*'s saved me more than once."

For the next few minutes, the agent said nothing to Sonus, instead monitoring the displays and issuing orders to his ship. Sonus could again see several veins beneath his translucent skin, one pulsing in a rather disconcerting way.

His attention was then drawn to a peripheral screen, which showed the Vitaari shuttle hovering above the trees.

"You were right," said Maktar. "The drones are already broadcasting. Let's see what the system says."

Sonus continued to study the displays but could make little out of it.

"It's identified the broadcast frequency and the components used. The transmitters are susceptible to an impactor beam. We might not knock them out completely but it should have an effect." Maktar turned to him. "It is... not without risk."

"To us?"

"The systems on that old shuttle won't know what's going on, but they'll probably analyze the drones later. Deactivated transmitters on every probe, with no other visible damage? They'll know it was a precise attack, and they'll know the rebels couldn't possibly be responsible. My orders are to remain out of sight."

Sonus took a deep breath. If Maktar were discovered, would the First Empire still offer their help? Or would they give up on Corvos all together if they couldn't stay in the shadows? Sonus didn't want to scare away the one and only source of hope he'd felt since the moment his combat shell crashed in the river.

But he also couldn't risk Cerrin's life.

"If those drones find the others, you might as well put me back on the ground. Please do what you can."

"Very well."

Once he'd given the order, Maktar monitored the displays

carefully before announcing that the *Spectre* had fired three impactor beams at the active drones.

"Thank you."

"Don't thank me yet. They're still… ah, one has stopped moving. Now two. Looks like we did something, at least."

Though Sonus had heard from Toll Maktar about the capabilities of his ship and its systems, it was something else to see them in action. He felt certain that he'd made the right decision. He began to imagine a full-scale rebellion, with a dozen combat shells—or something better than shells—raining destruction on the Vitaari.

As the *Spectre* gained altitude once more, he turned to the agent.

"What should I call you?"

"Toll, yes?"

"Toll, can you show me what's outside?"

"Of course."

Sonus could see beyond the forest's edge now—to where the ocean began in the far west and to the mountains that separated the forest from the desert to the south, where the Kinassans dwelt.

And as he rose farther, he felt the dizzying sensation that the horizon all around him was sinking faster than ground directly below. Yes—the curvature of the planet down and away from him was undeniable now, and he could see all of the way to the far edge of the single great continent of Corvos in every direction, where it touched the dark blue seas that ran endlessly around the planet.

Everything. Everyone.

Everything and everyone he knew was contained within that increasingly small section of land. The thought occupied him so fully that when he glanced at the screen again, brilliant blue sky had become an impenetrable black.

11

The crack of the shot echoed around loading bay five. The bullet thumped into the barrel but missed the daub of red paint entirely.

"Curse this bloody weapon!" yelled Talazeer, slapping the rifle. "It's pulling right. I'm telling you—it's pulling right!"

As Marl strode over to him, the Drellen's clawed feet scraped across the grilled metal floor.

"That accursed noise. When are you going to start wearing shoes, anyway!"

Marl halted, yellow eyes bulging.

"That was probably uncalled for," added Talazeer. "But you really should consider some footwear." He threw the rifle to his bodyguard, who snatched it out of the air with one hand.

"You did hit the mark once, sir."

"Out of ten shots!"

"Thirty meters is a long way."

"Not for me. Didn't used to be, anyway. It could be my injury. My eye was affected, you know."

Marl raised the rifle, which featured a long barrel and a sight with countless settings. He adjusted his domed, scaled head, curled one finger around the trigger and fired. He hid the red paint dead center.

"Congratulations," hissed the Count.

"Perhaps some rest, sir?"

"More bloody rest? I don't think so."

"You could visit the other mines."

Talazeer had covered another six the previous day. There had been little to concern him and the switch to terodite seemed to be proceeding well. He was happy to leave Rasikaar and his team to oversee this. The priority was still these damned rebels.

"You know what, I think we'll just go down to the forest ourselves—take a few troops, start at their last known position and see what we can find. At the very least, I might bag a few animals. All this waiting around is driving me mad."

"What did the commander say about the drones, sir?"

"Technical malfunction. They're looking into it. She thinks that sly bastard Sonus might have rigged some device to affect the transmitters. I don't see how he would have the time while running for his life." Talazeer removed his shooting gloves. "Two days. I shall have to report to High Command—even though I already told them the problem was resolved. They probably have spies here, anyway. That wretch Rasikaar, perhaps."

The Drellen gazed at the open bay door as soldiers marched by. Often, Talazeer was glad that Marl didn't say much. On other occasions, it would be nice to converse with a being who offered more than a sentence at a time.

"Have you no more suggestions? You were of no use down on the ground and you're of no use now. Your race was hunted just as we're hunting these natives. Surely you must have some insight?"

Eventually the bodyguard said, "The commander is an anti-insurgency specialist."

"Very helpful." Talazeer put out his hand and Marl returned the gun. "Better to do something than nothing."

Though he didn't say so, the Count loved the thought of intercepting the rebels himself, capturing Sonus and Cerrin. That would wipe the fake smile off Elezz's face.

He hurried toward the door, past another shuttle where three men were conducting repairs. Upon reaching the corridor, he saw that the passing troops had been part of a guard detail. Four of them were escorting the Echobe prisoner, Kannalin. Commander Elezz had notified Talazeer that she was considering executing her back-up plan, but had said nothing to him that morning about proceeding immediately. He was about to turn right and make his way to operations to confront her.

Then he reconsidered and keyed his comcell. "Commander Elezz."

There was a short delay. "Yes, sir."

"I'd like to see you outside loading bay five."

A longer delay. "Yes, sir."

When she arrived, Talazeer found himself rather preoccupied by her appealing face and figure.

"I take it you're trying this subterfuge of yours?"

"In the absence of other alternatives, yes. I was going to consult you before the shuttle left. Do you object?"

"Do you really think it will work?"

"The device is transmitting perfectly, though we will need to bounce it off the Mine Three array. I'm dependent on the shuttle crew and the guards to carry out the plan correctly. We will stage a forced landing and ensure the prisoner has an opportunity to escape."

"What does he believe is happening?"

"That he is being returned to Mine Three. I had the guards beat him a little last night for some fictional infraction—to reduce his suspicions."

"I see. Nice touch."

"I will keep you fully informed, sir. Presumably, Rasikaar has not yet apprised you of the developments at Mine Thirteen?"

"No."

"The report only just came in. There have been sightings of Kinassan warriors beyond the walls. We wouldn't want trouble to flare up in the desert region again."

"Certainly. I've not been there yet."

As Elezz was taking action against the rebels, the Count knew the Kinassans must be his priority. There was little point solving one problem if he allowed another to develop. "I shall fly down immediately. What about this drone malfunction?"

"We're still investigating. Likewise with the madrin particles. I shall tell you what the technicians told me—they're keeping an open mind."

Hearing an approach behind him, Talazeer saw one of Rasikaar's staff slinking toward them.

"Sir, a call from Viceroy Ollinder."

"Patch it through to my comcell."

He turned and walked away from the others, grateful that he at least wouldn't have to talk to the viceroy face to face. He had delayed too long; he should have contacted High Command *and* Ollinder already—discussed the Corvos situation on *his* terms.

Talazeer touched the comcell on his collar and waited while the *Galtaryax* staff connected the call via the array.

"Talazeer, you there?" Ollinder, who was close to retirement age, already sounded annoyed.

"Yes, Viceroy, of course. How are you?"

"Let's not concern ourselves with pointless courtesies, young man. I understand that you still haven't cleaned up that rebellion. You sent assurances to my staff that it was already dealt with!"

Talazeer felt himself shiver. If Ollinder was angry, he could only imagine his father's reaction.

"Sir, there is no rebellion. Just a few escaped prisoners we need to round up. We apprehended several but there were some... complications. I can assure you that it will all be under control in a matter of days."

Talazeer was not about to tell his superior that there was now also trouble with the Kinassans.

"I do hope so. I've got a lot of people breathing down my neck about your terodite. I was at least glad to see that your last few freighters had tons of the stuff."

"Quite so, sir. And we will keep it coming."

"I expect your father's been in touch?"

"No. Why?"

"One of his advisers has been questioning *my* advisers about Corvos. Unfortunately, we did have to tell him that all is not well."

Talazeer resisted the temptation to kick the wall.

"I thought he might have contacted you personally," added Ollinder.

"No, sir. Though of course we're both very busy."

"You will apprise me of any major developments regarding the rebels?"

Talazeer wondered why the viceroy bothered; he clearly had at least one well informed source on the *Galtaryax*.

"Sir, they really are not worthy of the name. Rest assured that nothing will affect production."

"I do hope so, young man. I do hope so."

The great trees soared a hundred feet higher than the one they were sitting in.

There were almost no branches on the bottom half of the trunks, but toward the top they grew in great, dense clusters, forming an oval shape. Each leaf was topped with a dab of purple, giving it a distinctive tint. While the high, thick canopy would protect the rebels, the comparatively open ground below would allow them to move quickly.

"We'll have a bit more air under there, too," said Jespa, chewing on something he had foraged during the climb.

"We will," replied Cerrin. "What do you think—three miles?"

"About that. They're tired but once we tell them we're this close… even the Palanians might hurry up."

Cerrin smiled, unsure of the last time she had done so. In truth, the Palanians, and the rest of the rebels, had actually performed well. Repeating the pattern of walking at night, resting in the day, they had covered the ground quickly, no doubt all spurred on by thoughts and memories of the Vitaari attack.

"I think about him," said Jespa, running a finger down his angular jaw, "Sonus—where he might be, what he might be seeing. Do you?"

"I think about Kannalin. And the others."

That was the truth, but not the whole truth. She thought of

Sonus often. She wished they'd had a moment alone before he parted. She would have liked to embrace him, at least.

"We have to keep going. For them."

"We do. So, how's it going with Torrin?"

She'd not asked him about her directly before and Jespa blushed.

"How'd you mean?"

"Oh, come on. Anyone can see you two get on well."

"I get on well with lots of people."

"But you don't hold their hands. I've seen you—in the dark or when you think no one's looking."

He grinned. "She says we should take it slowly. In case... something happens."

"What do you think?"

"I think that's a good reason to enjoy life while we can. What do you think?"

"It's up to you. I hope it works out."

"Thanks," said Jespa. "We should head down."

It seemed to take an age to reach the ground. Cerrin knew her companion could have done it in half the time, but Jespa repeatedly warned her about taking the descent too quickly. According to him, more people fell off trees on the way down than the way up.

Their resting spot was not ideal; the thickest cover was patchy so they were spread over quite an area. Torrin had posted sentries and—though Jespa settled down to rest immediately—Cerrin wanted to check on all the rebels, who were divided into six groups. The Palanians had stuck together and she heard them before she saw them. They were with several Echobe within a copse of trees, and someone had just cried out.

"What's that noise?" she demanded as she pushed her way between two saplings.

She found the Palanians crowded around Koros; only Erras wasn't there. Koros lay on the ground, one leg resting on a pack, his wrinkled face twisted with pain. There was no mystery about why he was in such agony: a huge thorn had gone right through the bottom of his foot, the end showing just below his little toe.

"Cerrin, thank the Maker," said Dari, one of the Palanian women. "What do we do?"

"How did that happen?"

"I had to… I had to *go*," rasped Koros. "I know I should have put my boots on but it was an emergency."

"I told you about the malroot thorns. I told everyone."

"What's done is done," said Dari. "Can you help him?"

Cerrin put her gun down and squatted as the others made way.

"Torrin can make something for the wound but first the thorn must come out."

"It's barbed," said Dari.

"This accursed place," croaked Koros. "Just once, I'd like to walk a paved street or shelter below a proper roof."

"Where?" snapped Cerrin. "The capital? The Vitaari blew most of the roofs off."

"Are you going to help him?" asked Dari.

"I've never removed one of those before. One of you might as well do it."

Out of the corner of her eye, she saw one of the Palanians shake her head and mumble something.

"What is it? Not enough that I get you out of Three? Get you hundreds of miles from the Vitaari? Get you close to a safe place?

Should I hold this old fool's hand because he couldn't be bothered to listen?"

None of them said anything. Koros leant back, hands and face contorting with pain once more.

"Do it quickly if you can," Cerrin added, trying to regain her composure. "Then stitch the wound and bandage it. Torrin will bring something to help keep it clean. You should take some of Maktar's medicine, too. If you trust it."

Nothing more was said.

But as Cerrin walked away, she found herself face to face with a glowering Erras. They had not exchanged a word since the lake.

"Always so sure of yourself, eh, Cerrin? Even though you have made so many mistakes."

She did not say what she wanted to. She'd never much liked Erras. But he had clearly been close to Nuro and he'd had little time to get over what had happened at the lake. Without a word, she walked past him.

Cerrin quickly checked on the other groups, then found a place to rest beneath the fronds of a sprawling plant. There was only space for her, Torrin, and Yarni. When Torrin heard about Koros's injury, she departed immediately to prepare the treatment.

Cerrin saw that her blanket had been put out, her pack placed as a pillow. This was Yarni's doing. The child was turned away, apparently sleeping.

Cerrin put the gun next to her pack and laid down. The day was already a warm one; she didn't need to cover herself. She was almost asleep when Yarni stirred and turned over.

"Are the Old Giants close?"

"They are, Yarni. Very close."

. . .

Mine Thirteen was located on the edge of a depression ten kilometers wide. The sandy soil of the desert plain was more orange than brown, the flat terrain occasionally broken by an outcrop of rock or a handful of boulders. Like almost all of the other camps, Thirteen was enclosed by a circular wall and dominated by the central tower.

As the shuttle approached, Talazeer had been pleased to see the walls and tower gleam in the morning sun. In fact, he had complimented Governor Selerra. But once down on the ground, he saw that the installation did not compare well with the others.

Thirteen was one of the oldest mines and the yields of aronium lessened with every passing year. The Kinassans, though, were tough and durable. And because they seldom needed replacing and worked well in their native environment, costs were comparatively low. Additionally, the mine was so remote that the tribesmen didn't even operate in the area, meaning that a skeleton crew of guards was sufficient. Talazeer hoped that wasn't about to change.

"What exactly happened?"

The Count and Governor Selerra were standing beneath an awning, close to the landing pad. There, some of the workers were sweeping great piles of orange sand aside. Despite the wall, the stuff seemed to get everywhere, including Talazeer's mouth. He wished someone had warned him. The other Vitaari, Selerra included, all followed the Kinassan custom of wearing hoods and wrappings to protect themselves. Unlike the Kinassans, they also wore visors.

Talazeer blinked as a gust of wind blew more sand into his face. "Ugh!"

"Apologies, Excellency. We shall find a visor for you."

"I can't imagine why you haven't already."

As Selerra dispatched his assistant, Talazeer glanced at the two guards nearby. They wore long robes over their uniforms, as did the other soldiers. The garrison at Mine Thirteen numbered just thirty-two, the smallest on Corvos. The pair were both eyeing Marl, who stood at one corner of the awning, cloak wrapped around him, unconcerned by the sand.

"Well?" demanded Talazeer. "What about this sighting?"

He didn't think much of Selerra. He was a small man, young for a governor; rather ugly too, with one eye clearly higher in his face than the other.

"Yes, Excellency. It was last night. We are so unused to activity beyond the walls that we did not notice the approach until we heard a noise from one of those odd beasts they travel on. A pair of guards investigated and found something going on behind the accommodation block." Selerra pointed to the block, which was situated beside the generator station. "They saw grappling lines thrown over the wall. Two laborers were there, talking to the tribesmen on the other side. Fortunately, my men were able to apprehend the laborers."

"How impressive—you captured *prisoners*. I hope you don't expect a commendation, Governor. I assume the tribesmen escaped?"

"I'm afraid so, sir. To explain—we generally have little use for the combat shells. By the time we had them powered up and in the air, we'd lost them. The shells do struggle with the wind and the dust here."

"What about the wall? Why haven't you taken precautions—sensors?"

"Excellency, this is the first sighting in five years. We were told by Administrator Danysaan to save power where we could. Keeping the combat shells running is—"

"Yes, yes. Well, I suppose five years is a long time."

"I did send a patrol out this morning and they located the tracks of the Kinassan animals. There were six of them. Their trail was leading south. There is a rock formation forty miles away—they may have a well or some other water source there. Whether this was an isolated incident or a suggestion of a move in our direction, we're not sure."

"And the two prisoners?"

"They've not said anything yet, sir, but they will."

"How can you be certain?"

Selerra's face brightened. "I think you'll approve, Excellency. Perhaps if I show you."

The assistant had returned with the visor. Talazeer put it on, then followed the governor toward what was referred to as the pit.

He knew that when Thirteen had been constructed, the Vitaari engineers had dug an initial shaft that ran several hundred meters straight down into a seam of aronium. Due to the unstable soil, that shaft had been strengthened with a series of huge, circular metal ribs. Upon these a spiral walkway had been constructed, and Talazeer now saw what looked like most of the mine's inhabitants upon it. Some of the workers were descending, carrying empty receptacles on their backs. Those ascending carried great loads and moved at less than half the speed.

"The workers carry out waste material, Excellency," explained Selerra. "We use a lift for the aronium. If you study our latest yields, you will see that—"

Talazeer waved a hand at him. If a discussion about yields didn't concern terodite, he wasn't interested.

He *was* interested in the Kinassans. Those close to the surface kept their hoods up, and with their long, flowing robes, neither body nor face could be seen. On the lower levels of the shaft, some had lowered their hoods and all—male and female—seemed to have had their heads shaved. The Kinassans were not as dark as the Echobe, nor as large. Their faces were longer, more angular.

"Why do they have no hair?"

"An infestation, sir," replied Selerra. "Quite disgusting. The insects are called claw-ants. Fortunately, we've kept them away from us but the accommodation blocks need regular de-lousing. We have, however, found another use for the creatures."

As they walked, the Count's thoughts drifted to the messages he had sent to his brother and father the previous evening. He had done his best to explain the situation and assure them that any problems were strictly temporary. He'd have preferred not to involve them at all but felt it important to present his side.

He had not yet received a reply.

Selerra led Talazeer past a great pile of sacks. Four native women sat on a bench nearby, repairing the sacks with large needles and thick thread.

"Looks like something from a prehistoric village."

"The women are very skilled and quick, sir. It's far cheaper than using automation."

As he passed, Talazeer noted that the hooded women all possessed the same pale green eyes. They also had rings in their noses.

Along with Marl and the two guards, the Count and the

governor continued around the edge of the pit until they reached the walkway entrance.

"Our would-be rebels," said Selerra.

Close to the entrance, two near-naked Kinassan men had been strung up from poles sunk into the sand. Their feet were inside a half-buried box, and when Talazeer looked closer, he saw the sand there was alive with insects, each a good five centimeters long.

"Claw ants," explained Selerra. "We don't expect these two to hold out much longer."

One man's eyes were closed. He did little more than groan as drool dripped down his chin. The ants had made their way up most of his body, leaving gouges all over his skin. Many were now climbing up dried rivulets of blood.

The second man was alert, eyes locked on the Count. If anything, his injuries were worse. The claw ants had ravaged his legs and stomach and were now scouring his chest and neck. The Kinassan bared his teeth, green eyes shining with defiance.

"Tell that man to look away or I will have Marl do something that will make these ants seem like a slight annoyance."

"Of course, Excellency."

At a signal from Selerra, one of the guards yelled at the prisoner.

"Use Vitaari, man!" bawled the Count.

"My apologies, Excellency," replied Selerra with a ridiculous bow. "These natives are incredibly stupid. They understand only a few words. It is simply more efficient for us to use their tongue."

"And yet he is still looking at me."

The native shouted a single sentence, then repeated it over and over, his entire body shaking from his bound hands to his mutilated feet.

"What's he saying?"

"I'm not sure, sir. Nonsense. He's lost his mind. Shall we move on to—"

Marl spoke then, his first utterance since they'd arrived. His yellow eyes were set on the guard. "*You* understand. Tell Count Talazeer what the prisoner said."

The guard turned to Selerra, who nodded reluctantly.

"He's been saying it since we caught him," admitted the guard. "Hail the heroes of Mine Three. Hope will never die."

12

After the *Spectre* left the Corvos system and entered what Toll Maktar referred to as trans-light, Sonus gazed, entranced, at the maelstrom of movement and color beyond the viewport. Maktar had patiently explained the key concepts, particularly the ship's anti-matter engine, but Sonus was struggling to make sense of it all. After he had bombarded the agent with dozens of questions, Maktar eventually suggested that he use the facilities aboard the ship.

Sonus had just spent a wondrous half an hour showering, scrubbing several weeks of dirt and grime off his skin, out of his hair, from beneath his nails. Maktar had also promised to buy him a new set of clothing on Xerxa Minor, but for now he had to make do with his holed and malodorous work overalls. Even so, he felt greatly refreshed as he returned to the cockpit.

Toll Maktar was slouched on the seat, a flask of his nutrient water in one hand, studying the screen. Upon it, small passages of text were scrolling upward. "How was that?"

"Marvelous, thank you. I feel a little guilty though."

"About your compatriots?"

"Yes." Sonus ran a hand through his newly clean hair and sat down.

"They have survived much, yes?" said Maktar. "We can only hope that they repay your faith in them."

"And I your faith in me?"

"Time will tell."

Sonus pointed at the screen. "What's all that?"

"Intelligence updates. We agents are given limited access to the First Empire's communication network. The updates help us avoid difficult entanglements."

"Why only limited access?"

"Remember, we are Ikasaran: clients of the First Empire, not members. There are things they believe they must keep from us. I have informed them of my decision to assist you. They will await my report. I just read another—by the Vitaari, regarding the breakout and the assassination of the viceroy. What was his name?"

"Mennander."

Sonus had never really considered the word *assassination* though it was certainly correct. He would never forget the sight of that great ship crashing into the desert sands outside Mine Five. Even now, it barely seemed possible that he was responsible for such destruction.

"I thought I had a reasonable chance of getting out once I had the combat shell. And once I reached Mine Five, I thought I might damage the shuttle. But to bring it down..."

"When the news reached Vitaar, there must have been some very shocked individuals."

That elicited a moment of pride from Sonus, but he more often felt disquiet when he recalled his escape. There was a seductive element to suddenly acquiring that much power—and he would not mourn any of the Vitaari he had eliminated—but, for all his earlier boasts to Maktar, it was not something he could ever really celebrate. He would do what he had to: but only to achieve peace.

As a child, as a young man, even in his early days as a slave, he could never have imagined himself a warrior. He had no choice now but to fight, not if he wanted to banish the Vitaari and free the people of Corvos.

Maktar continued, aiming a finger at the screen: "It seems Count Talazeer has returned. He was ordered to fix his own mistakes. Very curious. Vitaari are not known for giving second chances."

Sonus recalled his brief encounter with Vitaari nobleman after he had shot down the ship. He remembered the damage to his face and the rage in his voice.

"They have also reinforced their number with a new contingent of Colonial Guards led by a Commander… Elezz. You said you hadn't faced the hunter drones before, correct?"

"Correct."

"Perhaps the commander arrived with some new equipment."

Sonus glanced again at the viewport. The maelstrom was strangely hypnotic and he forced himself to look away when his eyes began to ache. After a time, his thoughts returned to his enemies.

"One of the Vitaari back in Mine Fourteen told me a little of their history. He told me about these families, these 'circles.'"

"There are twelve," replied Maktar after a sip from his flask. "All of the males within them are noblemen of some type, including your Talazeer with his little title. They seem to occupy the top positions in every sphere—political, administrative, military. I'll have to refresh my memory of the Count now that he's returned. As I recall, he's a member of Circle Za-Ulessor. A powerful clan, but not as powerful as Circle Za-Ili. They have dominated in recent years."

"How big is a circle?"

"There are hundreds of petty noblemen in each, along with a handful of genuinely powerful people. Only males, of course—females are afforded very few opportunities in their society. The current leader, Imperator Zensen, is part of Za-Ili. He's been around a long time, and seems to have kept the circles together well enough. But there are always undercurrents, rumors, enmities. We—and the First Empire—have occasionally exploited them. The Vitaari are a curious race. They are extremely patriotic and tied to their history, yet they often put personal ambitions first."

"They believe themselves superior," said Sonus. "That is why they treat other races with such disdain and cruelty."

"By the terms with which they judge achievement—monetary gain, territorial expansion—they have been very successful. They have largely gone unchallenged."

"Until now," said Sonus.

Maktar offered a grim smile.

Not long afterward, Sonus fell asleep, only to be awakened by an urgent beeping. For the first time since leaving Corvos's atmosphere, he actually felt the ship move and the first thing he saw was Toll Maktar hunched forward, his expression tense.

"What is it?"

"Good question." Maktar continued to study the display for some time.

Sonus did the same. "We're not in trans-light anymore."

"No. It could be... yes. I'll explain in a moment."

Maktar issued instructions, then conducted a conversation with the female voice. Sonus noted that his calm tones almost matched his automated counterpart. By studying the tactical and navigational displays, he began to understand what was happening.

"We're heading for that moon."

"It's actually an asteroid. Most in this system contain high levels of senisium."

"I've not heard of it."

"Neither had I until I became an agent. This is a trick I picked up from an old hand. The Vitaari like to scatter interrupter relays across their territory—even in neutral areas. They transmit false signals that emulate planets, other ships, and so on, so that ships drop out of trans-light. Which is what just happened to us." Maktar tapped a small display screen. "The blue hexagon, that's the interrupter. And the red triangle there is another ship, probably a Vitaari interceptor on its way to check out who fell into their trap."

"So, the senisium..."

"Is impenetrable to scanners."

"Ah. So we hide behind the asteroid?"

"Precisely. Even if that's not an interceptor, I don't want them to get a profile of the *Spectre*. That information could reach Xerxa Minor."

"The Vitaari have ships there?"

"We don't actually know exactly what they have there, but there is certainly a presence."

"Are we behind the asteroid yet?"

"The *Spectre* is still moving, trying to keep the core between us and… whatever that is."

Sonus watched the red triangle move across the screen.

"No identity code," continued Maktar. "Every ship is supposed to broadcast one. Needless to say, Vitaari interceptors don't advertise their presence."

"I don't suppose you do, either."

"Quite so. Ah, there's the code."

A small ship icon and several sentences of text appeared. The agent leaned back; the tension gone from his body.

"It's just a freighter. And a small one at that."

"Where from?"

"It's registered on Orp IV but that doesn't mean it came from there on this trip. In any case, nothing for us to worry about." Maktar gave the ship more orders. "We'll steer clear of the relay, then return to trans-light."

"How long to Xerxa now?"

"Around eight hours. The ship hasn't finished the new calculations yet. It'll be done by the time we're away from the relay."

"Have you been to Xerxa recently?"

"Fairly. I was procuring some ammunition for a group of, well, there's no other word for it: pirates."

"Which system are they from?"

"Various. But they operate three ships in the Ninth Sector. Ever since their leader was eliminated by the Vitaari, they've been carrying out quiet—but very effective—sabotage operations. One of our agents was killed while helping them. I took over from her."

"Some agents are female?"

"Yes. We're not like the Vitaari. I didn't know her myself but she'd been very successful."

"How did she die?"

"Somebody cut her throat. She was found in a trash compactor. On Xerxa Minor."

The first real danger came as they approached Unt. Sonus had been disappointed to find that almost the entire surface of Xerxa Minor was covered by cloud, so that he'd seen nothing from the viewport. According to Maktar, it was tiny planet, just six thousand kilometers in diameter, the only indigenous life a few scraps of hardy vegetation. The *Spectre* descended through the planet's atmosphere with barely a bump—but shortly afterward the little ship began to shudder and shake.

"You weren't joking about the winds."

The agent was so preoccupied that he didn't reply. Suddenly, Sonus felt movement behind him. He turned and saw that two narrow holes had opened up in the seat. The same had happened behind Maktar, who took out the straps within and fitted them over his shoulders and around his waist, locking them in place over his stomach. Sonus did the same and was soon grateful for the stability.

"Don't remember it being this bad," said Maktar. "Let's lose some more altitude."

After a time, one of the displays showed a visual of the terrain below. Great swathes of snow and ice were punctuated only by the odd strip or patch of striated rock.

"Not far to the Drop now."

"The Drop?"

"It's the biggest hole left behind by the Vitaari. That's where Unt is—the port is a couple of kilometers underground."

"Is the air breathable?"

"It would be if it wasn't so cold. Unt is completely sealed. There's not much space but they pack a lot in."

"Seems odd that anyone would want to live here."

"Mostly they come for trade. There aren't all that many places where neither the Vitaari nor the First Empire holds sway. As you'll see, most are passing through. The ones that live here are usually hiding from something—or someone. Anyway, better tell the spaceport we're coming in, yes?"

Maktar gave the ship some orders, and after a few moments, a gruff voice came through, speaking a language Sonus assumed to be *Standard*. He knew of it but had never heard it spoken. Maktar conducted a brief discussion, during which time various documents appeared on one part of the display.

Sonus's gaze was drawn to the viewport, where he could see snow flurries and a wall of rock that seemed alarmingly close. He recalled those early moments in the stolen combat shell back in Mine Four, when he'd guided the vehicle along the flank of Mount Origo.

"Good news," said Maktar. "There's a private bay for us. I don't want too much attention for the *Spectre*. I've already paid the dock-chief a bit extra so hopefully he'll keep his mouth shut."

"You've paid him? How?"

"Sorry, I forget how much there is to explain. Computers carry out the transactions. They use the old galactic currency here—like most independent systems and planets. Same with the language."

"*Standard*," replied Sonus. "The Vitaari I mentioned told me about it. A language shared by all."

"Actually, the Vitaari prefer not to. It's used across the First Empire though. Most people know some."

Sonus shook his head; all of these different races and planets had been interacting for millennia. Though the astronomers at the university in Okara had predicted there must be planets around other stars, no one on Corvos had any inkling of life on other worlds until the arrival of the Vitaari. Not for the first time, Sonus wished that this discovery had been made via telescopes or some other far-seeing technology.

His ruminations were interrupted by the appearance of a large ship on the screen. Its shape reminded him somehow of the bulky Vitaari rifles, and as the *Spectre* descended past it, Sonus glimpsed a huge, faded image of a naked female.

"Brigands, probably," remarked Maktar. "That thing's a freighter. They run loads from one sector to another, make money off supply and demand—no questions asked, yes?"

The *Spectre* veered to the right, past three smaller ships ascending together. They were of an odd design, each consisting of a central oval section with a cube at each end.

"Private vessels. Probably rich types looking for something illicit. Unt has gambling dens, fighting pits, brothels."

"Unfortunately, we had a few similar places in my home city. They were sometimes built underground."

"This whole place is underground."

The *Spectre* eased under a great overhang of rock. Beneath it were three circular entrances, and as the ship approached the one farthest to the right, two doors separated. To Sonus, the aperture didn't look big enough even for the agent's ship but, once closer, he realized it was at least twenty meters across. The *Spectre* passed through, spun one-hundred-eighty degrees, then landed on a triangle of orange lights.

The straps retracted into the seat. Sonus stood up but found that Toll Maktar was still studying the display.

"Just waiting for our passes to come through—without them we can't move around. Second bribe of the day goes to the personnel chief. Ah, there it is."

Maktar took the bracelet from yet another hatch and fixed it on his wrist. "Everything we need is in here. Well, almost."

He stood and walked past Sonus to the rear compartment. When he returned, he was wearing a bulky ring on his right middle finger.

"Vulgar, yes? Strictly speaking, weapons are forbidden. Many ignore the rule though, so a little protection comes in handy." The agent held up the ring. "Stun-charger. Will knock most species out for several minutes—with no permanent damage."

"I suppose your armor would attract too much attention."

"It would. And there are more thieves in Unt than anywhere else I've been—so watch yourself."

Sonus shrugged. "I've nothing worth stealing."

"That's about to change."

The air outside the ship was very stale and smelly, but Sonus was glad to be outside and on the move. It was not until much later that he paused to reflect on the historic nature of his first steps on alien soil—the first Corvosian to ever set foot on another planet—and was struck by how he'd wasted the moment.

What would he tell the people back on Corvos when they

asked? That he'd timidly kept his frightened eyes on the back of his host, following closely in his footsteps, too anxious and over-whelmed to think a single thought worth remembering? Because that was the truth.

At the rear of the landing bay, they found a rough set of steps cut into the rock. More surprising still, green-tinged water was running down the steps and dripping from the ceiling.

"They don't exactly spend a lot on the place," commented Maktar as he led the way up the steps. Once at the top, they faced a metal door embedded in the rock. The agent held up his bracelet and the door retracted.

They turned left into a dank tunnel. From his experience in the mines, Sonus adjudged that it had been carved out with hand drills. By slaves of the Vitaari, no doubt. He took a few deep breaths to steady his nerves. No matter how far across the galaxy he travelled, he couldn't escape the signs of his oppressors. They'd been there first; they might still be here now, waiting for him.

At the end of the tunnel was a small security booth. As they approached, a great orange shape popped up. The creature's neck was far wider than its head, the eyes and mouth almost invisible within rolls of fat. It placed two blubbery arms over the side of the booth. In one hand was a small device.

Sonus froze. Maktar was the size and shape of a human, not much more different from Sonus than a Kinassan was from a Palanian. Even the towering, gray-skinned Vitaari had clearly evolved in parallel with the basic human form. But this orange blob in front of him, despite having two arms, two eyes, and one head, was something else... something monstrous.

His instincts told him to run.

But his mind was in control. And it told him to be ashamed.

He was the stranger here, no less alien than anyone else—and probably more than most.

When Maktar held up his bracelet, the device buzzed. He exchanged a couple of words in *Standard* with the orange blob, and the creature waved them on their way.

"A Modun," explained Maktar as the barrier retracted and they continued on. "Not the most sophisticated of species but they're to be found in every sector. I believe there are more than a billion of them, all told."

"A *billion*?"

"Yes, but if you do learn some *Standard*, don't bother engaging them in conversation. I've yet to encounter one with more brain cells than a kifla."

"A what?"

"Like a rat, yes?"

"I don't like rats."

The tunnel opened up into a high-roofed cavern where dozens of aliens were on the move. Sonus noted that four tunnels entered the cavern on the left side. To his right was a protected entrance containing a line of booths where short queues had formed.

"Checkpoints to get into the market," explained Maktar.

"Didn't we just go through security?"

"That was just the first of many. No one trusts anyone here. And, of course, every faction wants to collect its own fees and bribes."

Sonus could see more Moduns, all wearing blue overalls with huge open necks and sleeves to accommodate their bulk. The next most common species could hardly have been more different.

These creatures were tall and slender, their bodies obscured by vivid, multi-colored cloaks. Upon the head of each was a strange metal contraption with tubes passing into at least three orifices. Sonus could make out only thin mouths because the top half of their faces was covered by a mirrored visor.

As he and Maktar joined the nearest queue, they found themselves behind one such creature.

"Raxis," confided the agent. "They run this place, employ a lot of Moduns as cheap labor. Their home world is the closest inhabited planet; they developed this place after the Vitaari left. Their government wants nothing to do with it, however, so it's run by an administrative body called the Executive. Corrupt to its core."

"What's all that machinery on their heads?"

"Allows them to breathe here. Apparently, their atmosphere contains some unusual combination of elements. As for the visors, I've never been entirely sure."

Sonus was slightly proud of himself that he felt no panic at the bizarre appearance of the Raxis standing in front of them, nor any of the other strange species wandering about or waiting in line. Perhaps, after such a visceral reaction to the Modun, he'd gotten it out of his system. Or perhaps being surrounded by a dozen alien species made their presence feel more natural and less threatening than being confronted by a single specimen.

As they waited in line, Sonus began to study individuals of various races. One was a tiny figure not even as tall as a Lovirr. He travelled around on a hovering disc that kept his head at a respectable level. Sonus also saw two hulking figures escorting a female humanoid clad in a shimmering dress of scarlet. Her long, flowing hair was adorned with all manner of jewelry, something Sonus noticed right after realizing she had only a single eye. Her bodyguards were not of the same species. They wore only sleeveless tunics, and their imposing bodies seemed to be made up of pinkish plates, like a crab or tortoise. The heads were bizarrely small, hairless, and of a darker red. They were as big as the Vitaari and—though no weapons were visible—wore gloves equipped with metal studs.

Sonus shook his head in disbelief. He was so lightheaded that he almost felt like his mind was floating away from his body. He pledged to himself that one day—when there was time—he would record it all for his fellow Corvosians, not only this journey but everything that had happened to him since his escape from Mine Fourteen.

"This must all be disorientating for you, yes?" remarked Maktar.

"That's an understatement." Being stared at by Maktar only made the lightheadedness worse, so Sonus pointed at the first unknown species he saw. "What about the creatures with the veils?"

A trio of these beings was passing through the booth to their right. Their bodies were clad in featureless black but everything above their shoulders was covered by a circular veil at least two feet high. The material was pale, yet nothing could be seen.

"The Zelmekra," said Maktar. "They refuse to ever show their faces on religious grounds. They travel far and wide, great traders, but few people have any idea what they look like— beyond having two arms and two legs. Not very popular but they're tolerated because they tend to be exceptionally rich."

At last their turn came at the booth, which was manned by a Raxis in an azure cloak. Maktar held up his bracelet once more, but the words he was exchanging with the official did not sound particularly friendly. As they spoke, Sonus tried not to look at the

Raxis's facial apparatus, particularly the transparent cylinder, inside which some liquid bubbled.

Clearly annoyed—which was the most emotion Sonus had seen from him yet—Maktar removed his bracelet and handed it to the official. The Raxis nodded, then returned it. The barrier withdrew and the pair passed.

"*Vun Tak!*" muttered Maktar.

"What?" said Sonus.

"Sorry. An Ikasaran curse."

"What does it mean?"

"Something like 'Give me strength.' But we use it for everything, really. I told you this place is rotten to the core. That one didn't want a bribe that could be traced so I had to give him something real. Fortunately, I've encountered this situation before."

"Why did you give him your bracelet?"

"That was to cover the hand over. I gave him some Raxis coins. They're no longer used as currency but very valuable at antique markets—there's one over there."

"Ah."

Not far beyond the checkpoint, they came to a narrower section with stores on either side. Maktar strode purposefully toward one and led Sonus inside. The store was very small but stocked with a huge variety of clothing, some of which hung from the ceiling.

A Modun with an alarming skin affliction ambled toward them and offered an enthusiastic greeting. Maktar spoke to him briefly. The Modun took a device from a pocket and aimed it at Sonus, who started—but Maktar did not seem at all concerned. The Modun then retreated.

"You're a bit taller that an Orell," said Maktar, "but you look close enough to pass. I've asked for clothes in their style. If anyone tries to speak to you, pretend to be dumb."

"What did you tell the Raxis official about why you're here?"

"I told him I'm returning to Ikasar with a criminal."

"So, I'm a dumb criminal?"

"No offense, yes?"

Maktar's bracelet beeped one of its various tones. He activated the screen and gazed down at it.

The Modun returned holding a baggy pair of black trousers and an equally loose gray shirt. These he gave to Sonus, who was encouraged by the incredibly light and smooth feel of the material. A younger Modun with some kind of pipe clamped in his mouth then appeared. He offered a black coat that at least had some shape to it and a pair of matching boots.

The elderly Modun spoke; it seemed like a question.

Without looking up from his screen, Maktar replied, then addressed Sonus.

"There's a room at the back where you can change. We should get rid of your overalls immediately."

Sonus gave a noncommittal grunt: his best guess what a mute criminal might do in the circumstances.

Maktar pointed at his bracelet. "The *Spectre* just picked up a First Empire intelligence update. The Vitaari have expanded their spy network in response to the most recent engagements. It's likely that they have agents here on Xerxa. We will have to be very, very careful."

13

The canteen on the *Galtaryax* was a large space that seldom contained more than ten people. Founding Day, however, was a date of such significance that it could not be ignored, despite ongoing operations. The key traditions of the occasion included the playing of the imperial anthem, the recitation of the Domain Lists, and the consumption of historically traditional food—mostly *krasa*, a dried meat far too salty for Talazeer to enjoy—and drinks—especially *massis*, a syrupy cocktail so sweet that Talazeer would find it intolerable without the salty dried meats.

Count Talazeer considered the whole affair rather tiresome but as leader he had to show himself willing. All of the mine governors and virtually the entire crew were assembled in the canteen, where the ship's faded imperial tapestries had been hung. Having often received compliments on his singing voice, the Count did not object to leading the anthem. He was pleased to see that every last person present joined in.

The reading of the Domain Lists was shared between Talazeer, Deputy Rasikaar, and Commander Elezz, who seemed very keen to contribute. The list was exactly what its name suggested: a record of Vitaari military victories and colonial acquisitions. An abridged list was used and, unfortunately, Corvos did not merit a mention. Talazeer was surprised by the zeal with which Elezz recited her section (from memory). He concluded she was either nauseatingly ambitious, genuinely patriotic, or a combination of both.

With the readings over, the feasting began. The food and drink had been placed on two long tables in the center of the canteen. The crew of the *Galtaryax* was accustomed to a diet of preserved rations and they dug into the traditional fare with enthusiasm. Talazeer chuckled to himself, trying to imagine being so starved for real food that *massis* and *krasa* became cause for gluttony. If they were truly delicacies, people with the means, like himself, would enjoy them every day of the year and not just force down a bite or two on special occasions. The food and drink had arrived yesterday on the latest delivery from Vitaar, which had at least included some decent wine.

Marl took one mouthful of the *krasa*, then shook his head violently, eyes rolling.

"Try not to vomit," said Talazeer. "We wouldn't want a scene. Is that really your first taste of it?"

The Drellen nodded, then reached into his cloak and retrieved a flask of water. Once he'd drunk his fill, he replaced the flask and took out a small container. From this, he plucked pieces of raw flesh with his clawed fingers.

"Where does the chef get that stuff anyway?"

"From one of the mines, sir. A type of bovine creature dwells nearby."

"Tasty, is it?"

"I've had worse."

Talazeer sighed. It was another banal conversation with Marl, but he knew that the others going on around him would be insufferable. It was customary on Founding Day to share tales gleaned from families and ancestors relating to the triumphs on the Domain List. The Count possessed a good array of tales himself but could think of nothing less interesting than telling them again or hearing others. Though he enjoyed real military history, these stories were invariably embellished and exaggerated.

Fortunately, he had a genuine reason to leave the evening early: the attending governors had brought the latest figures on the terodite yields. If these were as promising as anticipated, he could send an update to High Command.

"Excellency, this is for you."

One of Rasikaar's assistants arrived holding a small package. "Blossom candies, by the looks of the box."

This was another foodstuff associated with Founding Day— and one Talazeer enjoyed more than he cared to let on.

"Ah. Thank you."

Having earlier noted one of Elezz's technicians enter the canteen and speak to her, Talazeer turned to face the approaching commander. He had never met any other female officers, so he wasn't sure if the heeled boot she wore was standard issue. It certainly accentuated her figure, which he had concluded was well above average.

"Commander."

"Excellency, the shuttle has returned. The guards assure me all went well. The prisoner Kannalin was given the opportunity to escape and took it. I even had the men aim harmless shots at him. His position is around thirty kilometers from the rebels' last known location. We couldn't make it too obvious but we have to give him a chance of finding them. The device is transmitting and we're currently tracking him."

"Very good, Commander. Any progress on the drones?"

"Analysis continues. My men think it unlikely that Sonus could have put something together but—"

"Unlikely, yes. I agree."

"Then again, he did single-handedly steal a combat shell, destroy most of Mine Fourteen, and bring down the viceroy's shuttle—so, not a man to underestimate."

Talazeer did not reply to that.

"We continue to question the other prisoners," added Elezz. "In the event that Kannalin does not lead us to his friends, we will move on to more... extreme techniques. Though it is, of course, possible that the rebels have changed their plans. I believe you wanted to discuss the situation at Mine Thirteen?"

"You've read the incident report from Governor Selerra?"

"I have. And I am more than happy to dispatch a unit to investigate these tribesmen."

"Sounds sensible. We must always be watchful. It's disturbing that the Kinassans are aware of what occurred at Mine Three."

"Yes, but history shows us that such news can spread quickly. I'll admit that I am beginning to understand your eagerness to capture the leaders alive. As you said, a broadcast upon screens in every mine can counter such talk. Let us hope we soon have every living rebel in our hands."

"That would make for quite a show," said Talazeer. "Here, Commander, have one."

The Count was referring to the blossom candies. He had opened the box while they'd been speaking and just popped the first one into his mouth. He did love candy.

"Ah, thank you. I… Sir, are you all right?"

Talazeer did not feel all right. His tongue seemed to have swollen and his throat felt tight. His breathing was painful. His next breath didn't come at all.

"Sir? Count Talazeer?"

He lurched away from Elezz and gripped the top of a nearby chair. As the lights of the canteen whirled, he felt himself sink to his knees.

A circle of faces looked down at him. Panicked, frightened faces.

"Count Talazeer, what is it?"

He tried to suck in a breath but nothing would come. His chest felt rigid, paralyzed. As he collapsed onto his side, his head cracked against the floor. He didn't feel it. The pain was elsewhere.

Then *everywhere*.

Something horribly rough and warm grabbed at his face and pried his lips apart. He glimpsed Marl, yellow eyes bulging right in front of him. He tasted blood. Raw meat. What was the Drellen doing?

Bile rose in Talazeer's throat. Convulsing, he felt himself spasm, then vomit onto the floor. Only then did a breath come, but with it more vomit.

When he finally regained his senses, he was looking down at half a red blossom candy, covered in blood and spittle. Next to it was a single chunk of the meat Marl had been eating.

The Drellen knelt beside him, a clawed hand on his master's arm. "What was it you said about not vomiting and making a scene?"

· · ·

The setting sun cast an orange glow upon the great trees. The light filled the spaces below the branches and illuminated the forest floor. It could hardly have looked more welcoming.

The rebels had stopped upon a rise that fell away down a gentle slope to the first of the Old Giants.

"We're almost there," said Yarni.

"Almost," said Torrin, anxiously fingering her necklace. Both of them were chewing on the rations Toll Maktar had provided. All agreed they didn't taste of much but they did seem to provide energy. The Palanians had tried them before the Echobe, but as they'd had little time to forage anything else, everyone eventually came around.

Cerrin was enjoying the view as much as the others but she was eager to keep moving, and not only because they were so close. One of the few traditions all Echobe shared was a belief that camp should be made while there was light in the sky. Cerrin had followed this without exception. She did not want to displease the gods, nor did she want to worry her fellow rebels.

For most of their long journey, this tradition had meant waiting until after sunrise each morning to halt their march. However, since Sonus's departure, they'd been marching not only all night but well into each day, sleeping only a few hours in the afternoon before moving on again at dusk. On this day, being so close, they had been on the move for nearly twenty-six hours straight, and dusk was approaching again.

Moving back through them, she could see their weariness but there were no complaints. "Almost there," she assured them as she passed. "Take a breather and we'll get moving."

Upon reaching the Palanians, she was immediately approached by Dari. "How far is it?"

"About a mile."

Dari cursed in her own language.

"Baros?" asked Cerrin.

"Yes. He can't walk."

The Palanian man had twisted his ankle that morning. Some of the Echobe had also experienced accidents, but Cerrin couldn't believe how hapless the Palanians were. It sometimes seemed to her that they were purposefully sabotaging progress.

"We've strapped it, but he's in a lot of pain," added Dari.

"What about Koros?" asked Cerrin, as Erras emerged from the tress and stood beside his compatriot.

"He's done his best," said Dari, "but I don't think we can move him any farther."

"We have to. The sun."

Erras answered. "What do you think will happen if the sun goes down? Will we all burst into flame? We can do no more today."

"Then we'll carry them."

"If it's only a mile," said Dari, placing her hand on Erras's arm. "We'll follow later. It doesn't matter to us about the sun. Perhaps you can come back and get us?"

Cerrin would not and could not forget her promise to Sonus. "We stay together. We'll carry them."

Count Talazeer awoke in the medical bay. The first thing he saw was the aged face of the ship's surgeon, a man with exceptionally bushy eyebrows and saggy skin beneath his chin. Talazeer's thoughts soon switched to his own condition when he recalled the terrifying events in the ship's canteen.

"Am I…"

It was a relief to hear that his voice still worked.

"Good morning, sir," said the surgeon, straightening up. "All things considered, I'd say you are exceptionally fortunate. Most of the poisonous material was expelled when you vomited. Quick thinking by the Drellen. A bodyguard indeed."

"Poison? The blossom candy?"

"I'm afraid so. Marl also had the foresight to preserve what was expelled." The surgeon walked over to a nearby table and returned with a metal tray. Upon it were the remains of the candy.

"We've begun an initial analysis. Not exactly my specialism but we should be able to identify the substance responsible. The rest of the package has been isolated."

Talazeer sat up. Only then did he realize that his throat was very sore.

"I've administered a relaxant for the affected areas," continued the surgeon. "It appears that the poison is of a type designed to inflame tissue. If you had fully ingested it, the damage would have been swift and catastrophic. You've a lot to thank him for."

The surgeon pointed toward the window. Though the medical lights made visibility difficult, Talazeer could make out the wide, flat shoulders and domed head of the Drellen in the waiting room.

"How are you feeling, sir?" asked the surgeon.

"Considering I almost died? Not bad."

Talazeer's recollection of the previous evening's events were tinged not only with fear but shame. How weak and idiotic he must have looked—collapsing, choking, then vomiting in front of his subordinates.

"All rather humiliating." He hadn't intended to say it out loud, but the surgeon swiftly responded.

"Humiliation is preferable to *elimination*, Count Talazeer.

You have survived two, sorry, three assassination attempts while here on Corvos. That is fortunate, no?"

"Or unfortunate, depending on your point of view."

"Shall I call for the commander? You might wish to—"

"No, no." He had no desire to see Elezz while in this condition. "Just send Marl in."

While he waited, Talazeer drank water from a mug on the table beside his bed. Realizing he could smell vomit, he also took a disposable wipe and cleaned his chin and neck.

Marl strode in and stood at the end of the bed, his reptilian form as usual almost entirely hidden beneath his cloak.

"Well. Once again, I find myself in the position of having to thank you, Marl. A novel solution but you performed exceptionally well. The surgeon tells me that, without your intervention, I might not be here."

The Drellen responded with an almost imperceptible nod.

"Poisoned," continued Talazeer, feeling his rage build. "On *Founding* Day. On *my* ship. How could such a thing be possible? It is one thing to be attacked openly by rebels, but this? What about that bloody assistant who gave me the package?"

"Sir, he claims that it arrived with yesterday's delivery from Vitaar—a point several others have corroborated. The package was kept in the cargo hold with all of the other... refreshments... delivered for this afternoon's celebration. Anyone could have tampered with it there, or it may have already been tampered with before it left Vitaar."

"What has Elezz said?"

"Sir, we have no idea who might be involved in this. I suggest that we conduct our investigations *personally*."

"You suspect... what? A conspiracy?"

The Drellen shrugged. "We don't have a motive yet. There's no reason to suspect the assassin is working alone, nor any reason to suspect otherwise."

"Assassin. There's no other way to put it, I suppose."

"If the assassin is on board, it's possible they might try to strike again. If, however, the operation was initiated on Vitaar, that raises other questions."

The rage was still there. "Why me?" yelled the Count, striking the bed with a fist. "What have I ever done to anyone!"

14

The route to the weapons market snaked through scores of ramshackle stores constructed from plastic panels, metal sheets, and chunks of rock. Some were tiny—little more than a hatch—while others boasted numerous employees and rack after rack of offerings. Tiny drones buzzed around the shoppers, each equipped with a miniature screen or an audio unit announcing offers: "Almana's Breath! Get it here! Best price in the quadrant!" Sonus couldn't help but notice some booths employed scantily clad males and females of various species to entice potential buyers inside.

Sonus was pleased with his new clothes. Not only was the material comfortable and light but the shirt, trousers, and jacket had actually changed size to fit him. According to Toll, this technology was common.

As they hurried past a Modun cleaning crew who smelled quite foul, Toll Maktar quickened his step.

"Fortunately for us, the weapons market is usually quieter." He lowered his voice. "Did you spot any Vitaari?"

"No."

"They have excellent methods of disguise but are limited by

their unusual height and size. Not very good at blending in—though they often use proxies for surveillance."

"Does the First Empire have agents here? Anyone who might help you?"

"Possibly. But if there are, they haven't told me."

After passing through the narco market, they entered a high cavern where a few azure-clad Raxis were directing a small army of slow-moving Modun. The Modun were all holding hand drills and shuffled into a gloomy tunnel.

"Always some work going on," remarked Maktar. "They need more space for stores. Twenty percent of everything sold here goes to the Executive."

They followed a narrow path through a storage area filled with ribbed cargo containers stacked four high.

No, not storage, Sonus realized, glancing into a couple of the containers with open doors. The lowly Moduns dwelt here. Some seemed to have a decent collection of belongings, but in one container he saw more than ten of the creatures laid out in cramped conditions. He knew that the inhabitants of Mine Three had been housed in such containers, though his home at Fourteen had been within freezing subterranean tunnels. Shivering, he zipped up his new black coat. Thoughts of his fellow rebels were never far away; he felt almost ashamed by his new set of clothes.

The weapons market was as noisy as the narco market but the sound was of a different type—mostly from a firing range where several prospective clients were testing out handguns. The merchants' booths were inside large, circular containers that looked to Sonus like converted fuel tanks. Any wall space not taken up by racks of weaponry contained a screen showing the weapons in action: dueling warriors, precision shooting, and endless explosions.

"Imagine having to work here," said Maktar.

"Why are they so noisy?" replied Sonus as he followed the agent past the firing range. "The Vitaari guns are fairly quiet."

"Some are cheap, so the engineering isn't effective enough to dampen sound. And some people like them noisy!"

They passed two humanoids with faces almost entirely covered by white hair. The pair wore some kind of military uniform and were deep in conversation with a Raxis trader. One aimed and fired a small rifle with a flash of green light that exploded impressively against a large concentric target.

Suddenly, a tiny figure appeared beside him. The creature possessed four arms and two legs and—like the one he'd seen earlier—was floating along on a circular disc. Clad in miniscule but immaculate clothing, the interloper possessed a pinched, bright yellow face. When Sonus instinctively recoiled, the disc zoomed over his head and was suddenly a foot from Maktar's nose, flying backwards. The creature squeaked at the agent, imploring in a very high-pitched *Standard*.

Maktar waved it away. With an offensive gesture, the creature flew off.

"Vun Tak," came the curse again. "She always comes after me when I'm here," he explained. "Made one deal on my first visit and she seems to think I owe her. Not very helpful when one is trying to avoid attention!"

The pair continued through the market, turning right along one of the corridors between converted fuel tanks.

"I did some research while you were sleeping on the *Spectre*. Given your group's lack of... sophistication with technology, I believe something low maintenance and easy to carry is best for everyday use. But we'll also want a few units of something that's going to really make the Vitaari sit up and take notice. Ah, here we are."

Maktar stopped beside a rack of weapons, each of which was secured by a chain. As soon as he halted, the proprietor appeared. This Raxis wore a comparatively mundane cloak of orange and red stripes. Like all of them, the lower part of its face was dark and wrinkled, the mouth a thin line. Sonus found the visors very disconcerting.

The trader said something to Maktar, who pointed at one particular weapon. It was one of the larger rifles: easily a yard long, with an odd barrel composed of two separate struts about three inches apart. The surface of the weapon was a dull black, apart from the metallic interior of the twin barrels, which gleamed under the cavern lights.

The trader unlocked the chain and handed the heavy-looking weapon to Maktar. The agent examined it and asked a series of questions. When the exchange finished, he offered the weapon to Sonus.

"Here, see how it feels. Put the strap over your shoulder to help with the weight."

Though smaller than the Vitaari assault rifles, the weapon was indeed heavy.

"The barrel components have to be balanced out by the stock," explained Maktar. "It's called a runner gun. See the two struts on the barrel—they create an electro-magnetic field that shoots projectiles four times faster than conventional guns. This carries very heavy ammunition."

Maktar bent down and ejected the magazine. He took out a

copper-colored shell, which almost filled his pale palm. "See the size? Only holds eight shots, but each will do a lot of damage. One or two shots might account for a combat shell. With a few of these, you could see off their shuttles, even lighter military vessels."

He turned and questioned the Raxis. When the seller answered, Sonus saw hundreds of tiny teeth in his mouth.

Maktar continued: "My funds will stretch to six, with the rest going toward simple rifles. What do you think?"

"How complicated are they?" asked Sonus. "What about maintenance?"

"Actually, there aren't too many moving parts so durability is an advantage. As long as they're kept clean and reasonably dry, they should work. But if one does break, repair is not an option. Neither is replacement, so be careful."

"Does he have six?"

"Yes. And he's happy for us to test them all on the range—not with real ammunition, of course."

Though the limits of the firing range didn't allow for a full test, Sonus had already seen enough to trust in Maktar's choice. With the weapons paid for, the seller agreed to have them delivered to the *Spectre* immediately.

Toll Maktar then visited several more vendors and eventually settled on twenty rifles manufactured by the Raxis themselves. They were cheap but this was an established, reliable model. Maktar also secured two thousand rounds of ammunition.

They passed another stall, where the agent swiftly obtained a hand-sized device housed in a box. "For the Vitaari drones. This will scramble their coms for an hour or more. There are better versions but they're not available here."

With durability in mind, he then purchased six handguns. These fired relatively weak plasma bursts but had one huge advantage: a single charge would generate two hundred shots. Maktar procured a charger, which could be carried in a backpack and replenished itself through solar and kinetic energy.

He said: "The plasma will bounce off most armor but any kind of hit will often blind the target. Better still, the charger will last for years. Even when the shells run out, you'll still have something to fight with."

His spirits surging, Sonus shook Maktar's hand. "My sincere thanks. These weapons will change everything."

"That's the idea. I'll arrange for delivery and then we'll see about the explosives."

"In here?"

"No. Even on Xerxa there are *some* rules. We have to head deeper underground."

They took a different tunnel out of the weapons market and Sonus soon found himself descending via an elevator. The two hairy military men were also present, as was another work crew of Moduns and a pair of the veiled Zelmekra. The elevator was just a broad metal platform but amazingly steady and smooth. Sonus watched sections of rock flying by and looked up at the now distant light above.

"I can't believe we're still going."

"It's *very* deep," replied Maktar quietly. "I believe the Vitaari used to drop their most powerful explosives down this shaft."

"I'm glad we haven't seen any," said Sonus.

"That doesn't mean they're not here."

At last, the elevator halted and they were ushered off by a pair of uniformed Moduns. Three armed Raxis were also there, and Maktar was required to confirm their identities once again. They then set off with the other occupants of the elevator along a broad tunnel. Several smaller corridors branched off it into little caverns that had been converted into well decorated establishments, all with more than a few customers.

"The gambling quarter," said Maktar.

"Why's it all the way down here?"

"I'm not entirely sure. Where there's gambling, there's usually violence. Perhaps the Raxis just like to keep it out of the way."

"Strange to locate so many people close to the bombs."

"Actually, it's a bit of a walk yet."

Sonus reckoned it took them quarter of an hour from the elevator. During that time, he observed a number of strange sights: First was a group of aliens crowded around something, all shouting and cheering. Through the sea of bodies, he spied two small dog-like creatures up on their hind legs. Both seemed to be fitted with some kind of shock device that gave off a burst of energy when they struck each other with their paws. A particularly strong blow sent one of the creatures flying through the air. The crowd roared.

Then two battling patrons were thrown out of a well lit cavern, one a tough-looking character with an eye patch and bulging muscles. His opponent was no more than three feet tall: a pink-skinned humanoid with black dots for eyes and tendrils upon its head that looked to Sonus like a squid's tentacles. The tough reached into his jacket and pulled out a curved blade, only for the squid-thing to leap up, use one tentacle to disarm his foe and two others to poke him in both eyes. The big man staggered backwards, slashing wildly but striking nothing but air. Before the pair could continue the fight, two Raxis guards appeared. Invisible blasts from their stunning weapons downed the combatants instantly. Soon, the guards were dragging the unconscious pair toward the elevator.

The gambling dens were gradually replaced by storage areas, some of them guarded. Sonus and Maktar then reached another checkpoint, though this one was very different to the others. The booth was mounted within a vast metal gate and four armed Raxis in dark blue cloaks were on duty. When the gate rumbled upward, Sonus saw that the metal was at least three feet thick. He and Maktar weren't the only ones entering the explosives market. Behind them were the two Zelmekra from the elevator and another Raxis who was treated deferentially by the guards.

On the other side of the gate were more caverns, each sealed by a reinforced door.

"As I remember it, the one we need is close." Maktar stopped to study a mounted display that listed the different dealers. "Yes. Over here."

A short walk took them to another door embedded in the rock. A screen flashed on and the face of a Raxis appeared. After a brief conversation, the door slid open and Maktar led the way inside. They were greeted by another Raxis, this one with a partially transparent visor. Sonus made out a pair of a large, inquisitive eyes that reminded him of a horse. The alien offered the prospective customers a tray holding some glasses and tiny plates of food. Maktar politely declined and continued into the store.

"Female," he confided quietly. "For some reason, their visors are less opaque."

Oddly, the female's cloak was comparatively dull. The male

who came forward to greet them was hurriedly putting his on. Sonus now saw that the Raxis were built very much like humans, though their underclothes seemed to consist entirely of wrappings. The proprietor's cloak was a vibrant mix of red and green squares. Once fully clothed, he adjusted his breathing apparatus and ushered the new arrivals forward.

They passed row after row of munitions—large and small—mounted in racks on the floor. Maktar was clearly specific with his request because the seller swiftly led them to a sample. Having inspected it, Maktar passed the explosive to Sonus. It was a heavy, semi-circular device with a control panel on top.

"Armor-piercing mine with magnetic lock. The interior contains hundreds of koridium balls that are expelled into the target upon detonation. Just one of these would take out a shuttle, no problem."

"If you could get close enough to plant it."

"Fair point. Also good for ground vehicles or an unmanned shell."

Sonus could already imagine numerous applications. "How many can we afford?"

"Five. What do you think?"

"You're the expert."

"I think we'll—"

There was clatter from the front of the store and the female cried out. Sonus spun around and saw several Raxis guards march inside, stun-weapons at the ready. When the female tried to protest, she was shouldered aside. Maktar spoke to the proprietor, but his eyeless gaze was fixed on the interlopers. The agent guided Sonus behind him. As the guards approached, his hand moved to his bracelet.

Sonus looked around at the variety of explosives.

He's not going to fight in here?

Other panicked thoughts flooded his mind.

What if we're captured?

What if we lose the weapons?

The first guard reached them and barked a command in what sounded to Sonus like *Standard*.

Toll Maktar raised his hands. "You should do the same, Sonus. Looks like we're under arrest."

"Vun Tak?" said Sonus, though it hardly seemed the moment for levity.

"Vun Tak."

With two guards ahead and two behind, they were escorted out of the store and farther along the tunnel. His worst fears realized, Sonus kept his eyes on Maktar but he could discern little from his expression. He knew he was still entirely dependent on the agent in this complicated, dangerous place.

The guards turned into a cavern and passed two more Raxis, who seemed to be watching over numerous stacks of cargo containers. Sonus was surprised to note that this pair did not wear uniforms. He was even more surprised when the guards led them between two stacks and stopped in front of what looked to be an impenetrable wall of rock.

"What's going on?" he whispered.

"I wish I knew," replied Maktar.

Just then, a square section of the rock abruptly disappeared, revealing a narrow, dimly lit tunnel.

Sonus didn't have much time to absorb this development.

With a shove in the back, he was sent into the tunnel beside Maktar, still surrounded by the guards. The tunnel veered to the right and Sonus had counted fifty-five paces when they emerged into a smaller cavern stuffed with yet more cargo containers.

From behind a nearby stack came another Raxis, this individual wearing a cloak of shimmering gray. The front pair of guards separated to allow his approach. He came so close that Sonus could observe the remaining two guards in his gleaming visor. Upon the skin visible between the visor and his collar were numerous scars. The mouth undulated as the Raxis reached inside his cloak and produced a small handgun. The barrel was soon aimed at Sonus's chest.

Please, no. Not here. Not like this.

The barrel inched closer, the mouth behind it twisting into a bizarre grin. When the Raxis's gloved fingers twitched, Sonus winced. "Toll?"

Sonus couldn't help feeling relief when the barrel moved to target Maktar. The Raxis spoke a line of *Standard*.

"What did he say?" asked Sonus, somehow hoping that if he kept talking, he could halt—or at least delay—something worse.

"He asked why we have purchased such weak weapons."

Only now did Sonus realize that his captor was holding one of their new plasma-firing handguns. "I don't understand."

"Neither do I entirely. But I do know this character. His name is Krii. He's a criminal, a smuggler."

At an order from Krii, one of the guards pulled a canvass cover off a nearby stack. Beneath were several boxes that Sonus recognized as the weapons he and Maktar had just bought. Then, from behind them, two more men appeared with a floating transporter. Arranged upon it were the mines.

"Our new purchases, yes?" added Maktar.

"So, what does he want?"

"What do all smugglers want? A deal."

Sonus spent the next few minutes watching as the four guards removed their uniforms (presumably disguises) and donned their own cloaks, all rather more colorful than their leader's. Observing their interactions, he realized that the Raxis used a lot of gesticulation, perhaps because their eyes were always covered. He and Toll Maktar were now sitting on empty fuel barrels, the agent engaged in a heated exchange with Krii. The smuggler had twice dropped a little red ball into his breathing apparatus, which provoked brief, exaggerated shakes of his head. Sonus guessed it was some sort of narcotic.

Maktar waved a hand at Krii, who walked away, kicking the cavern floor in anger.

The agent turned to Sonus. "This could be bad. He wants information. Of a type I can't give."

"What information?"

"From the First Empire network. Vitaari dispositions—the placement of their vessels and defensive systems."

"To help him smuggle something?"

"Initially I thought so. But he specifically needs information regarding the Za-Ili circle. It's odd."

Krii approached Sonus and spoke at some length.

Maktar translated: "He says you shouldn't judge him too harshly. He is simply a businessman, trying to better himself. The Vitaari and the First Empire are no different to him, seeking wealth and power by whatever means necessary."

"He'll get no argument from me. Are you going to make a deal with him?"

Maktar appeared as anguished as Sonus had ever seen him, several veins pulsing. "The First Empire has strict rules about such things. If they were to learn of this, I'd lose my position. In fact, I'd likely be imprisoned for treason."

Sonus chose his words carefully: "You're asking us to risk our lives and take the fight to the enemy, after everything we'd done to escape. After we've lost so many of our people. And we're ready to do it. We'll risk everything. But we don't stand a chance without those weapons. Yarni and the other children, they don't—"

"All right, Sonus," countered Maktar, for once a hint of irritation in his level voice. "I know the situation."

Maktar sat there in silence, his breath escaping as white mist in the chilly cavern. Krii muttered something to his men, then dropped another red ball into the breathing apparatus. After the inevitable head-shudder, he aimed a hand at Sonus and said something in *Standard*.

"He's telling you to talk to me," explained Maktar. "Persuade me to make the deal."

Sonus knew there was no point repeating himself. "You have family back on Ikasar, I suppose—people who depend on you?"

Maktar looked down at the floor for a while, tapping the top of the fuel barrel with his finger. Within only a few moments, he reached for his bracelet and activated the screen. Then he waved Krii over and showed him something.

The Raxis was evidently pleased by what he saw, for he immediately slapped his chest and gave a triumphant shout.

"You gave him what he wanted?" asked Sonus, surprised by Maktar's swift decision.

"I did," said the agent. "We've come too far to leave here empty-handed."

They saw four Vitaari on their way back through the narco-market.

The sight of those imposing bodies, silvery faces, and angular features was enough to halt Sonus in his tracks.

"Keep moving," whispered Maktar, nudging him forward, then neatly seeking refuge behind a loading vehicle. Sonus followed the agent's example, pretending to study a nearby screen, but they kept the Vitaari in their peripheral vision.

"No uniforms," added Maktar.

The Vitaari wore sharply cut garments of black and gray. Every outfit was slightly different and yet the quartet were unmistakably a unit. "Probably from the Intelligence Directorate," said Maktar. "A division of the Colonial Guard."

"Could they be looking for us?"

"Unlikely, unless one of the locals has sold us out—the Vitaari have a lot of money to throw around. Listen, Krii promised to deliver our weapons to the *Spectre*, but it may take a while. Until then, we should keep our heads down. Are you hungry?"

They found a quiet eatery not far from the spaceport. Maktar made an educated guess about what off-world foods Sonus could stomach, and they both dined on a spicy soup accompanied by a plate of sticks that to Sonus tasted a little like potato. They waited in the restaurant almost two hours before Maktar received confirmation that their purchases had been delivered.

Sonus found his stomach unsettled as they returned through the checkpoints and headed for their bay, although he wasn't sure the unfamiliar lunch could be blamed.

Outside their bay, several large containers had been stacked up. Sonus couldn't help smiling with satisfaction: He'd been right to come. Right to put his trust in Maktar. When the rebels next fought the Vitaari, they'd have the firepower to match them. As he stopped to admire the haul of weaponry, Maktar continued toward the door.

Those few steps made all the difference.

The agent froze, then spoke loudly in what sounded like *Standard*.

Someone answered from inside the bay. Maktar didn't look at Sonus but subtly pointed his thumb at the weapons. Sonus flattened himself against the containers, making sure he couldn't be seen.

Maktar continued the conversation—which did not yet sound unfriendly—and entered the bay.

Sonus listened carefully and didn't move until certain that the agent was close to the *Spectre*. He then slid along the chilly rock to the doorway and peered inside. Maktar was close to the rear of the ship, dwarfed by two Zelmekra, their odd veils lightly dancing due to some flow of air.

Did Maktar want him to hide behind the weapons? Or to arm himself? Sonus had no idea. His heart pounded in his ears. He also detected the rumble of some ship not far away. Was it sufficient cover noise to pop the latches on a container? Maktar and the two others were still conversing. This was his best chance. He eased it open.

A runner gun.

Heavy. Bulky. Awkward. Hard to aim at small targets like a person. But at least he'd been able to practice firing it.

Gently lifting the runner gun out of the foam interior, he located a single shell and loaded it, wincing at every *clack*.

With the heavy weapon in both hands, he eased to his right and peered around the stack. Either Toll Maktar saw him or his timing was perfect, for the agent suddenly spoke in *Trade*.

"Are you ready, Sonus?"

"Ready."

The agent raised his hand and fired the stun-ring. One Zelmekra tottered backwards and fell. The second reacted even more quickly than Sonus, lashing out with a high kick that struck Maktar in the chest and sent him flying.

Sonus tried to take aim, but the runner gun was too heavy for such a fast-moving target. Then the Zelmekra produced a hand-gun and Sonus had no choice but to pull the trigger and pray.

Nothing happened.

At least nothing seemed to have happened.

But when he looked down at the bay, black blood and chunks of flesh and clothing now covered the floor and the rear of the *Spectre*.

Coughing, Toll Maktar hauled himself to his feet, then flicked blood off his hand.

"Nice shot."

The agent got to his feet and checked on the first Zelmekra. Its veil had come loose when it fell. Beneath was the silvery skin of a Vitaari.

Sonus's hands were shaking and he could not summon a reply.

Maktar nodded toward the doorway and the stack beyond. "Next time though, try not to stand in front of a pile of explosives."

15

The rebels spent the morning camped around a single tree. The trunk of the Old Giant was thirty feet across, the lower stretches covered by thick, reddish bark and the occasional incongruous tiny branch. The ground was obscured by several layers of dry leaves accumulated over many years. Green-feathered lorri birds had made their homes in the lower nooks of the tree but their cries were soft and musical. As the camp stirred, Cerrin saw relief and excitement upon the faces. They understood what this place could be: a home.

And yet she was determined not to get ahead of herself. Though the canopy far above was thick, if the Vitaari got in here, they would have space to move; space to surround and attack. The rebels needed to construct a proper building and some kind of defensive perimeter. Though there had been no sighting of their enemy since Sonus left, Cerrin knew the hunt would not end. She had four sentries out, stationed a quarter-mile from the camp. The rebels—especially the Echobe—were already settling in. Even the Palanians—apart from Erras—seemed at last to understand the value of this place.

Cerrin would allow them to rest but this was a far-from-ideal location. They were also low on food. There were so many mouths to feed. And yet so many fewer than when—

Murrit was suddenly in front of her.

"What is it?"

"Now that we have reached the Giants, we must honor them and the spirits. Ask for their protection."

Cerrin had not once heard the gray-haired guider complain during their flight. She wondered if her connection to the gods and the forest fortified her.

"The Ceremony of Gratitude," continued Murrit. "I have spoken to many others. We would very much like to—"

"Of course. Gather everyone."

Thirty-four, thought Cerrin.

Sixty-six people had fled Mine Three, including Sonus. She'd brought thirty-four of them to the Old Giants.

Nearly half their number were dead, rotting away to bones on the forest floor—or worse: captured, back in the hands of the Vitaari, being tortured and interrogated.

That a single one of them had made it so far was a miracle, she reminded herself. Cause to praise the gods.

The others seemed to agree. They knelt in a circle, close to the giant's trunk. All of the Palanians apart from Erras attended, even the injured pair. Cerrin and Yarni had gathered branches, leaves, and seeds to symbolize this area of the Great Forest and placed them in a small pile. Murrit knelt in the middle of the circle, beside the collation. She pressed her hands to the earth, and all of the others did the same.

First, she called out to Esill, Mother Goddess of the Forest, giving thanks and requesting protection. All Echobe knew the words of the simple prayer, or variations of it; many murmured along with the guider, while the others repeated her words after her.

Murrit then addressed Lintar, God of Trees, and Usifar, God of the Sky. The rebels repeated her words and recited "The Branch and the Leaf," an eight-line chant that celebrated the unity of all natural things, including the people of the Great Forest, who had been granted permission to join the flora and the fauna at the dawn of time.

Cerrin was pleased to see the Palanians joining in the chant. The ceremony concluded with the burial of the collation by Murrit and Yarni.

Cerrin allowed a minute of reflection to pass, then stood and spoke to her fellow rebels.

"We are here and we are thankful, but now the real work begins. We must move farther away from the edge of the Old Giants. We must find a place where we can build, where there is water and where gardens will grow. A place that we can defend if we have to. I know you are all tired. Rest here for now, forage if you have the strength. I will spend the day trying to find our new home. If I do, we will leave when the sun goes down."

As the group broke up, Cerrin sent runners to recall Jespa and Torrin from their sentry duties. As she waited, Yarni charged up, holding the head of a mushroom in two hands.

"Look what I've found. No spots, so we can eat it, right?"

"That's right."

"Can I build a fire? I like them—"

"No fires. Never."

Yarni's face fell. "Never? Not even when we build our log-house?"

"Maybe one day. Just be glad with your find. Were there more mushrooms?"

"I'll go and look."

Before running off, Yarni split the mushroom in two and handed half to Cerrin. "To keep you going while you search."

"Thank you."

Cerrin walked to the tree where she had left her gun and spear. The gun was spotted with dirt; she knew that Sonus would tell her off for letting it get in such a state. She had tried not to think of him too much. She had barely been able to grasp Maktar and his ship, let alone imagine the alien world he had spoken of. It all seemed impossibly far away; in fact, it all seemed impossible.

Though they had disagreed and Cerrin was still suspicious of the agent and his masters, she had mentioned Sonus in her prayers. While the others addressed Esill and Lintar and Usifar, she spoke only to Ikala, God of Battle. So far, Ikala had answered more often than he had not.

"I don't know how you keep going."

Baros—the Palanian man with the twisted ankle—was lying against the tree, covered by a blanket. Nearby, the other Palanians were busy clearing the ground.

Cerrin did not recall speaking to Baros before.

"Before the Vitaari came, I believed in the Maker, the only god I knew. Now I know of *your* gods, the Echobe gods. I think they must be within you, Cerrin—giving you strength, driving you on. I don't know how else to explain it."

"What choice do we have but to keep going?"

"It's easy to say. But to actually do it? There is something very special about you. I think perhaps your gods have chosen you."

Cerrin realized that some of the other Palanians were listening. While at first she had felt touched and appreciative, that now turned to embarrassment.

"How's your ankle?"

"A little better."

Cerrin was glad when Torrin and Jespa returned.

"See anything useful?" she asked the pair.

"Lots of buba plants to the north," said Torrin. "You know them?"

Cerrin nodded. The red bulbs that grew among their roots were plentiful in the winter months when other crops were dormant.

"I saw a stream to the northwest," said Jespa. "Followed it for a while, seemed to grow wider."

Nobody needed to say that water was more important than food or shelter. Cerrin picked up her gun and her spear. "Northwest it is, then. By the way, as it's just the three of us, feel free to hold hands. I won't tell anyone."

Jespa blushed; Torrin gave a nervous laugh. But once they were away from the camp, they did exactly as Cerrin had suggested.

Count Talazeer was ready to leave the medical bay. He had changed into a new set of clothes delivered by Marl and had just thanked the two assistants who'd cared for him.

But first, he located a mirror in a corner of the bay and adjusted his collar and jacket. He was intent on showing his subordinates on the *Galtaryax* that he was in good health and altogether unaffected. In truth, his throat still burned from the foul liquids forced upon him by the surgeon, and the other end burned even worse from the evacuation those liquids had caused. But an analysis of the waste assured the surgeon that there would be no permanent damage.

Talazeer noted Marl in the mirror, standing motionless in that way of his that rendered him almost invisible. They had spent the last hour discussing how they would investigate the assassination attempt. The Drellen did not normally carry his gun on the ship but was now armed with it, as well as his sword. They had agreed that—when outside the Count's quarters—Marl would remain within three meters of his master at all times.

The ship's surgeon entered the bay. "Ah, Excellency, I hoped I'd catch you before you left us."

Talazeer ran his fingers through his hair for a final adjustment and turned from the mirror. "Yes?"

"The poison was a blend of diomorfite and excenta. This combination is centuries old and commonly known as—"

"Darkflower." Talazeer reckoned there weren't many Vitaari unaware of the term. The poison had been used on several imperators and countless noblemen. "Perhaps I should feel honored."

"Sir, it has so often been used because it is relatively simple to create and generally fatal. It is, however, only fully activated by the chemicals found in the stomach." He gestured to Marl. "Hence the successful intervention."

"Widely available, then?" asked the Count.

"I'm sure it is—in certain circles. And, of course, anyone with access to the right chemicals could create their own. Though that does require skill and research. In fact, I've been carrying out some of my own."

"And?"

"I have a friend in the Intelligence Directorate. He has provided a list of all recent uses within the last ten years. I have sent it to you."

"Thank you, surgeon. And for your treatment."

"Of course, Excellency. Your question about the equipment?"

"Yes?"

"I'm afraid we have nothing onboard that could detect traces of the poison elsewhere. The Intelligence Directorate might have such devices."

"I suspected as much. That will not stop us identifying the perpetrators. What you have started, we will finish."

Talazeer had not made much use of the garden. It had been installed by his predecessor in a spare loading bay. Though it was in need of attention, the Count did find the place restful. Upon the walls were discrete screens to emulate lakeside in one direction and far away mountains in the other, and through-out the middle were plants and flowers of the most vivid colors. He sat now on a bench with Marl, awaiting those he had summoned.

Rasikaar and Elezz arrived together, and the deputy made sure he was first to greet his superior.

"Excellency, how wonderful to see you up and about so quickly. I was so worried. And for such a thing to occur here—"

"Calm yourself, man," uttered the Count in his deepest voice.

"It takes more than some treacherous coward to keep a Kan Talazeer down."

Commander Elezz was less gushing but did at least flash one of her pretty smiles. "Sir, good to see you. Let me assure you that I will do all I can to bring this criminal to justice. This is an outrage. I'm happy to say there is some good news from another quarter."

As she spoke, Talazeer noted some small drops on her sleeves. It looked like blood. Red blood.

"Go on."

"Our friend Kannalin is on the move. He has walked steadily southwest for the last day. When he finally halts, we should have a good idea where the rebels are."

"You're assuming he knows."

"We surmise that if he were merely searching for them, his path would be less direct."

Talazeer supposed that made sense. And though finding the rebels remained crucial, it was no longer his priority. There would be little point securing that triumph if there were still an assassin—or *assassins*—on the loose. Whether the culprit was aboard the ship or back on Vitaar, he was in a race against time to identify him before he struck again. Of equal importance—the question of motivation.

"Mmm. In any case, we must get started on the investigation immediately."

"Of course, sir," said Danysaan, "I have already begun initial enquiries."

"Myself and Marl will lead. It is essential that no one be regarded as above suspicion. With that in mind, I will select several members of the administration—yourself included, Rasikaar—to carry out an immediate search of the ship. This is to encompass the personal quarters of all crew members and every single other area. As for the senior officers, their quarters shall be searched by *us.*"

Rasikaar and Elezz exchanged a glance. Unsurprisingly, it was the female who spoke.

"Am I not above suspicion then, sir?"

"It is simply a case of being thorough, Commander. With respect, I have only known you and your staff for a few days. Most of the other crew members were here during my previous stay. I do not recall any *previous* attempted poisonings."

"Sir, that package came from Vitaar. Surely that is where you will focus your enquiries?"

"I will leave no stone unturned, Commander." Talazeer took a deep breath. "Rasikaar, you will assemble the entire crew in precisely one hour. I will address them."

"Of course, sir."

"Is that all?" asked Elezz.

Talazeer gestured toward the bay door and she hurried away. "One more thing, Rasikaar. Young Yullasir who handles the array. He's your best systems man, correct?"

"He is, sir."

The Count stood, grimacing at a slight pain in his stomach. "I will need him to handle the technical side of things. Have him report to me immediately."

"Of course, sir." Rasikaar waited for the distant hiss of the bay door before speaking again. "Sir, have you heard about this morning?"

"Heard what?"

"Commander Elezz. She was interrogating the remaining

prisoners. Apparently, she didn't learn anything of use but… well, it's quite shocking."

"Speak plainly, man!" yelled the Count, who was anxious to return to his own quarters.

"I believe there was a male youngster with the captives. The guards told me that he spoke out of turn. The commander… crushed his head. By her own hand. I understand that some punishments are necessary but… well, one hardly thinks of a female being capable of such a thing."

Garra were common in the area of the Great Forest where Cerrin had grown up. Jespa and Torrin were less familiar with the animals, so they stayed away while she advanced.

The search for a place to base themselves could wait for a few minutes if Cerrin could bring down an adult garra. Six of them had gathered at the foot of a giant, where several bushes offered purple berries.

Cerrin knew her stalking skills were rusty, but she had approached from upwind and so far avoided any treacherous twigs. The lack of cover amidst the giants meant that she had to choose her route with extreme care to reach within throwing distance of her spear. Jespa had suggested using one of the rifles, but Cerrin said the impact from one of the shells would waste too much meat.

It also just seemed wrong. Nothing born of the Great Forest should be destroyed by a Vitaari creation.

Now within a hundred feet of them, she moved slowly around a giant, her left shoulder upon its bark. She seemed to feel a warmth from the tree, and it sparked within her an affection for these towering, ancient things. They were her guardians now. It almost seemed a shame to kill here.

Garra were known to be at their least vigilant when eating, and she hoped to get very close before flinging her spear. Her heavy boots were far from ideal for this task, and she kept her eyes on the forest floor—not on her prey—to avoid any misstep.

The noise of the garra munching away confirmed that they were very much occupied by the berries. She knew she would only get one chance, but the range was short and her chances good, even if she hadn't had much time for throwing practice.

She crept forward, choosing the placement of each step carefully, then lifted her eyes. The rump of one garra was no more than ten feet away; from the angle of her approach, the rest of its body and the herd remained hidden behind the berry bush.

The whole mottled brown body was shaking, so ravenously was it devouring the berries. Cerrin could hardly believe her luck. She had uttered a brief prayer to Priss, the huntress, daughter of Ikala, but had not expected such good fortune. She drew back her arm, ready to throw.

And the garra bolted.

Springing around the bush, she found them already thirty paces away and moving fast. The little herd suddenly changed direction when they glimpsed Jespa—then Torrin jumped up, right in their path, and the garra veered back in Cerrin's direction.

And Cerrin had thought they'd just been standing around, waiting and watching. She couldn't help but smile.

The fleeing garra weren't running straight toward her, but they'd come close enough for a throw. Fixing her gaze on a slightly fatter, slower garra toward the rear of the group, Cerrin adjusted her feet, drew back, and let fly.

It was not a good throw—a glancing blow on the garra's chest—but it was enough to disrupt its stride. The creature rolled forward over its head and slid on its back. Cerrin raced toward her spear, but as the garra bucked its way back to its feet, it was clear that the beast was too hurt to escape. It could do no more than limp away, bleating.

Cerrin reclaimed the spear and darted toward the beast, not out of fear of losing it, but out of sympathy—not wanting to prolong its suffering and fear. She flung the weapon into its haunch at close range. The garra managed a few more steps, then collapsed onto its side. Cerrin pulled her knife and slit its throat.

Jespa and Torrin arrived as hot red blood flowed over the pale leaves of the forest floor.

"Lucky," said Torrin.

Cerrin did not answer. She only offered thanks to the gods, Priss in particular.

They hung the animal to let it bleed out while they continued on, planning to pick up their prize on their way back to camp. Jespa soon located his stream, and they followed its meandering path northward. The water was no more than six feet across and never deeper than a knee, but Cerrin knew it would be more than enough for their small number.

Thirty-four.

So many fewer than when we began.

She shook her head to clear away the thought. The stream was clear and tasted fresh, and so they marched on, hoping to come across some buba plants or other edible vegetation that might make for an ideal location.

"I can always take a group to harvest the buba," offered Torrin, using her upturned spear as a walking stick.

"We may have to," replied Cerrin. "But I'd like to keep movement to a minimum. And we need to move out soon, away from the edge of the giants. I'd rather not have half our people wearing themselves out for hours picking bulbs."

Jespa gazed longingly upward. "I wonder if anyone's climbed to the top of one of these."

"Don't even think about it," said Cerrin. "You'd break your neck."

"Not me. I can climb anything."

"How?" said Torrin. "There aren't any branches for the first hundred feet."

"There are ways."

While they were all gazing up, a piercing squawk echoed through the forest. It wasn't the first time they'd heard it since reaching the Old Giants.

"Nesting hammer-bird," said Jespa, who was always keen to show off his knowledge. "Noisy things. They don't like visitors much. Hope they don't give us away."

"Probably haven't seen any people in years," said Torrin.

"We have bows," said Cerrin. "Good target practice. Shoot a few and the others will leave the area."

"Must say I'm looking forward to dinner," said Jespa. "There are hollows in the giants. We can cook the garra and keep the smoke out of sight."

"No fires," said Cerrin.

"But if the smoke—"

"No fires. It's not just the smoke. Remember what Sonus said about the heat? You really want to take the risk of popping up on some Vitaari's screen just so you can have a nice dinner, Jespa? We'll have to dry the meat."

"Have to find some sunshine first."

"We can eat it raw today, preserve the rest."

"The Palanians will love that," replied Torrin with a grin.

"I'm worried about Erras," said Jespa, once the moment of levity had passed. "He walks around on his own. He's not even saying much to the Palanians."

"He's a troublemaker," said Torrin. "Doesn't like being told what to do. Especially by an Echobe woman."

Cerrin said nothing.

A quarter of an hour later, Cerrin stopped. They had reached a point where the stream veered close to an Old Giant. Between water and tree, a patch of thick undergrowth had sprung up, in places as high as their heads. The brambly mess was covered in dark green leaves and small white thorns, and the winding stalks were so tightly twisted together than it was impossible to distinguish if it were all one plant or a thousand individual ones.

"No walking through that," Torrin said. "Should we cross over the stream?"

Cerrin pulled out her spear and poked at the ground at the edge of the undergrowth. "I've never seen these before," she said. "Do you know it?

Jespa and Torrin both shook their heads.

"It looks hardy, whatever it is. Do you think it could grow on a roof?"

Torrin gave a baffled look.

But Jespa understood at once. "Could be. And if it did, even a drone passing under the canopy might not recognize what it was seeing, unless it came very close."

"Camouflage?" Torrin asked.

Cerrin looked around at the many branches that had fallen from the high boughs over time. Some were rotten, but even they could be useful. "We'll need more wood, but we can make a shelter here large enough for everyone. We have the water, and the canopy is thick. We won't do any better."

16

The Kinassan warriors were surrounded.

Though the higher ground of the sandy crest might have bene-
fited them in a hand-to-hand fight against spears and swords,
against the Vitaari, it simply made them visible and vulnerable.

The combat shells landed in unison, then trudged up the
sandy slope, rays of sun sparkling on the angular, white armor.
Several were struck by arrows and spears, and one brave warrior
even charged them. He was cut down swiftly, the assault cannons
shredding his body.

The tribesmen formed a defensive circle, but their resistance
was mercifully short. Ten seconds of sustained fire ended the
battle. By then, more than thirty warriors lay upon the blood-
stained sand. Only one was still moving, crawling away from the
advancing line of soldiers, desperately clawing at the ground.

One combat shell stepped forward to pursue him, stomping
over the bodies of his fallen comrades until it towered over him.
The warrior stopped crawling, but he did not turn to face his
enemy. He merely lay still, defeated. A giant metal foot rose over

his head, then stepped down hard, crushing his skull into the ground.

"Was that really necessary, Sergeant Guldur?" asked Commander Elezz over the comcell.

The sergeant shrugged. "You did order us to kill them all."

"Fair point." Elezz leaned back in her chair in the *Galtaryax*'s operations room, then gestured at the screen in front of her. "With your approval, Count Talazeer, I will have video of the… *battle*, I suppose we should call it… sent to Governor Selerra. He can show it to the workers."

"Of course," said Talazeer, who had just roused himself from a lengthy slumber. He was happy to see action being taken against the Kinassans but more preoccupied by his personal concerns.

That morning, he'd received a terse message from his brother Deslat, stating his—and the family's—relief that Talazeer had survived the assassination attempt. Though Deslat had relayed personal sentiments from his parents, the Count was bemused that neither had reached out to him directly. He'd hoped that his brush with death might soften their view toward him. Evidently not.

Elezz stood and ushered him toward another of the operations room's screens, which one of her technicians was monitoring. Talazeer followed at a languid pace and found himself staring at live footage of a dense forest, with occasional glimpses of two large hands, one of which was holding a stick.

"Kannalin is moving quickly." Elezz pointed to a map on an adjoining screen. "It's not obvious from above, but there are unusually high trees here. We think that's where he's heading." Elezz turned to face her superior. "Sir, is there anything I can do to assist your investigation?"

"No, no. You clearly have plenty to occupy you, Commander. Keep me closely apprised of progress."

Talazeer had no instinctual feeling about whether Elezz could be involved in the attempt on his life. He was, however, sure of one thing: she was decisive, brutal, and ruthless.

Marl followed him out of the room, then over to a nearby viewport. The *Galtaryax* was now over the mountainous region of Corvos's lone continent. He could not make out which of the peaks was Mount Origo.

As he gazed down at the planet, the Count thought back to his first arrival all those months ago. He had expected the assignment to be no more than a stepping stone to greater things. He could never have imagined that so much would unfold out here in this remote system. For a moment, he was tempted to spit down at the pitiful world.

But no. That wasn't where his real enemy lay in hiding. The planet's wretched natives were barely worthy of his notice, let alone his enmity, with one or two exceptions. What were they but primitive creatures, biting and clawing and screaming and dying as all lesser animals did when confronted by a superior species? Let Elezz handle them.

The real enemy was a Vitaari. Not some beast lashing out, but a real person, a thinking person, a sophisticated mind capable of carefully plotting an intricate assassination attempt. And Count Talazeer had never felt more determined in his life to succeed, to overcome, to triumph over his enemy.

He turned to Marl. "Well?"

"A productive morning, sir. I have made it clear to Yullasir that we will accept nothing less than total effort and loyalty. He is setting himself up in your quarters. Unfortunately, we do not have the equipment aboard to examine genetic evidence. However, I have established the precise movements of the package, identifying those responsible for unloading it and moving it to the cafeteria. I have interrogated all four individuals and conducted searches of their accommodations. One man was in possession of some illegal pornographic material, but I found nothing else suspicious. I have also taken possession of their personal devices and passed them on to Yullasir. They did not resist my request."

"No surprise there."

"Deputy Rasikaar has assured me that the remaining searches will be complete by the end of the day." Marl reached into his cloak and retrieved a selection of key-cards. "For the quarters of the six senior officers. And, sir, what about the list obtained by the surgeon?"

"Interesting reading but I found nothing of significance. The answers we seek are aboard this ship, Marl. I am sure of it."

The *Spectre* shuddered, then bucked, throwing Sonus out of the bunk in the rear compartment. He hit the floor hard, jarring his left shoulder.

"Are you all right?" shouted Maktar from the cockpit.

"I think so."

Grabbing the handle of one of the weapon crates stuffed into the compartment, Sonus pulled himself up. The ship continued to shift back and forth under his feet as he hauled himself through the doorway and lurched over to his seat. Maktar was already strapped in, and soon Sonus was, too.

There was no maelstrom beyond the viewports, only the endless oblivion of deep space.

"Another interrupter relay?"

"No. After our run-in with the Vitaari, I was determined to avoid any such complications by skirting along the edge of the Sea of Traps, but it appears I might have come a bit *too* close."

"Sea of Traps? Doesn't sound like a nice place."

"It isn't. But we should be able to avoid any obstacles. Once the navigation has recalibrated, we'll get under away again."

"Why the name?" asked Sonus.

"The area covers almost twenty percent of this sector. Nobody's entirely sure of the origins, but it's believed that some ancient civilization tried to encapsulate its entire star in a giant sphere. Either the attempt failed catastrophically or else some enemy destroyed it, because trillions of fragments are scattered around for light years. The material is extremely magnetic... You can imagine the dangers, yes? Many ships have been damaged or destroyed, but no one has ever made a real attempt to clean it up."

"Have we been hit?"

"According to the ship, no. It just decided that we are too close to the danger areas. Did you get some rest?"

"Eventually. I was thinking about the Vitaari. They will know by now what happened on Xerxa. They'll be looking for the *Spectre.*"

"Probably. But she's very hard to find. And they won't know where we're planning to take the weaponry. There, the recalibration is almost complete. Only a few hours now, Sonus."

Not for the first time, he imagined the scene: the *Spectre* landing near the rebels, bringing out the weapons, putting one in the hands of every man and woman. And then he thought of Cerrin. There had been something quite inspirational about fighting beside her: man and woman, Palanian and Echobe.

He realized he wanted this mission to succeed for her sake more than all of the other rebels combined. She deserved this. She'd earned the chance to fight back.

And Toll Maktar had given it to them. He was risking his life—and may even have betrayed his own masters in Krii's secret cavern on Xerxa—to give Sonus's small group of frightened, starving rebels a fighting chance.

"You have a very dangerous job."

Maktar kept his eyes on the screen as he replied. "There are probably worse, yes?"

"You're away from home most of the time."

"True. Sometimes I think of *this* as my home."

"You have loved ones, though?"

"No."

"Surely there must be—"

"No."

The agent had answered with some force.

"I apologize, Toll," said Sonus. "I should not pry."

"Not at all."

Sonus decided to concern himself with the displays. It was clear that the navigational systems had recalibrated, for soon the *Spectre* returned to trans-light. The maelstrom appeared, then was lost as Maktar closed the viewport. He unstrapped himself and turned to Sonus.

"Life on Ikasar is difficult. It's a moon—small, barren, no atmosphere. It's not meant to support life. My parents... They were mining engineers. It's dangerous work, but always in demand. Excavation is a never-ending need for our growing population. They were both killed in an explosion when I was five years old. I was raised in an institution." Maktar paused for a long moment, then sighed. "I signed up for the military as soon as I was old enough, just to get out of that place. My aptitude tests said I was a good candidate for intelligence work. At first, I considered myself lucky not to be holding a rifle on the frontlines somewhere. Then it became clear what sort of missions they wanted me for. I suppose it's only logical that those without families take on assignments like mine."

"What happens if you marry? Have children?"

"I must complete my years of service first," replied Maktar.

"Would you like a life like that?"

"I don't know. I've never had the opportunity to try it. Would you?"

Sonus huffed, then smiled wistfully. "I think I would. To live like my parents did, like most people did, until the Vitaari came. Who knows when my people will ever have that chance again? Honestly, it would be enough for me to know that some future generation might find some normality, have a chance for happiness."

Count Talazeer had decided that he could leave the searches to Marl. It didn't seem becoming for a man of his station to be rifling through boxes, bags, and drawers. But with Marl occupied, this meant he had to remain in his quarters for safety's sake.

His only company was the technician, Yullasir. Talazeer felt it unlikely that this reserved character could possibly be involved in the assassination attempt, but he kept his sidearm on him at all times.

"Excellency, I must ask how you would like me to filter the data?"

"I told you—I want to see *every* message sent to or from Vitaar since I returned. It all goes through the array, correct?"

"That is correct, sir, but this will include *all* personal messages. We have over a hundred people aboard. The messages number in the tens of thousands."

"Prioritize it by keywords. But leave nothing out."

"Yes, sir, thank you, but I'm afraid there is another issue. Your security override allows access to classified messages up to Level 4—but there are a handful of officials who are authorized to send and receive Level 6 classified materials, including Deputy Rasikaar, the mine governors, and Commander Elezz."

"I'm authorized to see Level 6 materials," barked Talazeer.

"Yes, sir, but only if they're addressed to *you*. Level 6 materials sent to or by another person are locked. I can identify senders and recipients, but I cannot examine the content."

"Fine, start with that. I'll get you clearance to open the content soon enough. A message to High Command should suffice."

"Of course, Excellency. I will collate the data as swiftly as possible."

Seconds after Yullasir retreated, Talazeer received a call from Commander Elezz, which he took in the living area of his quarters to make use of the screen. "Sir, we've received an urgent message from the Intelligence Directorate."

"Regarding the assassination attempt?"

"No, sir. A separate matter. But one of the utmost importance. An Inspector Urttiek would like to speak with us both. Are you happy for me to patch him through?"

"Go ahead."

Within seconds, the screen divided into two, showing both the commander and the inspector. The shoulders of Urttiek's black uniform bore the double golden lines of the Directorate. He bowed cordially.

"Count Talazeer, greetings."

"Greetings to you, Inspector. What do you have for us?"

"One of our infiltration teams was attacked three days ago on the planet Xerxa Minor. Do you know it?"

Talazeer shrugged. "No. Should I?"

It was Elezz who piped up: "A smuggler's den, if I'm not mistaken. One of the galaxy's biggest black markets."

"That's right, Commander," said the inspector.

Talazeer sighed with impatience. "Fine. What about it?"

The inspector bristled. "We lost two operatives in the attack, Excellency. Their assailants escaped on some kind of stealth ship with a small arsenal of weapons, including runner guns and high explosives. Fortunately, our men were able to plant a tracking device on the ship before they were ambushed. We've had some difficulties with the signal, but a detector buoy picked them up within the last two hours. Their course suggests they're heading for Corvos."

"What do you know of them?"

The inspector shifted on his feet. "Our team is continuing their investigation, but we have video of two men—an Ikasaran and an Orell—buying the weapons. These men are no smugglers. Their ship is one of the most advanced types constructed on Ikasar and often used by agents of the Red Regent."

Commander Elezz held up a single finger. "Inspector, would this type of ship by any chance produce madrin particles?"

"Yes, it's a known byproduct of Ikasaran anti-matter drives. Have you—"

"Just as we thought," interrupted Talazeer. "We reported the detection of madrin particles to High Command days ago, Inspector. If you look it up, you'll see a cloaked ship was our immediate concern. But why would the First Empire be interested in Corvos?"

"We cannot be certain, Excellency. Perhaps intelligence-gathering or sabotage."

Talazeer wondered if they might be involved in the assassination attempt, though an insider seemed more likely.

Urttiek continued: "We are also aware of at least three recent examples in which Ikasaran agents seem to be assisting rebel movements in our territory."

Could it have been the Red Regent and not the Lovirr who coordinated the attacks on Three and Fourteen? Whether true or not, it would be worthwhile to encourage the idea—especially on Vitaar.

"It would explain how a handful of primitives managed to bring down a shuttle and kill the Viceroy." Talazeer scratched his chin, putting on a show of thinking through the implications.

Elezz jumped in: "If the Ikasaran vessel shows up here, we should detect it easily as soon as it drops out of trans-light, thanks to your tracking device, Inspector."

Elezz's transparent fawning might have made Talazeer roll his eyes if he weren't busy looking serious, but Urttiek seemed receptive.

"Indeed, they should be easy pickings," beamed the inspector. "And, ideally, we'd like at least one of the two agents taken alive. We are very interested to speak with them."

"Of course, Inspector," Talazeer assured him, then added, "And I thank you for your assistance." If Urttiek liked a little deference, it was an easy enough, if slightly distasteful, game to play.

"Until we speak again, then." With another bow, Urttiek ended his part in the call.

Commander Elezz now filled the screen, which to Talazeer was a pleasant state of affairs. "This business with the hunter drones, sir. Perhaps they had help from this Ikasaran agent. And now he is returning with weapons for their cause. Sabotage, disruption. There might even be a connection to the poisoning."

"I do not see how."

"Sir, up until now, I would not have thought it possible that there was an enemy agent operating on Corvos right under our noses. We must consider every possibility."

Talazeer was determined to do so. But was the commander being genuine? Or trying to deflect him somehow?

Elezz hadn't finished: "Sir, our shuttles have no air-to-air capability, but the *Galtaryax* is armed with a range of missiles. I can instruct the crew to begin drills immediately. However, disabling a ship that size without destroying it may not be possible."

"Capturing them alive might be the Directorate's priority but it is not ours. If those weapons are aboard, they must not reach the rebels."

They had achieved a remarkable amount in two days. The shelter was half-completed, and there was already space to house the injured, weak, young, and old. The stream provided all of the water required, and Jespa had organized the digging of a latrine. Two more garra had been killed by hunting parties and—for the first time since their escape—the rebels had eaten no less than four meals in the same location.

Cerrin had taken Yarni along on the second hunt. The girl

had been speaking to Murrit about the gods and seemed very interested in Priss, the huntress. Cerrin showed Yarni how to hunt garra, and when the beast was killed, she smeared both their faces with the blood. Tradition held that some of the animal's speed and strength would pass on to them. Those Echobe who'd been of age before the invasion had all been through such initiations. For Yarni, who had been captured as a two-year-old orphan, it was all new.

That morning, Murrit had led a ceremony of blessing for their new home. Even the Palanians were in good cheer, though Erras still seemed determined to remain a man apart. Yarni and the other three youngsters were now playing in the stream, though even they remembered not to make too much noise. Everyone seemed to understand that this comfortable situation might end at any time, so meat was being dried and water flasks kept full.

Cerrin stayed away as much as she could. She was unable to shake the feeling that this was all too good to be true. Most of the others seemed to believe this new home was the gods' reward for all of the fear and suffering they had endured. This only troubled Cerrin all the more. It was Ikala, god of battle, who favored her. Would he still do so when she was not fighting?

Perhaps she was only cut out for fighting. Perhaps that was all she was good for.

And if the gods were on their side here, were they also with Sonus? Cerrin pictured that handsome, thoughtful face, his slight stoop, his habit of frowning even when there was no need to. What had those kind green eyes of his seen out there among the stars?

One hand on her spear, she watched the busy camp for a little while, then moved on. She adjusted the rifle hanging over her shoulder and began yet another circular patrol route, the only way she could provide herself with something approaching peace of mind.

She had felt uneasy since dawn. Doubt gnawed away at her; she could not help feeling that it was dangerous to stay in one place, that danger was close once again. She was possessed by an urge to leave, yet she knew there was no sense in doing so.

Strange slashes and grooves in the side of a giant caught her eye; they were clearly unnatural, and she stepped slowly closer to investigate.

A carving. Done by knife.

Someone had clearly spent hours and hours on it. In places, the reddish bark had grown over the picture but the images were clear. Tents, garra, the sun, leaves, and so much more. Echobe— or a people like them—had lived here before and one had taken the time to depict scenes of their lives. The tribe had hunted, swum in the stream, sat around fires, prayed to their gods. Cerrin guessed they had been here years, decades, even centuries.

"I wonder what happened to them."

Cerrin spun around to find Murrit thirty feet behind her. She cursed herself for not hearing the guider approach.

"You'd already seen these?"

"I was drawn to them as soon as we arrived." Murrit crossed the clearing. Though she still wore her Vitaari overalls like most of the others, she had marked her hands and cheeks with natural dye—swirling patterns of green and red.

"What's wrong, Cerrin?"

"Nothing."

"I sense doubt in you."

"We're in the right place. As safe as we can be."

"And yet you still don't seem sure."

"Are *you* sure? What do the gods tell you?"

"I'm no prophet. They do not speak to me more than anyone else. As a guider, my task is only to teach what I know, to encourage respect for the gods and spirits, to help others commune with them. What is it? You might feel better for unburdening yourself."

Cerrin wasn't sure she wanted to.

Murrit smiled. "Have you offered anything to Ikala?"

"Yes. The garra."

"He might look kindly upon you, then. He will listen."

"I have already asked for guidance. It did not come this time."

"The gods do not always answer us."

Cerrin was surprised to hear Murrit say this, though she thought it an admirable admission from a guider. Her feeling that Ikala watched over her was no more than that. Perhaps he'd never answered her... perhaps he'd never even heard her. Other than some half-forgotten tales of his hatching full grown from the Wild Sun as an immense warrior armed with staff and bow, what did she really know of him?

"I shall leave you in peace, then," said Murrit. "Perhaps it is enough to know that he has been there for you before and that he will again." She turned away.

"Wait," said Cerrin. "The uriop. Might it help me see him? Hear him?"

"If that is his will."

Count Talazeer was rather impressed with himself. Patience wasn't usually among his many admirable attributes. However, while the rest of the ship slept, he, Marl, and Yullasir kept at their investigative work. Each sat at a separate screen, scanning through private messages now totaling over six thousand. Even Marl, with his limited understanding of computers or the written Vitaari language, was making steady—if slow—progress.

Talazeer had seen nothing of interest for some time. Leaning back in his chair, he let out a long sigh. "I'm glad I didn't choose the Directorate for a career. This line of work is really not for me."

"This work might save your life, sir."

"You almost seem to be enjoying yourself, Marl. Perhaps you prefer detective work to your normal role?"

"My duty is to protect you, sir. This is simply another way of doing so. Have you found anything?"

"I've marked some files for further investigation. And you?"

"I have some questions for you."

"Go ahead. All this staring at the screen is giving me a headache."

"I've noted three separate crewmen who have contacts in the city of Trentasi. That is the center of Circle Za-Arinu, is it not?"

Historically, they were the enemies of Circle Za-Ulessor, although Talazeer had never personally had dealings with them. "Yes, go on."

"The messages seem harmless enough but could perhaps conceal a code."

"Relations between the clans have been good of late. Honestly, I doubt we should concern ourselves with that."

"Then there is Governor Erinttus of Mine Fifteen. He has exchanged messages with two members of the Intelligence Directorate."

"Erinttus was with the Directorate before this post. Old friends, probably. Check the messages anyway. Anything else?"

"Another governor, Vullett of Mine Six, is in contact with a distant member of your own family, sir. A Baron Onkirr Kan Talazeer. Were you aware of that?"

"No." Talazeer closed his eyes. "Onkirr is a second cousin. Fat fellow, rather annoying, if memory serves. I'm not sure what he'd gain by getting me out of the way, but do forward the messages to me, though."

Yullasir spoke up. "Excellency, Level 6 clearance has come through from Viceroy Ollinder so I've added some more messages."

The Count moved instantly to Elezz's file and eagerly read her every communication with her superiors back on Vitaar. To his mild surprise, he found that she'd been careful not to openly criticize him, even regarding the forest attack. Then he moved on to her personal correspondence with friends; these were very few and without exception boring.

Then he came to several messages that could not be read. These were marked Level 7 and not even the sender was revealed. Talazeer didn't know whether to be surprised by this or not. The few messages in his life that he'd received directly from his father had all been classified Level 7, although none had contained secret or sensitive information. Elezz, to his knowledge, did not have any such notable relations in her family line, but she must have acquired some well connected patrons to reach her level of success in the military. A powerful mentor, perhaps? Or a lover?

Or both?

Talazeer chuckled to himself, then made a mental note to question Elezz about the messages.

Next, he moved on to Deputy Rasikaar's file. He discovered nothing of note until he came to a message sent to Rasikaar from an anonymous private account. When Talazeer opened the message, he saw only a short paragraph of unintelligible text. It seemed to be nothing more than a random series of words, which to the Count suggested a code. He checked the date of the message—it had arrived one day before Founder's Day, only hours before he had been poisoned.

With Murrit keeping watch a few yards away, Cerrin lay back in a clump of fern, eyes closed as the guider had instructed. She spoke Ikala's name ten times out loud, then repeated it twenty times to herself. She did feel odd. Murrit had given her only a little of the uriop, which had curiously little taste and an unusually soft texture that allowed it to slip down. Cerrin felt light, almost weightless, as if she were floating in water.

Soon she realized that she could not hear or smell the forest. The blackness seemed to have enveloped all of her senses, and she imagined herself drifting through it. She felt little emotion, only clarity.

Then she was walking through the forest. All was quiet.

She heard something above. Yet she couldn't look; couldn't turn.

The noise got louder. A flapping sound. A piercing cry.

Something raked her head. Talons. Pulling off skin; tearing her head to pieces. Blood ran down over her eyes.

She woke, saw Murrit squatting beside her, hand on Cerrin's arm.

Cerrin reached up, half-expecting to feel the wounds upon her head. There were none.

"Gods. It was so real."

"What did you see?"

"It was horrible. I didn't see Ikala. It was... I don't—"

"A vision?"

"Yes. I suppose so."

"They are not always pleasant. But they always mean something. What did you see?"

Cerrin got to her feet, taking deep breaths to compose herself. Murrit reached out but Cerrin walked away.

"Nothing good."

17

Toll Maktar brought the *Spectre* out of trans-light and guided his ship toward the atmosphere. As black turned to blue beyond the viewport, Sonus studied the displays. He could see no sign of Corvos's single landmass.

"We're over the sea," he said.

"Yes. I want to stay as far from the *Galtaryax* as possible."

"But they can't detect us."

"Not unless something goes wrong, yes? No technology is perfect. Best not to tempt fate."

Sonus saw the logic of that but they were so close…

He needed to know that the others were safe. That Cerrin was safe.

And, of course, he was excited to put the weapons in their hands. He wanted to see their faces when they saw what he'd accomplished. A restless giddiness raced through his body. He stood, walked to the left viewport, and looked down. Between swathes of pure white cloud below, he could make out the dark of the sea.

Though no one on Corvos had known it before the Vitaari

arrived, four fifths of their planet was covered by water. In recent centuries, the Palanians had built great sailing vessels, but they had never completed a circumnavigation of the continent, let alone the world. Sonus had often wondered if there were islands somewhere far beyond the known lands, perhaps where a free people dwelt. Would they be as sophisticated as his people or as primitive as the Kinassan?

"Descending to twenty kilometers," said Maktar. "We'll be over the western coast in a few minutes."

Count Talazeer raced into the operations room, Marl just behind him. No one present—Commander Elezz included—looked away from the largest tactical screen.

"You have them?"

"We did, sir," said Elezz. "But the signal is intermittent. We established a lock a few minutes ago but now it's gone."

"Why didn't you fire?"

"It's a question of range. We picked them up on the far side of the planet. Hopefully, we will reacquire the signal."

"Hopefully?"

When he'd been summoned by the urgent call, Talazeer had expected a bit more than hope.

"There!" One of the techs pointed at a flashing yellow cross. "Signal… steady. Targeting already locked on."

"Distance?" snapped Elezz.

"Just over nine thousand kilometers. They're in range. But that ship is fast."

"Not faster than the missile. Set bearings and fire."

The tech's fingers flicked across the keys and one display

switched to a feed of the *Galtaryax*'s hull. A hatch popped open and the projectile blasted out, exhaust blooming as it powered down toward the surface.

"The A-6 is locked on," said the tech. "Estimated time of impact—three minutes, twenty seconds."

"So, no one has ever explored the seas?" asked Toll Maktar.

"Some areas," replied Sonus. "As a boy, I had a book of maps—the areas that had been charted. But we never found much except more ocean. Now we know that we never would have."

"Open ocean is a source of power. The winds above it, too. I know of worlds where all their machines are powered by natural energy."

Sonus shook his head. "Where will you land, Toll? The Old Giants?"

"As long as we can find enough space. But detecting your friends might be difficult. I found you the first time by following your Vitaari pursuers, but hopefully they've been thrown far off the trail by now. Don't worry, though. It's just a matter of—"

They were both thrown back in the seat as the *Spectre* lurched forward.

"Vun Tak!" The agent's unblinking eyes moved from screen to screen. "Must have come from the *Galtaryax.*"

Sonus now spied the orange dot on the tactical display. "What is it?"

"Missile. Five thousand kilometers northeast. We have about ninety seconds before impact."

"How did they know?" His throat tight, Sonus stumbled over his words. "H-How did they detect us?"

Maktar didn't answer. For once, Sonus could actually feel the strain of their speed within the ship and in his body. The seat was juddering. His stomach felt hollow; his teeth chattered.

"At least we'll be over the land."

The implication of the agent's words was clear: they would be shot down, they would crash.

"We can't reach the forest but that might be for the best." Maktar pointed at the largest screen. "What's that low, flat area south of the capital?"

"The Elaran Plain. Mostly marsh and farmland."

Maktar issued a series of instructions. Sonus cringed as he heard three blasts behind the ship.

"Counter-measures," explained Maktar. "They try to trick the missile's guidance system, confuse it or lead it astray."

"Have they worked?"

Maktar struck the seat with a clenched fist. "No. I don't understand how that thing's tracking us! The *Galtaryax* weapons systems are virtually obsolete."

The panic in the agent's usually calm voice scared Sonus more than anything.

Sacred Maker. If you can hear me, I beg you to aid our cause. Let us survive. Let us help your people.

"Range fourteen-hundred meters. Impact in thirty-eight seconds."

"Is there anything else we can do?"

"Outmaneuver it. But we'll have to wait until it's close."

"Range nine hundred meters," declared the technician. "Fuel at eight percent."

"It's going to be close," said Elezz. She was gripping the back of the tech's chair.

Talazeer watched her: that sleek hair, those sharp cheekbones, those tempting lips. He hoped she wasn't involved in the assassination attempt. He didn't want her to be his enemy.

"Range six hundred meters," said the tech. "Fuel at five and a half percent."

Talazeer wasn't worried. They could always fire another missile.

"Hold on tight, Sonus. Initiating evasion sequence."

As Maktar uttered the last word, the *Spectre* plummeted toward the ground, prompting Sonus to grip the straps tight and plant his feet. The little ship seemed to have dropped like a stone and now veered away to the right. Outside, small clusters of cloud shot past. The *Spectre* dropped again, then angled upward. Sonus now felt every movement—and a growing, crushing pressure in his chest and neck.

"Three hundred meters," said Maktar, also pressed back against the seat. "Impact in fifteen seconds. That's a Vitaari A-6. Designed to take out space-going vessels. It's bigger than the *Spectre*, a massive warhead. It will blow us to pieces."

Sonus looked at the screen, desperate to have some idea where they were. Distances were hard to judge but he realized the ship was over the northern end of the plain, not far from the capital.

"If I don't survive, take my bracelet," said Maktar. "If another agent is sent to Corvos, it will help you."

"If I don't survive, you'll still try to get the weapons to the others?"

"I promise, Sonus."

Again, Sonus felt a profound sense of gratitude: for the risks Toll Maktar had taken and the sacrifices he was prepared to make.

"What's that noise?"

"The missile engine. It's right behind us."

"Fifty meters," said the tech. "Fuel two percent... now one."

"What's the calculation?" demanded Elezz.

Her other man answered. "We won't get much closer, Commander. And the fuel figure is not reliable. It could run out at any moment."

"We should detonate the warhead now. Sir?"

Talazeer nodded. Elezz gave the order.

The blast killed every screen and light in the *Spectre*. The little ship seemed to be caught in a wave, rolling end over end. Sonus found himself upside down, legs dangling, straps biting into him. He vomited and it splattered the wall as the ship continued to spin. Hearing a cry, he turned to see that Toll Maktar had somehow cracked the back of his head. Blood was pouring from the wound but he continued to talk to his ship. The world outside the narrow viewport rolled—blue sky, a blur of land and trees, then blue sky again.

Suddenly, the screens came back on and the *Spectre* righted itself. The ship was moving oddly, however, jolting every few seconds with a shriek of metal against metal.

"We're coming apart," said Maktar, "We need to set down. Where can we find cover?"

"I—I don't know where we are."

"Then look!" Maktar reached over and thumped the button on his strap connector.

Now free, Sonus wiped vomit from his chin and struggled to his feet. He slipped and scrambled to the nearest viewport and found the city right below them. His city. He knew these buildings.

"Quickly!" shouted Maktar. "Might be another missile on its way."

Sonus was surprised to realize how slowly the *Spectre* was moving. He spotted the ruins of the Church of the People and knew exactly where he was. "Go south. Look for the warehouses. There must be some buildings still intact. Some are very large, with high roofs."

"I'm on two impulsors here and they might not last long. I'll switch to manual control—you direct me."

"Turn to your right." Sonus crossed the cockpit for a better view. "Descend if you can."

The jolting continued and Sonus had to grip the edges of the viewport to stay on his feet.

"As you are. I'm looking for a location."

He scanned the buildings below, seeing several warehouses, none of which had open doors. Then he spied one that was half-collapsed with a gaping hole. But the roof over the rest of the structure looked solid enough.

"Turn to the left... stay like that. Do you see it, about two hundred meters ahead? The brick warehouse with the black roof. Can we fit in there?"

"Let's find out."

. . .

"What do you mean there's no signal?"

"It disappeared, Excellency," explained the tech. "The blast may have blown out the tracker or destroyed the ship—or both."

"Scan the area," ordered Elezz. "Look for wreckage."

"We'll need to reposition the *Galtaryax* for that, Commander. It will take time."

"Do it. But in the meantime, we'll get some boots on the ground. Tell Sergeant Guldur to assemble thirty men and take a shuttle. Whatever's left of that ship, I want every piece."

The rear of the *Spectre* was a black and mangled mess. Pieces of the anti-matter drive were jutting through gaping holes in the hull, and huge chunks of it were missing entirely—including the anti-matter storage cell, which Maktar said was a good thing.

Three of the four emergency landing struts had deployed, which was enough to hold the ship aloft without the anti-gravity impulsors, which Maktar had shut down to save energy.

As for the agent himself, he had swiftly deployed a miniscule medical drone to stitch and cover his wound. He seemed a little groggy but assured Sonus that the injury was only a gash and not a concussion.

Maktar got down on his hands and knees and crawled under the vessel. When he emerged, the grim expression on his angular face had worsened. He opened his hand and showed Sonus a small red disc.

"Tracking bug."

"What? How did you know?"

"It was the only thing that made sense. That old missile was a heat-seeker. Counter-measures should have stopped it. I realized they must have had a direct reading on us. Probably spotted us as soon as we left trans-light."

"The Vitaari on Xerxa?"

"Can't believe I didn't even check."

"We were in a hurry."

Maktar dropped the bug onto the floor and raised his boot. "Blast should have fried its transmitter but let's make sure." He stamped down on the bug, breaking it into several pieces.

"So they probably lost track of us when the warhead exploded?"

"Unless they had a visual fix, yes."

"Then they may not know we're here?"

"No, but they'll be searching. I imagine they'll send the hunter drones. Soldiers, too."

"Can you repair the damage?"

"Personally, no," said Maktar. "That's why I have this." The agent lifted a silvery cube from the same metal case that had held the medical drone. On one side of the cube was a small control panel, which Maktar activated. Within seconds, it seemed to melt into thousands of tiny globes. These all rolled across the ground toward the ship.

"Nano-drones," explained the agent. "They're linked to the ship's systems and will try to repair most damage. They can take on any shape and emulate most materials. It's only temporary but hopefully it will work."

"Hopefully?"

"I've had to use them four times with the *Spectre*. Twice they couldn't complete the repair. There are limits to their capabilities.

The anti-matter drive is a loss, of course, but working impulsors are all we need to move around in the atmosphere."

"When will we know?"

"Soon."

Sonus glanced toward the sunlit street. "I'll get one of the runner guns, keep guard."

"Good idea."

Count Talazeer left operations and returned to his quarters with Marl. The Drellen agreed that the message to Deputy Rasikaar was suspicious, but even with Yullasir's help they'd been unable to make anything out of the code. Talazeer had initially considered a direct approach to Rasikaar himself but knew he had little evidence until either the code was cracked or they uncovered more.

Yullasir was now taking a well deserved break after working solidly for twenty hours. As they considered their next move, Marl sat and continued his carving. Talazeer fetched himself some wine, even though the afternoon had barely begun. He'd taken only a few sips when the bodyguard looked up from his work, carving knife in his hand.

"Sir, even if the deputy is involved, he would not have needed to tamper with the package. It may have arrived with the poison already implanted. I found nothing suspicious in his quarters."

"What could his role be, then? To report on me? On the result of the attempted poisoning? He hasn't even replied to the message, nor has he ever received any other message from that sender."

The door buzzer sounded. Marl put his carving aside and opened it, one hand on his sword hilt.

Talazeer was relieved to see only an unaccompanied Elezz.

"Commander. A development?"

"No, sir. I wanted to talk to you about the messages. May I come in?"

He gestured for her to do so. Marl moved aside, but not too far away.

The commander ran two fingers down a strand of hair, a gesture that the Count found rather sensual. "Sir, I daresay that by now you've come across the protected communiques within my message list."

"Yes—level 7." Talazeer gestured toward his workstation. "You can unlock them personally if you like."

"And you will remain suspicious of me if I don't."

"A man in my position must be suspicious of everyone."

"Count Talazeer, I will be perfectly frank. Those messages are between myself and a *very* high-ranking Colonial Guard officer. They are confidential and I would endanger my career if I even asked him for permission to allow you access. I wish I could tell you more, but for the moment I cannot. What I can give you is my word that those messages do not concern you."

"Then I shall have to take you at your word, Commander."

Elezz glanced at Marl and clasped her hands behind her back. "Perhaps there is something else I can do to convince you that I am no enemy of yours."

At that moment, Talazeer rather wished that the bodyguard wasn't present. He soon realized, however, that Elezz wasn't being suggestive.

"My... contact... is a very influential man. I can ask him to assist your investigation on the planet side, if that would be helpful to you. He has many ways of gathering intelligence discreetly. I know it must be difficult for you to investigate things that happened on Vitaar before the package arrived here on the ship."

At face value, it was a very generous offer. She'd be calling in a favor she might rather use for herself later. On the other hand, it was an easy way for Elezz to feed him false information if she were somehow involved in the plot.

But he didn't believe she was. It seemed clear to Talazeer that she was primarily trying to divert him from whatever was contained within those secret messages.

So be it. Let her keep her secrets, especially if she's willing to offer something so valuable in exchange for the privilege.

"Very well, Commander."

"Then I shall contact him immediately."

"Level 7. He must be very high-ranking."

She ignored this point. "Have you made any progress elsewhere, sir?"

"We have a number of promising leads. As I said, Commander, no one is beyond suspicion. No one."

Sonus crouched in the shadows at the end of the warehouse, gazing out at the city.

Fifteen years.

Fifteen years since he had walked the streets of Okara. The warehouses opposite were largely intact but engulfed by weeds. The rusting, faded sign upon one of the buildings was still readable: it had been a timber merchant. Birds had nested atop the sign. They did not make a sound. There was only silence in the capital now.

He wasn't sure why he was sweating, why his hands were

shaking. He didn't think it was the shock of the missile attack. The strange feeling had only struck him when he looked out. He had seen awful, nightmarish things in these streets:

Two children trying to rouse their clearly dead parents.

People running from burning houses with their hair and clothes aflame.

Long paths of blood on the ground where dozens of bodies had been dragged away after a massacre.

Screams. Fear. Death.

Sonus put the Raxis rifle down and wiped his clammy hands on his trousers.

In his daydreams of returning to Okara, it was always in a distant future when the city was once again full of life. He never imagined being alone, the only one of kind left in the entire city, staring out at silent, empty ruins.

A cat sprang from a bank of weeds between two warehouses. Clearly afraid, it bolted across the potholed street and sought refuge in a length of pipe. Sonus was glad to see the creature, but his smile faded when he saw what it was fleeing.

He had only ever seen ko-kyri behind glass in the city zoo. Normally, these lumbering lizards lived in the marshes far to the south. This particular specimen was at least eight feet long, so it was clearly thriving here in the abandoned city. Perhaps this was the same one he'd seen behind the glass so long ago, or perhaps it had been drawn here from the wild by the scent of death.

Startled by a noise behind him, Sonus was relieved to see it was only Toll Maktar. The agent crouched beside him.

"Anything?"

"Only animals. What about the ship?"

"Looks like most of the auxiliary fuel cells are intact. I've got the proximity scanner working, too—no signs of enemy ships yet, though it might not pick up ground troops."

"And the repairs?"

Maktar grimaced. "That's why I came over. As I said, the nano-drones have their limitations. Two of the three impulsors need new regulators. But regulators get hot when the impulsors are working—too hot for the nano-drones to use their own bodies as replacement parts. They'd melt away within minutes of takeoff. A big fall, yes?"

Sonus nodded. He stared out at the street and the warehouses and the weeds. All was quiet again. Had he really seen that ko-kyri? "What do we do, then?"

"We need a heat-resistant metal for the nano-drones to work with. Cobalt would work. Or tungsten, or vorsfeld. Perhaps there might be some in these warehouses?"

"Possibly," answered Sonus. "But I know where we can almost certainly find vorsfeld, and it's only about a mile from here. The university."

18

When she finally returned to the camp, Cerrin found the place in uproar.

She didn't have to make her way through the crowd to discover what was going on. The object of their excitement stood a foot taller than most of them, and his tear-stained face radiated relief and happiness. When Cerrin did make her way to him, Kannalin threw himself forward to embrace her. Cerrin held him close and felt tears forming in her own eyes.

Yet, at first sight of the crowd, she'd hoped it was Sonus who'd returned, and her joy was tinged with disappointment.

They separated. The big warrior looked exhausted: his hands and face were grimy, his clothes soiled and torn.

"I didn't stop. For three days, I just walked and walked."

At that, Cerrin glanced around until she saw Jespa. "Retrace his trail. Go as far as you can before nightfall. Somebody, go with him."

Another man volunteered himself and the pair jogged out of the clearing.

"There's no need," insisted Kannalin. "I wasn't followed. I

checked every few hours. I told them you were headed for the Black Hollow. I put them off the scent."

"We have to be sure," she replied. "How did you escape?"

"They were returning me to Mine Three. There was some problem with the shuttle so we made an emergency landing in the forest. They opened up the craft to make repairs and I took my chance."

"They didn't cuff you?"

"They did. Took an hour to saw through the plastic bands with rock. But that was after… after I ran."

Erras appeared then, pushing his way between two Echobe. "They let you go," stated the Palanian. "They let you go so you would lead them to us."

Kannalin's eyes widened with anger. "I told you I wasn't followed."

"They don't need to follow you, idiot," blazed Erras. "They've many ways of tracking you. Have you checked your clothing?"

Some of the Echobe were clearly angry at the Palanian's tone but—like Cerrin—they knew he had a point.

"What do you mean?"

For all his courage and determination, Kannalin had never been one of the brightest. Cerrin couldn't believe that the thought hadn't occurred to him.

"We must check you over," she said.

"They shot at me!" he snapped. "They chased me for more than an hour, but there were only a few guards. I'm telling you, I was *not* followed."

"And we're telling you that you can't know that," said Erras. "We must examine you and your clothes."

"We must," said Cerrin.

"Very well."

The shelter was too dark so Cerrin ushered him toward the nearest tree.

"I'll come, too," said Erras, now striking a more reasonable tone. "I know what to look for."

Once they were behind the tree, Kannalin began to disrobe.

"I am sorry," said Cerrin, at first averting her eyes but then realizing it was pointless. "Once this is done, we'll get you some food."

Kannalin didn't answer at first but then managed a smile. "The camp looks good. You were right about coming here."

"Where's your necklace?"

"When I woke up it was gone—must have come off during the fight."

"Torrin will make you a new one."

Once his boots, socks, trousers, and shirt were off, they set about searching them. Kannalin gestured to his undergarments, still about his waist. "What about these?"

"You can do it," said Cerrin, feeling along the seams of his shirt for any hidden bumps or strands of metal.

They searched each garment twice but still found nothing. Even so, Kannalin couldn't hide his embarrassment. "I don't know why I didn't... I was just so relieved to be free."

"Let's get that food," said Cerrin, leading him toward the shelter. "And you can tell us the whole story."

All of the skeletons were picked clean. The people, the horses, the sheep, the dogs: everything that had died in the streets of the capital had been ravaged, every ounce of flesh consumed.

Birds had probably started on the work immediately, Sonus thought. Then the ko-kyri had come north and established themselves in the city to finish the job. As he made his way through the eerie, empty streets, Sonus spied two more of the giant lizards, thankfully at a distance. He wondered what they fed on now.

Rats, cats, squirrels, whatever, he thought. *Nature fills any vacuum with life.*

He wished Maktar were with him, though he understood why the agent had to remain with his precious ship. He realized how swiftly he'd grown accustomed to having a well educated and knowledgeable companion to ask questions of and share ideas with. But out here in the open, Sonus primarily missed the comfort of knowing Maktar had so many defensive gadgets on his bracelet and about his person.

At last, Sonus stood before the one-hundred-foot bronze statue of Yoruss—father of Palanian science and a founding member of the university—who now stood vigil over an empty, broken city. Sonus wiped his eyes as he waded through the tall grass surrounding the statue, which was up to Yoruss's ankle and Sonus's waist.

Both hands on the Raxis rifle—as they had been for every step of his journey—he found the sloping path that led into the heart of the institution. The pavement was crumbling and bright green moss filled all of the cracks.

The door to the physical sciences building was locked, but most of the ground-floor windows were broken. He cleared the remains of glass from one and clambered inside.

The stock room of the metallurgy department was also locked and presented more of a problem. By searching several offices, he eventually located the key. The contents were well organized and labeled, and he quickly located a shelf holding boxes of vorsfeld in the form of thin silver bars. Another box held bars of cobalt, as it turned out, but he'd promised to retrieve vorsfeld, so he ignored it. He packed four one-hundred-gram bars into his backpack—twice as much as Maktar said they needed—and left the building via the broken window once more.

As he passed the statue of Yoruss on his way out, a distant rumble made Sonus look up in time to see a Vitaari shuttle slide out from the clouds.

The Vitaari troops had spread out from the shuttle and were now patrolling the streets in groups of three.

Sonus hid beneath the decaying wood belly of an old trolley cart, not far from the warehouse. He could see a drainage culvert about four feet deep that would take him in the right direction and, if he kept low, keep him hidden from view.

Cursing the bright sunlight, he darted toward it, dropped down to the ground, rolled over the edge, and landed as quietly as possible at the bottom of the ditch. Then he froze, listening for Vitaari footsteps or voices.

Nothing.

He moved as swiftly and quietly as he could, which wasn't as easy as he'd hoped—there were piles of sludge and refuse blocking the way at several points. The culvert became a dark tunnel where it met a grassy embankment. Sonus had no interest in taking his chances underground, not when the warehouse was only two blocks away. He'd have to climb back up to street level.

Should he just make a run for it? He hadn't heard the sound of Vitaari boots since—

Since now.

He chanced a peek over the edge of the culvert. A trio of Vitaari soldiers, even bulkier than usual in their armor and helmets, was making a perfunctory search of the street and its buildings, not even stopping to look through windows.

They weren't looking for people hiding out in the city, that much was clear. Whatever they wanted to find, it must be something big, much bigger than a human, too big to hide in a house. *The wreckage of a spaceship, maybe.*

Or maybe it had nothing to do with him at all. Sonus couldn't chance it. He needed to warn Maktar. The warehouse would hide the *Spectre* from satellites and aircraft, but the gaping hole in the front would reveal everything to a passing soldier on foot.

Fortunately, the troopers turned onto the next street, marching steadily away from him. He waited until he could no longer hear them before moving off.

Once across the street, Sonus edged between two small outbuildings to find himself behind another timber warehouse. Spying an open door, Sonus reckoned he was better off going through the building than around it. Pausing at the door to check he wasn't being watched, he slipped inside.

He raced across the dusty floor, under a high metal gantry, and between long rows of yellow-gray lumber stacked twenty feet high. At the far end of the cavernous warehouse was the main loading bay—he didn't dare try to slide open its giant, rusted, noisy doors, so he slipped through an open door into the front office instead.

He ran down a short hallway and into a small lobby. Its front door was intact, including the window. Sonus forced himself to stop and clear the dust from the glass in order to observe the street rather than simply throwing open the door.

Thank the Maker he did.

He could see three more soldiers loitering in the street, no more than twenty paces away.

The trio were deep in discussion, two consulting their arm-mounted units while the third made some adjustment to his clothing. The *Spectre* and Maktar were only one block away. The agent could likely defend himself against three Vitaari, but if any of them alerted the *Galtaryax* to the ship's location, the game was up. There would be no time to make the repair, let alone escape.

Lost in these thoughts, Sonus suddenly heard a puff of breath behind him. Spinning around, rifle at the ready, he saw a ko-kyri lumbering down the hallway toward him.

Only when Sonus raised the rifle did he realize he should have brought the silent plasma gun. The Raxis weapons were not as loud as the runner guns, but they were more than loud enough for the Vitaari to hear.

He might not have a choice. The beast closed in, eyes black and lifeless, slobber dripping from its snout.

It was then that a bloody lump landed on the floor.

A dead rabbit.

The ko-kyri instantly lost interest in Sonus and pounced on the easier prey instead, teeth tearing at fur and flesh.

Sonus looked up. Peering down at him through a missing ceiling tile was the small, inquisitive face of a Lovirr. Sonus jumped onto the lobby's reception desk and scrambled up into the ceiling next to his unexpected savior.

The Lovirr waved cheerily and then motioned for him to remain quiet. Below, the ko-kyri was making such a noise with the rabbit that Sonus feared the Vitaari would hear and investigate. A moment later, the doorway below exploded.

A single Vitaari stepped through the ragged hole where the wood door had been, saw the snarling ko-kyri, and blasted it in the head with his assault rifle.

The soldier laughed at the mess, then stepped over it to give a quick look around the warehouse space. He returned less than thirty seconds later and marched out the door again. He exchanged a few words with his compatriots, and the sound of their voices faded.

The bearded, diminutive Lovirr grinned and spoke in *Trade*. "Hungry?"

His name was Kakura. Sonus instantly noted how well equipped he was—he carried a large pack and hanging from his belt were a knife, an axe, and a Vitaari jolt-rod.

"It is fortunate that we met," said Kakura, in the mellifluent, almost musical voice shared by most Lovirr. "You are the fourth."

"The fourth what?" asked Sonus, still breathing hard after his narrow escape. They stood in the warehouse space now, between the tall stacks of lumber.

"The fourth Palanian I have met in the city. That is why I am here, you see—to make contact."

"There are still Palanians here?"

"Not living here, no. But survivors show up from time to time to see if anyone else is here."

"Why are you doing this?"

"To help the survivors, of course. To lead them to the camps and the hidden pockets of free peoples, so they're not alone. They are not easy to find, as you can well imagine." The Lovirr's smile faded a bit. "I know what the other races think of us, but we are not all collaborators."

"I know that, believe me."

The Lovirr's small, dark eyes changed. He suddenly reached forward and gripped Sonus's arm. "Wait a moment, you're *the* Sonus, aren't you? The hero of the breakout. The man who killed the Viceroy."

Sonus froze, clearly shaken—and that was enough for the Lovirr.

"Gods preserve us," replied Kakura, his words coming quickly. "What an honor, what a privilege. We thought you were still in the Great Forest with those who escaped from Mine Three."

"You know about them as well? How?"

Now Kakura smiled. He pulled his backpack over and opened the top. Under a blanket were several tiny cages containing birds no larger than the Lovirr's hand.

"Small but quick and strong. We Lovirr have always kept them. They never fail to return home, no matter how far you travel with them. Tie a message to its foot, and off it goes back home."

"That is a long journey."

"It took me twenty-five days to get here. The birds are much quicker, maybe five days. I'm supposed to head back in a week, and I am not looking forward to the journey. Especially the Karlay."

"That's what you call the Grassin mountains."

"It is. What about you? How did you get here from the Great Forest? I don't see any wings or feathers under your shirt."

"I wish I could tell you. Someday, maybe I'll get to."

It wasn't that Sonus didn't trust this little Lovirr, or not *exactly* that. He was certain Kakura would never betray him to him to the Vitaari. However, he was concerned that news of the First Empire and their secret assistance not spread like wildfire through the native peoples, either. Too much of his doings—and Cerrin's, too—were cause for gossip among the Lovirr resistance, apparently. That was a disturbing discovery, and it left Sonus eager to keep his secrets close to his chest.

"Kakura, listen to me. I wish I could stay and talk but I have to go. Is there some way for us to remain in touch? A place where we might leave messages for one another?"

"Yes. Well, not *me* in particular, but there's a way to reach my people. Some of the Palanian camps leave messages for us in a place just south of the parliament—"

"The Maker's Fountain."

"Yes. On the eastern side, close to the ground, is a loose brick. They leave messages there, behind it."

"I'm glad to know there are Palanian camps out there."

Kakura nodded. "I wish I could tell you more about them, but…"

"Believe me, I understand."

Suddenly, the Lovirr laughed. "They will never believe this back home. They will never believe that I met you."

He did not see any sign of the Vitaari during his brief trip back to the warehouse. Though he trusted Kakura—based largely on gut instinct—he made sure that the Lovirr couldn't see the route he took. Maktar greeted him with immense relief, then took the vorsfeld and placed it on the case beside the nano-drones. The little globes soon awoke and surrounded the strips of metal.

"How do they shape it?"

"Magnetic disintegration and manipulation," said the agent, now watching the case's display screen. "It will take fourteen minutes to fashion the components, nine to install them."

"Will it work?"

"It should. But no technology is perfect."

"So you keep telling me."

Count Talazeer took the call from Commander Elezz in his quarters.

"Anything from the city?"

"Not so far, sir, but they've only been searching for two hours. Better news from the Great Forest, however. Kannalin is no longer on the move. He's been in the same place for thirty hours straight, in fact. Either he has collapsed and died from running so hard, or he's found the place he was looking for."

"Your next move, Commander?"

"We'll recall the soldiers in the capital, then attack tomorrow. There will be no escape this time."

19

Everyone wanted to hear Kannalin's story. As darkness descended upon the Old Giants, they gathered at the shelter's doorway, listening intently as he described the events following his capture. They heard about the female commander who had first threatened young Nartinn and then shown mercy when Kannalin told them of the Black Hollow. By the time he described his escape, Cerrin had decided to leave.

She soon found herself crouching by the stream, cooling her hands in the water. For once, there was no one else around. But it was not solely a desire for solitude that had drawn her away. She had only just begun to order her thoughts when she heard someone coming.

Erras emerged from the shadows.

Cerrin was still wary of him and she found her hand wandering toward her knife. But he clearly wanted only to talk and crouched beside her, his gaze also on the water.

"You don't believe it either, do you?" he said. "That Vitaari bitch nearly crushes Nartinn's head, then she just decides that Kannalin's given her all she needs. No torture? They just send him back to the Mine Three? Without even raiding the Black Hollow first?"

"The Vitaari can't be everywhere at once. They only have so many soldiers. Maybe capturing us isn't as important to them as we think."

"Your judgment is far from perfect, but we both know you're smarter than that."

"What's the truth then, Erras?"

"I don't know. They may be using the other prisoners as hostages—if he leads the Vitaari here, Nartinn and the others get to live. Perhaps they promised him—"

"He is no traitor."

"I don't want to believe it either, but his story doesn't add up. And if you don't do anything about, I will."

"Go away, Erras."

"If Sonus were here—"

"He isn't. But he is at least was useful. Kannalin is worth ten of you."

She knew she was speaking with emotion, not sense, but she was sick of Erras and his opinions.

The Palanian stood up. "To you, *any* Echobe is worth *any* ten Palanians. You were happy to sacrifice Nuro, but not Kannalin."

Erras walked away.

Cerrin knew she should follow him, that he might well follow up on his threat. But she needed time to think. Despite her defense of Kannalin, she did know something was wrong. This was a trap, a trick, somehow. Then again, she'd felt the need to run even before Kannalin returned. Even if she ordered everyone to pack up and move on, to build a new shelter somewhere else, would it be enough to shake this feeling?

Or would she always feel hunted?

She stood up and walked back to the camp. Erras was sitting with the other Palanians, apparently keeping his opinions to himself for the moment.

Kannalin was eating inside the shelter, still surrounded by well wishers. Many were pestering him for information on the other captives; he did his best to reassure them that they would be returned unharmed to the mines.

When he'd finished his dinner, Cerrin quietly led him outside. It was very dark now and the camp was beginning to quiet down.

"I'm sorry but we need to keep searching. What about your shoulder? I'm concerned that they may have planted something in the bandages, perhaps even in the wound itself."

Kannalin said nothing but followed her back to the stream. A small sliver was exposed to the moonlight, which glittered on the water, providing a little illumination.

"I just… We need to be sure."

Again he did not reply. He knelt by the water and removed his shirt. As she stood over him, pulling away the little strips of tape that secured the bandage, Cerrin admired the bunched muscles on his shoulders and back. Trying to put the intimacy of the situation aside, she thought it best to say something.

"Enjoy your dinner?"

"Very much. I don't remember the last time I had garra."

"Jespa shot that one. Took him three arrows, mind."

"Cerrin… I wish it wasn't only me. I wish they'd all come back."

"I know."

With all of the tape off, Cerrin now gripped the edge of the bandage, ready to remove it.

"Wait," said Kannalin, his voice no more than a whisper. He reached up and took her hand away. He moved it toward his face, then higher, to his forehead. He gripped her middle finger and placed it in the middle of his brow.

"Do you... do you feel something there?"

"What do you mean?"

"A bump or... It feels strange."

"I'm not sure. Maybe. Why?"

He looked down at the ground as he spoke. "Since I stopped moving, I've had a slight headache. My brother got headaches all the time, but not me. Not ever. When I press there, it hurts. Is it possible that... I didn't want to believe it, but—"

Kannalin took a deep breath. He pulled Cerrin's knife from the sheathe on her belt and offered it to her.

"Open it up. Like you said, we have to know."

Though she took the knife, Cerrin didn't want to do it. She didn't want to cause more pain to this poor, brave man and she wasn't sure she actually wanted to know. This was the first time their number had grown, not fallen—they were thirty-five again. Yet there was something chilling about his confession.

"Please be quick," said Kannalin. He picked up a nearby stick, brushed off some loose bark, and placed it between his teeth. He then pointed her toward the exact spot.

Holding his head gently, Cerrin shifted it slightly to make best use of the moonlight. She cleaned her blade on her sleeve, placed the tip against Kannalin's skin, and began to cut.

After the discovery of the strange message to Deputy Rasikaar, Count Talazeer decided to review all his files once again. Even assuming Commander Elezz's offer of help was genuine, it would take her associate some time to discover anything, and Talazeer was determined to remain on the front foot.

There were, in fact, no more communiques with the mysterious sender, but the Count elected to focus on all of the deputy's messages around the time of the poisoning. Two in particular caught his attention. These were between Rasikaar and his son, and there was no actual written content. The pair had simply exchanged pictures attached to a blank message. Both were images of a well known beauty spot in the Vitaari polar region. Due to the nearby glaciers, the town of Mavvarrisa attracted tourists from all over the planet and beyond; the shores of the town were packed with holiday homes for wealthy Vitaari.

When he called Marl over, the Drellen peered at one image, then the other.

Talazeer said, "Rasikaar sent his image one day after the attempt, and his son replied the following day."

"Sir, the exchange of the images could mean a simple pre-determined message and acknowledgment."

"Indeed. Or there might even be something within the image itself. I'm sure the Directorate has a way of analyzing such things but I'm not sure how we can."

"Did he send any similar messages?"

"No." Talazeer nodded over at Yullasir, who was still sorting the messages. "He couldn't find any either. The timing itself is… interesting."

"Perhaps the time has come to question him directly?"

"As before, we have nothing solid, Marl. But Rasikaar has been here a long time. The rest of the administrative staff know him very well. We shall talk to them all."

• • •

Kannalin had borne the pain with tremendous courage. With a small patch of skin pulled back, the bump was clear to see, although the fast-flowing blood made it impossible at first to identify what it was. She had to cut away more skin, then use strips of cloth torn from her shirt to stem the blood flow, before she finally recognized the color of the foreign object: yellow.

It was the unmistakable yellow of the surgical plastic used by the Vitaari to replace or hold together broken bones.

"They did surgery on you?"

Kannalin slowly lifted his hand and removed the stick from his mouth. Tears squeezed past tightly clinched eyelids and rolled down his cheeks.

"My shoulder," he grunted.

"Your head, as well."

"No, they—"

"Yes," said Cerrin. "They did."

She then went to fetch Torrin and Erras. The Palanian man accepted an apology from her with good grace. To his credit, he seemed to take no satisfaction from being proved right.

Upon examining Kannalin, both agreed the bug was there.

"It might not be in his brain," suggested Erras. "It might even be attached to the other side of the surgical plastic, simply slid into place."

It was a grim hope—removing the plastic was likely to kill him, if not immediately, then by infection. Cerrin told the group this.

"Do it," groaned Kannalin.

• • •

Removing the plastic had been easier than Cerrin feared. The skull had not yet had time to grow tight around the plug and seal it into place. But the transmitter had not been attached.

The hole in his skull had revealed itself to be about an eighth of an inch and perfectly circular—the work of a surgical drill. Through it, she had seen the glint of clean steel. There would be no removing the device without killing him.

Kannalin now lay back, hand pressed against the bleeding hole, eyes barely able to focus. Although Murrit had given him some herbs to help with the pain before the extraction began, they were mild and he had mercifully passed soon after Cerrin began probing the edges of the plastic with her knife.

"I'm sorry," he murmured. "I'm sorry."

"Perhaps there's another way to get it out," said Torrin, fighting back tears.

"Not outside of a hospital," said Erras gravely.

Cerrin couldn't speak, couldn't look at him. There was no time to ask Ikala or the other gods for answers. She was in no doubt about what they had to do now. For all she knew, the Vitaari were already closing in.

Torrin seemed to sense it. "He can leave, lead them away."

"He can barely move," said Erras.

"I… I…" Kannalin slumped back into Torrin's arms.

"We have to leave, Cerrin," continued Erras.

"Go and get them organized."

Torrin seemed uncertain. "What will you—"

"Just go!"

As the others left, she sat behind Kannalin, holding him up. His head lolled back. She removed her necklace and tried to tie it around his neck, but it was too broad. He offered his hand and she placed it there, gripping hard. "You are one of us again, Kannalin. Now and for always."

His head tilted toward her as he lost consciousness. She was grateful for it. She pulled out her knife, reached over Kannalin's shoulder, and cut his throat.

By the time she reached the camp, all had been awakened but the darkness made their task more difficult. They had at least prepared for a moment like this. The preparations included stretchers for Baros and Koros, neither of whom had recovered sufficiently to walk.

Cerrin and Jespa had already scouted three escape routes, and she now elected to head northeast. This was the quickest way to escape the Old Giants. Nowhere amid their mighty trunks would be safe for them now.

If the Vitaari came before they'd left the giants for good, Cerrin's last resort would be to divide the rebels and order them to scatter in the hope that some at least would survive.

A small figure trotted up. "Here, Cerrin. Everything is in there. You're all ready."

"Thank you, Yarni." Cerrin took her pack and pulled it on. She was already armed with spear and rifle. "Torrin, you bring up the rear."

"Why are we leaving, Cerrin?" asked Yarni.

"I'll tell you later. It's complicated."

"Some of them are unhappy. They think we should stay. They say we'll never find anywhere like this."

"Is that right?"

"I told them that you'll find us somewhere even better!"

Cerrin put her hand on Yarni's head. "You're right, as usual. Go with the others now."

Cerrin ignored several people who tried to ask her what was going on. It was very dark close to the tree, and she had to call Jespa's name to locate him.

"Ready?"

"Think so. Sentries all recalled—no reports of anything unusual."

"That's something. You're with me at the front—make sure we follow the right route."

"We can't cover our trail, Cerrin. Not with this many people. If the Vitaari get here, they can follow."

"Which means all we can do is get as far away as possible."

"Are you going to talk to the group?"

"No. Talk means discussion. Discussion takes time. We don't stop until I say so. Let's go."

Cerrin did not glance back at the tree or the shelter or the stream. She was glad now that she had spent so little time there. She wished they had left sooner. Had the vision sent by Ikala been a warning of imminent danger? The bird had wounded her head as Kannalin had been wounded. Had Ikala offered a sign that she had ignored? All she had time for now was a prayer.

Ikala, god of battle, watch over us.

Again, she led them into darkness, and into the unknown.

The nano-drones had already failed three times. On every occasion, Toll Maktar set them back to work. The second attempt took longer than the first, and the third took longer than the second. Sonus now realized the limits of the agent's technical knowledge. He understood what all of his machines did, but not how, or how to fix them when they didn't work.

There was very little to be learned from the display on the side of the case, either. It merely showed the component to be created, and when each attempt failed, it displayed a two-word message that Maktar translated as "NO CAPTURE."

At least they had the cover of darkness now, but they'd seen the lights of a Vitaari patrol not long before. Maktar suggested the soldiers might not grasp how small the *Spectre* was, as they seemed to limit their search to larger structures.

"Vun Tak!" Maktar kicked the ground and lurched away when the fourth attempt failed.

Sonus looked at the screen—and the slowly rotating three-dimensional rendering of the component. The regulator was small, barely three inches across.

"Which part is made of vorsfeld? All of it?"

"No," replied Maktar. "Just the U-shaped tube here." He tapped the image on the display. "The fuel runs through the bend and the mechanism ensures it's a consistent temperature. Any temperature fluctuations will trigger quark/anti-quark generation instead of a stable anti-gravity field."

Sonus ignored the parts of the explanation he didn't understand. "Is it just the vorsfeld part that the drones are having trouble with?"

"I'm not certain."

"What about asking it to manufacture the two pieces separately? Is that possible?"

Maktar shrugged, then dragged the case across the ground and began speaking to it.

After several clearly frustrating minutes, he turned to Sonus.

"Didn't make any progress until I tried talking to it through the *Spectre*. Ah, there's your answer."

The display screen now showed two separate rotating pieces.

"It's ready," added Maktar.

Sonus gestured toward the block of vorsfeld and the irregular mass of nanodrones beside it. As soon as Maktar activated the program, about a fourth of the drones swarmed the vorsfeld as usual, while the others formed separate lump unto themselves.

"That's new," said Sonus.

"Look at that!" said Maktar, pointing at the vorsfeld. One end of the bar was warping slightly—but noticeably—under the blanket of drones. "Well done, Sonus. But even if it can make both, how do we join them together?"

"How would the drones do it?"

Maktar looked annoyed, but he consulted the display again. After a few more minutes of questioning the device, he said, "Simple welding, it looks like."

"How hot are those plasma weapons? They'll need to be at least three hundred and ten degrees to melt vorsfeld."

The agent consulted his bracelet. "I'll check—your degrees are not the same as what we use, nor the same as the manufacturer of those guns... Yes, the average temperature of the beam is three hundred and fifty degrees."

"Then we can stick the components together ourselves."

Sonus had barely completed the sentence when they heard a shout of Vitaari from the street. Maktar grabbed another of the Raxis rifles and followed Sonus around the stern of the ship. The only light came from the case screen, which was hidden from the street behind the *Spectre*.

Reaching the damaged doors, the pair crouched down and

looked out. White beams from three flashlights were approaching, the figures behind them invisible. Nearing the warehouse, the Vitaari turned toward it. They had taken only a few steps when they suddenly stopped.

From somewhere high above came the drone of a shuttle engine. The three soldiers were quiet, but another voice could be heard through their comms systems. Then, one soldier laughed and another shook his head. They abruptly turned around and marched back the way they'd come.

"Lucky," said Maktar.

"*Very* lucky."

Count Talazeer was awakened from a deep sleep by a shudder that seemed to reverberate through the entirety of the *Galtaryax*. He didn't get up because he had felt the shudder many times and knew what it was: the shockwave of a freighter full of ore breaking free of orbit before starting its trans-light journey.

Talazeer did sit up to check that Marl was where he should be. Each night, they moved one of the couches to a position across the bedroom door and Talazeer could see a slender, clawed foot hanging off the end.

Earlier, Talazeer had seen him changing the wrappings that served as the only clothing he wore under his cloak. The bodyguard generally seemed shy about his body, and this time the Count had caught him unawares. Though he covered his scaly back swiftly, Talazeer had noted the marks and scars upon the skin. Before becoming a bodyguard, Marl had fought as a champion in the fighting pits that were still popular in some regions of the Domain. Apparently, his patron and owner had been an immensely wealthy member of Za-Arinu. He had released Marl from his service at the pleading of his children, who wanted their father to cease his interests in the pits. Talazeer had often pressed Marl on his past, but the Drellen seldom offered much.

The Count had almost drifted back to sleep when a call came through. He accepted it using the comcell beside his bed and was not surprised to hear the direct tones of Commander Elezz.

"Excellency, apologies for disturbing you. I was awoken myself only minutes ago. It appears that the rebels have discovered the tracking device. I have ordered the troops in the capital be recalled and the entire complement land as close as possible to the rebel camp. We should have boots on the ground in ninety minutes."

"You are prioritizing them over this secret ship?"

"Sir, four hours of searching has yielded no results. I presumed that you would not want to risk losing the rebels again. From the information gathered, we believe that they are in one group. Data from the tracker suggests that the female Cerrin was the one to find and remove the device."

"That does not surprise me. And I concur with your decision, Commander. Keep me closely apprised of your progress."

Within fifteen minutes, the two components were complete. Devising a way to make a weld with the plasma rifle took considerably longer.

Toll Maktar had kept watch while Sonus experimented with the plasma weapon on some stones and scraps of metal from the warehouse floor. Now, the agent put down his rifle and knelt beside him.

"Anything out there?" asked Sonus.

"Not a single light. Perhaps they're chasing your Lovirr friend."

Sonus preferred not to think about that possibility. Not when he was aiming a plasma gun at one of two quarter-inch vorsfeld pegs that stuck up from the U-shaped tube to attach it to the mechanism.

"You know, I didn't expect the nano-drones would succeed in making both components," admitted Sonus. "I was just trying to figure out which of the two components they were having trouble with."

"And are you expecting this to succeed? Welding two parts together with a plasma weapon, when Ikasar's finest nanotechnology failed?"

"Well—"

"I am joking with you, Sonus. I have more faith in you than I do in any of these machines."

Sonus lowered the gun and looked into Maktar's eyes. He saw nothing but sincerity there.

"Thank you. Now let's see if your faith is well founded."

Sonus aimed once more, let out a slow breath, then pulled the trigger. After only five seconds, he halted. "See there—it's beginning to melt."

Then he began heating each peg five seconds at a time, back and forth between the two, until he was pleased to see a molten circle at the end of both.

The regulating mechanism made by the nano-drones appeared to be a shiny yellow rectangular box with two small black insulator pads on top. Whatever the drones had built inside the box apparently didn't interest Maktar, and so Sonus's curiosity would have to go unfulfilled. Sonus lifted the box and placed it gently against the twin pegs so that the melted ends covered the insulator pads precisely.

Maktar carefully placed several stones around the regulator to hold it in place as the molten vorsfeld cooled, and only then did Sonus let go.

"Nicely done," said Maktar.

"A bit messy, actually. I suspect some will drip down from the top of the pegs. But the main thing is that the seal holds."

"So, what now?"

"Give it a half-hour to cool. Then, we fit it and see if it works."

"If it doesn't," said Maktar, "and it falls apart three kilometers in the air, at least we won't be disappointed for long."

20

She only stopped when they had passed the last of the Old Giants. Her people were making speedy progress. Better still, they had just crossed a wide stream, taking a short diversion through the knee-length water to obscure their trail. But ahead lay unfamiliar territory.

Cerrin was glad to be moving, glad not to have to dwell on Kannalin. She did not feel guilt for what she had done, only sorrow that the brave warrior had met such an end.

There were but thirty-four of them again.

She knew now that Sonus had been foolish to think they might ever strike back at the Vitaari. They would never be able to stop running. Never stop dying. She would keep as many of them alive as she could, for as long as she could—and that was all. Thoughts of building a new home, a new life, had been fantasy. This was their life from now on, until they fell one by one to their enemy.

It might take a year or more until the last of her people was dead. It was more likely to take a day.

An hour earlier, they'd heard a shuttle's engines to the east, so Cerrin knew that soldiers were on the ground and following them. She'd made sure that the stretcher-bearers were regularly changed, chided the slow, ignored the complaints, and kept the pace quick but steady. She had done all she could.

Occasionally, she heard others talk about Sonus and Maktar, imagining some dramatic return, some great rescue. Cerrin could not afford such thoughts; he was gone, and she could neither expect nor rely upon surprise help from above.

So much had occurred since he'd left. She did not expect to ever see him again.

She stood now between two jagged outcrops of rock—a rare sight in the Great Forest. Ahead lay undulating ground only partially covered by trees. Clouds had veiled the moon, and they could risk no torches or flashlights. It would be a treacherous walk, and she'd be lucky not to have a dozen more rebels in need of stretchers by daybreak.

"We continue in one minute. Pass it on."

Torrin did so and Cerrin listened as word went back along the column.

Then Jespa came bounding forward. "I saw their lights. More than twenty. Less than a mile."

Cerrin had already made up her mind. "All right. Find yourself a rifle."

As Jespa went to do so, Cerrin called Torrin over.

"There's a little wind and the clouds are patchy. It will clear. Follow the Ever Star and do not stop until I return or the sun comes."

"I will," said Torrin. "What are you two going to do?"

"Give the Vitaari a little surprise."

. . .

Once back across the stream, Cerrin and Jespa waited until they could see the lights in the distance. They had left their spears behind but both had rifles with full magazines.

"You take the left," she instructed. "I'll go right. Don't get closer than two hundred feet and don't do anything until you're on their flank. Make sure you hit at least three or four. Let's see how they like having wounded slowing them down. Retreat directly away from them before heading east. Meet back here."

"Got it."

Cerrin saw a flash of teeth in the gloom—Jespa's smile.

"Ikala is with us this night," he said. "I feel it."

The Vitaari were not difficult to locate. Those at the front and back were using their powerful helmet lights, illuminating the giant bodies of their compatriots. Cerrin tracked them for a while, estimating that there were around thirty.

She then got ahead of them, finding a good position with a clear field of fire, no more than eighty feet away. As the lead Vitaari came level with her position, she clicked off the rifle's safety and selected fully automatic fire. She knew the soldiers would be wearing armor. She also knew that the rifle's bullets would shred it.

The three at the front with lights went past. Cerrin dug the butt of her rifle into her right shoulder, steadied herself, and opened fire.

Impacts. Shouts. Cries. The beams of light suddenly flashed in every direction. She kept firing, swept the barrel to her right, grinned triumphantly when she heard the bullets strike.

There was little in the world that made her happier than hurting Vitaari.

Then the lights swung toward her.

Just as she ducked down, Jespa opened up. The lights moved again. Some of the Vitaari were keeping their heads, voices steady. Others were shouting and shrieking as they realized they were caught in a crossfire.

Cerrin placed the gun back over her shoulder, pulling the strap tight. She waited for a beam of light to move out of her path, then sprang away, heading back for the stream. Twice she stumbled. And three times she stopped, not looking toward the enemy but simply listening for any suggestion of pursuit. The beams of light still seemed to be coalescing around her firing position, but she was already two hundred yards away from there. Jespa was still attacking; she was surprised he still had any bullets.

On she ran, until at last the weight of the gun and the night's journey began to tell. Yet still she moved quickly, so quickly that she almost splashed straight into the stream.

Not recognizing any of the surrounding terrain, she tracked right until at last she reached the point where they'd parted. If she'd been asked, Cerrin would not have been able to identify a single feature—but it *felt* like the right place, and she knew from experience that Jespa would find the spot in the same way.

In the distance, she saw the odd flash of light, but it seemed the Vitaari hadn't advanced. At the very least, they'd now be concerned about another ambush and have several casualties to deal with.

She waited there, rifle in her hands once more, sweat cooling on her back. Two minutes. Four. She couldn't be sure but it seemed like at least some of the Vitaari were moving again—toward the stream. Jespa was as quick as her through the forest, if not quicker; he should have been there by now. Cerrin knew something had gone wrong.

Then she heard him: breathing ragged, steps irregular and

unsure. It was so unlike him that she raised the rifle as he lurched out of the shadows. He was coughing badly, and when he came close, Cerrin smelled the metallic scent of blood. She put her hand on his shoulder. "You're hurt."

"Yes. Side. I—I—won't get far."

Cerrin lowered her hand to find the wound. Before she even located it, her fingers were covered in blood. He was right.

"Oh, Jespa."

"Sorry, Cerrin. I think I kept firing for too long. They were shooting blind and one just got lucky."

For once, she had no idea what to do. Jespa had his own answer. "I've still got a few bullets left. I'll try and lead them away, take as many with me as I can."

Cerrin's hand was still on his shoulder. She squeezed it. She had no words.

"Tell Torrin I'm sorry. I really hoped… Just tell her I'm sorry."

Marl approached the table where Count Talazeer sat waiting for the next of Rasikaar's team to arrive.

So far, the interviewees had offered little insight regarding the administrator's history and character. The Count had at least been able to discount the mysterious coded message. It was nothing more than a random attempt to infect as many computers as possible with a key-logging virus. Such garbage was usually filtered out at the relay station, but occasionally a message slipped through.

"She's outside, sir. Anything from the commander?"

"Sergeant Guldur's unit was ambushed before dawn this morning. Five casualties, but one of the rebels paid for it. Guldur remains in pursuit. We must be ready, Marl—I don't want to miss all the action."

"Yes, sir."

Talazeer waved at the door. "Send her in."

Berevikk was a middle-aged woman who had worked as Deputy Rasikaar's personal assistant for many years. She seemed even more anxious about the situation than the previous two and sat opposite Talazeer with her hands clasped in her lap, occasionally casting a furtive glance at Marl.

Talazeer did his best to put her at ease and began with some simple questions about her role, her relationship with Rasikaar, and so on. He then turned to the subject of the deputy administrator's son, whom he'd exchanged those odd pictures with. The Count was surprised to see Berevikk's face brighten. "Well, I think everyone was pleased. I've met Master Rasikaar's wife on several occasions and I know she was very happy to see them back in contact again."

"There were issues between Rasikaar and his son?"

"For some time. It's difficult for lone children—expectations can be so high."

"Explain."

"I probably shouldn't say anything, but the young man had been in trouble. I didn't hear anything of this from the deputy, of course, but there was some… gossip. I'm not sure I should—"

"As I explained, anything said in this interview will not be shared, certainly not with the deputy."

"Nothing ever reached court," continued Berevikk. "I believe the wider family brought some influence to bear to ensure that. But apparently the young man was mixed up in some intrigue between clans—the selling of secrets or something. After that, the deputy refused to meet or speak with his son for several months. I'm so glad they're finally talking again. I'm afraid that's all I know."

"Do you remember who you heard this from?"

"I honestly don't, sir. It was some time ago. But I do know that the son is back at college. Architecture, I think. I believe he's into his second year of study now."

Talazeer pressed her on the subject of the son but learned nothing more of use. Even so, he felt this was a breakthrough of sorts; Rasikaar's boy was of questionable character and had exchanged these odd picture messages with his father around the time of the poisoning.

Berevikk knew nothing of the pictures, nor of any recent communication between the two.

"On the day of the poisoning, did you notice anything about Rasikaar's behavior?"

"No, Excellency, other than shock. We were all shocked—and relieved that you recovered so swiftly."

To her credit, this deferential reply was quite convincing.

Talazeer dismissed her and continued the interviews. Not until the last one—which was with the *Galtaryax*'s captain, Nemmetor—did he hear anything more that interested him.

"We talked about the son, yes," said Nemmetor, a quietly capable man whom Talazeer might have admired if he'd come from a better family. "Honestly, I've had some trouble with one of mine—very directionless, more interested in women."

"Did you discuss their relationship recently?"

"No. I know the young man is studying."

"Which the deputy is pleased about?"

"I expect so."

"You haven't discussed it with him?"

"I've known Rasikaar a long time, but we're not close these days. He used to be a regular in the officer's lounge of an evening."

Talazeer had attended these functions only once: he'd found the local officers to be a terminally dull bunch.

"But not recently?"

"Hardly at all. Over the past few weeks, he's become rather reticent. Then again, I suppose he's been busy with the terodite switch."

Talazeer wasn't convinced by this. Though anxious and eager to please, the deputy seemed to delegate as much work as possible. "Or preoccupied by something else?"

Nemmetor grimaced. "Sir, I am aware that this is all in relation to the poisoning. I do not believe for a minute that the deputy was involved. He has been out here a long time. Yes, he's made mistakes, but he is committed and loyal—a good Domain man. He would not involve himself in a plot against you."

"And yet, you have observed that his habits have recently changed."

"I have."

"Thank you, Captain. That will be all."

As Nemmetor left, Talazeer turned to Marl. "The time has come to question Rasikaar himself."

It was a beautiful day but Cerrin could not help wondering if it would be her last. The Wild Sun had risen into a cloudless sky, casting a brilliant glow onto the uneven, marshy ground. Only an hour earlier, they had seen the star live up to its name, releasing what looked like spouts and wreathes of flame. Murrit seemed to think this a portent of success while other Echobe thought it might signal suffering and death. All knew that the sun grew wilder with every passing year. The eruptions were blindingly bright, yet they enraptured every one of them until Cerrin forced them on.

They had at least negotiated the tougher terrain without serious problems; she had just called a halt in a dense copse of trees barely a hundred feet across. It was precarious but the best she could do. Though there was sufficient undergrowth to obscure them from the ground troops while they attempted to sleep, the canopy was patchy and thin. Cerrin felt sure that either a shuttle or the dreaded drones would appear soon to direct the soldiers. The old tactic of staying put in daylight would have to be forgotten. She and Jespa might have slowed the Vitaari down, but they could not be far behind.

Yet there had been no choice but to stop. After sixteen hours on the march, the rebels were worn out. Crouching behind a tangled bush, she glanced back at them, most sitting or lying or drinking water. Koros and Baros lay on stretchers beside an Echobe woman who had fallen badly in the night. There was only one chink of light: The Kannalin episode had at least brought Erras back into the fold. He was once again showing energy and leadership, to the Echobe as much as the Palanians. No one had put in more shifts carrying the injured.

An hour earlier, the guider Murrit had taken Cerrin aside. She reported that three Echobe had told her of visions: all of the same object—a Vitaari skull. Despite their situation, the guider seemed sure that it was a promising sign from the gods. Cerrin didn't know what to believe.

Torrin walked over and knelt beside her, carrying a handful

of black akay berries, which were abundant in the area. Cerrin took them gratefully and popped them one by one into her mouth. They were soft and sweet. She was glad to see that Torrin was coping. Telling her about Jespa had been one of the hardest things she'd ever done.

"You all right?" asked Cerrin, squeezing her arm with her spare hand.

"Jespa and I kissed yesterday. I'm glad."

Torrin broke down then, the tears coming easily until her tunic was wet through. Several times, she glanced back at the others, as if fearful someone would see her. Cerrin found her eyes were pricked by tears, too. They had lost not only a precious warrior and scout but a good man. Not the first, not the last.

Thirty-three.

Torrin wiped her eyes on her sleeve and gazed out at the terrain behind them: an area of high grass dotted with young saplings. The ground was soft; in daylight, the soldiers would easily follow their trail. "Any sign of them?"

"Not yet but it won't be long. I don't know what to do. We're exposed. I should never have taken us this way."

"You're wrong." With a weary smile, Torrin pointed to the left. There, amid a line of dark trees was one without bark. "It was struck by lightning. My father showed it to me. I know where we are. About five miles northeast is the Crystal Lake."

"You're sure?" Cerrin had some idea that the lake wasn't far from the Old Giants, but her mental map was vague.

"Islands," Torrin continued. "There are islands on this side. Hundreds, and thick by trees. Some close to shore. It might be our best chance."

"It might be our only chance."

"Especially if we can take out a few more Vitaari."

"What do you mean?"

"Koros and the other injured folk have been talking. They know they're slowing us down and they don't want to be responsible for getting anyone killed. They *won't* be. They want to stay here, wait for the Vitaari—do what they can to give the rest of us a chance."

Koros, Baros, and four others who'd elected to stay were given bows and arrows. As they prepared themselves in a defensive position amid the trees, Cerrin found the sight almost pathetic. But when she said her farewells and led the rebels away from the copse, she felt a burst of solemn purpose and a renewed strength within. If she didn't get the rest to safety now, all of these sacrifices would be in vain.

Twenty-seven.

With Erras at the rear of the column, Cerrin led at a trot, navigating between clumps of undergrowth and stands of trees, ordering the rebels to keep low and close together. She had told them about the Crystal Lake, and having a target destination ahead seemed to spur them on. Someone even mentioned the "island folk" in hopeful whispers, which Cerrin thought very strange. They were merely a legend, and not a pleasant one: a savage tribe who lived in the Crystal Lake and ate children who wandered too far away from their parents.

It was hard not to constantly scan the skies or pause to listen for their pursuers, but she kept her attention on the terrain ahead. After two hours, she halted in an area of thick vegetation dotted with bright orange blooms, each as wide as a hand.

Ordering the others to rest, she ran ahead, toward what looked like open ground. Reaching the edge of the trees, she couldn't stop herself from smiling. She found herself at the end of a tongue of water connected to a larger body that stretched out of sight to the northwest.

It had to be the Crystal Lake.

The waters were a brilliant blue, the surface calm, adorned here and there by flocks of pink birds, the like of which Cerrin had never seen. She couldn't spy any islands from her position, but the lake was bordered by a narrow beach of gray sand; they could follow it north and stay hidden in the tree line.

She was halfway back to the others when she saw Torrin running toward her, her face tight with fear.

"Vitaari soldiers, twenty at least, moving quickly. No more than half a mile behind us."

The first attempt with the newly made regulator was a failure. The nano-drones fitted it into the impulsor, but the system had neither started nor determined what was wrong.

Sonus examined the component once more and observed that the surface of the welded pegs was very rough. He suspected that the ship's internal scanners assumed it was still damaged and therefore dangerous to use.

Using some sand found in a corner of the warehouse glued to a scrap of cloth, he was able to smooth out the join and polish the rest of the makeshift regulator. Toll Maktar seemed impressed by his improvisational skill but doubtful that this simple refinement would work.

And yet it did.

"Two impulsors," said the agent, clenching a fist. "Enough to get us in the air, yes? Well done."

Sonus glanced toward the sunlit street. "And we haven't heard any shuttles for a few hours. Straight to the Old Giants?"

"We must. Who knows how long that regulator will last? No offence."

"None taken."

The pair hurried inside and Maktar closed the hatch.

"But what if it does fail?" added Sonus. "Can the *Spectre* function on one impulsor?"

"With one, our only hope is that we survive the crash, yes? I've had to disable the safety protocols as it is. Ready? I suggest we strap in."

Sonus took his seat beside the agent and watched the screens. He held in a breath as the *Spectre* lifted from the ground and did not let it out again until they were free of the warehouse and into the daylight. Though no alarming noises could be heard, the little ship's movements were far from smooth. Maktar took them up to a hundred meters, then set off on an easterly course.

"Power's fluctuating. I'd say that regulator's doing the job but only just. Stealth measures are at less than thirty percent. I'll stay low, use ground clutter where we can. I'll keep the speed down, too, to reduce our heat signature."

"How long to the Old Giants?"

"Around two hours."

Sonus's stomach dropped. That was a long time to spend imagining the *Spectre* falling out of the sky, and he could think of nothing else—fearing at every moment that his repair would fail.

• • •

The deputy administrator stared warily across at his superior. He seemed unwilling—or unable—to look at Marl, who occasionally tapped a clawed finger on the table.

Count Talazeer had initially enjoyed the investigation, taking the initiative to uncover his enemies. But he needed answers quickly, before events down on the surface reached a conclusion—or before his foes struck again.

"Have you identified any suspects yet, Excellency?"

"Oh, several," replied Talazeer. He pulled his chair close to the table and leaned forward. "It goes without saying that we must pursue every piece of evidence."

"Of course."

"One such piece is a pair of messages exchanged by you and your son. Well, in fact, there is no message—just images."

"Images?"

"Yes, of Mavvarrisa."

"Ah yes, those," said Rasikaar with a nervous smile. "My son asked me to send him that one in particular, from our last trip. I didn't ask for the one he returned, but it was a nice picture. Photography was a hobby of ours—when he was younger."

"Before he got into trouble?"

For the first time, Deputy Rasikaar looked more angry than afraid. "You... know about that? Berevikk, I expect. The silly old bitch never could keep her mouth shut."

"Now, now, Rasikaar. There's no need for that. What exactly happened?"

The administrator looked down for some time but eventually composed himself and answered. "Ullavar has always been rather naïve. I think he inherited it from his mother's side. He wasn't interested in the academy or even university, so I set him up with a work placement with my uncle—a chief engineer at a naval yard. While there, Ullavar was… befriended… by a young woman. He believed it to be true love. We did meet her—and, frankly, I was rather suspicious—but my wife persuaded me to leave it alone." The administrator paused for a few breaths before continuing. "It was Za-Duss Viskar who set it all up. They hired this woman to break into the shipyard computer system by any means necessary, and she thought my son could get her access. It might have worked, too, if my uncle hadn't figured the whole thing out first. Ullavar was devastated, of course. My uncle was very good about the whole thing, and thanks to his influence, we were able to keep Ullavar's name out of the official investigation. It was a difficult time. I'd hoped we'd put it behind us."

"I'm sure," said Talazeer. "And you have done well to keep it from me. The taint of such dishonorable conduct can be hard to remove."

"My son was naïve, Excellency, *not* dishonorable."

"It seems you are close. And yet neither of you added any kind of message to your recent missives. In fact, you have not communicated in over a month. Not even a greeting. Quite odd."

"Young people can be like that."

"Of course, but nothing from you?"

Rasikaar was clearly becoming exasperated. "Ulla doesn't respond well if he feels I'm prying. My wife keeps me up to date."

"Let us be very clear. You categorically deny any connection to… recent events, then?"

Rasikaar was now gripping the sides of his chair. "Count Talazeer, I am prepared to cooperate but there *must* be limits. I am a senior officer with seven years of service here. I will not be treated like some common criminal."

"Was that a denial?"

"Sir, you cannot do this!"

At the outburst, Marl took a step closer.

Rasikaar squeezed his eyes shut, then slumped back before composing himself once more. "I do not understand why suspicion has fallen on me when there is good reason for this... attention to be directed elsewhere."

"Go on."

"Sir, this is very difficult. I cannot afford to incur the anger—"

Talazeer thumped the table. "You cannot afford to incur *my* anger!"

"Very well, then. Sir, Commander Elezz has been conducting secret communications."

"I am aware of that. She assures me that these Level 7 messages are with a senior commander and do not relate to me."

"Sir, I am not talking about messages sent using the array. Last week, my staff informed me of an unusual energy reading from the loading bay where her staff keeps their equipment. I went there myself and made a note of everything. As it turns out, they have a laser interferometer in there using seventy-three times more power than it should."

The administer paused again, but Talazeer only raised an eyebrow expectantly.

"Hidden inside the interferometer is a portable coms array. Energy readings suggest that it has been used regularly since she arrived. I suppose I should have told you immediately but the commander is very well connected. I did not want to risk offending her, but of course my first loyalty should be to you."

"Indeed, it should. I appreciate your honesty, Rasikaar, belated though it may be."

"It is hardly conclusive, sir, but—"

"Conclusive? Perhaps not. But certainly *instructive.*"

21

The islands were their only chance.

Cerrin had led the rebels along the trees beside the beach for more than two hours. They halted now in the shadows of slender palms, upon sandy soil, only twenty paces from the water. The island closest to the edge of the lake was about two hundred yards away. The interior was thick with palms and vines, offering good protection.

The Vitaari were no more than a quarter-mile behind, and Cerrin had already dropped back twice to watch them. All around her, the rebels were shoving everything, including their shoes, into their packs and preparing to swim. Out in the open water, they would be easy targets. All twenty-seven of them needed to be hidden within the trees of the island before the first soldier looked out across the lake.

Murrit was leading several Echobe in a prayer. Torrin, Erras, and a few others were collecting branches to use as floats for the weaker swimmers. Cerrin had recruited two Echobe warriors—Allarin and Purrik—to help her build a barricade. If it came to it, they'd keep the Vitaari's attention away from the lake and swimmers with suppressive gunfire, then lead them on a chase back into the forest.

Leaving the pair there—facing south, rifles ready—Cerrin hurried over to Yarni, who was staring anxiously at the water.

"All right?"

"What about the snappers?" asked the youngster. "Everyone knows there are snappers in the Crystal Lake."

"Not at this time of year," said Cerrin, who knew absolutely nothing about snappers. "They're sleeping on the bottom. Now listen, you do as Torrin tells you and don't look back until you reach the island."

Cerrin grabbed a short but thick branch from the pile. "This will help you. Take it steady. It's quite a long way."

"You will come later, won't you, Cerrin?"

"You know I will."

"But Jespa didn't. Kannalin didn't."

That startled Cerrin, but she found an answer. "They might come later."

"They're dead. I'm not stupid. I know they're dead."

There was no time to say any more. Cerrin kissed Yarni on the head and ran over to Torrin. "Go now. Watch Yarni."

Allarin called out to her; the Vitaari were close.

Cerrin immediately began grabbing the more hesitant rebels and corralling them toward the water. She didn't leave until a dozen—Yarni included—were actually swimming. Satisfied that she could do little more, Cerrin sprinted back to the barricade. She picked up her rifle and followed the line of Allarin's outstretched arm.

The Vitaari were staying in the trees for the moment, but the sun sparked off their guns and visors. Then the soldiers advanced.

• • •

Count Talazeer reached the elevator at the same time as Commander Elezz. She had notified him just minutes earlier that Sergeant Guldur was about to engage the rebels and that she was flying down to observe the final stages of the operation. Talazeer was bemused to learn that the unit had sustained casualties from some ambush, but Elezz seemed sure that the endgame was near.

He gestured for the commander to enter the elevator first.

"I see you have your hunting rifle, Count Talazeer. I do hope you have a chance to use it this time. I gather the weather is rather more clement today."

"So, the rebels have reached a lake?"

"Indeed. An odd tactic, but I suppose they are running out of choices—and numbers. Unfortunately for them, it's likely to prove their downfall. In an open area, we can make the most of the shuttles and the shells if we need them."

"Fine, but I want her alive, Commander."

"Her?"

"Yes, the leader. And the one who took the shell, too, of course."

But, in that moment, it was only Cerrin he thought of. He imagined holding her close, cradling that strangely captivating face in his hand, running a finger down the scar he had given her.

The *Spectre* flew just above the treetops, screens showing the dense forest beneath them. The Old Giants were below but, of course, Sonus did not expect to see any signs of the rebels from the air. Cerrin was far too clever and cautious for that.

Toll Maktar pointed toward a suitable clearing, then turned the ship toward it.

"I had no idea how large this area is," said Sonus. "We might be ten miles from them. Farther."

"Once we're down, I can transfer more power to the scanners. We'll find them. If…"

The agent never completed the sentence.

"What were you going to say?"

"If there are any of them left. We've had no contact with them for several days, Sonus. Anything could have happened."

"And what if we can't find them? What if they are… gone?"

"My suggestion would be that we fly back to the capital and try to make contact with your Lovirr friend. We have the weapons. They must be used against the Vitaari."

Despite his questions, Sonus couldn't see that far ahead. He believed that Cerrin and the others were still alive. He *had* to believe it.

Bullets thumped into the sand and peppered the logs of their makeshift barricade. Cerrin, Allarin, and Purrik ducked down, aware that at least five Vitaari were firing at them. Cerrin glanced back at the water, relieved to see that everyone was off the beach. But they were already strung out; and progress seemed perilously slow.

Purrik risked a quick look over the top. "They're staying in the trees. Think I saw a few going left, trying to flank us."

They had arranged the logs at right angles, to cover this eventuality. Allarin positioned himself on the left flank. "I'll keep an eye out."

Cerrin waited for a pause, then leaped up, aimed at a flash of movement, and shot off a few rounds. Ten seconds after she'd ducked down, Purrik did the same. Up went a cry from the Vitaari.

"Eat that, shenk!" As Echobe insults went, it was the harshest there was.

"Can't believe it's just us now," said Purrik. "I really thought Sonus might get back in time to help."

"He should never have left," replied Allarin.

They heard an unusual wailing sound just ahead of them.

Allarin frowned. "What was—"

The grenade detonated, blowing the logs into the air. Cerrin felt a great pressure in her ears and instinctively ducked her head. She looked up just as the logs crashed back down in front of her, showering her and the others with sand. Cerrin shook her head and wiped it from her eyes.

Purrik said something but Cerrin found herself deafened. "What?"

He held up four fingers, then pointed to their left flank.

As soon as the ramp touched the forest floor, Sonus headed for the doorway. He had one of the Raxis rifles with him and was desperate to get out of the *Spectre*.

"Wait," said Maktar, who was running the first scan since their shaky landing. "I know everything's at minimal capacity, but I'm not reading any humanoid life signs. What I am reading is one of the shuttles."

"Where is it?"

"Currently descending, headed for…" Maktar's eyes moved from screen to screen. "Headed for that lake northeast of here. I can't think of many other reasons why the Vitaari might be going there."

"You're right. Let's go."

The agent hesitated. "That shuttle might contain drones or combat shells."

"Then we better get there first."

Toll Maktar nodded. He issued some commands: the ramp retracted and the door closed.

"How far?" asked Sonus.

"Six minutes."

"Time to landing, eight minutes."

The pilot's voice came through clearly to the hold. The troops were in an excitable mood, enjoying the ride down, ready for combat.

Count Talazeer was sitting with Commander Elezz to his left and Marl to his right. The Drellen had asked him to consider staying on the ship, arguing that he was taking an unnecessary risk. Talazeer overruled him without explanation: the truth was that he had to see the rebels beaten; he craved that reckoning with Cerrin and Sonus.

"You did reiterate to Sergeant Guldur that the leaders are to be taken alive?"

"I did," replied Elezz. "But this is combat, sir. We can guarantee nothing."

The screen ahead showed the visuals from Guldur's helmet camera. Elezz called her subordinate. "Sergeant, leave those in the water—we can round them up later. You are to press your attack on those still firing. Try to take them alive, if possible."

"That won't be easy, Commander."

"I'm sure you'll do your best."

Talazeer was already editing the footage in his mind, complete with how the battle would end: Cerrin bound and gagged in the mud amid the managed corpses of her fellow rebels, all severed limbs and heads. He looked forward to sending the video to Deslat and his father. Perhaps he would one day watch it with his mother; perhaps she would at last praise him as she did her other sons.

"Are we flying at maximum speed?" asked Talazeer. "I wouldn't want to miss all the fun."

Purrik cried out and fell on his back, dropping the rifle.

"Stay where you are, Allarin," ordered Cerrin. Her ears were still ringing; even her own words sounded oddly distant. She turned to check on the injured man.

A thick splinter of wood was sticking out of his right shoulder.

"Could have been worse," breathed Purrik with a brave smile.

"You want me to pull it out?"

"Nah, leave it in." Purrik sat up without assistance and recovered his rifle. "I'm down to twenty rounds."

"Fifteen," said Allarin.

"Go, Cerrin," said Purrik. "You can't do any more here."

She turned toward the lake. The slowest of the rebels were now a hundred feet from the far beach. She could probably catch them before they reached shore.

"He's right," added Allarin. "They need you."

Cerrin took the rifle from her shoulder and placed it on the ground. "Got to be thirty left in there." She slapped both men on the shoulder, picked up her spear, and ran for the surf.

. . .

"Do you see any sign of them?"

Sonus studied the main screen, which showed one side of the lake and a line of islands. "No. Can you use the scanners?"

"Can't spare the power," replied Maktar.

Suddenly, a piercing alarm sounded and the *Spectre* lurched to the right as it began to descend.

"Vun Tak!" bellowed Maktar. "An impulsor's gone. We're flying on one."

"Not now! Not now!" Sonus smashed a fist into the rifle he was holding between his legs.

As the safety straps emerged once more, the pair pulled them on.

"Eighty meters," said Maktar. "We're going down."

The *Spectre* continued to veer to the right and rotate onto its side.

"Hope we don't come down on the roof," said Maktar between gritted teeth.

Sonus found himself gripping the straps as the little ship continued to lose altitude.

"Forty meters," said Maktar. "Thirty. The reserve booster should kick in about now."

The *Spectre* righted itself, but kept falling. Then—the sound of thunder raging against the bottom of the ship as it smashed through branches of the canopy. Then—a full second of silence.

Sonus's head snapped forward at the same moment the main screen shattered. Sharp, searing pain shot up his back and neck.

All was still.

The ship's computers and displays were black and lifeless.

Both viewports were partially covered by branches. Leaves fell upon the rest and in moments all was dark.

Cerrin had tied her spear to her ankle, ensuring that she would keep at least one weapon with her. She forced herself to concentrate on her swimming for a count of fifty, refusing the constant temptation to look behind and ahead. Then she allowed herself one look back at the shattered barricade.

At least ten Vitaari had broken cover and were now bolting across the sand, firing as they ran. One rebel (Cerrin couldn't tell which) was cowering as the lump of wood was shredded all around him. The other looked to be dead.

Suddenly, more Vitaari sprang out of the trees—the four on the flank—and the first soldier shot the last rebel in the back.

Cerrin couldn't help crying out and she swallowed a mouthful of water. *Twenty-five.*

Spitting out what she could, she turned and looked forward. Ahead were bobbing heads and flailing arms and legs; it was difficult to see who was who. She had expected to see the quickest of the rebels already on the island but they seemed to be swimming around it. Then she saw what hadn't been discernible at distance: there was no beach, only a steep, rocky shore with no easy method of getting out.

We're trapped.

This is it. It's over.

Ikala, please. Help me. Help us all.

She was a hundred feet behind the stragglers so she put her head down and powered on, only taking breaths when she needed to. Relieved to hear no more firing, she only stopped when she caught up with the slowest rebels. The group had now bunched up, with only a hardy few swimming on around the island.

"No!" yelled a woman.

Cerrin turned back toward the beach and saw the Vitaari dragging Purrik and Allarin along by their feet. She was glad to see that neither of them was moving. The rest of the soldiers were walking toward the surf, guns at the ready. Cerrin guessed the range was at least a hundred yards, but the Vitaari had all the time they needed. It would be a massacre.

She wondered why they were hesitating until she heard the familiar drone of an approaching shuttle.

"Cerrin!"

Yarni splashed over, thankfully still holding the branch. The girl looked panicked and desperate.

"It's all right. Stay calm. Just keep moving your legs."

"All courage," breathed the girl.

"Look there!" It was Torrin now pointing up at the shuttle descending rapidly toward a wider section of the beach about a mile to the south. Cerrin knew then that it was truly over. Even if there were no combat shells in that shuttle, it could follow them and strike from above.

But that didn't mean they had to give in.

"Come on!" Though she had no idea where she was going, Cerrin swam on through the rebels, knowing every yard gained at least gave them time. She'd save as many as possible for as long as possible, even if that time was measured in minutes. "This way!"

Her hearing at last back to normal, she didn't stop until she reached two men looking for a way onto the island. One of them was Erras.

"These accursed rocks. We'll cut ourselves to pieces and they'll pick us off from the shore."

"They haven't yet," said the other man.

"The shuttle," said another. "They're waiting for something."

"By the Maker," said Erras. "Look there."

Cerrin could only assume it was some other horror—combat shells approaching or another shuttle over the lake.

She could not have been more wrong.

Cutting through the water toward them, staying close to the far side of the island, were five canoes. Powering them along with swift, steady strokes was a number of bare-chested men, each with a head of unkempt, curly hair. There were two in each canoe, and they were careful to stop where the Vitaari couldn't see them. The man in the lead boat raised his hand and beckoned to the rebels.

"I don't believe it," said Erras.

"The island folk," said Cerrin.

"They're real," added Torrin. "They're really real."

The lead man was still urging them forward while the others seemed to be busy with ropes. Cerrin turned to the rebels, many of whom could not yet see the islanders. "This way. Quickly."

She treaded water as the others swam past, ordering them to do nothing that might draw attention to their unexpected allies.

"Who are they?" said Yarni when she caught sight of them.

"Just keep moving. All of you, keep moving."

Cerrin looked back at the beach. The ramp of the shuttle was down and a large group was marching toward the soldiers.

Only when the others were all past her did Cerrin get moving. By then, she could see what the islanders had been doing with their ropes: they'd attached little loops to the sides of their canoes. The vessels were at least fifteen feet long with a man at the bow and stern. The ropes provided handholds for six people on either side.

The rebels were offering profuse thanks, but the islanders did not speak. Up close, Cerrin saw that they were as dark as the Echobe, their noses and ears pierced by fishbones beneath their wild hair. The leader pointed at a spare rope and she gladly took hold. Without a word, he set their canoe away, turning in a tight circle so as to remain unseen.

And in purposeful silence, the saviors transported the rebels away from their enemy.

Count Talazeer, Commander Elezz, and Marl trudged across the sand, accompanied by twenty Guardsmen. Talazeer noted that the Drellen was scanning the dense forest to the right, no doubt concerned about some unseen threat. The Count knew he should share that concern—not to mention the continuing uncertainty about Elezz—but he somehow felt cheerful. It was a quite beautiful day, sunlight sparkling on the lake, and he was looking forward to at last facing Cerrin.

As his party neared Sergeant Guldur and his troops, Talazeer shaded his eyes and looked toward the island. The glare was extreme and he could no longer see any figures in the water.

"Where have they gone?"

"Just the other side of the island, sir," said Guldur. "Don't worry, they won't get far."

"Do we have any boats?" asked the Count.

"Er, no, sir," said Elezz. "We do, however, have four combat shells on their way from Mine Seven. They will be here within thirty minutes and drive the rebels back to the shore."

"Ah, good idea. Glad we didn't miss out on anything."

Elezz wandered over to the bodies of two fallen rebels, riddled with bullet wounds, blood coloring the sand. Talazeer followed her and was glad to see that neither was Cerrin or Sonus.

"And the other dead—the two leaders weren't among them?"

"No, sir," replied Sergeant Guldur.

The Count took his hunting rifle from his shoulder and walked along the beach. "Lovely day for it."

"That was a shuttle. I swear I heard a shuttle."

Sonus slapped a vine out of his way and looked up toward the sky. He could see only a tiny piece of it through the canopy.

Maktar had made a start on clearing the debris from the *Spectre*, but the ship was still battered and sitting at an odd angle thanks to a broken landing strut.

"If it *was* a shuttle," he added, "we're probably too late. Can you scan?"

Toll Maktar threw a branch aside and shot Sonus an impatient glare. "The systems are barely running as it is. Let's clear all this so we can at least get to the drive."

"I could go on foot, get some of the weapons to them."

"Sonus, it's several miles—and look at how thick this stuff is. The *Spectre* is still in one piece. We have one good impulsor and we may be able to get the other going."

Sonus considered this and eventually clambered back over a tangle of logs and vines.

"You're right. We did it once. We can do it again."

"*We?*" said Maktar. "I'm depending on *you.*"

22

The islanders still did not speak. Their leader, a broad-shouldered man with a tough, purposeful bearing, occasionally signaled the other boats with his hand. Cerrin eventually realized that he was ensuring they remained hidden from the Vitaari.

From behind the first island, they angled across open water before passing two islets, one to the left, one to the right. Neither of these were wider than a hundred feet but they were tall enough to obscure the low-lying canoes and oarsmen. Reaching open water once more, the locals increased their pace, striking out for another island about a half-mile away. This one was quite large and covered by dense forest.

"They saved us," said Yarni, who was on the opposite side of the canoe and seemed to be enjoying the ride. "The island folk saved us."

Cerrin belatedly realized she could smell something, and when she peered down into the canoe, she saw a number of silver-green fish in a basket, some still moving. This was a fishing party, not a rescue mission—but, seeing their plight, the islanders had saved them anyway.

"You speak *Trade?*" she asked the leader.

He turned from the bow but did not answer.

"*Trade?*"

This time he didn't even turn.

Cerrin couldn't keep her eyes off the sky, again in fear of a shuttle or drone. She was still towing her spear upon her ankle, so recovered it and placed it in the canoe. The oarsman at the stern watched this but did not react.

Cerrin reckoned that the islanders must have seen the Vitaari before, even if the invaders weren't aware of them. How much did these strange tribesmen know about the world away from their islands? Did they know that the Vitaari came from another world? That they'd slaughtered and enslaved the other races?

Now close to the island, Cerrin saw that this one was also protected by a rocky shore but possessed a narrow inlet. As the canoes slid into the sheltered inlet, the rebels glanced anxiously at the shore. But other than a few little lizards upon the rocks, they saw no sign of life. Soon the terrain became dense with dark undergrowth and curtains of weeds hanging from branches; bulbous roots stuck up out of the water, rather like a swamp.

The inlet widened to about fifty feet, becoming thick with foul green algae, and veered toward what seemed to Cerrin to be the center of the island. On the far side of the marsh, she spied a crude timber dock up ahead. As the canoe reached the side of the dock, the leader nimbly put his oar out to steady the craft. He and the others then climbed out, secured the canoes, and helped the rebels out of the murky water. Soon, they were all standing there, dripping water and shivering.

The fishermen swiftly led them away along a well worn dirt path. Yarni found Cerrin and they followed hand in hand. The path took them through a picturesque palm grove, the weathered trees crested by vivid green fronds that shook gently in the breeze. The palms were well spread out, the grove carpeted by high grass.

Across the grove was a village. By the time they reached it, at least fifty islanders had emerged from ramshackle houses with conical thatched roofs. All boasted the impressively wild hairstyles and piercings of bone. Some of the younger women bore babies in their arms. Cerrin was relieved to see that most of the faces were more curious than hostile.

At a gesture from their leader, the fishermen began inspecting the rebels and taking any weapons they saw. Some looked to Cerrin first, but she readily handed over her spear and so they followed her example. Erras gave up his knife but glanced suspiciously at the village.

"I hope they're not going to chop us up and eat us."

"Not a chance," said Murrit, running a hand through her wet hair. "The gods sent them to save us. They are children of the Great Forest, just as we are."

Approaching now was an older man whose voluminous hair was entirely white. He was flanked by two tall warriors, both holding curved cleavers with blades made of bone. He wore as little as the other islanders—nothing more than a skirt of hide around his waist and a similar circlet around his neck to protect his shoulders from the sun—but around his forehead, neck, wrists, and ankles were strings of shells, stones, and sun-bleached fish skulls.

Cerrin and the other rebels watched as the chief conducted a brief conversation with the leader of the fishermen, who explained himself in a calm, deferential tone. The chief asked several questions of him and at one point seemed angry.

"So they can talk," said Erras.

His comment attracted numerous looks of annoyance from the islanders, which at least saved Cerrin from shushing him.

When the conversation fell silent, the chief clasped his hands and gazed at the ground for some time. Then he walked up to the closest rebel, which happened to be Yarni. The chief tapped her twice on the head, then moved on to the next rebel and did the same.

Whether it meant they were accepted or condemned, Cerrin did not know—but the process continued until every rebel had been so touched.

At least we will live or die as one.

Count Talazeer sat upon a log, watching Elezz. She was talking with Sergeant Guldur and looking up at the four combat shells, which had just taken off to scout the islands. The shells hadn't been on the beach long—just long enough for Elezz to explain the situation and what she expected.

Talazeer fondled the trigger guard of his rifle and toyed with the idea of an "accidental" shooting in the forthcoming firefight. If the commander really were involved in the assassination attempt, her death would be a significant blow to his enemies, possibly even provoke them into revealing themselves. But this was not the right place nor time; with so much still unknown, it was a risk he could not yet take.

Marl had spent some time selecting a few pieces of driftwood, presumably for his carvings. He stood close by now, watching the combat shells as they reached the first island and separated to begin their search. Talazeer imagined the rebels clinging to rocks, desperately trying to scramble up onto the island. He supposed a few might have perished in the water, perhaps some of the young and the old. It was all rather pathetic.

Elezz snapped an order into her comcell, then threw up her hands in disgust.

"A problem, Commander?"

Shaking her head, she strode across the sand.

"Only a temporary one, sir, unless they have mastered the art of magic." She waved a hand toward the island. "According to those four, there's no sign of the rebels. They've disappeared."

Toll Maktar handed the remains of the regulator to Sonus. The vorsfeld tube was holed and warped. He held it in his hands and sat down on a nearby branch.

"The nano-drones might be able to—" began Sonus.

Maktar shook his head. "They draw power from the case. The cells are drained."

Sonus looked at the *Spectre*. Every muscle in his body was sore from the crash, and his neck gave him a white-hot jolt of pain when he turned too far in either direction. "Then we each grab a crate of weapons and start walking."

"Do you think your friends have that much time?" Maktar shook his head. "You fixed the *Spectre* once, Sonus. You can do it again."

"It's getting dark, Commander," said Count Talazeer.

Elezz stood with hands on hips, gazing toward the island. She did not reply.

Guldur and the other soldiers had removed their helmets and armor and were now milling around the beach.

"What's the bloody holdup, anyway? The drones have been up there for ages."

"Only thirty minutes, sir. Ah, perhaps we have something."

One of her faithful technicians was approaching, a mobile unit in his hand. "Commander, we're reading over one hundred humanoids on an island approximately three kilometers away. It is small, scarcely a kilometer wide, and not visible from here."

"Over a hundred?"

"Yes, Commander. It appears there's some kind of permanent settlement. Well, a few huts and boats. The drones have found no other traces in the area. I think the rebels must have found a few locals willing to hide them."

"Is there a suitable landing area for the shuttle?"

"No, Commander, but we can create one with munitions. The vegetation is nothing like as thick as the forest."

Elezz turned to Count Talazeer. "Sir, as you pointed out, it is getting dark. Not an ideal time to launch an assault. I would also prefer to gather more combat shells—ten, at least—to surround the island before landing and attacking."

"*Another* delay, Commander?"

"Unless you'd prefer to bombard the island from the air right now, sir? We could eliminate them all in three minutes, locals included."

Talazeer only glared at the commander.

"We can patrol the island with shells throughout the night. The rebels aren't going anywhere. And daylight will make for better video of our victory to show the laborers at the mines. Shall we attack at dawn, sir?"

Talazeer couldn't fault the commander's logic. "Very well, but you are entirely responsible for ensuring that there are no more surprises, Commander. I want this settled tomorrow."

Neither the Palanians nor the Echobe could understand a word of the islanders' language. Nonetheless, it was clear that their execution was not imminent. Instead, they had been provided a welcome meal of fresh fish and fruit, hosted by the chief.

Now, he led them back to the center of the village, apparently keen to show them something. While he went to fetch it, Cerrin and the other rebels stood in a group, surrounded by the villagers, who still could not take their eyes off them. Cerrin had never been so grateful to have the young ones with them. Yarni and the other three children had been invited to play a game involving sticks with the local children, and this gave them all something to watch while they waited.

Erras walked over to Cerrin and Torrin. "They don't have much."

"No metal and not much wood," said Torrin. "All those cleavers and knives are made of bone."

"Not much use against the Vitaari," said Cerrin. "They could be here at any time. Do we really want to drag these people into our fight?"

"What choice do we have?" asked Erras. "They must have known the risk they were taking."

"I wonder how many more there are," said Torrin. "On the other islands, I mean. Incredible that the Vitaari missed them."

Cerrin had already given that some thought. "Like you said— no metal. Which means no mines."

The locals and the newcomers all turned as the chief reappeared, followed by six warriors, including the leader of the fishermen, now carrying a bone cleaver at his waist. Cerrin was stunned to see that the men were carrying three skeletons, one that of a child. The heads of the skeletons had been wrapped with more of the shell bindings like those the chief wore. The islanders treated the remains with great care, and the locals knelt respectfully as the bones were lowered to the ground.

Torrin quickly matched the gesture, then Cerrin. Soon all of the rebels were also on their knees, including Yarni and the children.

The chief stood solemnly, now holding a long staff crowned by a great fish jaw full of teeth.

The fishermen's leader—who was clearly an individual of some standing—crouched over the skeletons and pointed out marks on the bones. These were not cuts or abrasions; they were burns— the result of energy weapons or bombs. Such sights were nothing new to Cerrin and the other rebels.

"Killed by the Vitaari," she whispered to Torrin. "But when? During the invasion?"

"Maybe. Maybe they fled here."

One of the other men opened a bag made of fish-skin and retrieved a much larger skull. The size and shape of the head were unmistakable—a Vitaari.

Feeling eyes upon her, Cerrin turned to Murrit, who responded with a knowing nod.

"Gods," whispered Torrin. "They killed at least one of them, then."

The chief came forward, facing the newcomers. He spoke for some time, his expression growing fierce. For a moment, Cerrin wondered if his anger was directed at the rebels; was that why he had shown them the dead?

Then the chief raised his staff high and brought it down with both hands, splintering the Vitaari skull.

Talazeer dined in his quarters: one of the better efforts from the ship's chef, which he ate with a passable wine. As Marl returned to his carving, the Count sat at the table and reviewed the latest reports from the mines. The terodite switch was now largely complete and yield results were at record levels. Better still, there were no reports from Governor Selerra of any further difficulties with the Kinassans.

Everything was coming together perfectly. Talazeer smiled as he imagined the dramatic events of the next morning, then putting together an edited version to be viewed by every laborer on Corvos.

And, of course, his father.

He did not want to devote any more time to the poisoning investigation until the rebels were eliminated. He needed a good night's rest. But just as he rose from the table, a call came through. An anxious-looking Yullasir informed the Count that Viceroy Ollinder was requesting an immediate interview.

Talazeer put his discarded jacket back on and smoothed down his hair. Soon Ollinder's aged face filled the screen, his expression grave.

"Viceroy, to what do I owe this unexpected pleasure?"

"Talazeer, I must discuss a most important matter with you, but first of all, how are you feeling?"

"I'm fully recovered, thank you, sir."

"Good, good. Unfortunately, yours is not the only alarming incident I am dealing with at the moment."

"Sir?"

"Something is afoot, Talazeer, something deeply concerning. In the last week, there have been three assassinations in my sector. Two men were shot, one poisoned. It all points to some kind of plot, but… I can't say yet against whom. One of the victims was a member of Za-Ulessor like yourself, one of Za-Iddi, and one of Za-Yorrik. Why would anyone target all three families? It has been suggested to me that these are the first blows struck in some kind of clan war, but nothing like that has happened in centuries. I must ask if you have made any progress in identifying suspects. It is in the interests of all loyal Vitaari that we put an end to this before it gets out of hand."

Talazeer hesitated. He had no reason not to trust Ollinder, but something told him it might be dangerous to openly admit his suspicions to the Viceroy. And if this plot were real, could he be certain that Ollinder would act in his best interests?

"We have no definitive evidence as yet, sir. Might I ask what this plot is all about?"

"What is it always about? Power. Wealth. Individual family are always at each other's throats, quarreling over some personal slight or business rivalry. But this… To attack three circles at the same time, it's unheard of in modern history. It suggests a broad alliance of circles are moving against their rivals together. I have been in contact with other regional commanders. We are considering a direct appeal to Imperator Zensen. Some don't want to believe it, but we must bring the other clans together to act in concert if we are to avert disaster. Are you sure there's nothing you can tell me?"

"Viceroy, please be assured that if we have any reliable evidence, you will be the first to know. Do you really think this plot could have spread as far as Corvos?"

"From what I have heard, yes. On Oksaa VI, the investigating authorities uncovered some kind of communication network. The actual messages destroyed themselves upon inspection, but it seems they were using a state-of-the-art portable system to communicate covertly. Some kind of sub-space technology."

Talazeer watched Marl out of the corner of his eye. The Drellen had stopped carving.

23

The forest is silent. The rebels lie in a clearing, bodies broken and burned. Their eyes are open. He knows them all: Erras, Torrin, Yarni. Cerrin.

One hand is clenched in a fist, the other still grips her spear. Her dead stare is an accusation.

I wasn't there. I couldn't help them. I did nothing. Now they're gone.

Sonus opened his eyes, sat upright in the darkness. Toll Maktar had three small lights on.

"Are you all right? You cried out."

Still partly in the grip of the dream, Sonus shook his head and wiped his eyes. "What's going on?"

"I tried it again. The remaining impulsor still won't run."

Now it came back to him with a horrible clarity. Sonus had used a plasma beam to reshape and reconnect the vorsfeld tube to the regulator. He had done so three times, but on each occasion, the system had rejected it. Sonus wasn't surprised; the repair was rough and imprecise.

"Why did you let me sleep?" he said, hauling himself to his feet and stumbling through the maze of broken branches left by the *Spectre*'s crash landing.

"Don't you remember? You dropped the weapon and almost shot yourself in the leg."

Sonus did remember, but the canopy above was now daubed with smudges of light. "It's dawn."

He knelt and picked up the vorsfeld tube. After all the melting and reshaping, every inch of the surface was filled with grooves and knots, like tree bark.

He looked at the piece of bark on the ground, lying next to the pale, smooth wood it had fallen away from.

"A mold. We need a mold."

"Sure, but how's that easier to make than the tube itself?" asked the agent.

"We'll carve it from wood."

"Won't it just catch fire when we heat the vorsfeld?"

"We'll have to be very quick."

"I don't have any other ideas," replied Maktar. "Let's try it."

Sonus picked up a multi-purpose tool that included a blade he could carve with. "I'll need the right piece of wood."

Maktar gestured to the mass of broken trees that surrounded them. "Take your pick."

Cerrin was woken by Yarni.

"Something's happening."

It felt like the middle of the night—but Yarni was right. The village had become a hive of activity. The islanders were packing up their things or preparing weapons. Cerrin drank from the wooden mug of water Yarni offered her, then got up and went outside.

Though barely a word was being spoken, the villagers were hurrying this way and that—most of them carrying fish-skin bags or piles of wood or weapons. And Cerrin could see all this because the sun was already rising.

Torrin hurried over. "The old and the weak are gathering by the water. They keep gesturing to Murrit and the children. I think they're offering to move them off the island, too. Cerrin, they know the Vitaari are coming. They're readying themselves for the fight."

"Where will they take them?"

"I think the next island along. Do you want me to organize it?"

"Yes."

"Yarni, come on—that includes you."

The girl immediately shook her head. "I'm staying with Cerrin."

"I'll bring her along later."

"Very well," said Torrin, already on her way.

"I'm not leaving this island," said Yarni defiantly.

More of the other rebels were waking and emerging from various huts. Cerrin took Yarni's hand and knelt down in front of her.

"Yarni, I have a job for you. The old and the injured will need someone to look after them. You and the other children will have to do that. I know I can trust you to do the right thing."

The girl's face tightened with frustration. "But you need every-one to fight. *I* can fight. I can use a bow just like you showed me."

"And I know you'd fight well. But not today, Yarni."

"Please don't make me leave." She threw her arms around Cerrin. "Please."

"Listen to me. We might lose. If that happens, someone has to survive. Someone has to live on." Cerrin was gripping Yarni so tightly by both arms that the girl winced with pain. "There are only twenty-five of us left. Tomorrow, it may only be five. But we have to keep going. As many as possible, for as long as possible. Do you understand? You have to promise me you'll keep going, Yarni. Will you promise me that?"

There were twelve canoes and Yarni had taken her place in one. But she hadn't said a word to Cerrin, merely casting an accusing look back at her. Among those departing were several pregnant women who took charge of the oars along with some of the older islanders. Cerrin assumed farewells must have already occurred, because none of the other islanders were there to see them off.

Throughout the village, there was an air of steadfast purpose. The islanders were clearly a brave, practical people. She returned to find many already donning armor and practicing with their weapons. Some wore huge crab shells as gauntlets and chest-guards, and most were carrying the heavy bone cleavers, which looked like they could chop a limb off with ease.

An unarmored limb, she reminded herself.

There were women there, too, some as fearsome as the men. Cerrin wondered if any of them really understood what they faced.

As she made her way through a crowd that must have numbered a hundred, she saw Erras showing off one of the two remaining Vitaari rifles. The islanders clearly understood what it was, even if they had little idea how to use it.

Torrin led the village chief and the warrior-fisherman toward Cerrin. "I've made a little progress with names," she said as they drew near. "The chief is Ak-tra. And this—" he gestured to the other man— "is Uk-saa. They've already sent scouts out by canoe and on foot. I guess we'll know when the Vitaari are coming."

Cerrin didn't know what to feel. The kindness and courage of the islanders were inspiring, but she knew in all likelihood it was pointless.

Perhaps we should have died in the water.

If they had, the islanders might have carried on their simple lives in freedom. Now, their tribe would be wiped out forever. Murdered for a simple, unplanned act of compassion.

"You do realize that the Vitaari might just drop a bomb on us?" Cerrin said. "I don't imagine Count Talazeer and this Commander Elezz are very happy that any of us are still alive."

"We can't run forever, Cerrin. If we're to die, I want to die like this."

Erras appeared, and Cerrin realized that he wasn't alone. The islanders and rebels were all gathering around their two leaders.

Ak-tra raised his staff and all fell silent. As he spoke, Uk-saa took out his knife and began etching shapes in the sandy soil for all to see.

"Do they really know what they're up against?" whispered Cerrin.

Erras shrugged. "At least they have a plan."

"What exactly is the plan?"

Count Talazeer had intercepted Commander Elezz in the corridor between two loading bays. Every available trooper—

fifty-seven in total—would be loading onto the two shuttles for transport down to the island.

Elezz was again in dark fatigues, wearing a reinforced armored jacket with her usual sidearm in a holster. She had also tied her hair back.

"Sir, the drones and shells confirm that no one left the island during the night. Some scouts have been sighted, and a small party moved to a neighboring island about an hour ago."

"Why wasn't I—"

"Drone footage showed that the canoes contained pregnant women, young, and elderly. We can pick them up later."

"Ah."

"Were you aware of these islanders, Excellency?"

"Not at all," admitted the Count.

"It appears they have been generally overlooked. We cannot be sure what weaponry they have, but they seem primitive. My plan is to use the combat shells to clear a landing zone for the shuttles, then establish a perimeter while the first shuttle lands with ground troops. As soon as the troopers are clear, you and I will land in the second shuttle with the artillery team, if that's acceptable to you."

"Perfectly."

Elezz glanced around to ensure no one was close—other than Marl. "Sir, I've also received a message from my contact."

The Count was tempted to ask if it had come in via the portable sub-space transmitter. "Your Level 7 friend?"

"Yes. And he believes he has obtained crucial evidence regarding the attempt on your life. I will of course pass it on as soon as it arrives."

"Very good of you," said Talazeer evenly.

Elezz ran her fingers along the handle of her pistol. "Do you know, I actually feel rather sorry for them. They have no idea what's coming."

Talazeer watched her walk away.

Neither do you.

One of the islanders had spotted a drone, and Uk-Saa led Cerrin and Erras to the eastern side of the island to look at it. The four of them stayed in cover the entire time and watched the little machine ascend, far beyond the range of their rifles.

"So, what can we do?" said Erras. "They'll see every move we make."

She glanced at Uk-Saa, who frowned up at the drone. She doubted if he really grasped what the machines were, or the immense advantage they gave the Vitaari.

"We can't do anything from here," she said. "But at least we know. Let's get back to the village."

On the way, she and Erras used their best improvised sign language to try and explain to Uk-Saa how the drones worked. They didn't make much progress.

Once back in his village, Ak-tra seemed a man possessed. He marched up and down, bellowing out instructions. His warriors were digging four-foot-deep pits, mainly to the south of the village as there was little space for the Vitaari to land between it and the beach. As tactics went, Cerrin didn't think it a bad one.

As the Vitaari had monitored the island overnight, Cerrin had no doubt that they would now attack in great force. This would mean more troops than in the forest, at least one shuttle, and several combat shells. She would take one rifle, and Erras the other. They had eighty bullets between them: they would have to choose their targets carefully.

She couldn't stop thinking about the drones and the shells. Like birds, observing and attacking from above, they held every advantage. Unlike birds, they also had allies on the ground that they could direct using what they saw.

Cerrin knew she couldn't destroy those eyes in the sky. But maybe she could blind them.

Sonus could not just sit and do nothing.

His idea of using a wooden mold seemed to have worked. The wood smoked beneath the nearly molten vorsfeld, but it didn't immediately burst into flames. *Not enough oxygen between the metal and wood*, Sonus realized. This meant he could leave the tube in the mold much longer than anticipated, helping to ensure a smooth outer surface.

He and Maktar were now waiting for the metal to cool before removing the mold. While the agent stood over the component, wafting it with a broad leaf, Sonus set about clearing more debris away from the *Spectre*.

Looking up, he wondered how easy it would be to negotiate the hole they had created upon landing. The dream had been a powerful one, not the type that faded soon after waking. It stayed with him so strongly that he wondered if it was a vision, a premonition. He just hoped they could hold on a little longer.

"You heard that, yes?" asked Maktar suddenly.

"Heard what?"

"Sounded like a shuttle again. Maybe two."

. . .

The vessel descended, morning sunlight flooding the hold. Upon the screen, a tactical display showed the three drones and the eight combat shells surrounding the island. Two shells had been kept in reserve with a small maintenance crew on the nearby beach. Every single human life-sign on the island was being monitored by at least one of the aerial reconnaissance vehicles. Other than a few scouts, all were gathered in what appeared to be the only settlement.

"There is another way, sir," said Marl, who was sitting to Talazeer's right.

"Which is?"

"Talk to the rebels. Instruct them to surrender, so that the islanders are spared."

"Marl, I know you have a natural tendency to side with native populations, but those rebels have killed a number of our troops. Losses of this magnitude haven't been sustained on Corvos since the invasion. This is no time for half-measures. Their resistance ends today."

"No way to fight," muttered the Drellen. "Bombs and shells. No honor in it."

"Effective though," replied Talazeer. "And not everyone enjoys hand-to-hand combat as you do."

Elezz was to the Count's left, closely monitoring the screen. Today she had left her technicians on the *Galtaryax*. "Sir, the shells are in position. Shall I order them to strafe the village? Once the enemy is pinned down, we can drop the clearance-bomb and then begin landing Sergeant Guldur's unit."

"Go ahead, Commander."

. . .

Ak-tra seemed happy that his pits were finished, and so allowed Cerrin to employ some of his warriors. She had already made considerable progress building four great piles of foliage to the east of the village. Soon each pile was ten feet wide and five high, mostly wet leaves and sticks at the top with a good layer of dry wood at the bottom. She placed a trustworthy rebel beside each one, with a small fire already burning.

She now returned to the village, where everyone had once again gathered around Ak-tra. He and a few other men had produced several flasks and a number of tiny wooden cups. Ak-tra raised his staff to the sky and seemed to utter a prayer before pouring liquid from the flasks.

Erras pointed at the cups, then aimed a quizzical expression at Uk-Saa. The warrior-fisherman mimed drinking, then beat his chest and flexed his muscles.

"Makes you strong?"

"Could be alcohol," said Torrin. "Or something like it."

All the islanders drank the concoction and some of the Echobe, too.

"Why not?" said Erras, taking one for himself. "Might be the last drink I ever have." But having downed the contents of his cup, he grimaced. "Would have preferred a beer, to be honest."

Cerrin wouldn't tell her compatriots what to do, but she wanted to keep a clear head so she refused the drink.

As she looked on, Ak-tra emerged from his hut with a nasty-looking weapon she had already seen some of the men wearing. It was a thick gauntlet of fish-skin bristling with snapper teeth. Ak-tra gave Cerrin an approving grin, then offered it to her.

She took it and tried to appear appreciative.

"He must think a lot of you," said Torrin.

"Why do you say that?"

"Look around. None of their women are wearing them, only the senior men."

Cerrin couldn't refuse and reckoned it to be a useful weapon. She was about the same size as the chief and the gauntlet fitted well.

There were more surprises to come. Soon after taking their concoction, the islanders split into pairs and began fighting. But this was no half-hearted practice. They clashed fiercely, swinging the heavy cleavers one-handed, some also employing their knives. Blows were struck and soon many were bleeding.

"What in the Maker's name?" said Erras as they looked on.

By the time Ak-tra called an end to it, every one of the islanders had been cut, including the chief. He had fought with Uk-Saa, who was clearly his deputy.

"I guess they're ready now," observed Torrin.

In fact, there was one last piece of preparation. At the chief's order, several warriors came forward with little leather bags of stones, which each of them now secured to their belts. Cerrin noted that the stones were all of a similar size, heavy but ideal for throwing. She almost laughed at these most primitive of weapons but the reckless bravery of these people touched her. They really were like the Echobe.

Ak-tra then began directing the combined force of rebels and islanders toward the huts. As they began to move, a scout appeared, pointing to the south.

"Not good," remarked Erras. They could all see the line of combat shells advancing slowly above the trees, no more than a mile away. There was not a cloud in the sky, and the sun glinted on the white armor and transparent cockpits.

Torrin turned to Cerrin. "Is it time?"

"It is. I'll go. Erras, don't fire unless you're sure you can hit something. I might be a while."

Torrin began to speak but Cerrin was already on her way, gun over her shoulder. She sped along between the houses and defenders to her left and the intermittent line of pits to her right. She soon reached the first pile of wood and foliage, greatly relieved to find that the wind hadn't changed direction. Instructing the Echobe warrior there to light the pile, she continued south, stopping at each of the other three.

By the time the combat shells passed over the inlet, four thick trails of smoke were blowing across the approach to the village. Cerrin would have liked it to spread more but just hoped it would help.

She now sat with Lallan, a young Echobe warrior. They watched as the combat shells passed over the palm grove, engines rippling the blue-tipped grass. The machines spread out, arms lifting as they prepared to fire.

Then came a noise Cerrin had never heard before. A high-pitched whine, followed by another, then another. She realized small projectiles were detaching from the weaponry pods at the rear of the shells. One landed in the village and the first explosion went up, transforming a hut into a pile of sticks. Cerrin heard shouts from the defenders, then a second blast blew two islanders into the sky.

The smoke was at least growing thicker, drifting past the shells as they continued their slow advance above the palm grove. Cerrin imagined the soldiers inside the machines, recalled what

Sonus had told her about how the shells worked. She knew that the Vitaari generally used heat to identify targets on the ground. She thought of the inlet, and remembered arriving while holding on to the canoe. The lake water was very cold.

"Quite clever," observed Commander Elezz. "The smoke. It's hampering the drones and our sensors."

Count Talazeer snorted. "I wouldn't worry too much."

He was looking forward to seeing the battle footage but reminded himself to always behave in an appropriately heroic manner. It was, after all, essential that he play a starring role in this victory, or at least the edited version of it. Martial music and special effects could later be added to such presentations, enhancing the impact. Talazeer hoped the recording would become a revered part of his family's collection.

He watched as another hut went up in flames, sending the defenders scurrying into the pits they had dug, presumably to trap attackers.

"Ha! Commander, might I suggest that the shells switch to cannons—otherwise there's going to be nothing left for us."

"Yes, sir."

Sonus could do nothing more. He and Toll Maktar had replaced the repaired regulator and were now back inside the *Spectre*, waiting to see if the system would accept it. Only then could they try to actually start the last remaining impulsor. With the sun now up, the agent had also been able to activate an emergency solar power cell.

"It's happening," said Sonus, his whole body chilled by fear. "It's happening now and we're too late."

It had already been twenty minutes since Maktar had heard the shuttles.

"Here it comes," said Maktar, watching one of the smaller screens.

Sonus didn't need Maktar to translate the message. The system had not accepted it. The *Spectre* could not fly.

He had failed.

Maktar slumped back and shook his head. "It's only six kilometers. They're so close."

Tears taunted Sonus's eyes. He could not simply sit there.

"I'm going. I'm going to do what we should have done last night."

This time, Toll Maktar made no attempt to stop him.

24

Cerrin reached the inlet without incident. She hadn't actually spotted a drone but felt sure that the Vitaari could see her. She was well past the combat shells and now saw that they had ascended above the smoke to press the attack. They were at least using only the cannons, which gave the defenders some chance.

Cerrin slid down into the water, relieved that it was as cold as she remembered. She waded westward along the bank with the green sludge on top of the water splashing at her shoulders. Reaching a little cove, she lifted the gun up and rested it on a clump of grass, most of her body still in the water. Now she scoured the skies, searching for a gleam of white amid the azure sky and the gray smoke.

There.

The combat shell was about a hundred feet from the ground and three hundred away, the frame juddering slightly as the cannons fired. Cerrin had already selected semi-automatic; she couldn't afford to waste bullets. She told herself to ignore the sounds of the cannons and the shouts from the village.

Ikala, sharpen my sight, steady my hand.

She aimed carefully and depressed the firing stud.

She cursed. Her first shot was high.

But the second hit the shell, the impact visibly driving the machine backwards through the air. It spun around to face the unseen threat. She took a breath, fired five more shots, put most of them into the cockpit.

Eat that, shenk.

A small explosion on the shell's shoulder blew parts into the air. The vehicle veered left, then right, then began to spin wildly. Seconds later, it crashed into another shell. Somehow entangled, they spun around in a bizarre death grip, then abruptly dropped out of the sky.

A blast went up as they hit the ground. A cheer went up from the village.

Ikala, I thank you.

Cerrin slipped back into the water and set off again along the bank.

"Two?" exclaimed Count Talazeer. "How did they take out *two* that quickly?"

"Not sure, sir," replied Elezz, leaning forward in her seat to study the tactical screen. The second shuttle was in a holding position above the water, south of the island.

"Enough of this," said Talazeer. "Drop the clearance-bomb immediately. Once we're on the ground, this will be over in minutes."

"Perhaps we should wait a little longer, sir."

"So that we can lose more shells? Do you know how much those things cost? Drop the bomb—but make sure it doesn't take out the village."

"Yes, sir. Combat shells, withdraw to close cordon. Shuttle one, this is Commander Elezz. Use pre-sighted target point three. I want the southern half of that palm grove levelled."

"Acknowledged, maneuvering now. Dropping in one minute."

Sonus was already on his way. Using the sun to guide him, he ran with one Raxis rifle in each hand, two runner guns over his shoulders, and a backpack full of ammunition.

It was the first time since he'd crashed down in the river outside of Mine Three that he actually wished he'd had a combat shell to fly in. His legs were already aching. His spine was on fire.

He imagined himself racing through the air, rockets at his feet and on his back. It didn't help distract him. It only made him regret his failure with the impulsor all the more.

Flying with impulsors was smooth, graceful, nothing at all like a shell. The shell's thrusters were more like the *Spectre*'s reserve booster, crudely jolting you this way and that.

But at least it was still flying. Better than running. Better than lugging fifty pounds of guns and ammo on your shoulders. In shell, you didn't feel the weight of your weapons at all.

He imagined himself in a shell, carrying all the weapons in their crates—no, carrying the *Spectre* itself on his shoulders, hefting it into the sky, with only its reserve booster to help keep it aloft. Even better, he could fly with the *Spectre* on his back, racing straight into the battle, and toss runner guns down to Cerrin and all her people.

He might have laughed out loud at the thought if not for his lack of breath, if not for the burning in his legs and spine.

No, the *Spectre* was too heavy, even for a combat shell's thrusters. If not, the reserve booster alone might be enough to—

Sonus stopped running.

Then he turned and ran back for the shuttle without feeling the weight of the weapons on his back.

"Toll!"

The agent was sitting next to the lifeless shuttle. "What is it?"

"What if we strip the *Spectre* of everything but the reserve booster? Would it be light enough to fly?"

"What do you mean?"

"The anti-matter drive. The defensive systems. The computers. Any pieces of the hull that can be removed. Anything and everything."

Maktar looked away from Sonus and rubbed the middle of his forehead with two fingers. After a moment, he said, "If I understand you correctly, you want to dismantle my ship until it's nothing but a chair and steering column strapped to a primitive booster rocket."

"That, and fifteen crates of alien weaponry."

"Fourteen crates," said Maktar. "We leave the high explosives behind, yes? The landing may be a bit rough."

"But it's worth a try?"

"Definitely."

The shuttle blotted out the sun, casting a dense shadow over Cerrin as it slowly drifted toward the palm grove. Sonus had once told her that the vessel's fuel tanks were situated toward the rear, between the two back landing struts. These were not armored military vessels. They were vulnerable.

This was too good an opportunity to miss.

Cerrin threw her rifle onto the bank and dragged herself up. She looked behind her to check that there were no combat shells close by and found that she was clear. Scarcely able to believe her luck, she ran until she was amidst the grass of the grove.

Stop.

Stop and think.

She wasn't sure where the voice came from. Was it hers? Ikala's? Some other god?

Her hands didn't lift the gun, even though she was now in a perfect position to shoot. She simply looked up and noted the unusual module fitted to the right side of the hull. She hadn't seen one of those before. It was too small to be a fuel tank. What else—

She was already running, sprinting back toward the water, gun in both hands. With the combat shells now silent and the village some distance away, it was surprisingly quiet: so quiet in fact that she actually heard the bomb detach from the shuttle.

She dropped the gun as she reached the bank and launched herself into the air.

Everything went white.

The very air seemed to disappear, as if sucked into some invisible maw.

The shockwave hit, knocking all the breath out of her, propelling her head over feet.

Then came an ear-splitting, gut-wrenching explosion that seared her exposed skin.

She fell headfirst into the water, sunk low until the need for air sent her back up again. By then, the glare of the detonation was beginning to recede but the air tasted horribly bitter.

Almost the entire surface of the inlet was strewn with shattered trees.

At least they won't see me, she thought, before realizing she had lost the rifle.

Holding on to a nearby branch to keep steady, Cerrin splashed water on her still-warm face, aware that her eyebrows and hair had been singed. The bomb seemed to have wiped a quarter-mile of the island clean. Only a few spots of green remained where the palm grove had been. She could now see clear to the huts of the village.

The shuttle descended.

Count Talazeer watched as the first vessel touched down and the troops began to file out. His shuttle was already maneuvering, ready to land as soon as the other ship was out of the way. Beside him, Marl ran his usual checks over his alien weapon, having spent much of the morning cleaning and sharpening his sword. Talazeer imagined that the Drellen had mixed feelings about what was to come. He clearly had some sympathy with the out-matched rebels, but the bodyguard seemed to relish combat above all else.

"Sergeant Guldur's unit is down, sir. I've ordered him to advance on the village and begin the assault."

"Very good, Commander."

With a sideways glance at Elezz, Talazeer reminded himself to be careful and stay close to Marl at all times. As easy as it might be for him to arrange an "accident" on the battlefield, it would be equally as simple for her. Was she part of Viceroy Ollinder's plot? If Za-Ulessor really was involved, he was surprised that his father and brother remained in the dark. They might be very grateful—and very impressed—if he were the one to bring it to their attention.

By the time he snapped out of such thoughts, his shuttle had landed. Once the ramp was deployed, thirty troopers marched down onto the scarred earth below. Only then did Elezz rise from her seat, followed by Talazeer and Marl.

Talazeer was excited by the prospect of battle. He was a member of the Colonial Guard but had never really felt like a soldier. Occasions like this were to be enjoyed—something to tell the relatives when back on Vitaar, perhaps even on Founding Day. With the resistance crushed and the Corvos operation contributing to the Domain like never before, he would have much to be proud of.

Talazeer was about to lead the other two down the ramp when Commander Elezz spoke his name. She was staring down at the remote unit attached to the inside of her left forearm. But instead of the expected tactical display, it showed what looked like a message.

"Sir, my contact sent me this. I… think it's best that you see it now. I wouldn't want to delay something so important."

"What do you mean? What do you have there?"

Elezz rubbed the back of her neck, her expression unusually grave. "Sir, his investigators were able to access security scanners from Nexus Nine, where our supply freighters come from—including the one that delivered the poisoned gift. Apparently, most of the scanners at the facility were disabled by some kind of disruptor field. But there have been some recent thefts and a second level of security was installed—a fact the culprit clearly wasn't aware of."

"What are you talking about?"

"Sir, imager footage shows an infiltrator accessing one of the cargo containers—the one in which your package was placed. We even have his face."

Elezz approached Talazeer and showed him the screen. The footage followed a man entering the facility, then using some tool to open a cargo container and plant a package. On his way out, the imagers had obtained a very clear picture.

"You know him, I presume," said Elezz, reading the Count's expression.

"I know him. His name is Verresur. He works for my brother."

Sonus was amazed that they even got off the ground. Toll Maktar's description of a chair strapped to a rocket was greatly exaggerated, but he had dismantled the entire underside of the ship to remove all of its mechanical guts, computer systems, and engines. And he had not replaced the hull panels when he was done, leaving the belly of the ship looking skeletal, like a beast being eaten from the bottom upward.

Pulling out all of the cabling had taken the longest, but despite Sonus's impatience, they both wanted to be thorough. Any removable item, no matter how heavy or light, was ripped out and tossed aside. The pile of discarded machinery left at the crash site had looked twice as large as the *Spectre* as a whole.

On its way up, the ship took out more tree branches but somehow hauled itself into the air.

"Even worse than I thought, yes?" yelled Maktar as the ship lurched and shuttered its way across the bright morning sky.

Hands gripping the seat straps, barely able to stop himself vomiting, Sonus looked out of the nearest viewport. He saw only flashes of sky and forest.

Cerrin had also lost her spear. She ran with only her knife on her belt, determined to skirt around the first wave of Vitaari soldiers and join her people on the defensive line. They were two hundred feet from the southern edge of the village.

The first rain of arrows began to fall on the soldiers in their green armor and black helmets. Cerrin herself was the only one in danger from the falling projectiles, though she kept far to their right, hiding as best she could as she ran along the tree line. She just hoped there would be some close combat; surely Uk-Saa and his fellow warriors could do some damage.

She was approaching one of her smoke pyres, still burning and fuming, though it was now only as tall as her knee. The rebel guard was long gone, as instructed. Cerrin halted there for a moment to check on the Vitaari. She was ahead of them now, but even more troops were emerging from the second shuttle. The engines of that vessel were quiet at last, but she could hear something else: an intermittent blast coming from above and behind her. She turned and looked up.

There, careening through the air in fits and starts, was the skeletal remains of *Spectre*. Despite the state of the stricken craft, Cerrin's spirits soared.

By all the gods, Sonus did it! He's here.

And she knew instantly what she had to do.

. . .

As the floor rolled out from under him once more, Sonus threw his hands out and somehow held tight to the edge of the viewport.

He'd removed his straps and stood up from his seat because there were no longer any sensors or computers to tell them where to land—it could only be done by eye.

When the *Spectre* spun to the left, he at last spied the line of islands stretching away across the vast lake. And there could be no doubt about where the battle was unfolding: Several patches of forest were on fire and a Vitaari shuttle had landed on a broad, uneven circle of scorched ground.

"Where is it?" shouted Maktar. "We've only a few bursts left. We have to get down now!"

"The island is dead ahead. There's a Vitaari ship we need to stay away from."

"Find us somewhere to land!"

Then he saw it. Puffs of smoke rising at regular intervals. Just south of some sort of settlement.

As they got closer, he realized he could see small figures moving around. He didn't know if it was the rebels or someone else but they certainly weren't Vitaari.

"Looks like we're being signaled. To the right. Lose altitude if you can."

Maktar obeyed—and it was all Sonus could do to hold himself in place and not get flung across the cockpit.

Then he heard a thrumming on the rear of the *Spectre*.

Cannon fire.

Cerrin threw aside the branch she had used to control the smoke and watched the combat shell pursue the *Spectre*. Fire was blooming from its cannons and she heard the impacts as Maktar's ship zoomed overhead, dropping at an alarming rate. Cerrin cursed, even before she saw a second shell join the pursuit.

The *Spectre* began to pitch forward but again somehow corrected itself. Then it dropped suddenly—a hundred feet, at least—only to halt in mid-air, veer toward the water again, and drop behind a cluster of palm trees. Cerrin heard a loud impact but there was no explosion.

Please be alive. Please have the weapons.

Then came the familiar clatter of the Vitaari assault rifles. Cerrin was close to the east side of the village, roughly parallel with the first rank of attackers. She spied islanders and rebels sheltering behind the remains of the houses and dropping into the pits. Bullets plowed into the sandy soil. A fleeing islander was hit in the back, dropping in an instant behind a red puff of blood.

Cerrin broke cover and ran for the nearest hut.

Talazeer had not moved. Dragging his eyes off the screen, he now stood staring blankly down the ramp. The troops were already long gone. Commander Elezz and Marl remained by his side.

"Sir, I know this must be difficult for you. I apologize for the timing but I thought you'd want to see that right away. May I join the soldiers?"

Talazeer didn't reply.

He had first told himself that it couldn't possibly be true, that the footage must have been doctored, that Elezz was manipulating him, that this was some elaborate ploy. And yet it was by far the most illuminating piece of evidence he'd seen. It pointed the finger of guilt squarely at his own brother, even his own father, an idea that should have seemed beyond comprehension.

And yet it was not. Cold logic told him as much. His father had not even wanted to see him and his mother wanted to disown him. Had one or more of them decided that—after his failure to immediately defeat the rebels—he was too much of a liability? That it was better for the family and the clan if he were simply eliminated?

It would hardly be the first time a Vitaari had been betrayed by his own—sacrificed for the greater good of his clan. It wouldn't even be the first time in his own family. And yet, it seemed almost impossible to accept.

"Sir?" said Marl, one hand on his master's arm.

Talazeer sensed pity in the Drellen's voice and it sickened him. Whatever anyone else—even his own family—thought of him, he was still a nobleman and still the Administrator of Corvos. And he was about to lead the concluding action of this anti-insurgency operation. The accursed rebels would now taste defeat and suffering.

He shook Marl off, glared at him. "This… other matter can wait. Come, both of you. Let us see red blood run."

Count Talazeer took his hunting rifle from his shoulder and led the way down the ramp.

Ak-tra's pits were doing some good. Islanders and rebels alike had jumped into them, avoiding the worst of the Vitaari gunfire and fighting back by flinging stones. The islanders used slings and were well practiced, striking the soldiers again and again in the facemasks. To Cerrin's surprise, the constant barrage was slowing their advance, impeding their aim, and even cracking some of their visors. One stone knocked the rifle right out a soldier's hand, and the islanders sent up a cheer.

But slowing the soldiers was not the same as stopping them. Another fifty feet, and the Vitaari would be looking down over the edge. Then, the pits would go from sheltering the defenders to pinning them in while they were mowed down from above. Before that happened, they'd have no choice but to climb up and charge into the gunfire, praying to reach the giants and swarm them in hand-to-hand combat.

Those prayers would go unanswered, Cerrin knew. Death awaited them either way. Unless—

"You saw Maktar's ship?"

It was Torrin, spear in hand, running toward her from behind one of the huts.

"Yes. Do you know where it came down?"

"This way—hopefully not in the water."

The pair sped through the trees, away from the noise of gunfire and the hail of stones.

"There!" cried Torrin, turning to her left.

Cerrin followed and soon spied the *Spectre*—intact, but half-buried in sand.

The hatch was open, and three boxes had already been pushed out onto the ground.

"Sonus!" cried Cerrin.

But it was Toll Maktar who leaped out, body covered in his metallic armor, holding a bulky gun with a strange double barrel.

Before he could say anything, bullets pinged off the far side of the *Spectre*. Cerrin saw the two combat shells approaching from the water, arms raised, cannons firing.

As Cerrin and Torrin sought cover behind the stern, Maktar ran past them. He knelt down, took aim with the new gun, and fired.

His first shot missed. Cerrin thought that the second shot missed, too, because the combat shell barely moved.

Then she saw debris strike the water. Seconds later, the vehicle simply dropped out of the sky, hitting the lake with a great splash. The other combat shell turned and fled.

Torrin turned to Cerrin, eyes wide. "Gods alive!"

Two more boxes were chucked unceremoniously out of the hatch. Then Sonus leaped down—to find himself right beside Cerrin. Clad in strange black clothes, he started to speak but stumbled over his words. And so he shook his head instead and offered a broad grin.

Cerrin smiled, too, and resisted the temptation to throw her arms around him.

"You're alive," he said. "I knew it."

"For now." She pointed back at the village. "They're defenseless."

With a nod, Sonus reached for the nearest box and opened it. "Not anymore."

Each carrying a runner gun, the four of them sprinted toward the village. The plan was to force the Vitaari to fall back from the pits through the pure surprise of meeting genuine resistance. It would likely only take one or two deaths for the soldiers to retreat and regroup. As soon as they did, Maktar would start leading rebels and islanders back to the ship to distribute the rest of the weapons. He had already activated the scrambler he'd purchased on Xerxa, which would hopefully deal with the Vitaari drones.

Sonus would have preferred to be with Cerrin, but she was at the front, followed by Maktar. When they split off to the right, Sonus had no choice but to follow Torrin to the left.

They approached the combat zone from behind a hut. Climbing in through a low window, they crossed the dark interior and crouched by the doorway. The line of Vitaari soldiers were almost on top of the pits now, but only half were firing their weapons. Then Sonus saw what the other half were doing— pulling and prepping grenades from their belts.

"We have to hit them now," he said.

"I'm ready," said Torrin, crouching beside him.

"Aim low," replied Sonus. "These things have quite a kick."

Sonus aimed at a big man with a grenade in his hand. The blue diamond on his sleeve denoted the rank of sergeant. When a stone bounced off his armored chest, the Vitaari laughed.

"He's mine," said Sonus, settling on one knee to steady himself.

He was the first to fire. The range was no more than forty feet and the sergeant's head simply disappeared, showering the troops near him in black blood. As the headless corpse tottered backwards and crashed to the ground, the surrounding soldiers seemed to freeze.

Either Cerrin or Maktar fired next. The shot tore the arm off one Vitaari and struck another behind him, toppling both men. Then it was Torrin's turn, and she punched a hole through the center of a soldier's chestplate.

As the other three kept firing, Sonus turned to watch Torrin. With unblinking eyes, she unleashed two more lethal shots.

"Be sure of your aim," he advised. "The magazines are small."

The panicked Vitaari clearly had no idea where their new foes were firing from. A few retreated, but others were shooting blindly at the huts. Sonus and Torrin were forced to lay low—but the volley abruptly ended.

Sonus looked up to see the soldiers all staring at their guns, thumping them or shaking them, apparently unable to make them work.

Then he remembered Toll Maktar's boast about his armor's scrambling capabilities. The Vitaari couldn't fire.

The islanders reacted first to the enemy's sudden confusion. Without hesitation—and seemingly without fear—they hauled themselves out of the pits and charged the Vitaari, weapons high and shouting.

"Ha!" shouted Torrin. "Uk-Saa will show them how a real man fights!"

The soldiers towered above the island warriors, who hacked away at knees, stomachs, and groins with their cleavers. Some strikes bounced off the armor, but others knocked away the plates or found gaps.

The soldiers answered by wielding their rifles as clubs and swinging wildly at their swarming enemies. Some of the rebels began to rise from the pits now, armed with spears and ready for blood.

Sonus lifted his runner gun, tried to find a target, then lowered it again. He did not trust his aim enough to fire over the heads of his friends and allies, especially not at a moving target. Nor was he certain his gun would work while Maktar's scrambler was active.

But he was certain of one thing: the Vitaari were not in a

position to retreat. Surrounded by raging islander warriors, they'd be unable to withdraw even if they wanted to. Plans to lead the rebels back to the *Spectre* had been swept away by the tides of battle.

If he hoped to arm his friends, he'd need a new strategy.

"Torrin, stay here," he said. "I'm going to get the rest of the weapons."

25

"Why aren't you men moving?" demanded Elezz.

The second rank of soldiers—the ones who'd travelled with them in the shuttle—were huddled up a thousand meters from the settlement, watching the melee from afar.

"Trying to get updated intel on the enemy, sir, but... the drones aren't transmitting," said the group's leader, a lieutenant by his insignia, though Talazeer didn't know his name.

"How much intel do you need on a bunch of savages with fishing poles, Lieutenant?" scoffed the Count.

"The first group are not firing their rifles," observed Marl quietly.

Elezz reached for her coms. "Sergeant Guldur, what—"

"He's dead, Commander," said the lieutenant bitterly. "Decapitated. They have some kind of ballistic weaponry. They've killed several of ours already."

"The ship on the beach," said Elezz. "Delivering weapons. Allied to the Red Regent, as we suspected."

Talazeer looked past the troops and saw a Vitaari soldier grab one of the primitives and fling him ten feet through the air. But then the soldier was swarmed by three more warriors, fell to his knees, and was lost to sight amid the melee.

"This is shambolic, Commander," hissed Talazeer. "We *must* prevail. What about the shells?"

"Not suitable for close combat," murmured a soldier.

"They'd kill as many of ours," said Elezz. "We'll do this the old-fashioned way. Guardsmen, with me." She drew her handgun and marched past the soldiers, who obediently followed.

"Sir," said Marl. "Your body armor may not be sufficient against these new weapons and your head is not protected."

"I'm not wearing a bloody helmet," spat the Count.

The Drellen scratched his scaly cheek. "Then it might be wise to hold back, at least until we have the upper hand."

"And miss all the action? Marl, sometimes I really don't think you understand me at all."

A Vitaari soldier retreated from the prodding spears of three Echobe and never saw Uk-Saa behind him. The bone cleaver sank into the back of the soldier's knee, and he crumpled to the ground. Uk-Saa leapt on top of him, wrenched his helmet up, and unleashed another swing that colored the air with black blood.

Cerrin was preparing to charge from the hut, knife in hand, when Toll Maktar gripped her arm.

"What?" she snapped.

"Your friends are winning. We can do more against *them*, yes?" The agent pointed beyond the melee. A second line of Vitaari troops was now stalking along the path toward the village.

Cerrin glanced at his bracelet. "Can that thing disable *their* guns, too?"

"Not from here. It won't work much longer anyway—not enough power. But it's not the only surprise under our hats, yes? Let's move. We can spring another trap."

Sonus had collared Erras and four other rebels on his way to the *Spectre*. Now he was showing them how to load the Raxis rifles. It wasn't a difficult process, and in less than minute, he was ready to lead them back into the fight.

"Not you, Erras," he said, lifting an open hand. "See that box—there's another runner gun. You take it, shoot at any combat shell you see. Protect the ship and the rest of the weapons."

"Got it."

Sonus set off back toward the village.

As the second rank approached the battle, an injured soldier limped toward them from the first. He was gripping his thigh, where one of the islander's cleavers had left a nasty wound.

"You there," said Elezz. "Where are the projectile weapons shooting from?"

"Not sure, Commander. Seemed to come out of nowhere. But no weapons seem to be working now, not on either side."

Elezz surveyed the area in front of them. "Even so. They weren't in the pits with the others or they would have fired on you sooner. They must be on the flanks."

Talazeer looked on, impressed, as she dispatched squads of five to both sides of the path. "Guardsmen, do not get involved in the battle. Your job is to look outward, find the source of any incoming fire, and take them out."

. . .

Despite the noise of the nearby melee, Cerrin sensed a presence behind her. She turned but could see no one nearby the thorny bush where she and Maktar had stopped. And when she looked back toward the path, the Vitaari were fanning out in their direction.

The first of them halted at the path's edge, barely twenty feet away.

"Ah," said Maktar with a grimace. "It appears somebody wants to avoid making the same mistake twice. But perhaps we have another opportunity."

"What do you mean?"

The agent nodded toward the great metal fin of the shuttle visible beyond the palm grove. He then aimed a thumb at the small pack on his back. "I have an iridium mine here—designed for hardened targets. That shuttle is a civilian vessel. The mine will take it out easily."

Cerrin didn't answer at once. She didn't like the idea of abandoning the defense.

"Then you and I can strike the second battalion from behind, yes?" added Maktar, as if reading her thoughts. "But we must be quick."

Cerrin was about to tell him to go alone when she heard the rattling of a weapon, followed by an agonized cry.

She eased to her feet and looked back at the village. Armed with a smaller type of gun, Sonus ran up beside Ak-tra and fired at a Vitaari, hitting the soldier in the helmet with several rounds. As the visor shattered, the Vitaari fell. There were perhaps now only fifteen of them standing. As more rebels climbed out of the pits, Sonus handed them weapons. Three others appeared, also bringing guns.

Cerrin was already moving. "Maybe you're right."

Though still nauseous and shaken from the crash landing, Sonus was almost enjoying himself. He switched from target to target, picking his moment to ensure that when he fired, he didn't endanger those on his side. Occupied with defending themselves from spears, cleavers, and slings, the Vitaari stood little chance. One blast from the runner gun easily put them down.

Sonus had already seen many wounded and dead friends. But for once, the rebels held the advantage; he was not about to waste it.

The Raxis rifles rattled. The runner guns emitted their low thumps. Plasma beams flashed at the attackers.

All around him, the Vitaari fell.

The gray-hulled shuttle sat on three landing struts, the underside coated by dust. Behind the cockpit was the bulky body, atop that the tall fin bearing the insignia of the Vitaari Colonial Guard. Thanks to the bomb dropped by its sister ship, the shuttle was a hundred paces clear of any cover, so Cerrin and Toll Maktar took an arcing route around to the right side. Planting themselves behind palms, they each targeted one of the two guards beneath the bow and stern of the ship.

As she aimed, Cerrin now realized her vision had been affected by the bomb blast. Her first shot with the unwieldy runner gun missed, and by the time she was ready to fire again, Maktar had done her work for her. The two pilots in the shuttle cockpit were oblivious; they had not seen the guards fall into the dust.

"Let's go," said the agent.

Sonus was seeking his fourth victim when something grazed his leg. He only realized that something was a bullet when pain shot into his left calf and he fell. Looking down, he saw that the shell had torn a hole in his trousers. He was bleeding—but not badly.

One of the islanders crashed to the ground beside him, face shattered by another bullet. Sonus looked up to see a second wave of Vitaari approaching.

"Back! Everyone back!"

Sonus took five painful paces and slid over the lip of the nearest pit, finding himself beside the white-haired warrior who seemed to lead the islanders. Both were forced to duck as bullets thumped into the sand inches from their faces.

When he looked back, he was astonished to see a Vitaari female waving the soldiers onward. And with her, two familiar figures: Count Talazeer and his reptilian bodyguard.

Once in the shadow of the shuttle's wing, they halted. Cerrin reckoned it unlucky that the shuttle's ramp wasn't still down, but Toll Maktar already had a plan. He hurried over to the three-clawed landing strut and looked upward.

"We have to attach the mine to the hull. It will take most of this side with it and hopefully ignite the fuel tanks. How are you at climbing, Cerrin?"

She pushed away thoughts of Jespa. "Better than you."

With a grin, Maktar put his pack down and retrieved the mine, which was semi-circular in shape and clearly quite heavy. He pointed out a small dial in the middle of the device. "Hold it against the hull and turn this to activate the mag-lock." He then flipped open a little door. "Timer. Three minutes?"

Cerrin looked up at the strut. It was about twelve feet high but there were plenty of holds.

"Make it two."

Sonus was no longer sure which way the battle would go. As soon as the defenders started diving for the pits to avoid the strafing gunfire, the few surviving Vitaari soldiers had fled to join the approaching battalion. In the chaos, there'd been no way to count how many rebels or islanders were left alive, but Sonus's best guess was around thirty—roughly the same as the soldiers marching their way.

Even numbers.

Even weaponry.

It was more than he might have dared to pray for just a few weeks ago, had he been inclined toward prayer. Even so, he couldn't say the odds were even.

What the soldiers did have was leadership. They advanced slowly but steadily, not faltering when one of their number was wounded or killed. The runner guns were taking quite a toll. Sonus had downed another Vitaari himself and seen three more taken out. Yet he could still hear the female commander: her voice resolute and clear.

At her order, the soldiers on the flanks split away toward the forest, a clear attempt to surround them. Sonus called out to those in the closest pits to target them, but no one could hear over the gunfire. He knew in time the soldiers would get around behind them. Then there'd be no doubt which way the battle would go.

A grenade rolled into the pit next to his. The detonation was muffled by the sand, but a great blast went up and the ravaged body of a rebel landed close by, showering Sonus and the white-haired leader with blood.

Though they continued to lose men, the new Vitaari battalion was now within twenty paces of the pits—weapons still working, still spraying bullets and death.

The white-haired man moved toward the body lying close by and touched the dead woman's face tenderly. Then, with a roar, he pulled himself out of the pit. All of the other islanders—thirty at least—began to clamber out, too.

"No!" cried Sonus, but realized there was no stopping them. "Fire! Everyone, fire! Give them a chance!"

Several warriors were cut down as they raced toward the enemy, but—whether because they'd heard Sonus's words or they all had the thought—the rebels rose and fired their weapons as one. Black and red blood sprayed through the air.

The warriors met the Vitaari with cleavers raised. Knowing speed was their only chance, they again hacked and slashed at their foes. The white-haired chief grabbed the barrel of a Vitaari rifle but was pulled off his feet as the soldier lifted it. Sonus aimed for the soldier's chest but tore a foot-wide hole through his stomach.

Close enough.

Sonus searched for the female commander, hoping to bring her down next, but found Count Talazeer. The sleek nobleman was down on one knee, his rifle aimed directly at—

Sonus threw himself to the ground and heard the bullet whizz past his head. He'd kept his hands on the runner gun. Staying low, he returned fire.

Talazeer heard a loud crack and the rifle was torn from his grasp. He looked down at his hands in shock, then gingerly flexed his wrist—it stung but wasn't broken.

Marl grabbed his shoulder. "Sir, we *must* fall back. The rebels have the advantage now."

The Count looked to Commander Elezz. Handgun ready, she had stopped barking orders for the moment. It was the first time Talazeer had ever seen doubt on her face.

"Marl is right," she said. "We can take off and drop the second bomb."

"We *cannot* lose!" hissed the Count. As the shame of another defeat struck him, he suddenly found himself gripping Elezz by the collar.

She glanced down at his fingers, then at his face, unmoved. "Sir, remove your hand or I will remove it myself."

He did so, then spoke again in a calmer tone. "We cannot lose, Commander."

"We *will* not!"

A plasma beam shot past, the Count feeling the heat of it on his face.

With a last shake of her head, Elezz turned and ran back toward the shuttle.

Cursing, Talazeer shook off Marl's hand and followed her along the path.

. . .

Cerrin dropped to the ground beside the landing strut. "How long?"

"Thirty seconds," said Toll Maktar.

They set off toward the trees but had only taken ten paces when they heard a cry: "Cerrin!"

The voice was one she knew. One she loved. Cerrin froze, unable to turn. Unable to breathe.

How could that voice be here?

Maktar spun around, and only then did Cerrin do the same. She saw Yarni on the far side of the clearing, running toward the shuttle.

At once, Cerrin sprinted at the girl, her face burning with fury. As she passed under the stern of the shuttle, Yarni seemed to realize something was wrong and stopped running. "Sorry, I only just caught up and I didn't want to lose you a—"

Cerrin grabbed her hand and—barely breaking her stride— dragged her violently toward the trees ahead. They had almost reached cover when the mine detonated. She threw herself over the girl and they both crashed to the ground.

Cerrin's immediate fear was being pierced by shrapnel or crushed by falling debris. She clung tightly to Yarni, covering as much of the girl's body as possible. She heard heavy pieces of metal crash down, but it seemed the sounds were far behind her. Only then did she realize her eyes were closed and force herself to open them.

One flaming wing of the shuttle had been ripped away and thrown into the trees on the far side of the clearing. Thick black smoke poured from the gaping wound on the shuttle's side, but there was no sign of fire until a second explosion tore the craft in two.

Superheated air rippled across the clearing, forcing Cerrin to turn away. Metal shrieked as the cockpit tipped forward into the ground, crushing the bow.

"So *that's* what you were doing!" said Yarni.

"Why are you here?" demanded Cerrin, gripping the girl's arm hard.

"I didn't want to miss the battle," she replied, eyes wide. "I stole a canoe. I know I shouldn't—"

"Idiot!"

Footsteps. Cerrin rolled to her knees, knife at the ready.

"We need to get back to the village," said Toll Maktar.

Sonus was out of ammunition.

But only eight Vitaari were left on their feet, and the islanders had them surrounded. One held up his hands in surrender, then the others did the same.

Sonus wasn't surprised that the warriors did not stop. Their cleavers continued their grisly work, hacking off limbs and slicing up faces, leaving the earth dark with black blood.

He dragged himself from the pit and surveyed the battlefield. For the first time, he was struck by a sense of pride. Every last rebel was armed with a worthy weapon. One of *his* weapons.

Everything would be different now.

Torren was approaching him, a Raxis rifle on her shoulder, a grim look on her face. Only now did he feel the pain in his leg, even though it was hardly bleeding.

"There are still Vitaari out there," he said. "Five on each side, hiding in the woods. We've got to hunt them down. Don't give them a chance to regroup."

"You're injured," she said.

"I'm all right."

"No. You stay here with the wounded. I'll get a group together to search the forest."

Sonus nodded. His leg was trembling now. It would be best to sit down. But not yet. As Torrin trotted away to gather a team, he began searching the bodies. Not those of his fellow rebels; he could not face that now. Instead, he examined the Vitaari.

He had seen Talazeer here. And, although he knew it was unlikely the Count was among those face down in the dirt at his feet, he had to look.

Cerrin walked swiftly for the village, Yarni and Maktar at her heels.

Talazeer was racing for the shuttle, with his shiny green bodyguard and an armored soldier close behind.

They spotted each other at the same moment.

Marl was first to react. His bulging yellow eyes shifted from Cerrin to Toll Maktar, and his slender white gun flashed. The shot was deflected by the agent's silver suit, which was still snaking its way up to his neck.

Maktar immediately returned fire with his runner gun. And yet Marl had already leaped, and the shell shattered the trunk of a palm tree.

"Shoot her!" yelled Count Talazeer.

The soldier—a female—*the* female Kannalin had told them about—raised her handgun. Cerrin matched the movement but her runner gun was heavier, slower to lift. Too slow. She'd be dead before she even got a chance to pull the trigger.

The Vitaari didn't get the chance either. Yarni flung a stone that struck her in the neck and sent her reeling. Now it was Cerrin's turn, and she aimed for the head. But a giant silver hand snatched at the barrel of the gun.

Count Talazeer held the gun down and swiped at her with his other hand. It was a clumsy attack, but his reach was so long and his arm so strong that when it connected, Cerrin was knocked clean off her feet. She landed on her side in the sand, head pounding with pain.

Talazeer scrambled for the gun, which she'd dropped on the ground between them. Cerrin drew her knife and darted forward, slicing at his arm. The Count was forced to retreat, that oddly perfect face of his riven by fear.

You cut me.

Now I cut you.

Dimly aware that Maktar and Marl had moved away, Cerrin advanced in a fighting crouch.

"Well, well," he said, covering his fear with a smirk. "What a pleasure it is to see you again."

On the final word, he kicked at the ground, sending sand up at Cerrin. It splattered her eyes, and she slashed blindly to keep him away from the weapon.

Only, he didn't go for the weapon. His hands clasped her wrists like shackles, and he squeezed until she dropped the knife.

Cerrin stopped struggling. She knew he could pull her hands off if he wanted to.

"Very well done, sir," said the female.

Cerrin tried to blink the sand out of her eyes, and the first thing she saw was the female approaching her, one hand on Yarni's neck, the other aiming the handgun at her head.

"Thank you, Commander," replied Talazeer.

"What about Marl?" she asked.

They all turned to see Toll Maktar discharge the runner gun at the Drellen, who leaped up onto one side of a palm, only to reappear halfway up it on the other. He returned fire but was foiled again by the agent's protective suit.

"He can take care of himself," said Talazeer. He leered down at Cerrin. "At least we've salvaged something from this mess."

"There is still the other bomb, sir."

"Are you blind?" asked Cerrin, nodding toward the smoke.

The female frowned, then spoke into her coms system. "Shuttle one pilot, this is Elezz... Shuttle one pilot, respond."

Despite her situation, Cerrin took some satisfaction from the look on the commander's face. It lasted only a heartbeat.

"Shuttle two pilot, report."

"Standing by, Commander."

"Land in the cleared area immediately."

"Yes, Commander."

With that, Elezz hurried away through the blue-tipped grass, dragging Yarni along with her.

Cerrin shivered as the Count placed his hand around her neck and pushed her forward. She would have rather have found herself in the grip of a mordyn. The Vitaari glowered down, black eyes shining. "I have waited a long time for this, Cerrin. I am so looking forward to... getting reacquainted."

· · ·

With his injured calf, Sonus could only sustain a kind of limping jog. As he entered the palm grove, he heard engines and saw the second shuttle descending toward the ruined first. Then another sound reached him—the low boom of a runner gun. Spying a blue laser blast up ahead, he readied his own weapon. A minute later, he came upon Toll Maktar.

The agent was crouching behind a palm, his armored suit apparently malfunctioning. The section covering his right arm had disappeared entirely. Even so, he poked his head out and fired—Sonus could not see his target—then dropped the gun, evidently out of ammunition. Maktar touched his gauntlet blaster, then peered out once more.

Sonus was fifty feet away and about to call out when the creature Marl appeared out of nowhere, landing on the palm ten feet above Maktar's head. Half his cloak had been blown away and he had lost his white gun—but he still had that long sword Sonus had seen him use to devastating effect before.

"Above you!"

As Marl dropped toward Maktar, the agent looked up and raised the blast gauntlet just in time. The Drellen somehow contorted his body so that his clawed feet pushed off on the palm, propelling him over his opponent and onto the sand. Before Maktar could turn, Marl heaved the blade down at him. Metal shrieked and sparks flew. Thankfully the armor protected his neck and back but he was thrown off balance.

Sonus kept moving, not daring a shot with the imprecise weapon at that range.

Toll Maktar swung desperately with his right arm and the blast gauntlet connected. With a concussive flash, Marl was sent flying backwards into the grass.

When he appeared again, he had lost his sword. Maktar advanced, gauntlet at the ready, but the Drellen rolled and disappeared into the grass...

...only to reappear ten feet away, the sword reclaimed. Then he flung himself at the agent and the square tip of the sword caught Maktar full in the face.

"No!" yelled Sonus. He stopped running and raised the runner gun, but Maktar was directly between him and the Drellen.

As the agent stumbled backwards, the Drellen pounced. His claws flashed three times and Maktar crumpled to the ground.

Sonus fired.

It was not a good shot—but good enough to rip the body-guard's arm off just below the elbow.

As the severed limb fell into the grass, Marl looked at it, then at the crimson blood leaking out of his mangled stump.

Sonus fired again. At least, he pressed the trigger again. But the runner gun was empty.

The Drellen wasn't screaming. He stood there staring at Sonus with his monstrous yellow eyes. Then he tore the remains of his cloak away and wrapped it around his mutilated arm like a tourniquet. After calmly collecting his sword from the ground, he turned and walked away into the trees.

Sonus dropped the gun, then ran to Toll Maktar.

"Is it bad?" mumbled the agent.

Sonus couldn't speak. Maktar's face was unrecognizable. The Drellen's claws had torn his mouth and nose apart, leaving terrible rents as wide as a finger. Thankfully, his eyes were intact. Blood, more orange than red, dripped down between them from out of his hair. It was then that Sonus saw the sword wound to the top of his head. It split both skin and skull.

"Toll…"

"It's bad. I know. What *was* that thing?"

"Talazeer's bodyguard."

He took Maktar's hand in his own. The fingers did not move. The arm was heavy and limp.

"Did we win?" asked the agent. "The battle?"

"We won, Toll. Thanks to you, the rebellion has really started now."

"*You* started it, Sonus," said Maktar, somehow summoning a smile from his ruined mouth. "You and Cerrin. And you'll finish it. You'll finish it."

As they passed the wrecked shuttle, neither Elezz nor Talazeer showed the faintest interest in the screaming pilots still trapped inside. The other shuttle was already on the ground, and at a signal from Elezz, it lowered its ramp.

Elezz led the way forward, gun still against Yarni's head. Showing courage beyond her years, Yarni tried to pull away, only to be clubbed on the ear by Elezz.

"Don't even think about it, you little shit."

Cerrin bucked in Talazeer's grip before she even realized she was doing it, but his fingers were like iron.

"Now, now. None of that. Do you know how much trouble you and your little friends have caused me, Cerrin? Mark my words—you will pay for it a thousand-fold. You are mine once again."

As Cerrin and Yarni were marched into the shuttle's gaping mouth, there came a scrapping and gasping sound behind them. Cerrin turned to see Marl climbing up the ramp, his slender pink tongue showing as he breathed deeply. He had lost most of his right arm and now collapsed to his knees.

Talazeer actually looked shocked. "Marl... are you..."

The bodyguard lifted himself up, yellow eyes rolling, crimson blood spotting the ramp. "I'm fine, sir." He staggered on past Elezz and Yarni, who also looked on in amazement.

The commander recovered herself swiftly. "Pilot, we're aboard. Take off."

A blue laser bolt sizzled into the ramp.

Cerrin spun around and saw Sonus running toward them, Marl's white rifle in his hands.

"Take off *now*!" bellowed Elezz.

"Commander, the ramp," protested the pilot.

"Do it!"

The shuttle floor began rattling slightly as the engines raised in pitch. Cerrin felt the weight on her legs grow as the craft eased from the ground and slowly began to ascend.

"Sonus, fire!" screamed Cerrin. "Now!"

"Come on!" snapped Talazeer, dragging her away from the ramp and hiding himself from Sonus's sight.

The sizzling sound of a laser burning through metal echoed again and again through the walls of the shuttle bay. Whatever Sonus was aiming for now, it clearly wasn't the open door.

The cockpit?

The engines?

The shuttle's ascent began to pick up speed. The laser rifle wasn't doing enough damage.

Then it did. The vessel lurched violently, knocking them all off their feet and sending them sliding toward the ramp.

Yarni cried out, flailing for a hold she didn't find. Free from

Talazeer's grip, Cerrin scrambled after her, grabbing her arm just as her legs slid off the ramp and into the open air.

Cerrin glimpsed the earth below; the shuttle was already quite high.

She knew she had to take the chance. The only chance.

"Yarni, we—"

Suddenly the Count's hand was on her again, a vise on her forearm.

"No!" he yelled. "You're not slipping through my fingers again, bitch."

The shuttle was still rising. She couldn't waste another second. She twisted her wrist with all her strength—not trying to slip free of Talazeer's grasp but to grind the sharp teeth of her gauntlet against his fingers.

At the first attempt, he cried out; at the second, he screeched.

And suddenly they were free.

Cerrin turned to see the naked fear in Yarni's eyes as they slid off the ramp and into the suffocating heat left behind by the shuttle.

"All courage!" screamed the girl.

"All courage!"

As Yarni was torn from her grip, Cerrin felt herself tumbling through the air. All she could do was wait for the pain.

26

Talazeer found himself alone in the medical bay. His wounded hand had been treated and the scars removed; now, the ship's surgeon was doing what he could for Marl's arm in the operating room.

No other wounded soldiers had been rescued from the island to require the surgeon's attention. No other soldiers had returned at all, save the two pilots and Commander Elezz.

The Count was content to be alone, and so was not the least surprised when company almost immediately arrived.

Commander Elezz approached the bed he was lying on, hands clasped behind her. Spots of black blood could be seen on her uniform and her face was still covered in grime. He supposed he couldn't blame her entirely for today's defeat.

Her usual composure had clearly been shaken by the events of the day. "My sincere apologies, Excellency. I… should have done better."

Talazeer said nothing, barely able to summon a coherent thought. If his family had been willing to resort to poison to rid themselves of him before, they would likely be willing to blast the entire *Galtaryax* from orbit now.

He hoped Cerrin and her little friend had broken their necks.

He had not yet been able to summon the energy or courage to inform the mine governors of what had occurred. The thought of contacting Viceroy Ollinder appalled him. There was nothing ahead for him but darkness.

Elezz continued: "I should have foreseen that with the stealth ship still active, an intervention by the agent was possible. But we should remember that the rebels have suffered grave losses, too. I will request reinforcements immediately."

Talazeer could simply not be bothered to reply. In fact, he was about to curse at her when she stepped closer to the bed. And when he glanced at her full, tempting mouth, he couldn't quite bring himself to be unpleasant.

She spoke in a whisper. "Sir, there is also this."

Elezz placed a remote display unit in his now fully healed hand.

"Further evidence uncovered by my contact. Intercepted communiques between your father, your brother, and his assistant. I am sorry."

As he read them through, any remaining doubts evaporated. The messages were written very much in his father's and brother's voices. They discussed the poisoning quite dispassionately, as if the act had already been decided upon. His father had left the details to Deslat, commenting, "Your mother and I never wanted this. But these continual failures shame us all. He was always weak."

The Count dropped the device on the bed and looked away, his mind numbed by those words. He'd endured many a tirade from both his parents and always known he was something of a disappointment to them. As it turned out, they'd been right all along.

"Leave me alone, Elezz."

"Excellency—"

"Don't call me that. I have no... don't call me that."

"Sir, there is something else I *must* tell you. Something that might change everything." Elezz glanced over her shoulder, even though they were alone in the bay. "My contact is General Hudiss Kan Lennesher."

Talazeer knew the name, as would all Vitaari of any rank. Lennesher was a senior member of the High Command, an exceptionally powerful and influential man.

"As you know, he is a member of Circle Za-Yirrok, as am I. He, I, and many others are... part of something. A movement seeking to displace Za-Iddi and the established order."

Talazeer thought instantly of what Viceroy Ollinder had told him about the recent killings and his fears of a burgeoning civil war.

"Is that what the sub-space transmitter hidden in your interferometer is for?"

If Talazeer could feel anything, he certainly would have enjoyed the look of shock that alighted on Elezz's face. But he couldn't.

"Yes." She paused, clearly anxious. "Count Talazeer, you know that I am taking a great risk in telling you this, but I believe we can be useful to each other. My circle—and others—believe that Imperator Zensen is taking the Domain in the wrong direction, risking our entire future."

"You certainly are taking a risk," he countered. "The Za-Ulessor are aligned to Za-Iddi. Why would you tell me, knowing I can expose you and Lennesher? Some bloody trick, I suppose!"

"No. I'm telling you because we both know there is no way back into your family. They've tried to have you killed."

Talazeer did indeed know that, but it was another thing to hear it said.

"Sir, your path to power does not lie in that direction. It cannot. But there are other paths. Corvos is more important than you know. *You* are very important."

"You mean the terodite. Why is it so damned crucial?"

"Have you heard of the Nisibia system?"

"Only the name. My accursed brother wouldn't tell me any more."

"The Nisibians are exceptionally advanced. Most of the technology upon their planet is run by some sort of artificial intelligence network. It is so sophisticated that the Nisibians are merely required to monitor it. The network controls everything—cities, ships, factories, even the weather, apparently. We Vitaari are no strangers to automation, but the Nisibians have achieved something unique. One can imagine the military applications. A campaign fought with maximum efficiency? Zero error?"

"Why isn't this common knowledge?" asked Talazeer.

"The sector is very remote and has never been fully mapped—which is why the existence of the Nisibians has only recently come to light. They've never made any serious attempt to make contact with other civilizations—something to do with their religion, as I understand it. Imperator Zensen sent an envoy last year, but it soon became evident that the Nisibians are already closely aligned to the Red Regent. We don't believe that she has exploited their technology herself, but she evidently understands the value of keeping it from the Domain. Nisibia may well be the key. We're moving forces to neighboring systems, and so is she. It seems likely that the Imperator is considering an invasion. If he can seize Nisibia, he will deny the Red Regent an advantage and give us the chance to exploit this network technology."

"You want it. You and Lennesher and your dissident friends. You want the Nisibian technology."

Elezz gave a little smile, then gripped his wrist, her hands surprisingly soft. "We already have agents on Nisibia, gathering information. If you work with us, we can protect you. And there *will* come a time when we will be the ones in charge. For those who take the risks now, there will be great rewards later. What shall I tell the general, sir? Are you with us?"

The Vitaari dead were dragged into the pits and buried. The fallen islanders were placed on a pyre in the middle of the village. At Torrin's suggestion, the dead rebels were placed there, too.

Including Sonus, only fourteen rebel fighters had survived.

Though covered in bruises and cuts, the formidable Ak-tra joined Uk-Saa in leading a brief ceremony honoring the dead. Then, the pyre was set alight. Amidst the pile of Echobe and Palanians and islanders was only one being not from Corvos. Toll Maktar.

As Sonus gazed into the flames, he spoke to his fallen ally, thanking him for his sacrifice, pledging once more to honor him by continuing the rebellion.

He did not know how he might contact the Ikasar, but he wore Toll's bracelet now on his own arm. He had already salvaged what he could from the *Spectre*, then surrounded it with firewood and set it alight. His friend would not have wanted his ship to fall into enemy hands.

Only five hours had passed since the end of the battle, but everyone understood that they could not remain in the village. Torrin seemed to be best at communicating with the islanders, and it had been agreed that they would all move by canoe to the neighboring island to join the others. Sonus had no idea what would happen then.

He had a fully loaded runner gun over his shoulder and now looked at the pile of weapons and equipment close to the largest hut. It included all they had liberated from the dead Vitaari: rifles, ammunition, grenades, armor.

Sonus turned away from the pyre and entered the chief's hut. Inside were two litters bearing Cerrin and Yarni. He guessed that they had fallen around forty feet, and he knew he would never forget the terrible sight of it.

Even though Cerrin had told him to fire, he knew he had made the wrong decision. Cerrin had come down on her left leg and fractured her ankle. She had also snapped two fingers, which had been stabilized with wood and twine. She'd remained conscious throughout and had done nothing but ask about Yarni, pleading with Sonus to tell her. In the end, he had done so.

The girl had come down on her back. She was still unconscious, and though her neck seemed all right, Sonus felt sure she had sustained serious internal injuries. He did not expect her to live.

When Sonus knelt beside Cerrin, she stirred. The first thing she did was turn to her right and look at Yarni. With nothing else she could do to help, she simply reached out and pushed the blanket covering the girl up to her chin.

She turned back to Sonus. "What's happening?"

"We're getting ready to move. We can't stay here. We're going to the other island."

"And then?"

Sonus shrugged. "The Vitaari will come back," he said after a time. "They always come back."

Cerrin smiled. "So did you."

WILD SUN: BECOMING

BOOK THREE OF THE WILD SUN SERIES

Coming Soon

Ehsan and Shakil Ahmad simply love the art of storytelling. It's a passion they've shared since their childhood in New York, the first-generation American children of immigrants from Pakistan.

Today, the brothers are back in the city of their birth, working at separate tech startup companies while collaborating on novels and screenplays.

Ehsan and his wife welcomed their first child into the world in 2018.

Also from Uproar Books:

THE WAY OUT by Armond Boudreaux (2020)

When a virus necessitates the use artificial wombs for all pregnancies, two fearless women discover the terrifying truth behind this world-changing technology.

WORLDS OF LIGHT AND DARKNESS (2021)

The best science-fiction short stories from the pages of *DreamForge* and *Space & Time* magazines, including works by Jane Lindskold, Scott Edelman, and more.

WE by Yevgeny Zamyatin (2020/1924)

The original Russian dystopian masterpiece that inspired George Orwell's *1984* and became the first novel ever banned by the Soviet Union.

FORETOLD by Violet Lumani (2021)

A high school student who struggles with OCD and anxiety can't help but imagine tragedy and death all around her, but some of her visions are coming true.

For more information, visit uproarbooks.com